FINDING SUPPORT

EMERSON GAIL

Cover by Erin

Edited by Brittany Montano at Brittany Montano Management, LLC

Published By Brackish Publishing
brackishpublishing.com

Prologue

Jagger

A few short minutes after I finish setting up everything in the hotshop, noise fills the lobby as tonight's group filters in. The employees from Paradise 11, a bar in Anchor Point, are taking a glassblowing class from me as their company Christmas party. I think it's a cool idea, fun and interesting, instead of boring and mundane like most office parties.

The next two hours are going to be a blast if the energy emanating from the group is any indication. They are already having a great time, joking around. Since it's Christmas, I'm having each person make an ornament. I premade several in case we have any disasters. Glass is delicate and I don't want anyone to go home empty handed.

"Hi! Welcome to Coastal Glass Studio. I'm Melanie," my sister greets the group. I appreciate her being here to help with the class. She has her own job and a husband but jumps in to assist me anytime I need her.

"Hey, Melanie. I'm Ryan." I hear the man who booked the class respond.

"It's nice to meet you. Is the entire party here?"

"Yes, we're all here."

"Great! Follow me."

She's leading them into the small room next to the studio where they can leave their jackets, bags, jewelry, and phones. Cubbies line the walls giving everyone has their own space. For everyone's safety, it's important for them to keep most items out of the studio. We do allow phones as long as they are kept in a pocket when working.

After their belongings are put away, Melanie brings the group into the studio and goes through a list of safety instructions and passes out safety glasses. I stand a little behind her waiting for her to finish.

"This is a blowpipe." She holds up a long pipe and one of the guys snickers, drawing my attention. He's tall and skinny with short, blond hair dyed red and green at the ends. 'Tis the season, I guess. The girl standing next to him elbows him in the ribs. "Never raise the pipe above your head. Do not swing the pipe in the direction of another person," Melanie continues, ignoring him, but it's no use.

This time, the guy with the red and green hair and another guy start to laugh. "I always swing my pipe in the direction of others," the other one whisper-yells to dyed-hair guy, causing me to snicker. This is going to be an eventful night.

"Hush," Ryan scolds while clearly trying to hide his own laughter.

"Okay," Melanie smiles, doing her best not to bust out laughing, too. "The instructions I gave you are posted around the studio." As she finishes, I step up next to her. "This is Jagger, or Jag. He owns the studio and will be leading your class."

"I'd like to see his blowpipe raised," dyed-hair guy mutters.

Embarrassment floods me, and my face and ears heat. I take him in for a brief second, clearing my throat, I stare right at him completely infatuated. He's fucking hot, wearing a pair of tight, black jeans and a cropped shirt that shows off his flat stomach. Not the best option for glass blowing, but I like it on him.

"Welcome to Coastal Glass Studio. If you will each choose a marver, but don't touch anything yet." No one moves. "Choose a steel table. They're called marvers."

The group spreads out around the room, each choosing one of the tables. Everything they need is there, ready for them to work.

"On the tables, you'll find pens and name tags. Go ahead write your name on a name tag and stick it on your shirt," Melanie instructs as I walk to the table in the front of the room and pick up my blowpipe.

I take a minute to read the names as they put on the tags while Mel collects the pens and trash. I like to be able to call my guests by name, and there is no way I will remember everyone's name. Carrying the blow-pipe to one of the large furnaces, I gather a layer of molten glass on the end. As I work, I explain what I'm doing.

"Once you have a layer of glass on your blowpipe,

bring it back to your marver and roll it like this, keeping it in constant motion." They watch as I continue the demonstration. "You'll have to return to the glory hole-" The entire room erupts in laughter, cutting off my explanation. Okay, I should have known better with this group.

Matt and Ellis, the two guys making comments earlier, fall into each other, almost knocking over a shelf of glass. We've barely gotten started, and I'm already enjoying this group more than most.

"As I was saying," I continue doing my best to stay professional, but it's impossible to keep the laughter out of my voice. "You'll have to return to the glor... furnace."

"Smart save." I read her name tag— Chelsea— as I nod a thank you.

"Several times," I keep going, not missing a beat. "The glass must be kept above 1000 degrees to keep it pliable so you can work with it. Now, I'm going to have each of you bring your pipe to the furnace to get a layer of glass. Melanie and I will be walking around the room to help you roll your pieces."

Once everyone is working on their glass, Mel and I visit each table, giving individual instructions based on what ornament they are making, and giving them time to work independently, but also helping them add color and shape the glass.

"Okay," I walk up behind Ellis, the guy with dyed hair. It might not be the smartest idea, but I want to be close to him. "Now, you're going to blow into your pipe with a big puff to create a bubble."

"I'd like to blow into your pipe." My breath hitches at his daring comment. There's no way I'm not every shade of red in existence. It takes a minute for me to compose myself, so Melanie continues my instruction, demonstrating with her own blowpipe. I never let a man get to me like this, especially at work. I pride myself on remaining professional. This isn't the first group to make these types of comments, but I can usually ignore them and move forward.

For the rest of the session, the crude jokes continue every time the words pipe, blow, hole, or hard are mentioned. It's bordering on ridiculous, but it's funny as shit, too. This might be my favorite group ever.

"Hey, Manny," Grayson calls. "Your blowing skills are top-notch." I take my eyes off Ellis long enough to see what's happening, and poor Manny's face flames red as everyone turns to look at him.

"Damn," Apollo jumps in, looking over at Manny. "How are you so good at blowing?"

"Maybe you should come over to our side," Matt adds with a wink.

"Enough, children. Did you ever think he's this good because he uses his mouth for other things?" Chelsea tries to save him, but with this group, it falls flat.

"That's the point, Chels. *He* practices blowing."

"Apparently a lot, if he's this good. I mean, I've sucked my share of cock and I stink at glassblowing," Matt laughs.

"Who else needs help?" Melanie grabs the attention off Manny and redirects everyone to their glassblowing. Manny took the teasing in stride, but Chelsea looks annoyed. Those boys are going to have a long night.

Glassblowing isn't an easy process, but the whole group works hard for over an hour, and the ornaments turn out pretty good. It has also been a riot to work with them.

The session wasn't without a couple of issues. Apollo dropped his first ornament halfway through the process and had to start over. I broke two pieces while demonstrating because I got distracted by Ellis' innuendos. Okay, maybe it was just him. I haven't been able to take my eyes off him the whole time.

At the end of the session, I help each of them place the finished pieces in the annealing oven where they will rest overnight.

When I approach the first table, Grayson looks relieved. "Where's your bathroom?" he asks as soon as his piece is safely in the oven.

"Go back to the lobby. It's across from the room where you left your personal items."

"Thank you," he gets out as he rushes off.

After the rest of the group has their pieces in the oven, they walk back to the lobby and gather their things, then head outside. Melanie starts cleaning the studio up while I walk the group to the lobby.

Ellis hangs back, and I'm not disappointed. "Hi! You're kind of hot," he says with a flirty smile, squeezing mu bicep.

"Just kind of?" I question with a raised eyebrow.

He rolls his eyes. "Fine. You're super hot." He steps

into my space and I gasp softly. He smells good, like the beach— coconut and salt. Fuck, it's intoxicating. Ellis lowers his voice as if anyone else is in the room and says, "And you know it." My cock twitches as his warm breath skates over my ear.

Ryan chooses that moment to leave the bathroom. He glances at us briefly, and Ellis quickly moves out of my space.

"Thanks," Ryan waves. "We had a great time." He joins the rest of the group outside, looking a little flushed and disheveled.

"What was that about?" Ellis asks as he leans against the wall, looking at me like I'm his next meal. That would be a welcome feast.

I rest a hand on the wall next to his head and lean close to him. Ignoring his question about Ryan, I say, "I think you're hot, too." Ellis shivers at my words, and my dick hardens. Fuck, I wish he wasn't leaving with the group.

The bathroom door opens again, and Grayson walks out. Now I know why Ryan looked guilty. I don't care what they did in the bathroom as long as they cleaned up.

"Quit trying to get in that poor man's pants and let's go have dinner," Grayson teases.

Ellis' head snaps in his direction. "Maybe he's trying to get in *my* pants," Ellis retorts. It's true, but I don't say anything.

"History tells a different story, friend," Grayson taunts.

Ellis slaps his hand over his heart and inhales sharply. "I *never* tried to get in your pants."

"Day one, Ellis. The moment Ryan introduced us."

I smile at their exchange. Yeah, I can see that. I don't even know Ellis, but he seems like a giant flirt. The thought of being with Ellis has me horny as fuck, and Grayson's words aren't helping. Knowing Ellis is probably up for a good time has my mind reeling. I glance at him, ready to ask if I can see him again, but he's already walking toward the door.

"Bye, gorgeous," he purrs as he pushes the door open and disappears onto the sidewalk. Ellis is different than the guys I usually date, but I'm drawn to him. Something about him intrigues me, and I know I need more of him. I make a mental note to visit Paradise 11 as soon as the holidays are over.

CHAPTER 1

ELLIS

Pushing myself up, I yawn and stretch, hearing things pop that should not be popping at my age. Why am I awake this early on my day off? I didn't get home until almost three, and fell asleep on the couch, which is entirely too small for my six-foot frame... fine, five foot eleven, but every man deserves an extra inch. I never sleep well on the nights I don't make it to my bed.

After pulling on a pair of sweatpants, I walk over to what qualifies as a kitchen in this small space I call home and make myself a cup of tea. I can't bring myself to enjoy coffee. It's bitter and disgusting, like drinking liquid dirt and no amount of cream and sugar fixes it. My mom loves hot tea, so I grew up drinking it like a little old lady.

After my tea is ready, I sip on it while I make a poor man's breakfast of eggs and toast. I can't afford frilly extras, like fancy fruit or bacon. My trailer isn't much, but it's mine. Okay, well, not mine exactly. I rent, so technically, it belongs to my landlord. But I pay the bills by myself without any help. That might not seem like a big deal to most people, but I'm proud of myself for getting this far on my own.

The one-bedroom Airstream is just over two hundred square feet. There's enough room for me and my meager belongings, plus the rent is super cheap, which is good because I can't afford much. My job as a server at Paradise 11, a local bar here in Anchor Point, pays decent. Yet, it's not enough to cover rent, utilities, food, and entertainment, not that I need money for that last part. A few months ago, I took a second job at a call center. At least the call center job is remote, and I can do it in my underwear. It's exhausting being on my feet all night, running from table to table. If I have to work a second job, I'm glad I don't have to leave the house or put on clothes.

I'm working over seventy hours a week, which doesn't leave much time, or energy, for anything fun. Well, I do make sure to find a hookup, or two, each week. Sometimes it's guys who come into the bar. Other times, I find men on a dating app. I'm upfront that I'm only looking for sex. Relationships are not for me. One, I don't have time to invest in something long-term. And two, it's not like anyone wants to have a serious relationship with me anyway, so why bother setting myself up for disappointment?

Dropping a piece of toast onto a plate, I slide the two eggs on top. When I cut into the over-easy eggs with my fork, yellow goo flows over the toast.

"Perfect," I groan, swallowing the runny concoction.

My mind wanders back to all the fun I'm not having. No one wants to do *anything* with me, let alone anything fun. I mean sure, fun for a night, maybe, but nothing long-term. I'm twenty-one years old and have never had a boyfriend. The dates, if you can even call them that, have only been to get to the sex part of the night— a few drinks, maybe dinner, then a quick fuck. Never to see the guy again.

I'm not necessarily complaining. I have a *very* active sex life, and a ton of guys fuck me. But for once, I'd like to go on a real date, maybe a few dates with the same person. Getting to know someone on a deeper level than what his soap tastes like, or how his dick feels in my ass, is total life goals at this point. Goals I'll never reach. I sigh heavily, shoving the last bite of breakfast into my mouth, resigned to the fact that love is not in the cards for me.

"Ugh!" I groan, pushing myself up while grabbing my plate and gathering the other dirty dishes off the counter and table. This mess isn't going to clean itself. I *hate* cleaning. Despise it to be honest. I try, and fail, over and over at keeping the small area tidy. I put off everything cleaning related until I can't stand it, or until I spill something making a bigger mess. If I ever get a well-paying job, the first thing I'm doing is hiring a housekeeper.

Forcing myself to get started, I wipe down the small counter. I've made that mistake one too many times, forgetting to clean the surface and having nowhere to set the clean dishes until I can dry them.

Twenty minutes later, the sink is finally empty, and

I'm putting away the last few dishes when there's a knock on the trailer door. I'm not expecting anyone, but my BFF, Megan, tends to show up unannounced whenever the mood strikes her. She's gotten an earful of loud sex noises multiple times, but it doesn't deter her. Once I even found her sitting on the bottom step waiting for me when I walked my latest fuck to the door. Her fault if she heard me scream. That man *definitely* took me on the ride of my life like he promised. Whew, he did *not* disappoint.

When I open the door, I'm met with a very distraught Matt. His hair is a mess and his clothes are dirty. Matt is several years older than me, and we work together at Paradise 11 where he's a bartender. We're work friends and have hung out a few times, but we aren't close, and I'm a little surprised to find him at my door on our day off.

"Hey, Matt. What's up?" I do my best to cover my confusion with a smile and an upbeat tone.

He shoves his hands into his pocket and stares at the three small steps leading up to the door. "Ellis, uh... hey. Yeah, sorry. I should go." He glances around in complete confusion as if he's not sure how he got here.

"Come on in, Matt. I'm not doing anything important," I tell him, hoping it will put him at ease. Cleaning can wait. Matt might not be my BFF like Megan, but he *clearly* needs a friend.

"Are you sure?" he asks, perplexed

This sad, meek guy is not the crazy, confident bartender I work with, who flirts with everyone and laughs at the stupidest stories just to get a big tip. He's happy, confident, and doesn't seem to have a care in the world. The only time I've ever seen him look remotely concerned is the day Ryan, our boss, called him into his office back in October after Matt no called, no showed for a couple of days. We all thought he was getting fired. And even then, he looked better that he does today.

"Absolutely," I assure him, stepping back and holding the door open. When Matt doesn't move, I reach out and pull him up the steps and into my home.

He freezes just inside, and I barely have room to close the door. Matt is in some weird daze and doesn't follow me when I take a few steps toward the couch. With no other choice, I turn to face him. "Do you want something to drink?"

"Beer." His answer is immediate and confident.

"It's nine in the morning," I say, trying to figure out what is happening right now.

"Oh. So, no to the beer?"

I guess we're having beer. I open the mini fridge and pull out two beers, replacing them with two from the box under the sink. I set them both on the table and sit on the couch, still waiting patiently for Matt to join me. Slowly, he trudges across the microscopic space, dragging his feet as if it's the hardest thing he's done in weeks. He falls onto the couch next to me, picking up the beer, and popping it open. He empties it in a few large gulps then crushes the empty can. What the actual fuck is going on?

"What's wrong, Matt?"

"Nothing. I'm all good. Got another beer?" He eyes

the one sitting front of me. I don't want to drink this early in the day, but I also don't want him to down another one that fast. There is such a thing as pacing yourself.

"Let's talk first. Maybe have some food. Then I'll get you another beer," I suggest, attempting to gain control of the situation.

"Nothing to talk about. Not hungry." He shrugs as he looks at me in confusion, like maybe he doesn't understand why I said that.

"Why are you here?" I finally ask, tired of playing this game.

He absently runs a hand through his greasy, disheveled hair only making it worse. When he lifts his arm, his sleeve falls, and I notice a few scratches. They are *definitely* new, not bleeding, but no more than a day old.

"What happened to your arm?" I ask with a gasp before thinking about my reaction. He quickly drops his arm and pulls his sleeve down, stretching it into his hand.

"It's fine. A little scrape," he rushes out.

Wrong. That's more than a little scrape. This is a bunch of angry, red scratches, making it hard to tell if they are from something or someone.

"Can I see? I can clean them for you," I offer softly, not wanting to frighten him. I need to help him, but if I act like it's a big deal, he might freak out and bolt.

"It's nothing, Ellis. I was working on my car. Yeah. I, uh, scraped my arm on something sharp. It's fine." He tries to sound casual, but his words are unsteady and clearly made up on the spot. What is he hiding?

"Well, I'm glad you're okay." What else can I say? He clearly doesn't want to talk about it.

Food. I need to feed Matt. Walking to the cabinet where I keep a few snacks, I pull out a bag of jalapeño chips and a jar of ranch dip, opening both and placing them on the table. I fill two glasses with water and carrying them over.

Feeding Matt and keeping him from drinking alcohol is the main goal right now. It doesn't seem like he's planning to open up to me, and I don't think it's a good idea to push him. I don't know much about how to help someone, but I remember when I was a teenager if I didn't want to talk, and Mom or Dad tried to force me, it only pissed me off more. Making me tell them something when I wasn't ready was a sure-fire way for me to keep things bottled up or lie to them. I can only assume it's the same for Matt.

After several agonizing minutes of silence, Matt shoves a few chips in his mouth. He grabs another handful and devours them just as quickly, coughing a little as he swallows them. He picks up the water and downs the entire glass.

"Damn, those are spicy," he chokes out, eyes a little watery.

"Jalapeño," I say, getting up and refilling his glass. He goes in for more chips, but this time, he dips them in the ranch before eating them. Yep, there's a reason I eat them with dip- masks some of the heat.

"Got any plans for Christmas?" I ask. Matt chokes

on the chips, and a look of pure devastation crosses his face. He covers it quickly, but there is a flash of sadness in his eyes. "Yep." He smiles. "You know- gifts, a tree, big dinner. The whole thing."

"Are you sure?"

"Uh huh. It's one of my favorite holidays," he exclaims with a wide smile and little too much enthusiasm. Matt is definitely hiding something. He wipes the chip dust on his already dirty jeans and stands abruptly. "Gotta go. Last minute shopping. Thanks for..." he trails off and runs out the door before I have a chance to stop him.

What the hell was that about?

CHAPTER 2

JAGGER

It's been a long week, and I'm glad to finally have a few days off. Who knew glassblowing would be so popular the week before Christmas? I've had two birthday parties and four Christmas parties this week, but January and February are probably going to be slow. My classes aren't as full and there are only two parties on the books.

Today is Christmas Eve, so I'm technically closed but came in for a few hours to finish up some paperwork. That way, I can enjoy three full days off. It's the only vacation I've taken since I opened almost a year ago.

Last January, I had no idea the business would take off the way it has this year. I've been blowing glass since I was a kid, and for years dreamed of opening my own studio where I could create pieces to sell and offer classes. For almost a year, I have worked six days a week without breaks or employees. Even on my day off, I'm usually preparing for a class or working on a piece. Mel has been a godsend. There is no way I could have pulled any of this off without her help. She works at the studio several hours each day for free and has her own business, a small gift shop in the next block. She has been in business for four years and has several employees to keep things moving when she's at the studio. It doesn't hurt that her husband is a doctor, and she doesn't have to work. She stocks my pieces in her shop, and they tend to sell quickly, especially this time of year. Before the studio opened, I spent months creating vases, bowls, ornaments, and abstract pieces so there would be plenty in storage ready to sell if she needed more inventory. That was a smart decision because I've created very few new pieces this year.

I'm not complaining, though. Not having time to create new pieces means I'm busy teaching classes and holding parties, which bring in decent money. If things continue to go this way, I'll be out of the red in about five months. Paying back the loan I borrowed from my dad and being able to turn a profit in just over a year is more than I expected when I started this adventure. By next holiday season, I might even be able to hire an employee.

"Jagger," Melanie yells my name as she taps my shoulder. I jump and my heart races.

"Damn, girl! Give a guy a heart attack," I gasp, clutching my chest.

"Well, answer when I call," she snaps back

"I did!"

"The fifth time."

"What?" I ask in disbelief. "No," I argue.

"Oh, you were deep in thought. I'm sorry I scared you." She smirks at me. "I bet I know what, or should I say *who*, you were thinking about." She never misses an opportunity to pick on me.

"If you must know, I was thinking about how proud I am for pulling this off." I motion around the studio. "It still floors me that it's been such a success."

"I never had any doubt." Mel hops onto one of the marvers. One day she's going to do that and get an ass full of glass. I will *not* feel sorry for her when that happens.

"And I appreciate the support."

Mel is two years older than me, and we get along great. She is my sister, and the person I trust most in the world. We have a bunch of siblings, including two older brothers and an older sister. I was born a twin, but Jax died when we were seventeen. Eight years later, and I still miss him every day. It doesn't help my parents have his room the exact same way he left it the night he died, like some shrine of sadness. It's the reason I moved out the day I turned eighteen even though he had been gone less than a year and I had over three months of high school left. I couldn't be in the house any longer without him, let alone with my parents. I don't know which was worse.

I've second guessed that decision for years. Did I leave too soon? My parents were mourning the loss of their youngest son, and I left them to deal with it on their own. It was time for me to heal. I was quickly drowning in an abyss of depression. Living in that house was slowly killing me, breaking me a little more each day. It's still difficult to be there, but I can usually make it through a visit if I avoid Jaxon's bedroom.

Mel snaps her finger in front of my face. "What?" I growl, shoving her hand away.

"Where did you go?"

"Nowhere." I shake thoughts of Jax away. "Sorry. Did you say something?"

"I miss him, too," she says in a small voice.

What?"

"That look." She points to my face. "It's your 'I'm thinking about Jaxon' face."

"You might have lost your mind. That's not even a thing." I shrug it off with a chuckle that falls flat.

"Were you thinking about him?"

"Yes," I admit. "Like I said, you have a tell." She hops off the table and wraps her arms around me. "It's okay to miss him. It's also okay to talk about him," Melanie mumbles into my chest. She's almost a foot shorter than me and her arms barely fit around my muscular frame. I follow her lead and wrap my arms around her, hugging my sister.

"Damn, I miss him so fucking much."

"Me, too."

"I should have—"

"No," she cuts me off. "Do *not* finish that sentence."

She's right. I've been through that night ad nauseam with my therapist, lying alone in bed, and talking to Mel. I shouldn't blame myself. Nothing would be better if it had been me instead of him. Our family would be devastated either way. There is nothing I could have done to save him that night. Logically, I know all of this, but I wish I could go back and change the course of events. Maybe then I'd still have my brother.

I grab the broom and start sweeping the floor, forcing my mind to focus on something other than Jaxon. It immediately wanders to the person who's been invading my thoughts and dreams for the past two days. In a year's worth of classes and parties, the group from Paradise 11 that came on Wednesday is by far my favorite. They were hilarious and an absolute blast to teach. They certainly kept me on my toes all night. It was hard to stay focused and teach with all the jokes and innuendos they were spatting. Being completely unprofessional, I chose to stand behind the hot, sinewy guy to demonstrate how to blow into the pipe. I couldn't take my eyes off Ellis the entire night with his short, blond hair, dyed red and green at the ends, lean muscles and tall frame, matching my height. Fuck, he was a dream. I don't even remember anyone else's name, well, except Ryan and that's only because he booked the event and paid the bill. But Ellis? Damn... I can't get him out of my head. Maybe I need to make a trip to Paradise 11.

"For all that is holy in this world, get your head on straight, Jag," Melanie whines, throwing her hands up in frustration.

"One, nothing about me is straight, and two, what are you going on about now?"

"As if I don't know that's your 'I'm lusting over a guy' face," she says smugly.

"I do not have *that* look. I gave you 'Jaxon sad face,' but I do not have a 'lust face.'" She laughs like a damn hyena. Doubled over, hands on her knees, laughing like she heard the funniest joke ever told. Dramatic much? "What is wrong with you?"

"Oh, sweet baby brother. I know you better than you think. You were not discreet in middle or high school, and I know your lust face. It's the look you get when you're watching porn."

"I don't-"

"Save it." She holds up a hand. "We both know you watch porn. *Everyone* watches porn. I'm a married woman and I watch it, sometimes with my husband. It gives us new ideas and keeps things spicy."

"Ew, gross. Never mention porn and Kevin in the same sentence again."

"Grow up, Jag. We all have sex. Now, tell me who you're lusting after."

"No one," I growl, proving her point.

"Oooh, is it the hottie from the other night? The one with the dyed hair? He was gorgeous and definitely wanted to blow something other than glass." Melanie taps her chin. "If I recall correctly, his exact words were, 'I'd like to blow into your pipe.'" She glances down at my crotch then looks up and winks. Instinctively, I drop the broom, covering my dick with my hands. I might die of actual horrified embarrassment. Why is my sister my friend? That girl crosses too many lines. Every. Damn. Day.

"Don't you have something else to do? Anything?" I ask, hoping she takes the hint and leaves.

"Well, I do need to check on the store and close up for the holiday."

"Go do that."

"Fine. I will leave you with your lusty thoughts." She gets all the way to the door then yells over her shoulder. "Be sure to clean up if you jerk off in this building. I don't want to find dried cum on any surface." The door clinks shut behind Mel before I find something to throw at her. Damn, I love that girl, but sometimes, I want to murder her.

CHAPTER 3

ELLIS

The smell of homemade biscuits and bacon frying wakes me entirely too early, but my mom thinks the Christmas celebration should start at the crack of dawn. Glancing at my phone, I see that it isn't even seven yet. What fresh hell is this? I have *got* to start sleeping at my own place on Christmas Eve. Then I can stroll in at a more reasonable hour like nine or ten or noon. Yeah, Mom would totally *not* go for that.

After a quick stop in the bathroom, I drag myself down the hall to the kitchen of the ranch-style house I grew up in on the northeast side of Anchor Point. It's in a quaint neighborhood a few blocks from the beach.

"Good morning, Mom. Merry Christmas," I greet, kissing her on the cheek.

"Merry Christmas, baby. Come sit. Let me get you some tea," she says sweetly, looking at me like I'm the only person in the world.

"I can get it, Mom. You have enough to do," I reply.

"Nonsense. I have a special Christmas blend, and I am happy to make it for you."

"Thank you." I take a seat at the table and wait for my mom to steep the tea. I'm perfectly capable of taking care of myself, but any time I'm at my parents' house, Mom feels the need to wait on me as if I'm still a child. It's a nice gesture, but I know she'll complain about it to dad as soon as I leave.

"Mornin', son. Merry Christmas." Dad strolls in with his travel mug of coffee a few minutes after me, patting me on the shoulder.

"Merry Christmas. Where have you been?"

"Went for daily walk on the beach."

Every morning for my entire twenty-one years, my dad has taken his mug of coffee and walked on the beach while Mom prepares breakfast. Why should today be any different? It's all a little too 1950s for me, but they are perfectly happy and have been married for forty-eight years. My mom was only eighteen when they married. My dad was twenty-three. They spent the first years of their marriage finishing school and building their careers. Dad is a financial planner, and Mom is a pediatric nurse. They are both old enough to retire but still choose to work. Mom did cut back to part-time last year. They were in their thirties when they decided they wanted a baby, and it took them over twelve years to get pregnant. The story has been told to me so many times, it's ingrained in my brain as if I was actually there through it all.

Mom hands me a cup of tea then turns back to the stove, putting the finishing touches on breakfast. We're all still in the pajamas Mom bought this year with reindeer frolicking in the snow covering them. Dad even went for his walk in them.

Every year, she buys us matching pajamas for Christmas and insists we wear them. Dad and I gladly indulge her. Mom once told me she and Dad started the matching PJs tradition the first Christmas they were married. With almost fifty years in the books, nothing is going to stop her now. Somewhere in a box are all the past sets. Mom makes me leave mine here each year as a keepsake. I have no idea what that means. Does she look at them periodically, or are they simply packed up in a box in the back of a closet, forgotten until it's time to add the next set? I often wonder what she does with them.

Mom hands Dad and I each of plate piled high with food— biscuits, bacon, eggs, and grits. It looks and smells delicious.

"It's nice to have you here, Ellis. How is work?" Dad asks as he takes his seat.

"Good. Late nights, but I enjoy it. I'm glad I took yesterday off so I could spend the evening here." It's only a partial lie. I do like spending Christmas with my parents, I just wish they didn't wake up so dang early.

"Maybe you should try to work somewhere that isn't open so late. You need your rest," Mom chimes in as only a worried mother can.

"I like working at the bar, Mom. I get plenty of rest. Don't worry."

"If you say so, dear. You can do better than working at some seedy bar."

I shovel a fork full of eggs in my mouth to avoid saying something I'll regret. My mom means well, but my parents didn't go about teaching me how to be self-sufficient in a practical way, and now they want to dictate where I work. Newsflash, Samantha and Bob, I have bills to pay, and working at a bar pays them. Well, some of them at least.

Dad must sense that I'm done with this conversation because he changes the subject. "You outdid yourself, Samantha. This breakfast is delightful." Dad always knows the right things to say.

My mom is a great cook, but there's nothing extraordinary about a simple breakfast. There's not much you can do to scrambled eggs, but he's always handed out compliments freely to my mother. To this day, he looks at her like they're newlyweds. I often envy their relationship. Maybe one day a man will look at me the same way.

"Dad's right, everything was tasty. Thank you." I'm smart enough to jump on the compliment train and keep the conversation off me.

"Thank you both. I'm glad you enjoyed it. Ellis, run along and get showered. We have to leave soon for church."

"Yes, ma'am." Leaving my empty plate in the sink, I head down the hall to the bathroom.

My parents aren't religious and have never been the type of people to go to church on a regular basis, but for some reason, they make an annual appearance on Christmas Day. It's part of our family tradition, so I've never questioned it.

THREE HOURS LATER, we're home from church, lunch has been devoured, and it's time to open presents. Different year, same routine. Soon, I'll be able to return to my humble abode and spend the rest of the night with my best friend.

Before we settle in the living room to open presents, I fire off a quick text to Matt. I haven't been able to stop thinking about him since the weird encounter at my place two days ago.

> Me: Merry Christmas!

> Me: You doing ok?

He responds almost immediately.

> Matt: Hey! Yep, all good.

I stare at my phone for several minutes expecting more from him, but nothing else comes through. He must be busy with his own family Christmas. Pushing my concerns away, I pocket my phone and join my parents in the living room.

Frugal is the best word I can come up with to describe Mom and Dad. Even though they both make good money, and Dad ensured they are set for retirement, they live in a modest three-bedroom home, rarely go out to eat, and have never taken an extravagant vacation. Short weekend trips, sure, but never anywhere exciting like Europe.

Each Christmas, we receive five gifts— something to wear, something we need, something to read, something we want, and something to eat. That's it. Five things. Not that I need more gifts, and I appreciate everything they give me, but... F-R-U-G-A-L. Frugal.

Being the amazingly-perfect son they raised, I am continuing the tradition this year. The first few years I was on my own, I couldn't afford to get them more than one gift a piece, but this year, I'm finally joining the Young tradition. I spend my money a little more freely than my parents do, so it took me months to save enough to buy each of them five gifts.

Another tradition my mother insists on is the order of gift opening— youngest to oldest, eat, read, wear, need, want. It's times like this, I realize how old and set in their ways my parents truly are. I have friends with grandparents, and even great grandparents, their age. Megan's grandfather and my dad were the same age. They were friends until her grandfather passed away at the age of sixty-five. I worry about that sometimes— losing my parents. It's a sad reality, though. I'll be facing that younger than most people I know, not that they are ill in any way, but time is not on their side. Even if they live to be ninety, I'll only be in my forties. I shake away the morbid thoughts and focus on the presents in front of us. I do love presents!

Mom hands Dad and I each a small bag and I do the same, handing each of them the snacks I chose. Being the youngest, I open mine first.

"Oh, yummy! My favorites!" I gush with excitement as I pull out Sour Patch Kids, Peanut M&Ms, a bag of jellybeans, and a large bag of Cheetos. All my favorite snacks. Knowing me, this will be my dinner, and I'll go to bed with a stomachache.

Next, Mom opens her gift revealing pretzels and caramels. Then my dad opens his bag of salted cashews and circus peanuts. He's a weird one. Circus peanuts are the devil's candy, but he loves them and always keeps a bag on hand.

We move on to the other gifts, and by the time everything is opened, I have a book about artists from the Renaissance, a new pair of khaki shorts and a polo shirt, a tool kit, and a bag full of hair dyeing supplies. The book is super cool, and I can't wait to read it. The clothes are not my style at all, but I'll shove them in the back of the closet to wear in front of Mom one day soon. I *definitely* need the tools but don't really know how to use any of them. Maybe one day I'll learn. The hair stuff includes ten different shades of dye, gloves, plastic caps, and some black towels. This is my favorite gift! Dark towels are the best idea. The first time I dyed my hair a bright color, my mom got really upset. After a while, it grew on her and she admitted she liked seeing what color I'll come home with next. Sometimes I only dye the ends, but other times, it's the whole head. I've ruined a lot of towels over the years, so these will be put to good use.

"Thank you both so much. These gifts are exactly what I want and need," I tell them, happy we have this time together. I love my parents even though we don't always see things the same way. They are good people and want the best for me. Sometimes their way of showing that is outdated.

"You are welcome, honey. You outdid yourself this year," Mom says with a smile.

"Thank you for the great gifts," Dad adds.

In addition to the snacks, I gave my mom an autobiography about an actress she likes who I've never heard of, new yarn for knitting, and a lightweight, blue sweater because she's always cold. I gave my dad a book about golf, a new golf shirt, and some balls and tees. He loves to play golf and still plays a few rounds every week. Together, I gave them a gift certificate to a nice restaurant in Orange Grove. They need to get out once in a while.

"Stay here. I'll be right back." Mom speed walks out of the room, coming back less than a minute later with two large boxes. I stand and take them from her. They aren't heavy, but I don't want her to lose her balance trying to carry them while maneuvering around the furniture. After setting them on the floor, Mom pushes one toward me and the other toward my dad. "This year, I made you each a little something special. Open them at the same time." My mother is practically vibrating with excitement.

Dad and I tear into the gifts at the same time, pulling out the contents.

"Mom! This is amazing. Thank you so much," I gush out. Dad and I are each holding blankets made from all the old pajamas she's been saving.

"Oh, Samantha, what a great idea."

"Hold them up so I can see." Mom claps her hands. I

smile at her request. She made the blankets but acts like she's never seen them. Dad and I indulge Mom and stand side by side holding our blankets.

After Mom 'oohs' and 'ahs' over them, we sit down. I take Dad's and spread it over me. There are so many patterns on his I've never seen, and I love looking at all the PJs they had before I was born.

MEGAN PLOPS DOWN on the couch next to me with a bottle of gas station champagne in one hand and two juice glasses in the other. We're young and poor. Cheap alcohol is the best we can do. Wine glasses are not at the top of my list of things I need to purchase for my home. My trailer doesn't exactly scream high class.

"How was Christmas with the parental units?" Megan asks once she's comfy.

"It was good. Boring. Same every year— a Christmas puzzle and hot chocolate last night then today five gifts and church with some food sprinkled in throughout the day. Oh, but I did get something cool." I take out the blanket and show my best friend.

"Wow, this is awesome. I'm glad she finally did something with all those pajamas."

"Me, too."

"Your mom loves her traditions. It's so dang cute," Megan muses wistfully.

"How was your Christmas?"

"It was great! Better than great! You know my family has zero traditions. Some years, we do everything on Christmas Eve; other years we save it all for Christmas morning. Last year, we skipped Christmas altogether and went on a family cruise. Well today, everything was decorated in shades of blue and pink. Weird, right? Like, it's Christmas. Those are totally the wrong colors. Then we all get a little box wrapped in Christmas paper, and my mom says we have to open them at the same time. She and Jane are both acting so giddy and strange as we tear into the packages. Inside are two ultrasound photos. *Two*. Then a little card that says, 'Baby Phillips Coming in July' and another that says, 'Baby Singleton Coming in July.'"

"Wait. What?" I blurt out. "You cannot be serious, Megs!"

"Serious as can be. I can't make this shit up. I'm going to be a big sister... again. And an aunt. In. The. Same. Month. It's weird, right? Like, it's weird for my sister and mom to both be having babies."

"It's not that weird. Your sister is twenty-three and married, and your mom is what? Forty something?"

"Thirty-nine. She was sixteen when she had Jane."

"Okay, definitely young enough to have another baby."

"True. And after raising Jane and me by herself, I'm glad she met Jim. They have a good life together and I *adore* having little siblings."

"That's all you did for Christmas?"

"Basically. We had a pseudo baby shower and celebrated the good news. We exchanged gifts like we always do, but all the food was centered around baby stuff like baby carrots, baby back ribs, pigs in a blanket, you know, because they are 'swaddled.' My mom can think of a million ideas like those. It was cute." She lifts her glass and takes a sip. Megan really does look happy with this development.

"You sound excited. I'm happy for your family."

"Thanks, Ellis. It was a good day." She drops her head to my chest and cuddles under my new blanket with me. "I'm glad to be here with you. I always need my 'E' time."

CHAPTER 4

JAGGER

Christmas at the Ward compound is definitely an adventure. Who am I kidding? Every day with the Ward clan is an experience like none other. And when I say compound, that is exactly what I mean. I grew up in a four-bedroom house on about a hundred acres of land between Anchor Point and Orange Grove. My parents own a huge citrus grove and grow oranges, lemons, and limes. At the front of the property, there is a small store where we sell the fruit and various citrus-related gifts. We also offer 'pick your own fruit' and sell to a few local restaurants and small grocery stores.

The modest house where my parents raised six kids sits at the end of a short drive to the left of the store. Behind their house, each kid has three acres where we've built our own homes. To the right of the store, seventy-five acres of citrus groves stretch along a small river that runs through the entire property. This land has been in our family for generations. My dad is an only child, so my siblings and I help run the farm. My oldest brother, one sister, and one brother-in-law all work on the farm full time. The rest of us help as needed when we aren't at our day jobs.

It probably sounds strange to most people, but all my siblings love living where we grew up. I have a small house on my plot, but I don't live there. Instead, I rent an apartment in Orange Grove right in the center of town. As much as I want to be near my family, there are too many memories of Jaxon here for me to live on the property permanently. I stay in the house during the holidays and sometimes if I'm here late at night.

We have a great time together, riding four wheelers, fishing in one of the three ponds on our land, working the farm, and generally goofing off. Running a citrus farm is hard work, but we make sure to play hard, too.

I'm stepping out of the shower in my two-bedroom house a little after six when there is pounding on my front door. Yes, pounding. Not some nice, civilized knock. It's got to be one of go to work or not, and he thinks everyone else should be awake, too. I feel bad for his kids when they become teenagers. They're never going to have a chance to waste a day lounging in bed.

"Come on, baby brother, you're wasting the day," I mock his words under my breath, not that he can hear me. However, he's kicked my ass a few too many times over the years and I don't want to take any chances. Damn him with his wrestling trophies and titles. I'm not a small guy, but I've never won a match against my oldest brother. In high school, Jax and I wrestled, too, but I was never as good as my brothers.

Shirtless with my long locks still dripping, I jerk the door open. "What? It's too early for your shit. I haven't even had coffee."

"Well, Merry Christmas to you, too, asshole," he snaps, unable to hide the teasing smile.

"Merry Christmas, Lex. Now, what do you want?"

"Duh, it's Santa's special day. Mom is already pulling casseroles out of the oven, and Melanie is on her second mimosa."

"It's six in the morning," I complain.

"Six-thirty-three to be exact," Lex corrects, glancing at his phone.

Instead of rushing to join my family and appease my brother, I meander into the kitchen and pour myself a travel mug of coffee to take with me, and then a smaller mug to enjoy now.

"Coffee?" I offer my brother.

"Seriously? Get dressed. There is coffee at the big house." It's funny that we all refer to my parents' house as the 'big house' since most of my siblings have larger ones. Mine is the smallest.

Lex groans when I sit at the table and take a long, slow sip from the Christmas mug Mom brought over. She has an entire collection and brings several to each of our homes every year on December first. Then she goes about decorating the entire property. Hell, some of the citrus trees even have colored Christmas lights on them.

"You're infuriating," Lex huffs out, taking a

matching mug from the cabinet above the coffee pot and filling it before joining me at the table.

"This is the last quiet moment we'll have all day. Savor it, Lexie. Savor it." He quirks an eyebrow at me but doesn't comment on the nickname he loathes. I coined it when I was around two, except back then, it sounded more like 'Wexie' because Ls are hard. When I was a kid, I had nicknames for all my siblings, but the only ones that stuck are Lexie and Wawa for my brother, Law.

After taking my sweet time drinking two cups of coffee, I amble into the bedroom, and as slowly as humanly possible, I get dressed. Spending extra time pulling my long, curly, brown hair into a ponytail then braiding it.

The doorknob wiggles, but when Lex finds it locked, he bangs on the door. "What is taking so long? Hurry up." Damn, he's impatient.

"You don't have to wait for me, Wexie. I know the way to the big house."

He growls at the use of the nickname he abhors. "I'll wait."

Doesn't he know I'm only taking this long because of how utterly annoyed he is getting? How can someone in his mid-thirties be so naïve? Once I'm ready, I sit on the bed and prop my feet up, scrolling through my phone for five minutes just for good measure.

When I finally emerge, Lex is pacing the living room, face beet red. Damn, he's gonna give himself a heart attack before he's forty if he keeps this up.

"Ready?" I ask nonchalantly, pulling the front door open and motioning for Lex to walk out.

"I was ready almost an hour ago," he growls, stepping onto the front porch. For a second, I consider closing the door in his face just to piss him off, but I don't want to keep Mom waiting. She looks forward to Christmas every year, starting on December 26th. Part of me is surprised she doesn't keep the decorations up year-round.

I follow my older brother out to the waiting golf cart. We don't use our cars on the property unless we need a truck to haul fruit. We own a bunch of golf carts and four-wheelers that use a lot less gas than cars. I don't argue when Lex climbs into the driver's seat. We sit in silence as he drives us down the short, winding road between my house and my parents' home.

By the time we arrive, the rest of the family is there, drinking mimosas or coffee and having lively conversations. There's a hearty round of 'Merry Christmases' when we walk inside then hugs from everyone as if they don't see daily and have several meals each week together. It is possible our family is a little too close. Being the outlier is uncomfortable sometimes. My mom wants me here more but has never made me feel guilty about moving away from the property. Nope, I guilt-trip myself without anyone's help.

"Everyone, grab a plate. Let's eat before it gets cold," Mom insists.

The entire kitchen table is covered with food—sausage and egg casserole, potato casserole, curried fruit, breads, muffins, coffee cake, grits, bacon, and fresh fruit. With our large group, there isn't room in the house. Years ago, when I was in middle school, Dad built a covered area outside with four large picnic tables. At the time, our family fit on two, but Dad hoped one day we would all live on the property and give him grandkids, so he built the others for the future. Between my siblings, their spouses, and my nieces and nephews, there are eighteen of us now. We still have room for a few more. Maybe one day Mel or I will add to the brood with kids of our own.

CHAPTER 5

ELLIS

My trailer is one of about twenty in a small park on the edge of town, just before the bridge that connects Anchor Point to the mainland. My entire life— work, friends, the beach, my parents— are all within a ten-minute drive, but today, I'm not interested in any of it. For almost a week, there has only been one thing, or more accurately, one person, on my mind. Nothing takes my mind off the hot as sin instructor at the glassblowing studio. Jag is everything I love in a man— sexy, long hair, muscles, tall. We're about the same height, but he has big muscles, especially on his arms. I bet he has a six-pack or possibly an eight-pack. God, how I want him to fuck me, so I can see every one of those muscles at work.

I'll never be anyone's boyfriend, or husband, and that's fine by me. I like having different sexual partners and experiences. That way, it never gets boring. I am a *slut* for cock. A cum slut in every meaning of the words. I knew I was interested in boys long before puberty hit. As soon as I was old enough to suck a cock, I found a hot baseball player and took care of him in the locker room one day after school.

We were probably too young to be doing it, but who cares? Lots of teenagers have sex. Living in a small town didn't lend itself to finding very many gay teens, so throughout high school, I spent many afternoons getting that baseball player off and letting him do all kinds of fun things to me. He never came out and we didn't have a relationship beyond the locker room. He went away to college on a baseball scholarship and will likely never return to Anchor Point. He wasn't the only guy at my high school who let me suck him off, but he was my first... well, everything. I guess in some weird way, I will always miss him. But I don't do the whole boyfriend thing. Casual hookups are the way to go. I've finally come to terms with the realization that is all I'm truly worthy of getting.

Without thinking about where I'm going, I drive the thirty minutes to Orange Grove and find myself standing outside Coastal Glass Studio. When Ryan, my boss at Paradise 11, brought the employees to a glass-blowing class as our Christmas gift and in place of a company holiday party, I never expected to meet the hunk of sex that is Jagger Ward. I only know his last name because I stalked his studio's website. I may or may not have jerked off to pictures of him on the website twelve times in the past week— the Twelve Wanks of Christmas. Not a bad way to spend the holi-day, but I would have preferred to spend one of those nights with him buried balls deep in my ass.

When I glance in the window, Jag is behind the front counter. No one else is in sight. Huh, he must not have a class right now. Confidence in my sexual prowess has never been an issue, so I swing the door open, ready to move from stalking my prey to pouncing on him.

Jag's head snaps my way, and his green eyes meet my brown ones. Damn, he's even hotter with his hair falling to his waist than he was last week with it pulled into a messy bun. Shit. I might be in trouble with this one.

"Hello, there. Ellis, right?" he asks with a smile.

"OMG! You remember," I gush and blush. "Yes, Ellis Young." I reach out a hand for him to shake.

"Jag, in case you don't remember."

"Oh, honey, I remember," I purr. His strong grip hurts a little, but I school my features and smile.

"What brings you in today?"

"Well," I say, seductively running a finger down his broad chest. "I thought maybe you can teach me something."

He laughs loudly in response. "I have a feeling you aren't talking about glassblowing."

"I'm most *definitely* talking about blowing."

Jag steps around me and walks toward the door. For a second, I think he's going to tell me to leave, but he clicks the lock and flips the sign around to the closed side. Then he stalks back and looks me dead in the eyes.

"How about a private lesson?" he asks, voice low and gravelly.

"Okay," I squeak out. What the hell? I never squeak. I am confident and willing when it comes to sex. Usually the initiator. I might not be a top, but I know what I like. When I want someone, I go for it without hesitation or second guessing.

With Jag, I feel out of sorts. Needy in ways I've never been with any other guy. *Nope. Stop, Ellis. Sex.* This is about getting fucked and moving on to the next guy. What was it the last guy called me? 'Cum and dump.' Yep, that's me. A depository of sorts, like a night deposit box. A cum bank.

Jag's strong hand pulls me toward the back where the glass studio is located, yanking me back to the present. I stumble a few steps before gaining my footing.

He kicks the door to the studio closed and pushes me against it, trailing his hands up my body from my waist to my shoulders. Jag leans in, fisting my hair with one hand and splays the other one across my back. He pulls me flush against his body, crashing his mouth onto mine. His tongue pushes past my lips and into my mouth, searching out mine. Well, this is something. I'm not big on the kissing part. Too intimate.

I sucked and fucked my way through high school, often with that baseball player before he finally kissed me on graduation day. Eighteen years old and having my first kiss was ironic. I'd been having sex since I was fifteen with half the 'straight' guys in town. Yeah, I do a lot of things ass backwards.

Why the hell am I thinking about another guy when Jag has his tongue in my mouth? Oh, yeah, that's right, because he has his *tongue* in my mouth. I try to kiss him back, I really do, but it feels weird and… personal. He's a good kisser and having his hands on me feels so fucking amazing, but I want to get to the good stuff.

Jag steps back and eyes me warily. "Sorry. Did I overstep? Misread cues?" He runs his hands through his hair, pulling it into a ponytail and wrapping an elastic hair tie around it. "I thought you were interested in…" He drops his hands to his side the same way he drops his words mid-sentence.

"I am interested!" I blurt out, my own voice sounding strained and unsure. I take a step closer to him. He's put too much distance between us. "Kissing isn't my thing. It's too personal. Most guys just want the sex part anyway."

"Oh, okay."

He looks a little sad or disappointed. Did I do something wrong? I've never had a guy give a shit when I wanted to skip the kissing or foreplay and jump right to the fucking. Ah, fuck. Did I find the *one* decent guy in Florida? Fuck my life.

"Sorry. I'll leave you alone." I turn to go and almost make it to the door before two strong arms come around me practically dragging me halfway across the studio.

"I like to fuck," he growls in my ear. "I hope like hell you're a bottom."

"Yes," is all I manage to get out before my shirt hits the floor. Damn, he doesn't mess around. I unbutton my jeans and push them to my ankles while he takes off his own shirt. His jeans are next then we're standing naked, face to face.

"Wait here." He walks to a small room on the other side of the studio. Great. Leave me here naked, cold, and alone. This feels fucking great.

Jag comes back quickly with a blanket, a condom, and a bottle of lube. He arranges the blanket on one of the marvers, patting and coaxing me onto the table. He drops the lube next to me and rolls on the condom.

Chapter 6

Jagger

When Ellis Young walked into my studio a few minutes ago, I never expected to end up here. I gently push him onto his back, and he goes willingly, spreading his legs for me. He's so ready and eager. That shouldn't surprise me. Ellis showed up here with one goal in mind. Literally walked in and basically asked me to fuck him.

Now he's lying on a blanket, open and waiting for me. Just sex. Nothing more. No strings. No awkward morning after. A quick fuck and he'll be gone. Perfect. Strings get messy.

Ellis said he wants to skip the kissing and foreplay, but I'm not ready to slam into him, yet. His body is gorgeous, and I intend to explore every inch of it. He's my height, but lean and sinewy, not muscular like me. That's fine because I'm rarely attracted to muscular men. Ellis is definitely my type with his shock of pink hair, small, silver hoop earrings, a few tattoos scattered over his skin with no rhyme or reason.

From the little I know about him, he's like a walking mass of chaos. The random seven or so tats inked over his arms and torso and the spiky hair that apparently changes color regularly fit that mold. A chaotic mess of colors and pictures with no theme. It suits him.

Tracing circles up his legs with my nails draws a stuttered breath from him. When my fingers graze over his stomach, he moans quietly. Dragging my nails over his nipples pulls a whimper from him. The more I touch him, the more cute little noises escape him. His cock hardens and leaks onto his stomach. I lean down and lap the precum up, making sure to avoid the head of his cock.

"Please," he begs, lifting his hips in an effort to reach my tongue with his erection.

It hits my chest as I move further up. Placing one hand on his lower abdomen and pushing him down, I kiss from one nipple to the other, biting down on the second one hard enough to draw a yelp from Ellis, but it turns into a moan as I lick the swollen nub.

"Get inside me already," he whines with need, practically vibrating under me.

"Bossy," I tease. He pins me with an annoyed glare. Okay, shit. He told me he wasn't into this foreplay stuff, it's just a quick fuck. But there is something intriguing about Ellis. I haven't been able to get him out of my mind for over a week and now that he's here, I want more than a quick fuck and run.

Jesus. Get yourself together. You can't be falling for someone you don't even know.

48

Shoving all the 'feeling' thoughts way the hell down, I stand up, admiring him for a few seconds while I coat my cock and fingers with lube. Stroking myself with one hand, my eyes graze over his body memorizing every bend, every lithe muscle, and every tattoo as I begin working one finger into him. If this is going to be a one-time thing, I'm going to commit it all to memory.

"Mm. More," he begs. I push in a second finger, scissoring them and opening him up for me then quickly add a third. "I'm ready. Come on. I need you inside me," he lets out breathlessly.

I line my aching cock up with his rim and push past the first ring of muscle. As soon as I do, Ellis grabs my hips and pulls me all the way in, balls deep, until I'm flush with his body.

"Stop being gentle and fuck me like you mean it." I pull out a little, slamming back into him hard, the sound of our bodies slamming together echoes off the walls of the studio. "God, yes! Do that again." Ellis screams, throwing his head back.

Setting a fast, steady rhythm, I slam into Ellis over and over. He immediately becomes an incoherent, babbling mess writhing under me. When I find his prostate, he lets out a loud moan that sounds something like 'there.' I hit that spot over and over. Sweat drips down my face, chest, and back. Ellis' body glistens and his fingernails sink into my hips, leaving marks and possibly drawing blood, but I don't care. His hole feels too damn good.

As I chase my own release, I grab Ellis' cock, using

his precum and the lube left on my fingers to jerk him at the same pace as my thrusts, pistoning into him harder and harder as he comes undone.

"Ung, fuck!" he cries out, emptying onto my hand and his stomach. Three thrusts later, I fill the condom.

"Fuck, that was hot." Breathing heavy, I lean over, dropping my hands on either side of his waist and using the table to hold me up until I can move. Slowly, I regain a little composure and stand up, pulling out of him and letting his legs fall back to the table.

Ellis' breath returns to normal while I dispose of the condom and pull on my boxers. Ellis pushes himself up and hops off the table, grabbing his own underwear and pulling them on. He's fully dressed before I get my jeans on.

"Thanks, babe. That was great." He waves as he heads for the door. I start to call his name as I pull my shirt on, but he's already gone, out the front door, leaving a trail of confusion in his wake. I know he said just sex. But... what the fuck?

Chapter 7

Ellis

Between Christmas with my parents, the huge New Year's Eve party at the bar and my afternoon with Jag, it's been a crazy couple of weeks. Showing up at Jag's studio for the sole purpose of getting fucked was new for me. Hooking up is the one thing I'm great at, but I usually find my men at clubs and on apps designed for finding for dates. But let's be honest, most of them of strictly for finding your next lay. Showing up at a man's job and asking him to fuck me is a new level of desperate. It's the truth. After more than a week of jerking off to images of the glass-blowing god, I had to see if he'd live up to my expectations. He most certainly did!

At the Paradise 11 New Year's Eve party, there were plenty of guys looking for a good time, but thoughts of Jagger clouded my judgement, and I turned down two different men. Two! I never say no! But, apparently, my hand and thoughts of Jag won out and I went home alone. Turns out it was worth the wait. Sex with Jagger Ward was the best quickie ever!

On the other hand, Christmas with my family was uneventful, per usual, with appetizers and wine on Christmas Eve, our annual trip to church on Christmas morning followed by lunch and gift giving. As soon as there was a break in the monotony, I bailed. Boredom set in hours prior to my exit, and I couldn't wait to get home. I love my parents, but I can only stand so much of the three of us together staring at the Christmas tree, or worse, putting together those godforsaken puzzles they like so much.

I was a late-in-life baby, and my parents are the ages of most grandparents. My mom was forty-five and my dad was fifty when I was born. Now they're sixty-six and seventy-one. They had long given up on having children and were both shocked and ecstatic when they got the news of my impending birth.

Having older parents has its pros and cons. In high school, they were too old and tired to stay awake and wait for me to get home, so curfews were always ignored. They believed sweet, innocent me when I promised I was in the house before midnight. The truth is, I was hanging out at parties I had no business attending and learning to give one hell of a blowjob behind dumpsters all over town. On the other hand, they didn't grow up with technology and didn't understand how important it was to my entire existence. We didn't have cable or streaming services or Wi-Fi. We had a landline! A landline! What the hell was I supposed to do with that? When I moved out at eighteen, I *finally* got my first cell phone. As if being gay in a small town wasn't bad enough, I was out of touch with… well, everything.

I love my parents, and they raised me well. They have no problem with me dating guys, which did come as a small shock to them. When I was sixteen and told them I was into boys, I expected some pushback, but they were amazing. It's still weird to me that they can fully embrace a gay son but live like it is the fifties when it comes to technology.

A gentle knock on the metal door startles me and I drop the plate I'm holding into the sink a little too hard, listening to it shatter. A broken plate is a later problem. Leaving the sink, I take two tiny steps and open the door.

"Hi, baby," my mom greets happily as she steps into my modest accommodations. I do *not* need this today. Sunday is the only day I don't work either job, and I require a little time to myself to regroup. She doesn't need to know I was off yesterday, too.

"Hey, Mom. What brings you by?" I do my best to force annoyance out of my voice, but I do not appreciate surprise visits from my parents.

She scrunches her nose as she looks around at the grime and dirt. "You need to clean this disgusting place." And there's one of the main reasons.

"Taking care of it today," I snip.

"I don't understand why you live in such a dump, Ellis. You should rent an apartment or buy a house. Those are so much nicer."

"And super expensive," I mutter.

"For reasons I can't fathom, you're killing yourself working two jobs. Surely, you can afford something better than," she waves her hand around, "this."

"It costs a lot of money to live better than," I wave my own hand, mocking her, "this. *This* is what I can afford. It's mine and I like it."

"Fine. If you want to live the life a poor boy, so be it." Why is she here ruining my day off?

"This *is* the *best* I can do." The tears stinging my eyes piss me off almost as much as my mother's words. "How about a little support?"

"Your father and I have always supported you," she retorts, astonished I would insinuate otherwise.

"Eh, support adjacent at best."

Unable to contain herself any longer, my mother starts picking up discarded clothing and shoving them on top of the overflowing basket in the corner. "What does that mean?" she asks through pursed lips.

"It means you were supportive until it wasn't convenient or no longer aligned with your vision of my future." I grab the shirt from her hand. "I can clean up my own mess," I snap.

"I can help." She walks to the counter and turns on the faucet, reaching into the sink.

"Stop." The harshness of my words startles her, and she quickly jerks her hand back. "Sorry. I dropped a dish and there might be broken glass in there."

I take a calming breath and look at my mom. We look so much alike. The same tall, thin frame, matching brown eyes, and wavy blond hair. Although, my hair is spiky with product and dyed a smokey blue.

I love my parents. I really do. But sometimes I can't stand to be around them. They mean well and probably view cutting me off as an act of love, but I was a *kid*. The only job I'd had at that point was working at a summer art camp for two years. It didn't pay much, and I was trash at saving. My parents paid for everything and never gave me any indication I was getting cut off at eighteen. The day they told me I had one month to find a place to live, I was shattered. It was a bitter pill to swallow, and I'm still pissed about the entire situation.

She looks around the small space. It is kind of gross right now. "We raised you to be better than this."

"You raised me to be myself, I won't argue that. But you put me out when I turned eighteen with no warning. I had no experience in the real world, and you gave me zero guidance."

"Oh, Ellis. Are we doing this again?" exasperation laces my mother's voice.

"Mother, please. I have things to do." I take a few steps toward the door.

"Are you telling me to leave?" she huffs.

I turn back to face her. "I don't have the energy to rehash this today. The past three years have been difficult. You gave me a month's warning. One month to scrimp and save what little I could and find a place to live. I was blindsided, but I made it work," I tell her. She may not approve of how I live my life, but I am doing my best and that's enough for me.

"What were your father and I supposed to do? You had these delusions of studying *art* of all things. We took drastic measures, hoping you would come to your senses."

"You cut me off, squashed my college plans *and* dreams of becoming an artist."

The door slams closed behind me, and my back stiffens. I can smell my father's cologne, some acrid, sixties version of what passes for smelling like money. It burns my nostrils, and I'm not even facing him. I can't believe they still make that crap.

"We gave you a dose of reality, hoping you'd come to your senses and choose a real major!" he roars, leaving no doubt that he was standing outside smoking his pipe, listening to ever word Mom and I uttered.

"Like finance or law?" I whip my body around to face him. "Yeah, it's old news, Dad. I'm never going to be a lawyer or have some fancy, corporate finance job, making huge amounts of money. There's more to life than wealth. I'd like to be rich in ways that matter to *me*."

"Money gets you the things that matter," he argues, eyes cutting into me.

"You can't buy love and friendship," I argue.

Dad scoffs. "Love has never been your strong suit. I don't see the boys lining up to date you, son. Did you ever stop to think it's because you are *poor*? Men don't want to date down." I gasp at my father's words as more tears sting my eyes.

I push past him and open the door. "Get out. Both of you."

"Ellis," Mom scolds.

"No, Samantha. Let's go." Mom follows Dad without question. I close and lock the door behind them before collapsing onto the floor, finally letting the tears I've been holding back fall.

CHAPTER 8

JAGGER

Ever since Ellis showed up at my studio last week, I can't get him out of my head. I think about him constantly— with both heads. After meeting him when his group of coworkers came for their Christmas party, I thought I had it bad. Nope, I was wrong. One afternoon of burying myself in Ellis' ass and, no matter how quick it was, I will never get enough of him.

"Ugh!" I scrub my hands down my face as I let out an exasperated groan.

He is all I can focus on lately. My glass skills are faltering. I'm ruining everything I try to create, and yesterday, I burned my left hand. It's not the first time I've burned myself working with extreme heat. It's a hazard of the job. Normally I'm very careful and take every necessary precaution. I was so entranced with thoughts of Ellis and the things I want to do to him that I wasn't paying close attention to my actions and caught the edge of a hot surface. The second-degree burn covers about a quarter of my hand and hurts like the devil. Thankfully, the first-aid kit at the studio is always well-stocked, so I was able to take care of the wound myself. No reason to involve a doctor and pay outrageous medical bills. Not having insurance is a sure way to force yourself to learn the basics. Mel tells me all the time to call Kevin if I need something, but I feel like I'm taking advantage of him. Having a doctor in the family has its perks, but I'm saving my call for a real emergency.

This might be the stupidest decision I've ever made, but I need to see Ellis. I figure, why not do the same thing to him he did to me and interrupt his workday? The drive to Anchor Point from my apartment is almost thirty minutes, enough time for me to make a better choice and turn around, but I keep moving forward. Honestly, I don't want to make a better choice. My heart races with anticipation as I drive over the bridge connecting Anchor Point to the mainland. As much as I love the beach, it's been years since I've been out here.

My heart constricts as thoughts of my brother invade my mind. Jaxon loved the water. The waves here aren't good for any kind of real surfing, but that never stopped Jax. We'd drive out on the weekends, or after school, and spend hours in the water swimming and surfing. Damn, I miss him.

It's been hard for me to do the things we enjoyed doing together like going to the beach, hanging out at the batting cages, and gaming. This is the first time in eight years that I've seen the beach. Panic sets in as I pull into a parking spot and step out of the truck. I don't know if I can do this. My chest constricts and my vision blurs as I steady myself with both hands on the truck door. Deep breath in through my nose, let it out slowly from my mouth. I practice the breathing exercises my therapist gave me, counting five in and five out in an attempt to calm myself. After spending more than a year being an angry kid with no direction and no future, I finally drug myself back from the brink and got some help. It was a long road, but my family stood by me and helped me heal even though I hadn't spoken to most of them during that time.

Parents are wonderful creatures who love their children unconditionally and are always there to pick up the pieces. Well, my parents are, not everyone is so lucky. I treated my family like shit after I lost my brother. I abandoned them and crawled inside myself. We were all broken after that tragic loss, but I refused to see anyone else's pain. All that mattered was how I felt and what I was dealing with in those months following Jaxon's death. My parents and siblings tried to reach out to me, but I ignored every phone call and text. For months after I moved to my apartment, I didn't contact them. They had already buried one son and basically lost me, too. I'm still not sure how I finished high school. That year is a blur, but somehow, I passed and got a diploma.

When I finally got my life together and came crawling back, my family was there with open arms. It hasn't been easy, but we've done our best to heal individually and as a family. Maybe 'healing' isn't the right word. We're living our lives the best we can but losing someone so young and unexpectedly isn't something you ever get over. Jaxon will always be a part of me and his memories will stay with me forever.

When my breathing returns to normal and I stop feeling like I'm going to pass out, I walk onto the boardwalk. My breath hitches again as soon as I see the beach. Hearing the waves is one thing, but seeing them is almost more than I can take. I grab onto the railing to steady myself again and watch the small waves lap against the shore. For a brief moment, I let memories of Jaxon effortlessly maneuvering his board through the surf take over. He was a natural and had big dreams of traveling the world to surf the best spots.

"Ellis. You're here to see Ellis," I remind myself.

My legs are heavy, and it's difficult to move down the pier. I didn't think it would be this hard to see the beach after so much time. I should have known, though. It's been eight years, and I still react every time I drive past the batting cages. It's an involuntary reaction and my body goes into a state of panic. As soon as I pass the cages, I relax, and everything returns to normal. Maybe I'm not doing as well as I think I am.

When I walk up to the open-air bar, I see Ellis inside effortlessly gliding through the space, smiling as he takes orders, and speaking to customers as he does his job. Is he flirting with that other worker? Shit. Maybe that's his boyfriend. They seemed friendly in the class, but I didn't think they were together. No that can't be right. Boyfriends would have been touching and maybe even kissing. Right? Although, that guy did make some sexual innuendos in class, so did everyone else. And surely, Ellis wouldn't have let me fuck him last week if he has a boyfriend.

Dammit, Jagger. Get it together.

What is happening to me? I'm inside the guy once and I'm already giving off stalker vibes, watching him work and freaking out with pure jealousy.

I yank the door open with my uninjured hand before I can change my mind. The bar is loud, patrons line the stools, and several tables are full.

"Sit anywhere you'd like," a short brunette calls to me. I recognize her from the night they all came to my studio, but I can't remember her name.

Working my way through a few people standing near the bar, I find a small table near the back with a perfect view of the water, not that any of the views in this place are bad. It sits at the end of the Eleventh Street pier, right over the Gulf of Mexico surrounded by water. With all the large windows open, the breeze is cool and the sounds of the waves lapping against the pier filters into the room.

I had never heard of Paradise 11 until Ryan, the owner, called to book the class for his employee Christmas party. After doing a little digging, I learned that he opened the bar almost seven years ago when the town was in ruins after Hurricane Nichole's devastation. He's done a great job with the place, but Anchor Point has been slow to recover from the devastation. Orange Grove had considerable damage, but being a little further inland, we didn't have the storm surge to contend with.

I pick up one of the menus that are wedged between the salt and pepper shakers and study it with my head down as Ellis approaches me. My nerves are suddenly on high alert. This might have been a terrible idea.

"Hi, welcome to Paradise 11. I'm Ellis and I'll be taking care of you. Can I... Jag?" he halts his well-rehearsed introduction when realizes it's me.

Sheepishly, I glance up. "Hey, Ellis. How ya doing?"

"Um, good." He gasps when he sees my bandaged hand. "What happened to your hand?

Are you okay?"

"I'm fine. It's a little burn, but I'll live." Even though my words are nonchalant, Ellis looks worried. He stares for a few seconds then shakes his head.

"What are you doing here?" he asks, his voice losing some of its initial vigor.

"Hungry?" The word comes out more like a question, so I clear my throat and try again.

"Hungry. Heard this place is good. And I happen to know at least half the waitstaff is sexy as hell." I offer Ellis a wink and lower my voice. "Especially, on his back, naked and spread open."

He falters, choking on whatever words he was trying to form. After several seconds, he shakes his head and beams. Damn, that smile. "I mean, Megan *is* hot," he responds flippantly.

"I don't see anyone but you," I state, holding eye contact until he glances at the device in his hand.

His demeanor changes and I can see the walls going up right in front of me. "Look, Jag, flirting isn't free here. If you aren't ready to order, I've got a table full sexy men waiting for me to come check on them."

A low growl bubbles up from the depths of my soul as a wave of jealousy soars through me. "I'll have an order of loaded tots, everything on them, and a water."

"Nothing from the bar?"

"No. Water is fine."

"Okay, BRB with that water, handsome," he flirts with a bright smile.

I watch him go. He shakes his ass, giving me a little show. Brat. I don't think I'll ever get enough of that man.

The smell of the beach— salty and fishy wafts— into the bar. I love that smell. I didn't realize how much I missed it until today. A calm feeling washes over me as I think back to the last time I was out here. Jaxon and I came out on a hot August Saturday, two weeks before our senior year started. A senior year he wouldn't finish. He surfed and I swam in and out of the waves. We spent hours in the water that day and even more time lounging on the beach. We talked about the plans we had for senior year, our futures. He told me he planned to ask Sarah, his girlfriend of three years, to marry him. He said he was going to wait until graduation day, but he knew without a doubt she was the only one for him. I truly believe they would have lasted a lifetime. That was the last time we spent an entire day together, just the two of us. Jaxon was dead less than a week later.

"Your food will be right out." Ellis sets the water down and turns to go, but I grab his wrist.

"Can you sit for a few minutes?"

He bites his bottom lip and shakes his head. "I have tables. I'm working, Jag."

"Sorry," I say, letting him go. "I know you're working, but I want to talk to you.

What time do you get off?"

"Tonight? Around midnight or so unless we get busy."

"I can wait."

He lets out a humorless laugh. "It's barely nine. You're going to sit here for more than three hours?"

"Unless you get busy and need the table." I look around to make sure no one can hear us and drop my voice. "You know how good my tip is."

Ellis' face turns several shades of pink. Huh... I didn't know it was possible to embarrass him. He's so free and open with his sexuality, constantly flirting with more confidence than I've ever had. He practically barged into my studio and told me to fuck him.

"Fine. If you want to wait three hours, then we can talk after my shift."

He doesn't wait for me to say anything else before he's off to that damn table full of 'sexy' men, putting on his flirtiest smile and gently touching one's shoulder then another's back. And the jealousy is back. Shit. I'm not normally so possessive or full of rage, but apparently, that's what Ellis does to me. How someone I've known two weeks can turn me inside out is a mystery. This is all new. I've never dated much and, truthfully, I don't have sex often. Apps and random hook ups aren't my thing, which makes what I did with Ellis that much more shocking.

Melanie will be proud of me if she finds out. Who am I kidding? Mel *always* finds out. She's like some weird sister ninja that knows everything about me—sometimes before I know.

My tots arrive, but the girl who greeted me brings them. Guess Ellis is busy. "Enjoy. I'll get you some more water." She returns seconds later, fills my cup and disappears. The loaded tots look and smell amazing. A plate full of tater tots covered in chili, cheese, green onions, sour cream, mustard, and jalapeños. Good 'ol comfort food is exactly what I need today between these crazy feelings I'm having for Ellis and all the memories I'm trudging up of my brother.

WHEN ELLIS finally gets off work, I've eaten my tots and an order of chicken fingers with fries. It's more food than I should have eaten this late at night, but I don't care. I needed something to keep me busy while I waited.

"Okay, so what do you want to talk about?" he asks, dropping into the seat across from me.

"I want to take you on a date," I blurt out. I spent three hours thinking of the best way to approach the subject. Apparently, spewing it out without a second thought was the move. Great. *Desperate much?* I silently scold myself.

Ellis guffaws at me, hitting the table as if it's the

funniest thing anyone has ever uttered. Wow, make a guy feel good. When I don't laugh, he sobers.

"Oh, you're serious. Sorry. Um… I don't really date."

"Why not?" Neither do I, not since the Ben disaster, but I want to date Ellis. I don't say any of that out loud.

"I liked what we did last week. We should do that again." The hopeful look in his eyes raises a bunch of questions. Is sex all he wants? Did I completely misread every cue? I thought he was interested in more than a one-night, rather afternoon, stand.

"I liked it, too, but I want to get to know you," I tell him honestly.

"Why?" he asks incredulously.

"Because I think you're interesting." *Interesting. Really, Jag? That's the best you've got?*

Ellis moves in closer. "Will a date get me laid?"

Leaning back in my chair, I force my features to remain impassive. "That can be arranged." As much as I want a real date with Ellis, I also crave him. I need to be buried inside him again. "When is your next day off?"

"Sunday."

"Then I'll see you Sunday. Do you want me to pick you up?"

"No. Let's meet somewhere."

"Give me your phone. I'll put my number in." He punches in his code before passing the phone over. I add me as a contact— Sexy Glass Blower then call my own number, so I'll have his. After handing his phone back, I add his contact— Best Ass.

He laughs when he reads what I put in his phone. "You think you're sexy?" he questions with a smirk.

"*You* think I'm sexy."

"Touché."

"What did you put for me?" he asks, shining that amazing smile at me again.

"Best Ass." I turn my phone so he can see. "And, yes, it means more than one thing." I push myself up and offer Ellis a hand. He lets me pull him to his feet. "Can I walk you to your car?"

"Not tonight. I promised Megan I'd stay and have a drink with her. She's waiting at the bar."

"Okay, Sunday then. I'll text you where and what time." I lean in, kiss Ellis on the cheek and whisper, "I can't wait for our date or to be buried in that hot ass again."

Ellis shivers at my words. I saunter away without looking back leaving him standing alone, hungry for more.

CHAPTER 9

ELLIS

Once the holidays are over, the bar is dead for several weeks then picks up slightly with island regulars through most of March before we get super busy. The spring and summer months are insane. I like this time of year. The temperatures are milder, but they will never be extremely cold in Florida. Once in a while we have a freeze, and everyone loses their minds.

Tonight has been slow, but it's nice to have a little downtime and get paid to hang out with my colleagues. I'm perched on a stool at the end of the bar because every table in the place has been empty for two hours. Ryan cut me about an hour ago, so I've been sitting here, sipping on a fruity drink and talking to Matt, Chelsea, and Megan when they aren't busy doing something else. I'm surprised Ryan hasn't closed the kitchen yet with only four people sitting at the bar.

Megan sips on her own drink even though she's

technically still at work. Ryan doesn't care when the place is this empty as long as we don't get drunk.

"Be right back," I tell Megan as I slide off the barstool and head for the bathroom. When I push open the door, I stop in my tracks. Matt has his sleeves rolled up with the water running, but he isn't washing his hands. He's staring blankly at his arms. I glance in the mirror, trying to meet his eyes, but it's like he's in a trance. He has no idea I'm even standing here. Through the mirror, I can make out several bruises on his arms. A couple are about the size and length of fingers. Some are smaller and some are larger.

"Matt," I venture. His eyes snap up as he tugs down his sleeves and washes his hands without actually speaking to me. "Are you okay?"

"Fine," he clips. He dries his hands and goes to step around me, but I block the way.

"What happened to your arms?"

"Nothing."

"Did someone hurt you?" I ask gently.

"What? No." He looks down as his face and ears turn bright red. "Sometimes, I like it a little… rough." He rushes the words out, looking sheepish and embarrassed.

"Oh, sorry. Okay, cool. Yeah, that's cool." I step aside and let Matt leave.

Who am I to judge what someone enjoys in bed? There's something nagging at me, but I can't quite figure it out. I have no reason not to believe Matt, but he looked almost scared. Maybe he just doesn't want anyone to know his sexual proclivities. It's not like I go around telling everyone I like to have sex in public places.

Once I finish in the bathroom. I return to the bar where the kitchen crew is now sitting. Megan, Matt, and Chelsea are doing their closing duties. There are only two patrons left and they look to be wrapping things up.

"We closing?" I ask Chelsea as she picks up my empty glass.

"Yeah. Ryan and Grayson left. Windows are shut, doors are locked."

"Cool. I'll go help Megan."

Walking over to my best friend, I hip check her and she swats me with the damp towel she's using to wipe down the tables.

"Need some help?" I offer.

"Nah, you're off."

"I'll sweep."

Megan mouths 'thank you' as I grab the broom and get to work. Anytime one of us is cut early, we usually hang around anyway and have dinner or a couple of drinks then help the other one out. What else do I have to do? Most of the other bars and clubs close at the same time, so unless I have the night off, I can't go out partying or searching for a hook up.

Plus, when I do get cut early like tonight, I smell like fried food and stale beer. By the time I get home and shower, I'm so exhausted all I want to do is fall into bed. I might as well hang with my bestie and help her clean up if I'm not going out to find a good lay.

As I sweep, I watch Matt wipe down the bar and

load dirty glasses into the large holder. He winces when he lifts it to carry it to the kitchen where the industrial dishwasher is located.

Worry settles inside me as I watch him. Is he telling me the truth? I guess if he likes rough sex, he could be sore from that. When he comes back, he's all smiles, joking with Chelsea, and being his usual jovial self. Maybe I'm looking for something that isn't there. Best to accept his story since there is no reason for me to think otherwise. I hate when people get in my personal business and try to force me to talk about something I'm not ready to talk about. Or worse, convince me there is something wrong with the things I enjoy.

Fingers snap in my face and I blink as I tear my eyes from Matt to Megan, who's standing in front of me. "Where were you? I asked you the same question three times."

"Sorry. Thinking about… a date." I say before I can think of something different. Fuck. Why did I tell her that? Out of all the words in the English language, I have to choose the one word I don't actually want to talk about. Eventually, I always tell Megan everything, but I have no idea what I'm doing with Jagger, and there is really nothing to tell. He thinks he has to wine and dine me to get me to fuck him. I tried telling him I don't need a meal. I'm easy. I'll fuck for free.

"A date. Oooh, do tell. Give me all the deets. Is it with that hottie from the glassblowing place? I thought you two were just fucking?"

"Slow down. Dang, girl. Breathe. If you must know, it's nothing. We're hooking up, and for some unknown reason, he thinks he needs to impress me or something. I don't need to be impressed to fuck a guy. Do you know how many drunken hookups I've had in bathrooms and dark alleys?"

"Yeah, too many to count. So... the glassblower." She winks. "What's his name? Jagger? Is that it?"

"Jagger, yeah." I can't control the huge grin.

"OMG!" She playfully smacks my chest. "You like him. He is definitely more than a hookup. Ellis is in *love!*" She sings the last sentence, and I want to crawl in a hole and die.

"I do not like Jagger that way. We are just fucking. That's it."

"Does he know that? Because a date sounds like more than 'just fucking.'" She air quotes the last two words. Megan knows me better than anyone. Hell, she knows me better than I know myself. Jagger probably does think this is dating or whatever, but it's not. It's sex. That's it.

"He knows," I lie with a frustrated growl. "He's a hookup. I'll have my fun then move on to the next one. It's what I do."

"Because you think that's all you're worth." She takes my hand and squeezes it tightly. "Jagger knows that isn't true. He sees more in you, or he wouldn't be taking you a date. Give him a chance. You're special, Ellis, and you deserve to be loved."

Damn, waterworks. I wipe my eyes with my free hand. "Fine. I'll give the date a chance, but I'm telling you, he's only in it for the sex."

"When you two end up together, I won't even say 'I

told you so,'" Megan teases.

"Yes, you will."

Megan shrugs, but we both know the truth. We will always love and support each other, but we will also call each other out in a heartbeat. Maybe she's right and Jagger actually likes me. I'm not stupid enough to get my hopes up. He'll figure out I'm not worth his time and move on, but a boy can dream about the day his best friend tells him 'I told you so.'

Chapter 10

Ellis

Shortly after finishing up in the shower and getting dressed in a pair of ripped jeans and a flowy, blue shirt, my phone dings with a text.

Jagger: Ready for our date?

Jagger: Meet me at the studio at 11.

Me: Kk!

I follow the response with a few heart emojis and drop my phone on the bed. Well, *that* tells me nothing. Where are we going? What should I wear? Is he just planning to fuck me again and send me on my way? I mean, I'm okay with that. I do love to be fucked, and it's not like a date would change anything for me. I'm deliciously fuckable but not datable. Like my dad has said on many occasions— men aren't interested in a poor, immature boy. And Jagger is *all* man with his strong, lickable muscles, and big cock. He also owns a business. He probably owns his house and pays his bills on time and can afford food whenever he wants it. My dad is right. No one is going to want me for more than a night or two of fun. It's a sad thought, but truthfully, I like my life. I love the excitement of jumping into bed with random men whenever I feel like it. I don't want to settle down. That sounds way too boring.

Glancing at my reflection in the mirror, I take note of my appearance. The blue shirt is more of a blouse with long, flowing sleeves and a V-neck. I love the way it looks on me, especially with my new blue hair color. This time I dyed more than usual, but not my entire head.

"It looks good," I tell myself. "Damn hot." If Jagger doesn't like it, I have the whole afternoon to find a hookup for tonight. Either way, win-win for me!

I pull on my combat boots, tucking my skinny jeans inside, and grabbing my keys and wallet then head out. The drive to Orange Grove will take about thirty minutes, and it's already a little after ten-thirty. Keeping a man waiting for a few minutes is a good idea, but being super late is not. I like my revolving door of men on their toes, but not to the point of being disrespectful.

As I pull onto the road that leads over the bridge to the mainland, my favorite song comes on my playlist, so I turn it up and belt out some Whitney at the top of my lungs. One amazing song after another blares through my speakers from my favorite playlist: Ellis and the Divas. It's seven hours of some of the best female singers of all time— in my opinion at least.

By the time I park my car in front of the glass blowing studio, I'm in a great mood. I always am after listening to my girls. One more quick look in the rearview mirror to make sure I still look amazing, as if I ever don't look like a slice of perfection, and I'm out of the car. Unexpected nerves hit me as soon as I step onto the sidewalk. *Deep breath, Ellis. He is no different from any other hookup you've had, and you've had plenty.* My silent pep talk does nothing to calm my nerves. It's a shock to my system. I don't get nervous around guys. Confidence in who I am and what I want from a man has *never* been an issue for me. Why now? Why with Jag?

"Ellis!" My head snaps up at the sound of Jagger's voice and I stumble back slightly. Damn, he looks hot in a pair of tight, black jeans, and a fitted red shirt that leaves nothing to the imagination, not that I don't already know what's under there. His long, curly hair hangs loose, almost reaching his ass. I offer a small wave as this god of a man approaches me. "Hey."

"Hey," my voice comes out raspy while his is strong and confident.

His eyes rake over me in appreciation. "Damn, you look fucking gorgeous," he says, holding a hand out to me. "Ready to go?" I hesitate to take it. Holding hands is almost as intimate as kissing.

"Yeah," is all I can manage, deciding to take his hand and let him lead me down the block. I have no idea what he has in store for us, but Orange Grove is full of things to do.

"How was the drive?" Small talk. Okay, Jag, I can do small talk.

"Easy. Fast." *Like me.*

"That's good. It does go by pretty fast. Do you like sub sandwiches?"

"Um, yeah." *Wow, Ellis. You're such a great conversationalist. That's gonna get Jag all kinds of interested.*

"Great!" His words sound forced and unsure, but he powers through and continues. "I ordered us some sandwiches and thought we could go sit in the park to eat."

"Subs sound yummy! How is your hand?" I ask, noticing it's still bandaged.

"Hurts a little. It'll heal."

"Is it a bad burn? Did you go to the hospital?"

"No hospital. Just a superficial second-degree burn. It'll be better in a few weeks and probably won't even scar."

"You're tough." I poke him in the side turning my flirt game up.

"You like tough guys?" he flirts back.

"I like naughty guys."

Jag lets out a low, guttural sound at my words and his face turns an adorable shade of red. Who knew I had the power to get someone like Jagger worked up with just a few innocent comments? Without another word, he pushes open the door to a sandwich shop and leads me inside.

After we have our food, Jagger leads me to a park bench. He opens the bag and pulls out two sandwiches, handing one to me. "It's turkey. I hope that's alright. I didn't think to ask about allergies."

"No allergies. I like turkey. Thank you." I bite into the sandwich full of meat and veggies. Mayonnaise squeezes out of the side and coats my two fingers. I lift them to my mouth and suck off the mayo. My eyes snap to Jag's lust-filled face when I hear him moan next to me. He adjusts himself while watching me intently as I make a big show, slowly sucking my fingers in and out of my mouth.

"For God's sake, Ellis. You're going to make me fucking come if you don't stop."

Smiling, I drop my hand to my lap and wipe the wetness on my pants. Jagger stiffens when I graze my lips. "Just giving you a sneak peek of what comes later," I whisper in his ear before gently biting his lobe. Jagger hisses as I lick the spot.

"Fuck," he groans, drawing the word out. "Eat fast."

"Nah, I think I'll savor the sandwich for a while," I tease.

Jagger lets out a low growl but doesn't comment. He adjusts himself again before taking another bite of his lunch. His bulge presses against his jeans, looking terribly uncomfortable. I'm going to enjoy watching him get off later.

Silence settles between us, and it isn't the comfortable kind. It's weird and awkward. This is the exact reason why I don't date. There is nothing interesting about my life or me. What do I have to offer someone like Jagger?

"Hey," Jagger says, bringing me back to the present.

His strong hand lands on my leg, sending fire through me. Well, I do have one thing to offer, but that's all I'll ever be to anyone. *Sex.* "Where did you go?"

I plaster on a beaming smile before turning my attention to him. "What do you mean? I'm here with you, enjoying this delicious sandwich." I pop the last bite into my mouth.

"No. You got this sad look in your eyes. Your mind was definitely somewhere else."

"It's nothing. Thinking about work." I make up the lie on the spot, hoping it's believable.

"No more thinking about work on our date. Relax." He squeezes my leg then gathers our trash and walks to a nearby can. My shoulders sag the second he turns his back. I don't think he actually believed me, but I appreciate him pretending even though it kinda makes me feel bad for being dishonest.

He sits back on the bench and takes my hand. My first instinct is to pull away. This is not the time to get clingy. Today is simply a means to an end, and that end is sex, not a relationship. Holding hands feels too intimate for the moment, but I allow it and lean against the back of the park bench.

"Tell me something about yourself," Jag encourages.

"W-What?" I stutter. I didn't think he was serious when he said he wanted to get to know me.

"This is a date. People usually get to know each other on these things. So, tell me something about Ellis."

"Oh, um…" I shrug. "Not much to tell, really. I work at a bar."

He turns, folding one leg onto the bench, so he can face me. "There is so much more to you than being a server. Tell me. I want to know."

Right. More. Everything that pops into my head is embarrassing and not something I want to share. He definitely doesn't need to know where I live. And I'm not telling him I'm a slut and not worth his time. He'll figure that last one out soon enough.

"I like to draw," I finally mumble the least embarrassing thing about myself. It's stupid because I'll never be good enough to do anything with my art. I enjoy creating it for myself, but that's all.

"What do you like to draw?" Damn, he's good at this date thing. Jag actually sounds interested. He could make a lot of money as an actor.

"Different things," I answer nonchalantly.

"Can I see one of your drawings?"

His question shocks me. I have a picture of the one I'm the proudest of on my phone, but Megan is the only one who has ever seen it. After years of discouragement, I quit sharing my art with my parents, and I've always been too chicken shit to show anyone else.

I pull out my phone and scroll until I find the drawing. I drew it about six months ago when I was sitting outside my trailer watching one of my neighbors. It wasn't meant to be creepy or anything. I was fascinated with her, so I did my best to capture the moment.

Handing my phone to Jag, I avert my eyes and stare at a tree in the distance. I want to give him time to fake his reaction. His first will probably be him trying not to laugh, and I don't want to see that.

"Ellis." The word is breathy and laced with emotion, causing me to look his way, forgetting that I'm trying *not* to see his reaction. He is staring intently at my phone with watery eyes. "This is beautiful. The way you captured her heartbreak… I've rarely seen a drawing full of so much raw emotion. I don't know her story, but I can feel her pain." Jag meets my eyes as he passes my phone back. "You are a phenomenal artist. Do you have more?"

I laugh at his absurdity as I shove the phone back into my pocket. "You don't have to be so nice. It's nothing. Just some doodling." I wave him off like it's no big deal, but his praise means a lot to me.

"What asshole told you that lie?" Jagger's words come out clipped as anger radiates from him. Well, okay, then. Scary.

"Everyone."

"Everyone is wrong," He snaps. "Tell me about the drawing."

No one other than Megan has ever shown any interest in my art. My parents, especially my dad, always told me to stop doodling and be productive. My teachers used to take my notebooks away for drawing in class. I was paying attention, but drawing helped me focus.

"She lives across from me. I don't know her name, and I rarely see her outside. This particular day, though, I was sitting outside. Suddenly, police cars and an ambulance tore down the road and rushed inside. A while later two officers came out with her. The police talked to her quietly, trying to console her. She was crying, but not a lot. Then the paramedics came out with someone on a gurney. The body was covered. She rushed to them and tried to pull back the sheet, but the paramedics wouldn't let her. The ambulance left. The police asked some more questions, I guess. She smiled at them, nodded that she was fine, I heard something about family on their way then the police left. She watched until everyone was gone then collapsed onto the ground, sobbing." I take a deep breath, gathering my thoughts. Jag offers me an encouraging smile.

"I've never heard that kind of anguish come from anyone. At first, I felt bad for drawing it, but I couldn't stop. It was a beautifully haunting moment. She stayed on the ground, sobbing for a long time and no one came. No family. No friends. Eventually, I went over and helped her up then walked her inside and gave her a glass of water. I told her my name and asked if there was anything I could do for her.

"She thanked me, but said she just needed to be alone. So, I left her. I still don't know her name. She moved out a few weeks later. Another neighbor told me that the lady came home from work that day and found her daughter dead. I didn't even know two people lived there. The daughter was in her mid-twenties, but I don't know how she died." I take a deep breath and dare a glance at Jagger. He looks sad. *Wow, way to bring everyone down, Ellis.* This is why I'm not dating material. I suck.

"That's a terribly sad story. You did a great job showing the agony she faced that day. Your drawing could win awards."

I scoff at his words. "Right."

Jag takes my chin in his hand and turns me to face him. "Do not underestimate yourself. I'm an artist, too, and I know raw talent when I see it. You are an amazing artist."

"Thank you," I whisper.

"Can I see more?" He lets go of my chin and drops his hand to my lap.

"Really? No one has ever asked to see my art."

"No one?"

"Well, Megan has, but she's my BFF, and pretty much my only fan. It's kind of like having your mom tell you that you did something good. She's kind of obligated to be supportive."

"Megan is not just being a supportive friend. She sees you."

"You don't even know her."

"I met her once and I saw the way the two of you interact. She doesn't strike me as the kind of friend who would tell you something is great if it isn't."

"She isn't," I concede.

"So, can I see some of your other drawings?"

"That's the only one I have on my phone, but I guess I can show you others one day."

"Perfect. Now I can ask you on a second date." Jag smiles like he's won the lottery. He'll realize soon enough I'm no prize and move on, but I guess I'll enjoy the ride while it lasts.

CHAPTER 11

JAGGER

Ellis' mood changed as soon as we started talking about his art. He has no idea how talented he is, but I am determined to show him. I'm not sure how I will make that happen, but I will figure it out.

"Do you use any other medium?" I can tell Ellis is hesitant to let me in, but I want to know everything about him. I don't know what happened to make him so shut off and afraid to let me in.

To him this might just be a date, but to me he is everything I've been looking for in a man. I shouldn't be this far gone for someone I barely know, but Ellis Young is going to be mine if it fucking kills me.

"I paint and like to make pottery, but that's not easy to do. It requires a lot of equipment, and I don't have room for it at my place or the funds to make that kind of purchase."

"Do have a space to paint?"

"No. My place is tiny. Like shoebox small. Studio

space is expensive." His voice is nonchalant as he tries to cover his disappointment. Art is clearly important to Ellis, but he tries to make it sound like it doesn't matter

"Is glassblowing your only medium?" he asks with a smile. With the focus on me, he appears happier and more interested in continuing this conversation.

I oblige and don't question the subject change. "Yes. I can sketch out a rough idea when I'm planning a big project, but I can't draw like you can. I've never been interested in painting. Pottery sounds fun. I wouldn't mind giving that a try. I've done some sculpting, and I'm pretty good at it, but it something I pursue."

"We should make art together some time." As soon as the words are out of Ellis' mouth his eyes go wide. "Shit. I'm sorry. That was a stupid idea. Forget I said it."

Leaning in, I run my nose from his chin to his ear. "I'd love to make art with you," I whisper. "Come to the studio with me." He shivers and lets out a small whimper. That's all the encouragement I need. I grab Ellis' hand and pull him up, dragging him behind me as quickly as possible without either of us falling.

When we get to the studio lobby, I close and lock the front door. The last thing I need is someone walking in on us. I don't let go of Ellis' hand until we're in my office with that door locked, too. My sister has a key and a bad habit of showing up unannounced. I should have taken Ellis to my apartment. It's right down the street, but it's too late now.

I rarely use my office, so my desk is clean, except for the laptop. Gently, I toss the laptop into the chair and pat my desk. Ellis jumps onto it. Placing a hand on either side of him, I lean in and press my mouth to his, pushing my tongue past his lips. My dick has been at half-mast since Ellis showed up a couple of hours ago. The blouse he's wearing is doing all kinds of things to my cock. Most of the guys I've been with in the past are jocks and built more like me. Ellis is tall and skinny. He has some definition, but he's not muscular. He's more my type, but for some reason, I end up fucking guys who are more like me.

Slowly, I unbutton his blouse, revealing his smooth chest. I wonder briefly if he waxes. Moving in again, I kiss from his navel to his neck, sucking a bruise into the sensitive skin. I flick my tongue over his nipples, biting gently on one while pinching the other.

"Oh, Jag. Do that again," he begs. I bite the other one, eliciting a loud moan.

His cock hardens against his jeans and it has to be as painful as my own trapped cock. Reaching between us, I unzip his pants then do the same to mine. A small sigh escapes him when the pressure releases. My hands flatten against his chest as I push him onto his back. Ellis lifts his hips allowing me to pull his jeans and underwear down. He places his feet on the desk without prompting, opening himself to me. Damn, he's gorgeous.

I push my own pants down, stepping out and kicking them to the side. As I run my hands down his legs, I notice how smooth they are under my touch. He has to wax. There is no hair on his legs or chest, and I fucking love it. I've never been with a man who waxes or shaves. It's fucking sexy.

Ellis lets out quiet mewling sounds as I caress his body from his legs to his hips then over his stomach and chest. Bending down, I lick his Adam's apple then trace my tongue up the side of his neck to his ear, nibbling on the lobe and drawing out another moan from him.

"Uh, Jag." Fuck, my name sounds good on his lips.

"You like that?" I rasp, grazing my lips across his as I move to the other ear. His only response is a sign, but I feel his cock twitch against my own and take the opportunity to grind against him. As I move my shaft against his, Ellis tenses and inhales sharply, arching his back off the desk.

"Oh, fuck!" Ellis pushes his hips off the table, grinding harder against me and I almost lose all control. I have to stand up and take a few deep breaths. Ellis cries out at the loss of contact.

"Give me a second, baby. Don't want it to be over yet."

"I want you inside me," Ellis begs, need lacing his voice.

Pulling the top drawer open, I blindly reach inside, wincing when my injured hand bangs against the side. Eventually, my hand lands on the bottle of lube, and I pop the cap with my thumb. Thankful my right hand isn't the one that's burned, I coat my fingers thoroughly before pushing two inside Ellis, scissoring them and twisting my wrist a few times before adding a third.

"Okay, I'm ready." My impatient boy.

I roll on a condom and push my cock inside,

slowly at first, but Ellis has different plans. He wraps his legs around me and plants his feet on my ass, pulling me in balls deep. I fall forward, dropping my hands to either side of his head. We're face to face, lips inches apart.

"Greedy," I muse with a smirk. He knew I was holding back for a reason. Feeling myself deep inside him is killing me. It takes everything I have not to come embarrassingly quick.

"Horny," he corrects. "Fuck me. Hard." Straight to the point. I like that. Pulling back, I slam into him. When he whimpers, I do the same thing again. It's hard but slow. Taking my time, I relish the moment, watching Ellis lose control and become a needy mess. "Please, Jag, fuck me!" he begs again, imploring me with every syllable. The neediness in his voice is tangible, spurring me on.

This time I give him what he wants, plowing into him hard and fast with no mercy. He cries my name every time I hit his prostate, and I almost lose myself when my name falls from his lips. I reach between us grabbing his cock and stroking it in time with my thrusts.

Watching this beautiful man come undone under me is possibly my new favorite sight. Ellis screams each time I slam into him, bucking his cock into my hand. He grips the sides of my desk as his eyes roll back in ecstasy.

It's not long before my back tingles and my balls draw up, and I can't hold back any longer. Ellis' breathing changes at the same time, and he falls over the edge with a loud yell, coating my hand and his stomach with his release as I fill the condom.

I rest against the desk, still inside Ellis, trying to catch my breath. Ellis' breathing slows. He reaches for my hand, taking it to his mouth and licking it clean without taking his eyes off mine. *Holy fuck,* that's the sexiest thing I've ever watched.

Once my hand is clean, he drops it. Pushing himself off the desk, he dresses quickly. It happens so fast, I barely have time to react.

"What are you doing?" I ask curiously, standing naked beside my desk that now holds one of my favorite memories.

He smiles and kisses my cheek. "That was amazing. Thanks for a great day."

"You're leaving?"

"Oh, yeah. Gotta be up early tomorrow." With that he turns to the door, flips the lock, and walks into the studio.

Early? It's barely four in the afternoon. "Hey, wait!" I call, pulling on my jeans, tripping and sucking in a deep breath when my injured hand smacks against the door jamb. Skipping underwear and not bothering with my shirt, I finally catch up with him in the lobby right before he clicks the lock on the front door.

"Can I see you again?" I sound desperate, but what the hell? We had a fun date and amazing sex. Why is he running off so damn fast?

Ellis freezes with his hand on the lock. "Um, yeah. I guess."

Then he's gone before I can form a response. What the fuck just happened?

LESS THAN FIVE minutes after Ellis leaves, the bell above the door dings and Melanie walks in with a huge smile on her face. Crap.

"Hey, baby brother."

"Hi." I'm still reeling from what just happened. I'm not in the mood for my sister, but I plaster on a fake smile and pretend all is well.

She hops onto the counter next to where I'm standing. I busy myself by going over bookings for the next month and making my schedule. "How was the date?"

"It was good."

"Good. That's all? Good wears a shirt," she teases.

I glance down at my bare chest. *Shit.* I was so confused when Ellis left, I forgot to go back and grab my shirt. I try to hide my smile. I really do, but when I think about Ellis, I get all goofy and lovestruck. It's problematic. "Fine. It was great!" Better than great, but I'm only willing to give my sister so much.

"The date or the sex?"

"Melanie!"

"What? I saw him leaving and he looked… satisfied."

"He was more that fucking 'satisfied,'" I bark, offended at her word choice.

"Ha! Gotcha. So, you did fuck him." She grabs one of my nipples and twists it, pinching hard.

"Ow, shit." I squeal, rubbing the sore spot. "If you

must know," I start, gaining some composure. "Yes, I fucked him. The date was fun, too. He's a very talented artist and we enjoyed getting to know each other. The sex was fan-fucking-tastic."

She stares at me for several seconds, looking me over like she sees something. "You really like this guy. Like, a lot."

"I guess."

"No, not 'I guess.' You're pining over him. Jagger and Ellis sitting—"

"I will murder you if you finish that song." Nothing quite like being instantly transported back to elementary school.

Melanie doubles over laughing.

"You think you're cute, but you're just annoying."

"You love me. Well, not the way you love Ellis, but you love me."

"We've been on one date."

"But you fucked him twice." She glances around the space with a look of pure disgust. "Can you maybe find somewhere besides the studio to have sex. You know you have an apartment close by, right?"

"Don't worry. We didn't do anything in here." I bop her on the nose, and she scowls at me. "If there is another date, I'll be sure to bring him to my place."

"I'm heading home. You coming to the big house for dinner tonight?"

"Not tonight."

"Fine. Leave me all alone."

"You chose to live on the property. And you have an

entire cadre of people with you, including Kevin," I remind her.

"Yeah, yeah." She stands on her tiptoes and kisses my cheek. "See you tomorrow. Love you, little brother."

"Love you, too."

Melanie leaves and I release my breath. I adore my family and I know mom likes having us all around, but I need my space. Having big family dinners almost every day isn't for me. If Jaxon was still here, things would be different.

CHAPTER 12

ELLIS

Jagger texted me a few times after our date last week, but I have mostly ignored him. I offered quick, one-word responses which was rude and stupid. Now it's been four days of radio silence, just what I deserve.

I want to like him. Hell, I *do* like Jagger, but I know how this will end. It's better to keep him at arm's length, so I don't get hurt.

Work is both amazing and horrible tonight. We are hosting a frat's winter formal, so the bar is closed to the public while we have about two hundred college kids here partying their asses off. The eye candy is amazing! Hot guy after hot guy as far as the eye can see. There are plenty of girls here, too, but I'm not paying attention to them. Most of them are drunk and obnoxious, but the bar is making bank. On top of the tip Ryan included in their contract, most of them are tipping us individually when we deliver food and drinks. Hot, drunk, rich guys— I can handle this for one night.

"You need to turn your flirt game on and take care of table seven," Megan states with a smirk.

"What? Why? That's your table." Color me confused. No server willingly gives away tables when high tips are flowing like water.

"Yeah, but the hot blond in the purple polo has been eyeing you for the past hour like you're part of the buffet."

Sure enough, when I glance in that direction, he's staring at me. When he sees me looking, he bites his bottom lip and winks. Swoon. "Deal." I don't bother waiting for Megan to respond.

"Hi, boys," I say in my flirtiest voice as I step up to the table, making sure to stand across from Hottie so I can watch him while I take everyone's order. "What can I get you?"

"IPA," the first one orders.

"Vodka tonic."

"Vodka Red Bull."

I write down the orders glancing up when the hot blond doesn't say anything. Vodka Red Bull guy laughs and elbows his sexy friend but doesn't take his eyes off me. "He'll take a tall drink of you." The rest of the table erupts into laughter and the poor blond guy turns every shade of red ever invented.

"Well, you are a cutie," I tell him, licking my lips in what I know is a seductive move. *This* I can do. Flirting and bathroom quickies are my specialty. He blushes even more when I wink at him. He was so confident when I was across the room, but now he's shy and embarrassed. His friends need to leave him alone. "What can I get you to drink?"

"I... um... I don't know. Something sweet?" he stutters over his words.

"We have a signature drink called Paradise 11 Sunset. It's got Southern Comfort, peach schnapps, pineapple juice, cranberry juice, and Sprite in it. It's sweet and delicious. You can't taste the alcohol."

"Yeah, that sounds good," Hottie says, smiling shyly at me.

"He's our resident light weight," IPA pipes in.

I look directly at him. "There is nothing wrong with not drinking or only having one. Leave him alone," I say as I jab my thumb over my shoulder at Mr. Hottie.

"Damn. Burn, dude," vodka Red Bull teases.

I walk away as the other two guys make fun of the one I just put in his place. Frat guys are so annoying. It's going to be a long night.

***

AT TWELVE-THIRTY, we cut them off. The party was only supposed to last until midnight, but Ryan let them keep going for a while. When the second fight in fifteen minutes broke out, he shut things down. Slowly, the guys make their way out of the bar and down the pier. I'm a little surprised when no one falls in the water. Thirty minutes later, I'm finally walking to my car, completely exhausted, but happy because I made almost five hundred dollars in tips, not including what I'll get from my cut of the contracted tip. That's the most I've ever made in one night and more than I've made during some of our slow weekends.

When I reach the end of the pier, Mr. Hottie is sitting on a bench. At first, I'm worried something is wrong. I only served him two drinks the whole night, but that doesn't mean he didn't order at the bar or from Megan.

He glances up and flashes a bright, sexy smile as I approach. He's not wasted. That's

good. "Hey."

"Hey." I freeze at the end of the pier, not sure what to do next.

The hot guy stands and rubs the back of his neck, suddenly nervous.

"Um, yeah. This might be a little forward or whatever, but do you want to hook up?"

"Hook up?" I question. I need a little more information than that.

"Yeah. You know, do you wanna fuck?"

I do my best not to act completely shocked. I've had more than my share of hook ups and most of them have been one-night stands with guys I've met on dating apps or at bars, but I've never been approached like this at work. Technically, I'm not at work, but still, the unexpectedness is throwing me off.

"You have somewhere we can go?" There is no way I'm taking him back to my place. I'm not stupid.

"Oh, huh. We can't go to the hotel. There are three other guys staying in the room with me." He looks around the boardwalk area. "Bathroom? Under the pier? Behind a building?" My cock hardens more with each suggestion he makes. Public sex is *such* a fucking turn on. It's kind of my thing. We also have to find somewhere we won't get caught. I do *not* need to get arrested. My first thought is the bathroom at this club I frequent. They're open all night and guys fuck in there all the time.

"You're twenty-one, right?" As soon as I ask the question, I feel like an idiot. Of course, he's twenty-one. He was drinking at the bar tonight.

"My ID says I am," he replies with a smirk.

Fuck. My. Life. I don't care that he isn't twenty-one, but I'm not fucking him if he's some weird prodigy that got into college at fifteen. "How old are you?"

"Nineteen," he replies sheepishly. I let out a sigh of relief.

"You have a fake ID?"

"Yeah."

"Good. Let's go. I know a place." I lead him to my car and drive the short distance to Cosmos, a club on the other side of the island. Letting a stranger in my car probably isn't the best idea, but he seems harmless enough. "What's your name?"

"Gavin."

"I'm Ellis."

"You don't think this is bad or anything, do you?" Gavin questions nervously.

"No, but if you're having second thoughts, that's totally cool. I can drop you off at your hotel," I reassure him. I don't want him to do anything he doesn't want to do.

"I'm not having second thoughts. I want to do this. I

just don't want you to think there's something wrong with me." Oh, God, Gavin is like I was in high school. Always so unsure when it came to sex. Slamming on the brakes, I turn to face him.

"Are you a virgin?" I am not all about taking someone's V-card tonight.

"What? No," he snaps then drops his head. "I've never had a one-night stand or fucked someone I didn't know."

Accepting his answer, I nod then continue driving. "Okay, then. There's nothing wrong with you. Sex is fun! I believe everyone should have sex as often as they want, as long as it's consensual." I pull into the parking lot at Cosmos and find a space right away. It's busy, but not like it is during the summer.

He chuckles uneasily. "I agree. It's just that I've never hooked up with a stranger."

"Stranger sex is the best. No strings. No attachment. No awkward getting to know each other phase. No dating."

"That does sound perfect." He sighs his relief.

"Come on. Let's go have some fun," I say as I put the car in park and open my door. Gavin climbs out and meets me in front of the car. "There's usually a cover charge, but it's only like ten bucks."

"Okay," he agrees a little breathlessly.

The bouncer checks our IDs, barely looking at them. We pay the cover and move inside. As we step through the doorway, I grab Gavin's hand and pull him to the back of the club where there are several bathrooms. We pass the first two, which are multi-stall bathrooms, and turn down a dimly lit hallway to the individual, private bathrooms. There are four total. They are all currently occupied, but there is no line.

A few minutes later, one of the doors opens and three guys file out. Gavin shoots me a questioning look. "We aren't the only ones here for this reason. The club knows exactly what happens back here. It's the reason they put in some private bathrooms." Not that I'd be opposed to having sex in one of the multi-stall bathrooms, but I don't want to scare Gavin off.

Being the one in control isn't my thing, but I'm fucking horny, and Gavin is gorgeous. My neediness takes over and I push him into the now empty bathroom, locking the door behind us. As soon as we're alone, he surprises me and pushes me against the wall and shoving his tongue in my mouth. The unsure kid in my car disappears and there's a strong, confident man in his place, manhandling me. And it's fucking *delicious*. Gavin is a few inches taller than me with large, strong muscles.

He breaks the kiss and steps back, putting one hand on my shoulder and pushing me to my knees while unzipping his pants with the other. By the time I'm on the ground, his hard cock is in his hand. He smacks my mouth with it, spreading precum over my lips. My entire body buzzes with need.

"Suck," he commands. Fuck, I love when a man takes control.

Without hesitation, I take his length to the back of my throat, hollowing my cheeks. I bob up and down, sliding my tongue along the vein on the underside of his cock. God, he tastes good. Like sweat and a musky, cedar body wash.

"Fuck, that feels good. Oh, God, just like that. Get me nice and wet for your hole."

Why are those words so hot? My dick twitches. I need release or at least out of these tight pants. I suck faster, bringing him closer to the edge.

He pulls out of my mouth long before I'm ready. I *love* sucking and choking on cock, sometimes more than I like getting fucked. Without a word, Gavin pulls me to my feet and turns me around, shoving my chest against the wall. My cock jumps again. He reaches around and finally unzips my black work pants, pushing them to my ankles right along with my underwear.

He bites my earlobe as he lines his cock up with my hole. "Sorry. I don't have lube."

He rubs the head of his thick cock along my entrance, using only my spit and his precum in place of lube. I do my best to relax. I've taken an almost dry cock before, but it hurt like a bitch.

Slowly, he pushes against my rim. "Hurry. Shove it the fuck in," I beg. I'd rather get the initial pain over, so we can get to the good stuff. "Please. Get inside me."

Gavin forces himself balls deep in me with one hard thrust. The pain pulls a cry out of me that can probably be heard over the music on the dance floor. Then Gavin starts to move in and out, hitting my prostate with each thrust. It's fucking glorious. My moans are obscene and slutty.

"Yeah, Ellis. Take it," he grunts, thrusting into me

over and over, hitting the perfect spot every time. I'm putty in his fucking hands. With every moan I let out, I sound lust-filled and sex-starved. Gavin grips my hip with one hand, forcing me against the wall with the other. Fuck, it drives me insane to be manhandled and used. I'm fucking feral. He slams into me relentlessly, groaning and grunting, chasing his release.

It doesn't take long before my breathing quickens. Every nerve in my body is on fire, sending shock waves to my dick. It's too much and I come untouched all over the bathroom wall with a strangled cry.

Gavin follows with his own release a few seconds later. When he's done, he pulls out of me and puts his cock away. I don't bother cleaning the wall. There's probably layers of dried cum on every surface in here. It's a disgusting thought, so I don't linger on it. After I pull my pants up, we wash our hands and walk out, passing the line of couples waiting for their turn.

CHAPTER 13

JAGGER

Gentry, Lex, and Law barrel into the studio as if they own the place. My best friend and brothers are nothing short of obnoxious when we all get together. Gentry drops two cases of beer onto the counter, while Lex drags in a cooler, and Law follows with two bags of ice. They fill the cooler and toss in several bottles of water for me, while I stand against the wall watching them with my arms crossed.

They're all going to be wasted by the time we get home tonight, which means they will be crashing at my place, or I'll be driving them all to their respective homes. That's fine, I don't mind being the designated driver. It's better than them driving, not that any of them would take a chance, especially now that my brothers have children. We all did stupid shit when we were younger, but those careless days have passed. Drinking and driving is one thing I abhor, and I would rather be the lifetime DD than have anyone get behind the wheel intoxicated.

Once the cooler is packed, we all grab our gear bags and toss everything in the back of my truck then drive twenty minutes to the paintball range. Gentry built the range on several acres he bought at an auction last year. The property had been foreclosed on, and he got it dirt cheap, not that he needed to save the money. His family is loaded. Gentry doesn't have to work, but he hates the spoiled rich kid life. Well, he doesn't hate it, exactly. He enjoys not having to worry about money and being able to help those in need. He spends his time running a youth center. Only those closest to Gentry and his family know the truth. His parents don't flaunt their money, either.

Two of our friends, Scott and Brice, along with my brothers-in-law, Andrew and Kevin, are meeting us at the range. We haven't had a paintball tournament in months. This will be good. I need to get out of my head and focus on something other than Ellis. He has consumed my thoughts for weeks.

When we arrive at the range, I grab my bag and start pulling on gear. I'm only wearing a compression shirt and a pair of cargo pants with some protection in the groin area now, so I shrug on a vest-style chest protector, a baggy t-shirt, and knee and elbow pads then wrap on a neck protector. We have rules about not aiming for the groin, neck, or face, but in the heat of the moment, people move and paintballs go rogue. Everyone else puts their gear on while downing a couple of beers. You'd think drinking would slow them down, but no, it makes them more vicious. I think it enhances their aim and abilities, too.

Once we're all geared up, guns loaded and pockets full of extra ammo, we split into two teams— Lex, Gentry, Scott, and me against Law, Andrew, Kevin, and Brice. Our paintballs are blue and theirs are red. So naturally, we become the blue and red teams. Creative, right?

Gentry has multiple game zones. Today, two of the areas, Military and Campground, are rented out for parties, so we're using the Western zone. This range is set up to look like an old town from a western movie with wooden buildings, a barn, trees, fake horses, and barrels to hide in or behind. Our team heads for the saloon and the other team heads for the bank, where we plan our strategy.

Gentry pulls a beer out of his pocket and cracks it open. "Okay, what's our plan?" he asks.

"Same as always," Lex replies with a shrug, drinking his own beer.

"Alright, so, no strategy. Just a free for all. Got it," I say sarcastically with a nod.

"It's not like they're going to have a plan." Scott points his thumb in the direction of the bank.

"True. At the rate Brice is drinking, they probably won't even have four players," I comment.

"If he isn't already passed out, he'll be an easy target," Gentry adds.

"Yep. Okay, if Brice comes out of the bank, whoever has a clear shot, take him out immediately. I'll go after Andrew. Scott, you go after Kevin. Gentry and Lex can gang up on Law," I suggest in an attempt to give us a little strategy. Brice is always an easy target. Law is their best player. Gentry and Lex being our best players, I think the matchups are fair.

"Cool. Once you take out your target, come help the rest of the team," Gentry adds as we pull on our face masks and goggles.

He presses a few buttons on his phone and the speakers around us blare with one long, loud beep, signaling the start of the game. The alarm will sound again at the end of the forty-five-minute session, provided there are players on both teams still in the game. If one team takes out all players on the opposing team before the alarm sounds, the game is finished.

We walk out the back door. Gentry and Lex peel off to the right, crouching low and staying hidden by the building and a water trough as they search out Law. Scott and I head left, keeping hidden as we search for our own targets.

I jump back as a ball flies in front of my face, and hits Scott in the back.

"Fuck!" I yell.

"What's wrong?" Gentry's voice comes through my earbuds. We have these cool walkie-talkie-looking things that connect to our earbuds so we can talk to each other during the game.

"Scott's down," I inform the others with an exasperated sigh.

"Shit!" Lex yells. "Already?"

"Yeah. They got him from behind. I don't know

where the bullet came from, but it almost hit me in the face as I stepped around the building."

"Scott, go back inside and keep your eyes open. Let us know what you see," Gentry instructs.

"You got it. Good luck, guys."

Scott pats me on the back as he makes his way back inside. I fall to my knees and crawl behind a fence, trying to see anyone from the other team while staying out of sight.

"Brice is down," Lex's voice comes through.

"Did you hit him or is he passed out?" Scott jokes.

"Hit. He was just standing in the middle of the damn street. No protection. What a waste," Lex complains.

"I think he just comes for the beer," I tease.

"Law is on the roof of the bank," Scott's voice breaks through. "I bet that's who took me out. Stay alert. He can see everything from that vantage point."

Staying between the fence and the building, I crawl out, to get a better look, hoping Law can't see me. I slowly peek around the building and find Gentry across the street behind a horse. How did he get over there without being shot by Law?

Movement to my left catches my eye and I see Andrew crawling in front of the saloon porch. Pointing my gun in his direction, I let several paintballs fly. The first three hit the railings, but the fourth hits him in the chest as he tries to roll away.

"Andrew's down!" I blurt into the small microphone.

Cheers erupt from my team until Scott interrupts.

"Gentry, behind you!" I look up in time to see Gentry shooting and turning at the same time. He hits Kevin but not before red splatters across his shoulder.

"Gentry's down!" Lex and I yell at the same time.

Kevin's still in since he hit first. Two on two now, and I am not in a good position to hit Law or Kevin. I retreat to the other side of the building, where there are more things to hide behind. When I get there, I see Lex has managed to wedge himself in the back of an old truck. Law is still on the roof, but he's crouched down and impossible to hit. I don't think he can see Lex from that spot.

"Stay put, Lex, and let loose as soon as Law moves. I'm going to see if I can get a line on Kevin," I order.

"Bet," Lex calls back to me.

When I glance around the side of the building, Kevin has moved closer, but he's not hidden well. I raise my gun and fire off a few shots, but before he can raise his gun, blue paint splatters against his chest.

"Fuck, yeah!" I cheer. "Kevin's out. "Alright, Lex. Let's bring home the win." As soon as the words are out of my mouth, my ass lights up as two bullets hit me back-to-back on the same cheek. I let out a yelp, falling to my knees. Fuck, that hurt. These pants offer zero padding on my butt.

"You okay, Jag?" Scott asks.

"I'm hit. Lit my ass up. Hurt like a fucking bitch," I whine. "It's up to you, Lex. You've got this. Take our brother out. Preferably to soft, exposed flesh," I growl as I walk into the saloon, joining Scott and Gentry.

I hiss when I hit the chair. One welt is a little higher

up, but the other is in the perfect spot to be rubbed every time I sit down. While I pout about my sore ass, I grab a bottle of water from the cooler and down it.

Ten minutes later, Lex cheers in our ears and Scott whoops from where he's watching out the window. "Law is down! We win!"

Lex comes barreling in the front door, yelping and covered in red paint. He grabs a beer, laughing, "Our brother is a sorry loser. He attacked me as soon as I hit him!" A few minutes later, the rest of the guys join us. Law flicks Lex off before, dropping into a chair and sulking into his beer.

"I hear you had a date." Lex drops into the chair next to me. Fucking Mel. Why did she have to blab to our brothers?

"A date?" Gentry questions, a tinge of hurt in his voice. I usually tell him everything.

"It was nothing." I try to play it off as if it is no big deal, but it is a big deal. I *really* like Ellis, and I can't wait to see him again. I'm not sure if I'm ready to share it all with my family and friends yet. Honestly, I have no idea what is happening with Ellis. He rushed out after our date and has only returned a few of my texts this week. He's distancing himself from me and I don't understand why.

"Tell your face it was 'nothing,'" Law teases. Maybe Mel's right. Apparently, my face gives everything away.

"It was a date. We had a good time. I don't know if I'm going to see him again," I snap

"Why not? What's the problem?" Lex asks.

"Can we talk about *anything* else?" I beg, making eye

contact with Gentry in what I hope is a 'please have my back' look.

Gentry winks. "Sure. Who's up for some pool? We can hit up Rooster's."

"Nah, I gotta get home. Mel and I have dinner plans." Kevin stands and Andrew follows.

"He's my ride." He motions to Kevin.

"You can ride with us if you want," I offer.

"Yeah, sure. Thanks."

Kevin heads home, and Scott bails, too. The rest of us pile into my truck and head to Rooster's, a dive bar a few miles from Gentry's place. Getting out today has been fun and it's kept my mind on something besides all the ways I might be fucking things up with Ellis.

CHAPTER 14

ELLIS

For the past fifteen minutes, I've been sitting in my car outside of Jagger's apartment contemplating whether or not another date is a good idea. Ignoring him didn't work. Hell, even hooking up with that frat guy didn't get Jag out of my head. When he texted a few days ago and said he missed me, I gave in and agreed to another date. The last date quickly moved to the sex part then I bolted. The more time I spend with Jag, the more things I feel for him. I keep telling myself to stay away. I'm only going to get hurt. I'm not good enough for him and eventually he's going to realize the truth.

"You're so stupid, Ellis," I chastise myself.

Why do I keep saying yes? Sex. The sex is fucking hot. That's why I keep coming back and now I'm catching feelings. This is why I never let the same guy fuck me twice. One and done. If I keep my distance, no one gets hurt. No feelings. No strings. Exactly what I want.

I don't even believe my own words anymore. I can sit in this car all afternoon and tell myself a thousand lies, but it isn't going to change the fact that I have feeling for Jagger Ward. Truthfully, I have for a while. It will hurt less in the long run if I end this now. He'll never want anything serious with me and when he grows bored, it's going to hurt a lot more than it will if I walk away now.

"You can do this, Ellis. One more date. A couple of orgasms then walk away." After my little pep talk, I shove the car door open and climb out. With a deep breath, I force my feet to move and make my way up to Jag's apartment. When I agreed to the date, he texted me his address and the elevator code. His place is right down the street from the studio.

Nerves eat at me while I wait for Jag to open the door. We have a whole night together, but I already miss him. Heartbroken for what I know is coming. I can't do this to myself again. Carefree and slutty, that's the life I should have. This bullshit with feelings is going to end with me lonely and depressed.

When the door swings open, I instantly switch to happy and shove all the other feelings deep down where they belong.

"Hey!" Jagger leans in and kisses me on the cheek. "You look hot." He takes my hand and leads me into the apartment. What is it with this guy and holding hands. "Have a seat. Can I get you a beer or glass of wine?" he offers as I sit on one of the bar stools where he's pointing.

My head is spinning. He's in a good mood, or maybe he's nervous. It's hard to tell. "Uh, beer. Thanks."

Jag grabs a beer from the fridge, twists it open then pours it into a frosted mug he gets from the freezer. Fancy. He sets the beer in front of me and refills his water glass.

"I made small plates, like little appetizers. We can munch on them on the balcony and talk if that's okay with you."

I practically choke on my beer. Talking feels intimate, like 'getting to know you better' stuff. That is *not* part of my plan for today, but I don't argue. I smile and sip my drink.

"Sure. Sounds nice."

I watch Jag work, plating serving dishes full of food on a large tray then he places two small plates, two forks and two napkins on the counter next to me before filling a glass with water from the freezer door.

"Can you carry the plates and your beer? I've got the food and my drink."

"Yeah." He leads the way out to the balcony where he places the tray of food on a table. I drop into one of the chairs, feeling a little out of sorts. This is all too boyfriendy and it's freaking me out. We need to get to the sex part so I can leave. I need to end this.

Oblivious to my mood, Jag takes the other seat and goes right into an explanation of what's on the tray, pointing at each item as he goes. "These are barbecue meatballs, mac and cheese bites, mini taco bites, caprese kabobs, and bacon wrapped dates."

"It all looks delicious," I say only half paying attention.

He shrugs as he hands me a plate and fork. "I like to cook and try new things. Sometimes it goes well, but other times it's a disaster. I baked a cake about a year ago and all I succeeded in doing was covering my kitchen in flour and burning the cake. Pan and all! I had to throw the pan away. When I opened the oven, smoke filled the apartment, and the fire alarm went off." He shakes his head sadly, but all I can do is bust out laughing. "Hey! Don't laugh at me," he whines in mock seriousness.

"Let... me... get this... straight," I croak out between laughs. "You literally work with fire every single day and keep the studio in one piece, but one attempt at baking a cake and you almost burn down an apartment building?" I can't stop laughing at the image playing through my mind.

"It wasn't *that* bad. There were no flames. Just a very black cake and ruined pan." He tries to sulk, but I can see him fighting a grin.

"I take it you didn't make dessert," I tease.

"Hell no! I will never bake again."

With my plate full, a little of everything on it, I bite into the fried ball of noodles and cheese first. Flavors assault my palette. "Wow! This is yummy." It's super cheesy and a little spicy.

"I melted cheddar, gouda, gruyere, and cream cheese then added a little cayenne pepper for a kick," Jag says with pride.

Dang, he really can cook. My heart falls a little

more for the man in front of me. It's getting more difficult to pretend my growing feelings don't exist. Next, I
try the mini taco bites, which are Phyllo dough cups
packed with everything that goes on a taco— ground
beef, tomatoes, onion, cheese, lettuce and sour cream
adorned with a small slice of avocado on top. The
caprese kabobs are a toothpick with a grape tomato,
piece of basil and mozzarella cheese. The dates add
some sweetness to the meal, and the meatballs have the
best sauce I've ever tasted. "What kind of sauce did you
use?" I ask, holding up my fork with half a meatball on
it. "These are good."

"I made my own," Jag states simply as if it doesn't
matter, but I am freaking impressed.

"You made your own barbecue sauce?" I squeal.
Wow, Ellis, attractive. My face heats, but either Jag
doesn't notice or he's being kind because he doesn't
make fun of me and my extremely embarrassing
squeal.

"Yep. I like to make my own sauces and dressings."

"That's cool." Man, I'm going to miss this. He's such
a great cook. My skills are limited to pasta, ramen,
PB&J, anything from a box or can, and eggs. I eat like a
teenager… mostly junk food and premade stuff.
"Everything is delicious. You're a good cook. Y-" I cut
myself off before I blurt out 'You can cook for me
anytime' because he can't. We aren't going to keep
doing this. Tonight is our last night together. My heart
fills with sadness at that last thought, but it's time to
walk away.

We eat and I drink my beer while we talk about

mundane things like work. The longer I sit here, the more agitated I get. We need to get this over with. I have to get out of here before I do something stupid like fall harder or tell him how I truly feel.

When the food is gone, I help Jagger carry the empty plates and leftover food inside. Then we clean up the kitchen together. When it's finished, Jag guides me to the couch. I was hoping for the bedroom, but the couch will do.

He pulls me down next to him, not on his lap, but close enough that our legs brush together, sending a rush of fire through me. Jag puts his hand on my cheek and turns my head to him. His lips brush across mine then his tongue flicks out, licking my lips. I open for him, and he dives right in. Our tongues rub over each other lighting up my entire body. My cock hardens as the kiss grows fierce. Man, he likes to kiss. I've kind of gotten on board with it, but it still feels too intimate.

Moving this along, I reach over and graze my palm over his crotch, but he grabs my wrist, stopping me. What the fuck? I break the kiss and jerk back a little. Our legs are still touching, but my hands and lips and in my own space.

"Sorry." He reaches to cup my face again, but I move back more.

"Aren't we having sex?" I narrow my eyes at him.

"Not tonight." I'm off the couch and on the other side of the room.

"What do you mean 'not tonight?'"

"Come on, Ellis." Jagger stands and motions for me

to come back to him, but I don't budge. "Can we have a quiet night, talking and getting to know each other?"

"Yeah, it was dinner conversation. Now it's time for the sex part," I snip.

"We had appetizers." A sexy, wicked smile lights up his face. "You'll have to wait for the buffet." He runs his hands down his chest. What the actual fuck? Is he serious?

"Fuck this. I'm done." I turn on my heels and bolt for the door.

"Ellis, wait! Why are you leaving?" He catches up with me, slapping his hand on the door, keeping me from opening it. "Please don't leave," he begs, panic lacing his words.

"Let me out, Jagger," I sneer.

"You're leaving because I won't fuck you?"

"Yep." I pop the 'p' loudly and glare at him. Jagger's body deflates as he steps back, allowing me to leave. Heartbreak is written all over his face. *Good job, Ellis. You ruined everything.*

I hold it together until the elevator doors close then the first tear falls. This is good. This is what I want, freedom to sleep around with no feelings and no strings. Good for me.

Chapter 15

Jagger

It's been almost two weeks since my last date with Ellis. He isn't returning any of my calls or texts, and I don't understand why. We have fun together and the sex is phenomenal. Sleeping is becoming an issue. I stay up late, thinking about Ellis and wake early with him still on my mind. Everything in my life is suffering— work, family, friends. I have three pieces to finish for an upcoming show that I haven't started, I haven't been home for a family dinner in over a week, and I've been ignoring my friends. Yesterday, I didn't even bother opening the shop, and I doubt I'll go in today. There are no classes on the books this week.

Lifting my head off the pillow, I glance at the alarm clock and find that it's not even seven. Rolling off the bed, I pad to the kitchen and start a pot of coffee then go to the bathroom to pee and take a shower. I'm not so far gone that I can't take care of basic hygiene, but I'm damn close.

By the time I'm clean and dressed in a pair of grey

sweatpants, the coffee is finished. I pour myself a large travel mug and retreat to the small balcony. The world below me wakes up as people start milling about and shops start opening. I like my apartment and being in downtown Orange Grove. The town is small, but having an apartment in the heart of the art district is ideal. I can walk almost anywhere I need to go.

My apartment is on the top floor of the tallest building in town, which isn't saying much since it's only eight stories. Shops fill the bottom floor of my complex and offices are on the second and third. The rest of it houses about forty apartments. It's a tight knit community, mostly people in their twenties and thirties without kids. It's quiet and the people are friendly.

My phone buzzes in my pocket and I immediately regret carrying it out here. I don't want to be bothered unless it's Ellis. A twinge of hope courses through me, but I'm quickly disappointed when I see my oldest brother's name on the screen.

Lex: Happy Birthday! Where are you?

Shit! Is it already the sixteenth? Damn, I'm losing it.

Me: Thanks. Home.

Lex: Where have you been?

Lex: Everyone is worried.

Me: I'm fine.

Lex: You haven't been around in weeks.

Me: It hasn't been weeks.

Lex: Close enough

Lex: What's going on with you?

Me: Nothing

Lex: Mel said you didn't go to work yesterday.

Damn my sister.

Lex: Are you sick?

Me: Nope

Me: Took a day off.

Lex: Why?

Me: I fucking felt like it.

He's pissing me off. I don't need to be interrogated. I walk back into the kitchen and refill my mug. As I go, my phone keeps dinging with messages. Probably birthday texts from my family. They do this every year even though I haven't celebrated a birthday since Jax died. I fucking hate this day. Leaving the phone on the counter, I retreat to the balcony. Again. I don't want to have any conversations. My ass has barely hit the chair outside when there is a loud knock at my door. Fuck! Why did I give my family the elevator code? The building is secure and without the code, you can't get to any of the residential floors. Like a damn idiot, I gave it to my siblings. It seemed like a good idea at the time, but that was when I was happily single with no prospects. Not wading through days of silence from the one person I want to hear from with sadness settling in and hating myself for driving him away. I can't believe I let myself fall so hard for someone who clearly doesn't feel the same.

The incessant knocking doesn't stop. If it's one of my brothers he will probably kick the door in if I don't answer.

"I'm coming," I bellow as I step back into the apartment. When I open the door, I find my sisters on the other side. "What?"

Is that anyway to great your two favorite sisters?" Max asks.

"You're my only sisters," I grumble.

"Well, we come bearing carb-filled birthday gifts, so be nice," Mel scolds, making herself at home in my kitchen. She opens a box full of pastries, doughnuts, scones, and bagels from the bakery down the street. One of the doughnuts has 'Happy Birthday' scrawled in blue icing.

"Thanks, but I'm not hungry." My stomach betrays me with a loud growl as soon as the words are out of my mouth.

"When was the last time you ate?" Max questions, assessing me like only a mother can. She's not my mother and I don't appreciate her treating me like her kid.

I start to respond but shut my mouth when I realize I don't know the answer. Thinking back over the last couple of days, I come up with nothing. "Yesterday... I think. Maybe the day before." Mel and Max share a concerned look.

"Sit," Mel demands, pushing me toward the small kitchen table.

As I drop into one of the chairs, I'm secretly grateful Ellis and I never shared a meal here. Almost every surface of this apartment reminds me of him. How did he ingrain himself in my life in such a short period of time?

A plate of food appears in front of me. It does look delicious. I venture a bite of a cheese Danish, hoping my stomach doesn't revolt. When that stays down, I take another tentative bite then another. My sisters watch me warily as I make my way through the Danish, a doughnut, and a bagel lathered with cream cheese. While I eat, Max refills my mug, emptying the coffee pot then making a second pot.

Satisfied with my food consumption, Max pours herself and Mel a cup of coffee then tops off mine again before joining me at the table. She picks up a large gift from the floor and hands it to me.

"Gifts and cards from the family."

"Thanks," I mumble. "I'll open them later."

"Now, tell us what's going on with you." Mel insists, accepting my decision.

"Nothing. Same thing I told Lex," I answer, dodging

the question and pretending everything is good even though it clearly isn't.

"How about telling *us* the truth." Busted.

"Max," I groan. Mel reaches over and takes my hand.

"You can talk to us," she assures me.

I consider what my sisters are asking of me. I know I can talk to them about anything. We have always been a close family. I'm the one putting separation between us because I can't deal with rejection. Hell, it's not even real rejection. Ellis made it very clear from the beginning that he was only looking for a hookup, but I thought he was just scared. I thought I could change him, make him like me. Jesus, I'm a fucking moron.

Scraping my chair across the wood floor, I stand up and walk to the other side of the room, It doesn't help that today is my twenty-sixth birthday. Jaxon has been weighing heavily on my mind lately. This happens every year. This day is always difficult for me. Celebrating without Jaxon seems pointless. It's also the day I left my home. Eight years ago today, six months after losing my twin, I moved into this apartment.

My sisters wait patiently as I pace the room, trying to work through my thoughts and decipher my feeling for Ellis. Is it worth telling them him. He means something to me, but apparently, I don't mean anything to him. That thought is a punch to the gut. I fall onto the couch as if I've been hit then bury my face in my hands.

Mel and Max sit on either side of me and Mel gently rubs my back. "Come on, Jag. Tell us what's going on. This is more than your normal 'birthdays suck' emotional rollercoaster you ride every year."

"You're kind of a dick," I tease. Mel smiles proudly at my insult. "Ugh! It's stupid," I groan.

"Not if it has you this upset," Mel replies.

I wish Jaxon was here. We told each other everything, and he gave the best advice. Fuck, I miss him so much. I shake those thoughts away. Thinking about him is only going to make me feel worse.

"There's a guy," I finally admit. "Or I thought there was. But I guess I was wrong."

"What do you mean?" Max asks.

"It was one-sided. Doesn't matter, now. It's over."

"He broke up with you?"

"No, Mel. We weren't together. We went on a couple of dates and had sex a few times. He won't return my calls or texts."

"Maybe something is wrong," Mel suggests. She knows who I'm talking about. I can see it her eyes, but she doesn't mention his name.

"No shit, Mel. It's me. I'm the something that's wrong," I snap.

"I think she means, maybe there is something wrong with him. Like he could have the flu or a family emergency." Max adds calmly.

"For two weeks?" I ask incredulously.

"Depends. Maybe."

"Wow, helpful, Max. Thanks." Sarcasm fills my words. This is not helpful.

"Don't be an ass. We're trying to help." Mel matches

my attitude. I sink into the couch, dropping my shoulders.

Mel is right. They are here to help and all I'm doing is taking my anger out on them. No, not anger. It's a feeling of worthlessness, like I'm not good enough for Ellis. *This* is why I can't keep a boyfriend. I fall hard and fast. Clinginess is a sure way to run off a man. I know. I've done it more than once.

"I'm sorry," I finally say.

"You should go see him." I scoff at Max's suggestion. "Why not?"

"Because no one likes a clingy man."

"That's Benji the dog talking." My family despises my ex, Ben, as if that isn't obvious in the disdain lacing Mel's words. She might actually hate him more than the rest of my family combined because she was privy to every miserable night I spent pining after a man who treated shit on the bottom of his shoe better than me.

"Tell us exactly what happened," Max encourages.

"Like I said, we've been on a couple of dates, and we've had sex a few times. Things seemed good. We texted some but didn't really talk on the phone much. About two weeks ago, he just quit responding. I even tried calling him. Now, I feel like it's bordering on desperate if I keep trying. He's clearly not interested," I rush out the words.

"Quit hiding behind the phone and go to him," Mel insists.

"I don't know," I say hesitantly.

"Ugh! You are so infuriating. Either get your shit

together and go see him or move the fuck on with your life," Mel snips, throwing her hands up. She has never been one to sit around and wait for things to happen to her. She makes them happen for her.

"Harsh," I mumble.

"Yeah, well you're being a dumbass."

"Mel," Max chastises.

"What? I'm right."

"Yes, but maybe say it a little nicer."

"Nice doesn't get Jag out of his head."

Max gives me a resigned look. "She's got you there."

It bugs me how on point my sisters are with their assessment of me. Growing up in such a close-knit family has its downside, but I appreciate their concern and desire to help even if they overstep sometimes. They want to see me happy. *I* want to see me happy.

"Okay," I concede. "I'll go by the bar tonight."

CHAPTER 16

ELLIS

Megan keeps watching me from the other side of the room. She's worried for no reason. Last night, we watched movies, painted each other's nails, and did facials. Not the fun kind of facial that I'd let Jag give me, but my skin feels great anyway. It was the perfect night of bestie bonding. I didn't even mention Jagger one time. I thought about him like a thousand times, but Megan doesn't need to know that little piece of info. It's bad enough that she acts like I'm going to fall apart if she doesn't watch me. Just because I drank one too many White Claws and they made a reappearance around midnight does *not* mean I'm sad or depressed or mourning the loss of a man I never truly had. She can keep her psychological assessment of my life to herself.

Jagger was a great lay, but now it's time to find the next one. Gavin was decent, and he took my mind off Jag for a night. Then I stupidly agreed to another date. There have been others since. It's not like Jag and I were exclusive. He was just another fuck with a few dates sprinkled in.

The hot, daddy-looking biker dude has been eye fucking me from the bar for the past hour. I was tempted to follow him to the bathroom, but Ryan is here, and I doubt my boss would approve of me sucking cock in the middle of my shift. Plus, he's been a miserable ass the past couple of days. Must be trouble in paradise. Grayson, his boyfriend, hasn't been at work lately, and I overheard one of the other bartenders say something about him quitting. That should make for some fun times.

This is why dating isn't worth it. You fall for the guy and eventually get your heart stomped on. Well, that's my assessment at least. I've never had a boyfriend, so I don't know for sure what it feels like to break up with someone. But from what I've seen friends go through, it's a big, fat nope for me.

"Boyfriend, five o'clock." I glance behind me then side to side. What the hell is Megan talking about? Five o'clock? What? Gently she turns me toward the door where I find Jagger standing awkwardly with his hands in his pockets.

"What the hell is he doing here?" I whisper-yell to Megan.

"My guess? He came for you." She smiles unhelpfully.

I scoff at her words. "Doubtful."

"We'll find out." She saunters over to him, and no matter how hard I try, I can't tear my eyes away. She says something, he chuckles. Then she leads him to a small table in the back. In *my* fucking section. After she spends several seconds talking to him, Megan walks to me.

"He's all yours," she singsongs, smiling with pride.

"I hate you," I say with no malice.

"You looove me. Now, go get your man."

I roll my eyes as I turn away from my best friend. Jagger is *not* interested in me. Okay, that's not entirely true. He's wants to fuck me, but that's it. No one will ever love me. Even my parents see I'm not worth it. So why waste time with the dating and getting to know you parts when we can skip to the sex. No matter what he's told me, he isn't going to want me long-term. He doesn't know me well enough yet to know I'm a waste of his time.

I take my time getting to Jag's table, stopping to check on my other two parties first.

"Is everything good here? I ask, stepping up to one table. "Can I get anyone another drink?

"Another round," one of the guys says, twirling his finger in the air.

"You got it," I say with as much enthusiasm as I can muster.

After typing their drink order into the computer, I walk to the other table, not even bothering to glance in Jag's direction.

Why is he here? After what happened two weeks ago, he should know not to come around again. We're done. I thought I made that clear. A searing pain shoots through my chest at that thought, causing my eyes to water. Why does it still hurt so much? I got exactly what I wanted.

"Hi!" I say excitedly, offering a flirtatious smile when I step up to the other table. "Can I get you anything else?"

One of the guys has been flirting with me for the past hour, and I was hoping to get a quickie after work, but now Jag is killing the mood by existing in my fucking space. The guy runs a hand down my arm and licks his lips as he eye-fucks me for the third, or tenth, time tonight. I've honestly lost count at this point.

"A side of *you* to go." As fast as the words fall from his mouth, his hand drops, and his entire body stiffens. I glance behind me, following his line of sight. Jagger is scowling at the guy in a possessive move that I do not appreciate. I turn back to the guy. He's not hot or built like Jagger. He's average at best, but he'll do for one night.

"Ignore him. Jealous of what he can't have," I snark, but as soon as the words are out of my mouth guilt eats at me. "I get off at 1." *And hopefully, you can get me off by 2.* I don't say the second part out loud.

He glances at Jagger again then looks at me. "Just the check, thanks." Fucking, Jagger, cock blocking me

"Of course," I say with a smile, pulling out the hand-held device. "Together or separate?"

"Together," the other guy responds. I can't quite decipher his tone, but there is a bitterness to it. My stomach sinks, suspecting I didn't meet their expectations, and I'm not talking about the service.

After pressing a few buttons, their ticket pops up on

the screen, so I hand the device to the one who said 'together' and he inserts his card, following the prompts on the screen then hands it back to me.

Seeing a three-dollar tip on an eighty-dollar bill confirms my suspicions. This pisses me off. Not only is Jag cockblocking me, but he's costing me money. Adrenaline courses through me.

"Thank you. Have a great night."

At the bar, I grab the drinks for my first table, but almost drop the tray when I see the two guys I just waited on walking hand in hand to the door. What the hell? They're *together* together? Okay, so, maybe that was going to be a bad situation. Or a threesome. I'm totally down for a threesome.

Ignoring Jag the past two weeks hasn't been easy, but it was necessary. Falling for him can't happen, and I didn't want to get my hopes up just to have everything come crashing down. It's been hard enough dealing with only little feelings. I can't imagine how it would be if I was in love with him. That would devastate me.

How did I let myself fall for this man? I've always been so good at keeping men at arm's length. As long as I stayed focused on sex and moving from one bed to the next, I didn't catch feelings. No feelings, no one gets hurt.

I arrive at the table with the drinks and hand them out to the waiting customers. With nothing else to keep me from Jag, I reluctantly head his way. Nerves eat at me with every step, my anxiety ratcheting up the closer I get. Why do I like him? Why can't it just be sex like with all the others? And what was that buffet comment anyway? It's been playing on repeat in my head since he shot me down that day. Why didn't he want to have sex? Am I that bad in bed? Is he already done with me? Maybe he's here to tell me it's over. Yeah, that makes sense. No, it doesn't, I already told him I'm done. My head is a fucking mess by the time I reach him.

Plastering a fake smile on my face, I step up to his table. "Hi, I'm Ellis and I'll be taking care of you tonight. Can I get you started with a drink?" I didn't plan for the bitch in me to pop out, yet here she is.

He lets out a guttural growl. Jagger actually fucking growls at me. "Don't give me some bullshit generic intro." He gestures to the seat across from him. "Who was that guy? He was all over you.

"He," I pause, taking a deep breath, trying my best to be nice. "He is none of your fucking business. You don't get to ask about guys I'm fucking."

Jagger looks like I punched him. He takes a few deep breaths then points to the chair across from him again. "Can we talk?" he asks in a calm, measured voice and it grates on my nerves.

CHAPTER 17

JAGGER

Ellis doesn't sit, but motions for me to continue. "What's your problem? I want to go out with you. I thought we hit it off, but then you quit returning my calls and texts." I bite out in frustration, sounding very whiny, and I do *not* whine.

Ellis lets out an exasperated sigh. "Can we not do this now? I'm working."

"If we don't talk now, then when? You've been ignoring me for two weeks."

"Fine. Speak," Ellis spits out, his words full of venom.

"Are you going to talk to me or just stand there?"

"I don't know, Jagger. Guess it depends on what you have to say."

I don't know how to deal with this version of Ellis. He's always so happy and upbeat. Seeing him angry and sullen is breaking me. I don't know what I did, let alone how to fix it. All I know is I like this man more than I have ever liked anyone and I don't want it to end before we have a chance to see where it might go.

"I like you," I blurt out like a damn teenager with his first crush.

Ellis looks shocked for a brief second before he masks his feelings. "It's just *sex*. That's all anyone wants from me. Well, except you." His words are flippant, but I can see a flash of hurt dance across his face, but he quickly readjusts with a laugh. "Am I that bad in bed?

His question throws me off. None of what he said makes any sense. "Sex isn't all I want from you." I reach for his hand, but he steps back. "And trust me, you are amazing in bed."

"I'm so fucking confused. You say you like me, but almost all we've done is have sex," he challenges.

"Because you won't answer my calls or return my texts. And when I took you out, you always wanted to get to the sex part as fast as possible." Keeping my voice down and my emotions under control is getting very difficult. "*You* ghosted me."

"Because you said I have to 'wait for the buffet,'" he utters with an eye roll. "What does that even mean?"

"That's why you're mad?" I almost laugh, but hold it in. This is not the time. "The point of that comment was because I want *more* from you. It's so much more than sex, Ellis."

"Bullshit," he scoffs. "Why do you want to get to know me when we're just fuck buddies?"

Anger rises in me. This conversation is going nowhere, and Ellis is pissing me off. He is not my fuck buddy. He means something to me, but I guess I don't mean anything to him.

"Did you ever stop to think you're the problem?" I snap. "Maybe all *you* want is sex." Standing up, I toss a fifty on the table. "For your time." I leave before he has a chance to say anything else.

Without a second glance, I rush down the pier to my car. If I look back and see Ellis watching me, I will lose my resolve and run to him, but if he's helping the next customer as if I was never there, it will break me.

It's still early when I leave Paradise 11, so I head out of Anchor Point toward Orange Grove. Instead of taking the turn that will lead to my apartment, I bypass the small town and drive toward my parents' home. When I pull up in front of their house, most of the downstairs lights are on and several golf carts are parked out front telling me my siblings are also here. I'm not surprised. At least one of them has dinner here every night.

When I walk inside, I plaster on my happiest smile and follow the cacophony of voices to the kitchen, where I find my parents, Law, and Andrew. The rest of my family is through the large double glass doors out on the large patio.

The weather has been chilly at night, so I'm not surprised to see a fire in the pit and my sisters-in-law helping their children make s'mores.

"Jagger! Happy birthday!" Mom squeals and rushes over, pulling me into her arms. "What a great surprise! Are you hungry?"

"I'm not hungry, Mom."

"We were just heading out to enjoy the fire. Come on, son." Dad picks up a tray of desserts and motions for me join them. I follow him out with Mom right behind me carrying plates, forks, and napkins. Andrew and Law walk out and start passing out beers and wine to everyone. I pour myself a glass of water from the pitcher on the table and take a seat next to Stephanie., Law's wife.

She bumps my shoulder. "Haven't seen you in hot minute."

"It's only been a month," I argue.

"You're like fifteen minutes away. Come visit more often."

I see the sadness in her eyes as she looks from me to our parents and back again. She is telling me my parents miss me, too. I get it. I know I should visit more often. There's no excuse for not coming to Sunday dinner but being here is still hard. I've spent a lot of time in the past eight years avoiding this house in some failed attempt to get over losing my brother. An impossible feat. That isn't something you ever get over. Sure, as the years pass, I have slowly started to heal, but it isn't something I will ever get over. In the process of avoiding dealing with Jaxon's death, I have put distance between my family and me. I didn't mean to do it.

"Yeah. I'll try."

"Why are you sulking?" Law asks from the other side of the fire.

"I'm not sulking," I pout with a slight edge to my tone.

"Great come-back," Andrew scoffs. I glare at him,

but he is not deterred. "Come on, smile! Whatever has your panties in a bunch can't be that bad."

"Fuck off," I snarl at Andrew.

"Ooooh, someone one is getting testy," Lex teases. I hate when he speaks in his mocking tone. It used to make me cry when we were kids. Now it just pisses me the hell off.

"I'm out." I push up from my seat and head in the direction of the citrus groves. I should go the other way to my car, but a walk through the trees will be nice. It's a cool night, but not too cold, and the light breeze feels nice.

Law steps in front of me, blocking my path. "What? You can't take a joke?"

"Move, Law." My voice and stance are pure challenge, daring him to make the wrong choice.

"No. Sit down and talk to us like a mature adult instead stomping off like a little kid."

"Are you fucking kidding me? You assholes are the ones acting like children."

"Nah, we were just teasing. It's not our fault you can't take a joke." I step around Law, but I only make it a few steps when he yells, "What's wrong? Your little boyfriend not putting out?"

Without taking time to think it through, I turn on my brother and land a punch to his jaw. He stumbles back but doesn't fall. Chaos ensues with Lex and my dad stepping between us so I can't go for Law again. I wasn't going to, but they don't know that. Andrew and Kevin hold Law back, forcing him into a chair. Stephanie puts an ice pack on Law's jaw. Max and

Amanda gather up the kids and load them into a couple of golf carts. None of this feels real. It's as if I'm watching from the outside. My dad is saying something to me, but I'm not listening. My head is a foggy and I'm feel like I can't breathe. I stagger away from the group, but when Dad tries to follow, I start running. I race through the groves, dodging low branches as I go.

I run until my lungs are screaming then I fall to my knees, breathing heavily from the exertion. Glancing up, I find myself in front of the tree we planted for Jaxon. His ashes are scattered here and a small headstone rests next to the tree. Someone has kept it up. The grass is cut and the tree above it is trimmed. The headstone is clean with fresh flowers placed in front. Birthday flowers.

Being faced with my brother's memorial, my breath hitches. It's the one spot on family property I've avoided for more than eight years. It took everything I had inside me to pull myself out of bed the day of his memorial and come out here with the rest of the family and our closest friends. I didn't want to be here. Logically, I knew he was gone, but a part of me was convinced if I didn't come here that morning, it wouldn't be true. He would still be alive just somewhere far away. But planting the tree and scattering his ashes made it real. Jaxon was dead. He was never coming home.

Tentatively, I run my fingers over the concrete, tracing his neatly carved name.

Jaxon Milard Ward
Son, Brother, Father
Forever in Our Hearts

"Hap-happy birthday. I miss you," I choke out. "Goddammit, Jax. I miss you so fucking much."

My knees are screaming, the ground is rough under them, so I shift to sit on my ass, never moving my hand from his name. A cold shiver rocks my body. I can feel Jaxon here. The citrus groves were his favorite place. He couldn't wait to go to college, but he knew he ultimately wanted to come back here and continue the family legacy. Jaxon was creative, too, and he enjoyed finding new ways to grow the business. Marketing was his strength, and he planned to major in graphic design. He also loved to cook and find unique dishes to make with the oranges, lemons, and limes we grow—pies, cookies, tarts. I could see him opening a bakery next to the gift shop. Maybe one day Mila will do that in his memory. Mom says she loves to bake.

"Things are kinda shitty right now and I wish you were here to tell me to get my head out of my ass. I met someone, but he doesn't feel the same way. Well, he might, but he's closed off. He doesn't think he's good enough. He's wrong, Jax. He's so fucking wrong. Ellis is everything. He's creative, smart, funny, sexy, and attentive. He has a beautiful soul, but no confidence in himself. He doesn't see what I see. I've already fallen for him, but I don't know how to get him to believe I'm all in."

I shake my head and laugh. "This is stupid." I wait eight years to visit and all I can do is whine. "I'm sorry," I blurt out. "I'm sorry I wasn't there for you that night. I'm sorry I didn't save you. I'm sorry I've pushed Sarah out of my life and haven't been there for Mila. Even when they are at the house for holidays and family events, I keep my distance. I can't face them. I failed your daughter the night I failed you."

Slamming the palm of my hand against the head-stone, I let out a strangled scream. "Dammit, Jaxon! Why the fuck did you have to die? All this time and I'm still angry, pissed off at you *and* Sarah. And I'm sad and heartbroken. For fuck's sake, I cry myself to sleep more often than is healthy. I can't get past losing you. Eight years, Jaxon! Eight goddamn years, and I'm still devastated. Ellis is the first person who has made me feel anything real in years. I- oh, fuck... Jaxon, I'm in love with Ellis."

My hand falls to my lap. I drop my head and stare and at the ground as realization hits. I'm in love with Ellis Young, a man I barely know but fuck if he didn't have my heart from the moment my eyes landed on him. Tears sting my eyes. I try to blink them back, but there is no use. Within seconds, my entire body shakes as uncontrollable sobs spill out of me. I cry for my brother and everything I lost that night. I cry for myself and the way I've not truly allowed myself to live since the accident. Most days I simply go through the motions and do the things I enjoy, but I haven't let anyone get close, not truly. I even keep my family and friends at a distance. With Ben, I was distantly clingy.

For two years, I refused to let him get to emotionally close, but physically I never wanted him out of my sight for long. It was quite impressive feat to be clingy as hell while holding the same man at arm's length. Honestly, it was exhausting.

Ellis is the first person since Jaxon died, I've truly let in and now it's too late. I cry for the man I love and for the relationship I'm afraid will never happen. For the first time in years, I'm allowing myself to feel and be vulnerable, but I can't find a way to get Ellis to do the same.

The rustling of leaves sounds behind me, then a heavy hand lands on my shoulder as someone sits beside me.

"Let it all out, son," Dad says, pulling me against his strong body. I don't fight it. I let my dad hold me while I sob into his chest like I did when I was a little kid. As the tears to subside, they turn into sniffles and hiccups, but I don't pull out of Dad's arms. It's been too long since I let anyone hold me.

After several long minutes, I wiggles away from my father and wipe my face with my shirt. "I'm okay."

"You are far from okay, Jagger. I've been here long enough to see that," he admits.

"Oh. What did you hear?"

"You're still blaming yourself for something that wasn't your fault, and you feel guilty for not having a relationship with your niece and for holding your family at arm's length for all these years. It's nothing we didn't already know, but I'm guessing you didn't fully realize what you were doing until today."

"That's not entirely true. I knew what I was doing. I just thought if I kept my distance losing someone else wouldn't hurt so much," I tell him the truth. I've been keeping too much inside for too long.

"That isn't how loss works, son."

"I know. Sitting here, I see how much I've been hurting myself. I turned my back when I needed my family the most. I didn't completely walk away, but I haven't allowed myself to be part of the family like everyone else. I stay away from Sunday dinners and I don't live here."

"Self-preservation can be detrimental," he says in his old, wise way.

"I thought self-preservation was a good thing."

"Not when you go about it the wrong way. You can't protect yourself from losing others. Sadly, it's part of life. Imagine how hard it's been without Jaxon. Now imagine how much harder it would be to lose another sibling or a parent when you have spent eight years pushing us away instead of being part of our lives."

"Dammit! I know you're right. Logically, I think I've always known that, but I convinced myself if I kept my distance losing Jaxon or someone else wouldn't hurt so much. If I don't care, it can't hurt!" Dad wraps his arms around me again.

"But you do care. You love your family, and you miss us. You've been hurting for years. It's time to come home, Jagger. And I don't mean moving back to the property. You love living in town and I will never make you feel like you have to live here full-time. I mean, it's time to let us back in and be part of this family. Let us help you," my dad says into my ear as he holds me tightly.

"What if I can't do that?" Tears sting my eyes as I form my thoughts. "It's been so long. I don't know if I can just flip the switch the other way."

Dad lets go, so he can look at me. "Then don't. I'm not asking for a complete 180 all at once. Commit to coming to one Sunday dinner. Then take it one week at time. If you can only make once every few weeks in the beginning, we understand."

"Dinner. I can do one dinner." As much as I want to agree to jump back into the way things were before Jaxon died, I know I'm not ready for that and I will not promise Dad something I can't deliver.

"Great! Now, let's talk about this boy you love," he says with a wicked smile.

"Oh, God, no!" I laugh as I groan out the words.

"Ellis, you said?

"That was a private conversation between Jaxon and me."

"Yeah, well, how about if I tell you what Jaxon would say?" I eye my dad with suspicion. I motion for him to continue. This should be interesting. "If you love him and he is all those things you said he is, then go get him. I don't know what happened before you drove out here, but you're running away from someone you obviously care about. Get your head out of your ass and go get your man."

"That's not what Jaxon would say," I protest with a grin, the first one I've managed in a while.

"Well, then, enlighten me."

"First off, he would have known I was in love before I did because he was so intuitive it was scary. He would have said, 'Stop being a dumbass and go show your man you love him. Telling him won't work because he isn't going to believe you.'" I stop talking and my eyes widen. *Shit.* Jaxon is right. Empty promises and words aren't going to work on Ellis. I have to keep showing him how much I care about him. Telling him is fine but only if I show him, too.

"Your brother was wise beyond his years," Dad states in all seriousness, but I can't hold in the laugh that bursts out of me.

"No, he wasn't. We were both dumb teenagers who did stupid shit like drink too much, smoke pot, and fuck around. But he always knew what to say to me when it mattered. If he was here today, that is exactly what he'd say."

We sit in silence for a few minutes, staring at Jaxon's headstone with Dad's arm around my shoulder. Dad squeezes my shoulder. "He's watching out for us, you especially. I believe that deep in my soul, Jagger. Jaxon loved us all and would want us to be happy. He would be proud of the man you have become. You're living your dream, Jag. That's more than most people get."

"Thanks, Dad. I want to make him proud, but I don't think I have done a good job. Jaxon would have never run from his family in their darkest moment. I'm sorry I did that to you and Mom," I choke out the words, overcome with emotion.

"Son, we never faulted you for the choices you

made. We were all processing Jaxon's death, and you had to grieve in your own way. None of us will ever hold that against you."

"I appreciate that, Dad. And for following me out here." I pause for a second, remembering the scene I left. "Is Law okay?"

"He's fine." Dad waves his hand in the air. "I'm sure you left a bruise, but after raising four boys, that wasn't even a real fight."

CHAPTER 18

ELLIS

Megan doesn't even bother to knock. She barges into my home like she owns the place. I'm stretched out on the couch in my underwear with an open bag of Cheetos resting on my chest. Megan looks at me then glances around the tiny space.

"It smells in here." She scrunches up her nose in disgust.

"So?"

"So..." She puts her hands on her hips and gives me that mom/teacher look she's somehow mastered even though she's neither. "*You* need a shower, food, and a cleaning crew. *I* probably need a hazmat suit."

"Stop being dramatic. It's not that bad." I drop the bag of Cheetos on the floor, ignoring the few that fall out then wipe my orange-coated fingers on my white boxer briefs.

"Oh, it's beyond bad. Bad departed days ago. This... this is disgusting. And I'm being nice because I'm your friend." She shoves my feet off the couch. "Get up. *Now*."

"Bossy," I whine, with a pout while following her command. Slowly, I plod to the bathroom. Every move is next to impossible. My body feels like it's wrapped in molasses. When I get to the bathroom, I drop onto the closed lid of the toilet.

"No, no. Up." Megan starts the shower then pulls me up.

"Stop," I whine again like a little kid.

Why is she even here? I was doing just fine with my emotional support Cheetos. This new bag doesn't even have ants in it. For breakfast, I was going to eat the bag I opened last night, but there was a family of ants enjoying them instead. That was a disappointing discovery. I considered eating them anyway because who cares... right? But instead, I opted for walking all the way to the corner store for more. The other bag is still around here somewhere. I didn't have the heart or energy to throw away their little ant home.

"Ellis!" Megan snaps, grabbing my attention. I don't bother answering or looking at her. "Either you get in the shower and clean yourself or I'm doing it for you." She reaches for the elastic band of my underwear.

Ew! That thought sends a shudder through me. She's my best friend and I love her, but Megan does not need to see me naked.

"Okay, okay. I'll shower." I shove her hand away. The last thing I need is Megan bathing me. She crosses her arms and stares at me like she doesn't believe anything I'm saying. "I promise."

"Fine. But if you don't come out in clean clothes, smelling like that fruity body wash you use, we're doing it *my* way." Megan closes the bathroom door with one last pointed look.

The water feels like pin pricks against my skin. I've been falling deeper into this depressive state since Jag came into the bar three days ago.

"Why did I turn him away? I know he's trying to get me to fuck him again," I lie to myself. This is all my fault. I've gone and caught feelings. Feelings I keep telling myself will never be returned by him or anyone else, no matter what lies they feed me, but somewhere, deep in my soul, I know that isn't true.

Everything with Jagger is different. I've never felt like this after sleeping with anyone. It's what I pride myself on... a good fuck and run. I feel things for Jagger and if the pain in his eyes the last time I saw him is any indication, his words are true, and he feels the same.

For two weeks, I hadn't been able to let go or get him out of my mind. Each day without him felt like another knife plunging into my heart. I pushed through the heartbreak for as long as I could, but when he showed up, it changed everything. Broke me in ways I never imagined. I ruined it all and I doubt it's fixable at this point.

I've called in sick to work for the past three days, completely ignoring the fact that I don't get paid if I don't work and I have bills to pay.

After I wash away the layers of nasty, I step out of the shower, smelling and feeling better than I have in days. I dry off before wrapping the towel around my waist and shoving the louvered door open. Quickly, I walk into the small bedroom and close the door behind me. Mistake. When I look at my reflection in the full-length mirror hanging on the back of the door, I gasp. Literally, gasp. Out loud. I clamp my hand over my mouth, hoping Megan didn't hear me.

I look like death. My blond hair has dejected streaks of a faded purple that was bright violet at one time, but now looks like I just rubbed purple chalk in it. My eyes are red and swollen and there are dark circles under them, a result of crying too much and not sleeping enough. And I've lost weight. I mean, I was skinny to begin with, but now I can see my ribs. The bag of Cheetos is the only thing I remember eating recently. Shit. I'm a fucking mess.

Turning away from the mirror as shame courses through me, I step into a pair of pink, fuzzy pajama pants with ice cream cones on them and a black hoodie then force myself out to Megan. If I stay in here much longer, she'll send out a search party. Slumping back onto the couch, I hope Megan will leave me alone. No surprise, luck is not on my side. She places a pillow on one end of the couch and pushes my shoulders gently.

"Lie back." I obey her order as she takes a seat on the other end and lifts my feet into her lap. "What's going on with you?"

"Nothing." The automatic response falls quickly from my lips.

"No offense, but you look like you've been run over by a truck. And you *never* call out of work. Ryan had to force you to take time off when you had the flu last year."

"It's stupid," I respond dismissively with a wave.

"Not if it has you this upset. Talk to me, Ellis," she pleads, softly running her hands up and down my leg. It feels nice. Relaxing. Supportive. Fuck! If anyone is going to understand and help me through this, it's Megan.

"Jagger hates me."

"What?" She stops rubbing my leg and stares at me in disbelief. "He came to the bar a few days ago."

"Okay. He might not hate me, but he should." I say meekly. "I've been ignoring him, and I was mean to him the other day."

"Oh, I overheard the conversation. You basically told him to fuck off after you ignored his calls and texts."

"Ugh! I remember." I throw my arm over my eyes.

"You told you were done with over one silly comment."

"I'm aware." Whatever she's about to say is going to be right, but I roll my eyes in annoyance anyway.

"The way I see it, you got what you asked for, so I don't understand the problem."

"Yes, you do. Stop being like this and help me," I beg with a whine.

"Melodramatic much?" she teases then pauses, furrowing her brows like she's formulating the perfect plan. "Call him. Text him. Hell, go to the studio! You have options, but sitting here sulking and pretending the bottom of the Cheetos bag has the answers is not going to solve anything."

"You aren't helping," I cry, kicking my feet like a toddler having one hell of a tantrum.

"Oh, I've helped. A lot. Look around."

I glance around the trailer. While I was showering and dressing, Megan cleaned the entire place. Dishes are washed and put away, the floor is clean, and she took the trash out. "Wow! It looks great in here. Thank you," I mumble still holding onto my attitude.

"You're welcome. I also cleaned out the fridge. Everything in there was old and moldy. It was gross."

"I'll go to the store tomorrow."

"What will you eat in the meantime?"

"I'm not hungry. I ate Cheetos."

"Look, Ellis. I'm fully aware Cheetos are your emotional support food, but they are not life sustaining. You need real food. Veggies and fruits and things that are good for you."

"I don't have the energy for the grocery store."

Megan sits up straighter and smiles at me like some evil genius. "I'll make you a deal."

"Oh, shit. What kind of deal?"

"I will go to the store and even pay for the groceries if you pull your head out of your ass, stop acting like a child, and go to the studio. Talk to Jagger, Ellis."

"That's a shitty deal," I grumble.

"How? You get free groceries, and you can find out for sure if there is something between you and Jagger. FYI, there is, but both of you are being stubborn asses." Megan flicks me on the forehead. Hard.

I clutch my chest. "Harsh! And ow!" I add, rubbing my head with the other hand.

Megan stands up and holds her hand out to me. "C'mon, get up. Let's do this."

"Wait. You mean now?" I squeak out. I thought she'd at least let me sulk for a few more days.

"Yep. What else do you have to do today?" She stands with her hands on her hips, daring me to challenge her.

Wallow. Eat Cheetos. Be sad. Cry. I don't list any of those out loud. I simply say, "Nothing."

"Good. Then put on shoes and let's go."

The drive to Orange Grove is lonely and the closer I get, the more my nerves eat at me. I told Jagger this thing between us was just sex, but I was lying. I've been lying to both of us for weeks. I knew the moment I met Jagger something was different with him. Each time we were together, my feelings grew stronger, and no matter how much I denied them, they only grew more. I miss Jagger. I really like him, and I want more with him than sex. I want a relationship.

When I park in front of the studio, it's closed, dark inside. Weird. He should be open. Worry washes over me. Is he okay? Did something bad happen? I opt to move my car closer to his apartment. By the time I'm in front of Jagger's building, I'm in a better mood than I was at home, happy even. A little concerned about the whole studio thing, but excited to see Jagger and tell him the truth. My feelings are still waging a war inside me and as I take the elevator up to his floor, they are all vying for the center spot in my brain.

I love him, but I don't want to love him. That word scares the shit out of me. He's the only one I want but am I ready to give up the freedom to fuck around with other guys? As much as I want my freedom, I also crave the idea of being in a relationship. I can do this. I can commit to one person. Right? Commit. That's a terrifying word.

Nausea washes over me as I stand in front of his door with my hand raised to knock. Hesitating, I force myself to breathe. *You can do this.*

CHAPTER 19

JAGGER

The knock at the door startles me. I'm not expecting anyone, but my siblings and Gentry tend to show up unannounced when the mood hits them. The last thing I want to do is face anyone right now. I haven't opened the studio since Ellis broke me three days ago. If I thought things were bad before I stupidly showed up at Paradise 11, I was gravely mistaken. This is pure hell.

When I left the bar on Saturday, I was pissed. Angrier than I've ever been. By the time I drove home from my parents' house and finally fell face down on my couch, I was devastated. I'm in love with Ellis, and nothing will ever happen between us. It was just sex for him. How? How can he not feel what I'm feeling? Guess I was kidding myself, thinking we were on the same page, wanting the same things and moving in the same direction. I finally showered this morning, but that's as far as I got. I'm still in my boxers, but I don't bother pulling on a shirt or pants. If my family wants to show up without warning, this is what they get.

Shock doesn't begin to describe how I surprise coursing through me when I wrench the door open and find Ellis standing right in front of me. Suddenly, I feel naked and exposed. I awkwardly cross my hands over my body in an effort to cover up as if Ellis hasn't seen me naked.

"Hey," he whispers with a small wave when I stare at him for too long. He's not his usual bubbly self. He looks like I feel— exhausted, scared, lonely, unsure. It's been a rough few days with little sleep, no food, and my back is sore from sleeping on the couch for three days. I only moved from the spot where I landed on Saturday to use the bathroom and then to shower today when I got sick of smelling myself.

"Hey," I grunt back after a long pause. "What are you doing here?"

"Can we talk?" he asks in a meek voice. I've never heard Ellis sound so small and terrified.

I scoff at his question. I asked that same thing three days ago and I was basically told to leave. The heart-broken part of me wants to yell at him and tell him no. The logical part of me wants to tell him to leave and never come back. The part that loves him is the one to finally respond. "Um, okay. Come in."

Ellis follows me inside, closing the door behind him. I grab a pair of sweats off the floor of the bedroom and pull them on, feeling a little less exposed. Ellis stands awkwardly next to the counter, and I watch him from the bedroom doorway.

"I'm sorry." He puts his hands in his pockets then takes them out before shoving them back in again. His shoulders are slumped forward, and his head is dropped, staring at the floor. I don't like this look on him- nervous and sad, fuzzy pajama pants, a black hoodie, and his hair isn't even colored. There are still remnants of the purple, but it's mostly been washed out. None of this is his normal look. Where are the ripped jeans or tight leather pants? Where are the blouses? I don't say any of that to him. I don't want to upset him. "For the way I acted on Saturday," he finally finishes after what feels like an eternity.

"You told me the truth. You were just dating me for sex. Can't fault you for being honest," I bite out.

"It's not like that."

"Isn't it, Ellis?"

"No."

"Then enlighten me. How is it?" Well, hurt is winning out. I thought logic might take over, but I guess I was wrong.

"I like you. I want to date you. But I've always been single. I like my freedom," he admits, but it doesn't sound like the truth. He sounds broken, like the words are being recited from memory, but he doesn't truly believe them.

"I don't share," I growl.

"Possessive much?" he mumbles.

"We're either together or we're not. I won't be with someone who is fucking other guys."

"Being with one person is a big commitment. I don't know if I'm ready for that."

"You're giving me whiplash, Ellis. Make a damn decision. Do you want me or not?" I ask bluntly, anger raising my voice as I speak. I can't do this back-and-forth bullshit. He is either all in or all out.

"Yes. I think so," he whispers.

Fuck this. I'm done with his crap. I'm gonna go for what I want. Taking several steps, I close the distance between us, grabbing Ellis by the front of his hoodie and slamming him against the wall.

"Stop me if you don't want this."

I give him a few seconds to speak. When he stays quiet, I crash my lips onto his, pushing my way inside. It's rough, all tongue and teeth. Needy. Desperate. Claiming what's mine. He hesitates at first but then he's kissing me back. He threads his hands into my hair as I hold him against the wall. My cock hardens and I press it against his, ripping a moan from him that gets lost in the kiss. Without breaking the kiss, I guide him toward the bedroom. It's a miracle we don't trip over each other or the discarded clothes and shoes I haven't bothered to pick up.

When his legs hit the bed, I break the kiss. In a bold move, I push his pajama pants down to his ankles then pull his hoodie over his head. He isn't wearing under-wear or a shirt. Ellis moans and his cock hardens, so I continue. I grab him by the neck, pulling him in for another quick kiss. Then I shove him onto the bed, pulling his pants and shoes off.

Crawling onto the bed still fully clothed, I straddle him. His hips are locked between my legs, and my hands rest on either side of his head. Leaning down, close enough to feel his breath, I look Ellis in the eye, and finally lay it all on the line. This is either going to be the heartbreaking end to everything or the beginning of something beautiful. Either way, Ellis deserves the truth. Somehow, I'll deal with the consequences if he runs from me.

"I'm in love with you, Ellis. You're either in it one hundred percent or we're done. No more fucking other guys." Ellis' eyes widen. "Yeah, I know I wasn't the only one. We didn't make anything official, so I didn't bring it up. But that stops *now*. It's you and me or nothing. Make a fucking choice." Ellis whimpers. Fuck, he's so responsive and it's turning me the fuck on. We're both rock hard.

Having Ellis under me is everything. Fuck, I love him. He's in the moment, but I have no idea what he's going to say. Ellis loves sex, and that might be all he truly wants from me. If that's what he says, I'll have to let him go.

"O-okay," he manages. His breathing is stuttered, his pupils are blown. He's turned on and I know he has trouble talking when he gets like this, but I need his honesty. I have to know what he feels before we move forward.

"Okay?" I snap. I'm trying not to get angry, but he has to give me *something*.

"I want this. I want you."

He looks away. I grab his chin and try to move his head to face me, but he resists. I don't want to hurt him, so I don't try again. He refuses to look at me. This can't be a good sign. My heart cracks a little more, physical pain burns my chest.

"Ellis?" I venture.

He sniffles. "I'm scared, Jag." His voice is full of emotion, and a few tears fall onto my hand. I let go of his chin, wiping at the tears with my thumbs. He'll look at me when he's ready.

"I'm not going to hurt you. I promise to love you fully, Ellis. I want you and no one else. This isn't a fling or a stop along the road to true love. Ellis, you are it for me. I'm in love with you. I'm all in, but only if you are, too. I can't do this if you aren't ready, and I can't force you to be someone you're not." The pain in my chest seeps into my words.

"I'm ready. I came here today to tell you that, but I got all up in my own head and ended up turning into a complete disaster before I got off the elevator." He wipes his eyes as he looks at me. "I…" Ellis trails off.

"Don't say anything you aren't ready to say. You want me, us. That's enough."

Ellis smiles. "Thank you for being patient with me. I'm sorry."

"Can I kiss my boyfriend?"

"Your boyfriend was hoping for a little more than a kiss. He *is* already naked." His smile

is flirtatious and… happy. It's so damn good to see him brighten.

"More than a kiss? Hmm, what could we possibly do?" I tap my chin.

"Jagger!" Ellis whines playfully.

He's been through enough. Today was hard for him, and I want to show him how much I love him. Still straddling Ellis, I pull my shirt off and toss it behind me then bend down and kiss him before jumping off the bed to get rid of the rest of my clothes. Ellis sits up and scoots to the edge of the bed, lowering himself to the floor. He looks up at me from his knees with lust in his eyes. Slowly, he licks from the base of my cock to the tip then lowers himself on my cock until I hit the back of his throat. I try to pull back, but he grabs my thighs, holding me in place and working my cock with his throat.

"Shit. I'm gonna come if you keep doing that. Damn, you feel good," I praise

He bobs his head up and down my cock, hitting the back of his throat each time. He doesn't choke or gag, but the sounds he's making are driving me insane. Spit pools around my cock and his tears mix with it, making a mess of his face. Fuck, he looks wrecked as he glances up at me through hooded eyes. Ellis loves sucking cock, but I need more than his mouth tonight. He pulls off me with an audible pop then licks down my length, teasing his tongue around my balls.

Throwing my head back, hands gripping his hair, I groan loudly. "Fuck, that feels phenom..." I choke on the last word as he sucks one of my balls into his mouth, stroking my cock. Incoherent noises fall from my lips. Pure ecstasy lights up every nerve ending. I step back, inhaling a ragged breath, willing myself to calm the fuck down. I don't want to come until I'm inside him.

"On the bed. Face up," I growl as soon as I can form words again.

Ellis climbs on the bed, letting his legs fall open. I love how confident he is with his body.

"When was the last time you got tested?" I ask.

Ellis averts his eyes. "You need to wear a condom."

I freeze at his words. "Because you've been with those other guys or because you have something?" My chest is tight waiting for his answer.

"I haven't been tested since December. I usually go a couple of times a year. A few times the other guy hasn't worn a condom." He sighs heavily. "I want to take you bare, but not until I've been tested."

It hurts to hear him say he took other guys bare. Fucking careless. Shoving those feeling deep fucking down, I look him in the eyes.

"Thank you for being honest." I pull out a condom and a bottle of lube from the nightstand and toss both on the bed. "I haven't been with anyone but you since my last negative test." I trail kisses from his knee to his thigh then across his stomach and down his other leg. "As soon as you get negative results, no more condoms."

"Deal," he squeaks out as I take one nipple in my mouth, sucking and biting it while I pinch the other. Ellis' eyes roll back and his cock twitches between us. "Uh, fuck."

He ruts against my cock, and I almost lose it. I'm worked up from his tongue and I'm going to blow as soon as I get inside him. I'm trying to make this last as long as possible.

"Fuck me. I need to feel you." Ellis drawls out in a breathy tone.

"Baby, I'm not going to last," I tell him, a little embarrassed by my admission.

"I don't care. Please."

"I have one stipulation." I trace my tongue up his neck. "You don't touch yourself. After I come, I'll take care of you." Biting on his ear, a moan escapes Ellis.

"Okay, yeah. Anything you want. Just get inside me."

"Greedy," I tease, working two fingers inside him.

"I used a toy last night. I don't need to be prepped. Hurry up." His voice is desperate and I fucking love it. I slide my cock in slowly. He winces as I pass the first ring of muscles, so I stop. "Keep going. I'm fine." I raise an eyebrow. "I won't lie about this," he promises.

Trusting Ellis knows his body, I slam the rest of the way in until I bottom out. *Fuck* he's tight.

"Are you okay? Am I hurting you?" I ask, running a hand through his sweaty hair.

"Yes. No. Shit. I'm good. Doesn't hurt."

He clenches around me, and I growl out a curse. Ellis laughs. He fucking laughs. Little brat knows exactly what he's doing to me.

"Do not make me come before I even move."

"It would be my proudest moment." He smirks.

"You're kind of a brat."

"You have no idea. Now stop talking and fuck your boyfriend."

Hovering over him, I steal kisses as I thrust in and out, getting completely lost in the moment. Ellis' wet heat and tight ass are going to send me over the edge. The sexy noises he's making aren't helping, either.

"Fuck, that's feels good. Damn, Ellis, your ass is perfect." I push his legs to his chest, giving me better access, slamming into him harder this time. The sound of skin slapping fills the room. I grunt and moan, not able to be quiet. I don't care if my neighbors can hear me.

Ellis wiggles his arms between us, reaching up and pinching my nipples, rolling them between his fingers, sending me over the precipice. I cry out, a mix of pain and pleasure.

Releasing Ellis' legs, I let my body rest on top of his until I catch my breath. Holy shit, that was mind-blowing.

"Are you alright?"

"Fantastic." I kiss him quickly then scoot down the bed taking Ellis' tip between my lips, working my tongue over his slit. He hisses and I cut my eyes to him, worried I hurt him. "Sensitive. I'm so fucking close already."

Moving so I'm between his legs, I devour his length until I gag then I pull up slightly. I'm not the cock sucking pro Ellis is, but my skills are decent. I bob up and down, running my tongue over his slit every time I reach his head. I love hearing him hiss. I reach between us and push two fingers into his sensitive hole, moving them in and out as I suck his cock.

"Oh, shit, Jag. Fuck. I'm gonna come." He tries to push me off him, but I suck vigorously. I want to taste him. A few seconds later, Ellis stiffens, lets out a strangled cry, and empties into my mouth. I swallow it all, licking my lips as I fall onto the bed next to him. He turns on his side, facing me.

"You taste delicious," I whisper as I lean over and kiss

Ellis turns red from chest to ears. "Don't say that," he mumbles against my lips.

"Why not? It's true." I shrug my shoulders, pressing a quick kiss to his cheek. "Be right back." In the bathroom, I clean up then bring back a warm washcloth and clean Ellis' cock and ass. After tossing the cloth in the sink, I pull on my sweats. "Are you hungry?"

"Yes! I was too nervous to eat today. But now, I'm starving." Ellis climbs off the bed and gets dressed, freezing as he pulls his hoodie on. "Is that an actual alarm clock?" He eyes the small device on my dresser. "You know cell phones are a thing and they have alarms, right?"

"I'm aware, but I need the incessant blare from that one or I'll never wake up. Don't judge me!" I try to pout but end up laughing instead.

"Then why is all the way over there and not next to your bed?"

"Because I also need it out of reach. Otherwise, I'll smack it off and go right back to sleep."

"If I ever stay the night, you're going to have to let me wake you with my mouth. We are not turning that thing on. It will give me nightmares. My parents didn't believe in giving a child a phone, so I was a senior in high school before I got one. And even then, I had to leave it charging in their bedroom at night." He points to the offending alarm clock. "An evil device monstrosity similar to that woke me every morning for years at six in the damn morning. Didn't matter if was the weekend or summer."

"Six?" I ask in disbelief. Shit, I'm lucky if I wake up by eight *with* the alarm clock.

"Yep. 'Sleeping in makes you lazy.' is my dad's favorite saying. My parents believed that everyone should be awake at six. Showered, dressed and at the breakfast table by seven. I even had chores to do before I came to breakfast."

"That's ludicrous."

"It is. Now I sleep as late as possible every day, which is still early, but not six in the morning early. My house. My rules." The defiance in his voice is adorable and... now I'm hard again.

"I don't blame you! And *when* you spend the night, I will happily let you wake me with your mouth." I grab Ellis' hand and lead him to the other room. "Sit on the couch. I'll bring over a snack."

My entire life changed today. The man I love is sitting in my living room, waiting for me to feed him. This is everything I crave, and I want it for the rest of my life.

CHAPTER 20

ELLIS

Last night, Jagger manhandled me and fucked me senseless or maybe fucked some sense into me, either way, it doesn't matter. The point is — now I'm ready to date him. Like for real. Jagger Ward is in love with me... swoon! It was impossible for me to sleep last night. I don't even know what to think. A boy actually loves me. My dad was wrong. I am worth something. To Jagger, at least. And that's all that matters.

I didn't say it back. Love is a scary word and not one I've said to anyone other than my parents on very rare occasions. That type of love doesn't mean the same as being in love. I've known for weeks that I have feelings for Jagger, but I never dreamed he would feel the same about me. That's why I kept pushing him away. I knew if I let myself believe there was something real between us, I'd end up getting hurt.

Jagger is a genuine guy and has always been honest with me, so I'm choosing to trust him and believe this is real. He invited me to spend the night, but I was a little afraid to be that vulnerable. Jagger asked for a compromise, so I agreed to breakfast, which is why I'm currently driving to his apartment.

Letting him see where I live is out of the question. It's embarrassing. If I bring him to my place, he'll know how poor I am and then he won't want me. Dad is surely right on that front. I spend the drive singing along with my 'Diva' playlist, belting out one off-key song after another. I love to sing, but I kind of suck at it. Megan's favorite thing to do is drag me to karaoke bars, get me drunk, and force me to sing. Drunk Ellis forgets how terrible he is, which Megan finds hilarious. But, alas, she's a great friend and never records drunk karaoke or posts any of my stupid decisions on social media. Besties for life!

Jagger apartment in downtown Orange Grove is much better than my place. Orange Grove is a bigger town than Anchor Point, but not by much. Still, I have to drive around for about five minutes before I find a parking spot two blocks from Jagger's building.

When I get to the complex, I open the door to the lobby lined with shops and walk to the back where there are two elevators. It's a little after eight on Monday morning, and none of the stores are open, except the coffee shop. Several other people mill about heading to their offices. Once on the elevator, I punch in the code and hit the button for the eighth floor. The elevator lurches slightly then rises quickly to the top. Stepping off, I walk to the right then realize I'm going the wrong way. Apparently, love makes me dumb.

Pivoting, I stroll down the hall and turn the corner before reaching unit 805. Jagger swings the door open and drags me into his arms, inhaling deeply as he hugs me.

"Are you smelling me?" I ask unable to contain my laugh.

"Yes. I love the way you smell all fruity and refreshing, like a cocktail on the beach."

"Okay, weird. Oddly specific and terrifyingly spot on. I used a coconut shampoo, and my current body wash is strawberry kiwi."

"Welp, my nose works." Jagger laughs awkwardly when his joke falls flat. It was cute, but I'm too nervous to focus on jokes. "Come on in. I need to check on breakfast."

"It smells great. What are you making?"

Jagger closes the oven about the time I reach the kitchen. The space is small, but it's an open floor plan so it feels bigger than it is. A counter with two barstools separates the kitchen from the living room. I hop onto one of the black stools. The aesthetic is nice. The kitchen has white tile counter tops with a red back splash behind the black stove. The other appliances are also black, and the floor is red tile. The rest of the room has a wood floor with white walls and two red couches. There are several paintings on the walls, and some of his glasswork is displayed on a few shelves that mostly hold books. I didn't really take it all in the other times I was here. The first time, we spent most of the date on the balcony then I lost my mind and ran. Last night, I was too emotionally drained to focus on aesthetics.

"Coffee?" he asks, holding up the pot.

"No thanks. I don't drink coffee."

Jag appears stricken at my words. "How do you function without coffee? I drink a pot every day."

"I don't like the taste. Most mornings I drink hot tea."

"I don't have any tea." Jag frowns. "Sorry."

"It's fine. I drink a cup while I was getting dressed. Water will do."

Suddenly, he brightens. "I have cinnamon rolls in the oven, bacon under the foil, and a bowl of fresh fruit in the fridge."

"Wow, that sounds great. Thank you for cooking."

He comes around the counter, placing a chaste kiss on my lips. "Thank you for coming over. I'm glad you're here."

Without thinking about it, I wrap my arms around Jag and rest my head against his shoulder. This is nice. Comfortable. Breakfast is not part of the one-night stand agenda, so this is a nice change even if I did run home like a coward last night. Baby steps.

Jagger hesitantly pulls out of my arms as the timer on the oven beeps. He takes the cinnamon rolls out, giving me a great view of his gorgeous ass. It looks damn good in his tight jeans. I watch as he fills two plates with fruit, bacon, and a cinnamon roll, his large muscles stretching the soft-gray Henley. My mouth waters and not because of what's on the plate he places in front of me. I focus on the food, so he doesn't catch me staring.

Is this for real? Can the sexy man sitting next to me

actually be my boyfriend? I never thought anyone would love me, much less someone as hot as Jagger.

"What are you doing today?" he asks, then shovels a forkful of fruit into his mouth.

"Well, I was supposed to work at nine, but I called out."

"Work? What time does the bar open?" he asks curiously.

I finish chewing and swallowing the mouth full of cinnamon roll before I respond. "Five, but we're not open on Mondays. I work a second job for a call center. It's remote, so I can work on my couch in my underwear, which is *awesome*."

"Do you work the call center job every day?"

"Usually Monday to Thursday from nine to three. Unless I take a shift for someone."

"What about the bar?"

"The bar is open Tuesday through Saturday right now from five until about 2 in the morning. I work all those days. In the spring and summer, I go in at noon Friday and Saturday. "Oh, so you must get off early those days?"

"Hell, no! I'm not giving up weekend night tips just because I go in at noon. That's pure insanity."

"You work a lot," he observes.

"Yeah, well, the bills aren't going to pay themselves," I use the most matter-of-fact tone I can muster.

I don't want Jagger to know how hard it's been for me to make ends meet the past three years. For the first two, I only worked at the bar and racked up a ton of credit card debt. The job at the call center is helping me pay it off. I'm doing a decent job. I had three cards that totaled close to twenty thousand dollars, but I've managed to pay off eight thousand since I started the second job. That's a huge accomplishment and one I'm proud of. Hopefully, I can pay off another eight this year. When I'm eventually out of debt, I'll be able to start saving for a better place.

"If it wasn't for those nasty bills, we'd all be rich," Jag says in jest

"Preach. Sista!"

"You really took the whole day off?"

"I did."

"Can we spend it together? Or do you have something else you need to do?"

"I'm free and all yours," I venture. I know he literally just asked me to spend the entire day with him, but I'm still having a hard time with this whole boyfriend thing.

"That sounds like the perfect day." Jagger gathers our empty plates and carries them to the kitchen. "More water?"

"No, thanks. Can I help?" I offer, starting to stand, but Jag waves his hands at me.

"Nah, sit there and keep me company. I'll take care of the kitchen."

Reluctantly, I sit back down. I don't mind helping, but I would be the same way if he was at my place. There's something special about taking care of someone else.

"How did you get into glassblowing?" I blurt out. The question has been on my mind since I met Jag in

December. He stiffens for a quick second then relaxes. If I hadn't been laser focused on him, I would have missed the slight movement.

"When I was a kid, I went to this sleep away camp for a week. One of the art classes they offered was glassblowing. I instantly fell in love with it. So, I came back here and begged my parents to find a class. Of course, there was nothing like that around here, but after some searching, my mom found a place in Orlando that offered classes on Saturdays. For six years, she or one of my siblings drove me to Orlando almost every Saturday. After the first two years, I had taken all the beginner classes. The instructor saw something in me, I guess, because he started doing private classes, since I couldn't take the more advanced classes they offered during the week. Anyway, it's been the only thing I ever wanted to do since I was like ten."

"Wow, that's cool. Did you go to college?"

"Yeah. I just got an associate's degree in business and took all my classes online. By the time I was sixteen, I was already selling my art, so my parents rented the studio space for me and helped me start my business. While I was in high school, I worked part time at a grocery store and used that money to buy some of the stuff I needed for the studio. My parents loaned me the rest. I started small and used the studio for myself and sold pieces at pop up markets. Then after I finished the associate's degree, I slowly started giving a few private lessons. At the beginning of last year, I started the business full-time, offering more classes plus doing school field trips and parties."

"Your parents sound wonderful. Supportive." A twinge of jealousy runs through me.

Jagger smiles and I can see the love he has for his family in it. "They are. I doubt I'd be where I am without their support or glassblowing. It's my job, but it's so much more for me. It clears my mind and calms the chaos that lives in my head sometimes." There's more to that last statement, but I don't want to pry.

"I get that. Drawing is like that for me." Even I can hear the sadness in my voice. I should have at least attempted to cover it. Jag is talented as fuck, but I don't know what other questions to ask.

"What about you? Did you go to college?"

"Ha, yeah, no. Being a lawyer or some financial planner was not for me." Jagger freezes with a dirty plate in his hand halfway between the sink and the dishwasher. Slowly he turns his head toward me with a quizzical look.

"You know there are other degrees, right?" The absurdity of the situation from the confused look on his face to the plate still hanging in the air to the thought of my parents supporting my art. It's all too much and I start laughing.

"Not according to my parents. 'We'll pay for college if you get a real degree like finance.'" I repeat my father's words in a fake deep voice. The laughter still lingering in my tone doesn't match the disappointment in my heart I still feel when I think about the night my dreams were ripped away from me.

Jagger snaps out of his confusion and puts the plate

in the dishwasher then continues loading it. "What did you want to pursue in college?"

"Art. Painting to be more specific."

"Your parents didn't think that was a good idea?" he questions as he loads the last dish, tosses in a soap pod, and starts the dishwasher.

"No," I scoff. "They think art is a silly hobby."

"Well, shit. They're going to hate my ass." He shakes his head with a nervous chuckle.

"You own a business and have a degree. They will like you more than they like me. Don't be surprised if they say you can do better than me."

Jagger snaps his head to me, meeting my eyes. "You're serious?"

"Yep," I respond flippantly.

"That's messed up."

I shrug like it doesn't matter, but it does, and it hurts. I hate knowing I'm a disappointment, but I also can't be the person they want me to be. I would die sitting in an office all day in a suit. Die!

The dishes are washing, the counter is clean, and the leftover fruit and bacon are in the fridge. Jagger brings refills my water glass and gets one for himself. Let's relax. I follow him to the couch and as soon as I sit, he pulls me against his chest. It feels nice— solid, comfortable, safe. *This* is where I'm meant to be. I'm happy. Truly happy for the first time.

Chapter 21

Jagger

My mind is reeling from learning that Ellis' parents don't support his art dream. I've only seen one of his drawings, but I'd like to see more. If the night he came to the studio with his colleagues is any indication, he's seriously talented and not just with drawing. His ornament was excellent, and he caught on very quickly.

I set my glass of water on the table next to the couch and offer to take his. Once both glasses are out of my hands, I wrap my arms around my boyfriend. I still can't believe he agreed to give us a shot. I should have manhandled his ass sooner.

"Have you ever taken art classes?" I ask once I have him relaxing on my chest. His body feels good against me.

"Yeah. I went to a local summer art camp every year until I aged-out at fourteen. I took every art class possible as my high school electives and built an impressive portfolio. I truly believed I was going to go to art school." The sadness is back in his voice and in the way he holds himself. I'm not even sure he notices, but I can feel how tense his entire body is. He's wound up tight. Gently caressing his arm with my fingers relaxes him a little. It isn't enough, but it's a start.

"Can I see more of your art one day?" I ask.

"Sure. I guess." His voice is wary. I wonder if he doesn't like to share his talent because his parents don't support that part of him. Anger rushes through me. How can anyone treat their own child that way?

Ellis adjusts himself in my arms and turns until he can see my face. "Tell me about your family. Are you close to your parents? How many siblings do you have?"

"We're pretty close. They all live here. Truthfully, I'm the only one who doesn't live in the house they built on their property."

"What? Your siblings all live in the same house?" The look of pure confusion on his face is comical.

"No." I reply with a small chuckle. "My parents own a citrus grove and have a lot of land. They gave each of us few acres and built us each a house on the land."

"Then why do you live here?"

Sharing this with Ellis is hard. I don't talk about Jaxon to many people outside of my family. No one wants to hear all the 'woe is me' shit that comes with losing someone you love, especially when it's been almost a decade. Most people think I should be over it by now as if grief is some easy process, like you go through these preconceived stages and then, bam, all better. That's not how it works at all. And everyone handles it differently. There's no 'one size fits all' when it comes to grief.

"It's closer to the studio." I tell a partial truth. Thankfully, Ellis doesn't question my reason.

"That makes sense. Tell me about your family."

"My parents always wanted a big family, so they had six kids."

"Six! Wow. That's a lot," Ellis muses.

"Yeah. But it was fun growing up in a big family."

"I bet. You must have always had someone to play with."

"I did." My mind wanders to Jax. We had a great time together. He was my best friend. Fuck, I miss him.

"Hey." Ellis nudges my ribs. "Where did you go?" he asks softly.

I shake my head attempting to clear it. "Sorry. Yeah, siblings. My oldest brother, Lex, short for Lexion, works at the orchard full time as does my sister, Maxine or Max, and her husband, Andrew. My other brother, Lawton, better known as Law, teaches middle school math, but helps out on the weekends and in the summers. Mel, the one who helped during your class, and I help when we aren't running our own businesses and my two sisters-in-law, Amanda and Stephanie, work at the store. In addition to selling fruit to local grocery stores and restaurants, we have a store on the property where we sell fruit, jams, drinks, and sweets."

"You have all shortened your names to three letters."

"Yep. My parents have this weird thing about picking names that can all be shortened to three letter nicknames. They also named us in groups of two: two L names, two M names..." I trail off, not sure where I'm going with this explanation. "We got picked on sometimes as kids, but by middle school Lex and Law were the biggest kids in school, so they put a stop to any bullying real fast."

"Um, Jag. You said there are six of you, so either I can't count, or you make number five." Ellis expertly picks up on what I was trying to gloss over.

I try not to bristle. I really do. But Ellis notices the change in my demeanor immediately. My mind goes numb. My chest aches. How can I still miss him this much? After all this time, it feels like I buried my brother yesterday. Ellis takes my hand and squeezes it. "You don't have to tell me."

"I want to tell you." I don't look at him. I can't. I'll break completely if I make eye contact, so I look out the window instead. "I have a twin. Had. I had a twin. Jaxon. He... I lost him when we were seventeen." My voice breaks as I try to choke back tears. Ellis lets go of my hand and pulls me into his arms. I rest my head on his shoulder. "We were at a party. You know how it goes. A bunch of high school kids drinking and being stupid. We were having a good time. One last blowout before the start of our senior year.

"At some point, Jax left with his girlfriend. She was sober and driving, so they made it to her house. Her parents were out of town. Every seventeen-year-old boy's dream, no parents and a gorgeous girlfriend. I'll never know exactly what happened, but they had a fight. Jax called me, but I was drunk and didn't answer.

I might have been passed out by then. I don't know. When I woke up the next morning, I had nine texts from him. I still have them saved on my phone, but I also have them memorized and they play on repeat in my mind often.

> We had a fight. Me and Sarah.
>
> She's pregnant.
>
> I can't be a dad.
>
> Answer your phone.
>
> I need you, Jag. Please.
>
> I have to get out of here.
>
> I need a ride.
>
> Fuck it.
>
> I'll sleep on a lounge chair.

I list off the texts in the order they came. "I failed him. I fucking failed my brother. The last time my twin ever needed me, and I wasn't there."

"His death wasn't your fault," Ellis assures me in a soothing tone.

I scoff at his observation. How many times have I heard those words? "All I know is I wasn't there when my brother needed me and when I woke up, he was dead. Drowned. No foul play and it didn't appear to be on purpose. The autopsy concluded that he slipped, hit his head, and landed in the pool. His phone was on the concrete, cracked and lying next to the pool."

"But you have a niece or nephew. That's something."

"Mila. My niece is named Mila. Jaxon's middle name is Milard, so Sarah named Mila after her father. My family has a good relationship with Sarah and my parents are very involved grandparents. I see so much of Jaxon in her. It's… just hard," I admit.

"I'm sure it's very difficult to see her, but you have a great opportunity to teach her everything about her dad. Let her get to know her father through your eyes. You knew him better than anyone else. His memory will live on if you share him with Mila."

Ellis' words are sweet, and he's right. I know I am missing out on important milestones in Mila's life because I can't move forward. I don't blame Sarah. She chose that night to tell Jaxon everything because her parents were out of town. She thought they could talk it all through and decide what to do. She should have waited until Jaxon sobered up. He was always an emotional mess when he drank too much.

"I know you're right. I'll try to be a better uncle." I sigh. "Can we talk about something else?"

"Sure! Does your middle name also start with an M?"

I laugh softly. "Well, of course. Lex and Law have middle names that start with J. Max and Mel have middle names that star with L."

"You know that's weird, right?" Ellis teases.

"Yep."

"So…" Ellis drags out the word, rubbing soft circles on my leg.

"So?"

"Tell me your middle name," he encourages.

"Uh, no."

"Oh, come on. I'll tell you mine," I try to make a deal.

"Is that similar to 'I'll show you mine if you show me yours?'"

"Something like that. But we've already seen each other naked, so all that's left is to share middle names." Ellis lifts one shoulder in a shrug.

"That's it, huh? Share middle names then what? We know everything about each other? We are officially official?" I tease.

Ellis barks out a laugh and I know I'll never get tired of that sound. It's glorious. "Officially official. I thought that happened last night when you manhandled the fuck out of me. I believe the exact word was 'mine.'"

Turning Ellis' head toward me, I press my lips to his. It's rough but quick. If I get us riled up, we'll end up fucking, and as much as I want that, I also want to learn more about Ellis, his art, and the things that makes him tick.

"Mine," I growl in his ear sending a shiver through him. His body flushes red and a sense of possessiveness runs through me.

After a beat, I let him go. "Marshall.," I state simply.

"What?" The word is gasp on his lips, and his face is full of confusion.

"My middle name is Marshall."

"Oh, I like it. Jagger Marshall Ward. It fits you."

"It does?"

"Yeah. Strong and confident."

"Time to show me yours," I tease.

"What?" There's that breathless word again. Damn, I love seeing how much I affect him with a simple question.

"Tell me your middle name," I implore.

He chuckles uncomfortably. "Sorry. It's Alexander."

"Ellis Alexander Young." I try his name out the way he did mine. "It's a good name," I conclude.

"I guess. I've never given much thought to my name."

"Well, I like it. What should we do today? The studio is closed on Mondays, so we have the whole day. We can stay here, binge movies and order takeout or we can go somewhere."

"Can we binge terrible reality TV?" Ellis asks, bouncing in his seat with childlike excitement.

"Anything you want."

"Then I want to stay here in your arms all day."

"Pick something." I hand Ellis the remote, pulling him a little closer. An entire day with my boyfriend in my arms sounds like the perfect day to me.

CHAPTER 22

ELLIS

J ag and I have been officially official for almost two weeks. I love when he says it that way. It's silly, but I feel special every time he says officially official, like it's some weird claim. Maybe it is. All I know is Jag counts every day of our relationship. Probably because it's new and the counting thing won't last forever, but it does something to my insides every time I hear it or see it in a text, like some kind of proof this is real. I'm probably just being stupid.

Every fiber of my being wants, no *needs*, to be loved by Jagger. I want to deserve him. To be good enough for once in my life. That fucking terrifies me. When he is finally done with me, the loss will be epic and I'm not sure I'll survive.

No one has ever treated me the way Jagger does. Part of it's my fault. Closing myself off was easier than getting hurt over and over. I know I'm nothing. Ellis 'Cum and Dump' Young. A cum dumpster for any man who will have me for a few hours. Hell, I'm rarely worth a few hours.

But Jagger is different. Everything about this relationship is different. Not that I've ever had a boyfriend, so maybe I don't know what I'm talking about. Shit. Why is this so hard? Jagger wants me. Me! Why do I question every single thing he says?

"Men don't want to date down." My father's words hit me in the chest. It's like he's in the small space with me. I hear him clearly. He's right. I live in a trailer, I'm poor, I barely graduated high school. *Poor, dumb, slutty Ellis. Every man's dream boyfriend.* Yeah, right.

My phone lights up on the counter with a text, but I can't look at it right away. I lost my appetite and can't finish eating breakfast. With my latest train of thought still fresh in my brain, I'm afraid to look. Jagger probably already came to his senses. Instead of picking up my phone, I fill the sink with soapy water and wash the dishes.

I've been trying to do a better job of keeping the trailer clean. After every meal, I wash the dishes and wipe down the counter. I even downloaded one of those apps to help keep you on track. I have a short list of things to do each day and each time I finish a task, I check it off on the app. It's been super helpful. For almost two weeks, I've lived by that app. At the end of the day, when I go to sleep with a clean home, I feel good about myself and my accomplishments.

When the last dish is washed and put away, I dry off my hands and hesitate before picking up the phone. It's a text from Jag. My heart races as I open the message. This is it, gone before I really had him.

> Jag: Good morning!

> Jag: Officially official day fifteen!

> Jag: Do you have plans tonight?

Relief hits me, my legs no longer able to hold me, so I fall onto the small couch and take a few calming breaths. There's the officially official message. *Swoon!* It makes my heart flutter and race for a completely different reason. It's going to hurt no matter what when Jag leaves, so I might as well enjoy the ride while I can. I quickly type out a reply to him.

> Me: No.

His response is immediate.

> Jag: Good. I'd like to take you out.

> Me: Okay.

> Me: Are you going to tell me where?

> Jag: How do you feel about surprises?

Each text pushes the negative thoughts further down and a smile slowly lights up my face.

> Me: I L-O-V-E Love them!

Jag: Good. Then it will be a surprise.

Jag: Dress is semi-casual.

Me: What does that even mean?

Jag: No shorts or t-shirts.

Jag: Jeans or dress pants and a nice shirt.

Jag: Does that help?

Me: Yeah, I think. Can I wear skinny jeans and a blouse?

Jag: Perfect.

Jag: Can you meet me at the studio at 6?

Me: Yes.

Jag: See you then, baby.

Baby? I like the sound of that. Ugh! But what am I going to do for the next nine hours? Okay, half of that will be trying to figure out what to wear. Skinny jeans and blouse cover like half my wardrobe. Which shade of jeans? Which blouse? Long-sleeved or short-sleeved? See through or not?

Forcing myself off the couch, I go to the closet and shift through the blouses. I skip over the blue one I wore the first time we had sex. I was horny as fuck night. The Twelve Wanks of Christmas was fun, but I was literally going to kill myself with lonely orgasms if I didn't stop jerking off to thoughts of Jagger and get a taste of the real thing. I never imagined that night would turn into being officially official.

It's one of my favorite blouses, and now it's full of Jagger memories. I'll have to burn it when the inevitable happens. I briefly mourn the future end of my relationship, and the loss of my favorite blouse before getting back to the task at hand.

See through is probably too much since I don't know where we're going and semi casual sounds a little more sophisticated than showing off my nips. My hand lands on a satin blouse I've never worn. I bought it a few months ago and adore it, but I haven't really had a place to wear it. I pick it up and run my hand over the soft, silky material. I have it in beige and black because those were the only two color options. I'm all over having the same shirt or pair of pants in every color if it will make the perfect outfit. Tonight, I think beige is the best choice. I love the cowl neckline with its deep v that shows off the middle of my chest without being too revealing. The material gathers just above my navel, and the sleeves are long and loose but cuffed at the wrists.

Gently laying the blouse on the bed, I walk to the small dresser and open the bottom drawer, rummaging through my jeans. Instead of pulling out jeans, I find a pair of maroon, skinny-legged, tapered dress pants I forgot about. I bought them on sale last year, and they've been living in the bottom of my drawer since. They will be a perfect match for the beige shirt. Paired with my signature black combat boots and the silver hoop earrings I never take off, this outfit is fire.

Okay, outfit problem solved! I glance at the time. It's only ten. Great. Eight more hours. This is going to be the longest day of my life.

Over the next several hours, I go to the grocery store and get what I need for the week, including more hair dye then I grab lunch from my favorite deli. Once I'm home, I take a shower and dye my hair. This time I go with a crimson red. It's not as deep and dark as wine, but it's not super bright and flashy like a pink. It's a decent match with my maroon pants, not that I coordinate my hair and pants often. This date feels deserving of something special.

By the time all of that's done, it's already five. *Thank fuck.* There's no way I can wait any longer without losing my mind completely. I pull on my clothes, add a little eyeliner and some lip gloss then head toward Orange Grove.

THE STUDIO DOOR is unlocked when I arrive, and Jagger has his back to it. I take him in for a minute— broad shoulders, long hair reaching his waist, black jeans, and a tight, fitted olive-green shirt. He doesn't wear his hair down often, but I wish he did. I'm one hundred percent here for it. Damn, it's sexy.

The bell above the door jingles when I push it open, startling me a little. I don't remember the bell, but sometimes I don't pay attention, so maybe it isn't new.

No need to ask and embarrass myself if it's been there all along.

Jagger turns to face me and his green eyes smolder as they rake over every inch of my body. He takes his time, assessing me from head to toe, licking his lips in sexy move and making an appreciative noise.

"Fuck," he groans. He takes three long strides to get to me, pulling me into his chest and wrapping his arms around me. "Damn, you're hot as fuck. Everything about this look is sexy perfection," he whisper-growls in my ear, sending a shiver through my body. I don't even try to hide it. It's way too obvious what he does to me. And if the shiver wasn't telling, the hard-on pressing against his pants is.

Jagger steps back taking me in one more time with a smile. "Thank you," I manage with a shy smile. Having his eyes on me like this feels good, but it's also a little embarrassing.

"I really like this color." He runs a hand through my hair. "Looks good on you." His gaze falls to my face. "Damn, your eyes are gorgeous."

"It's not too much? I wasn't sure if it was okay for me to wear makeup. A lot of guys don't like that."

"Fuck those guys. I love the eyeliner. You wear anything you want— bright colored clothes, makeup, hats, pajamas— I don't care. I like it all on you."

"Really?" Makeup has always interested me, but I got bullied in high school for wearing it.

"Really." Jagger's features change from happiness to concern. "Ellis, I like that you have your own style. It's one of the many things that attracted me to you. You don't wear makeup much, do you?"

"No." The floor suddenly becomes super interesting. This is uncomfortable and I don't want to have this conversation. "Why not? It looks amazing on you," Jag assures me.

"Makeup isn't for guys."

"Bullshit. What asshole told you that?"

"All of them. Can we talk about something else please?"

"Can I say one thing first?" I nod my head. "Ellis, never stop being who you are. As long as you are happy with what you wear, no one else's opinion matters. But, for what it's worth, I like everything you've ever worn, including the makeup and hair dye."

"Thanks," I reply, bashfully.

Jagger kisses my hand softly. "Ready to go?"

"Sure." Jagger steps away from me and I feel better and worse all at the same time. Better that the conversation and focus is no longer on me, but worse because he's on the other side of the room. I like him in my space.

He grabs his phone off a shelf and checks his pockets for his wallet and keys then walks back to me and takes my hand, leading me to the door. After Jag locks up, we head down the street hand in hand. I still have no idea where we're going, but it must be close because our cars are in the opposite direction.

"How did it go last night?" he asks as we walk.

Last night I attended the Current and Coast grand opening. I didn't invite Jagger. I thought about it, but it was by invitation only and I felt bad asking Ryan if I could bring someone. Jagger said he understood and encouraged me to go enjoy myself. It felt weird going without him, but invitations went out before we were boyfriends.

"The restaurant is gorgeous, and Grayson is going to slay the whole chef gig. His food is the best stuff I've ever eaten."

Jagger clutches his shirt with his free hand. "Better than my food?"

"You are a great cook, but you aren't a trained chef. I said what I said. Sorry, not sorry."

"It's a good thing I like you." He laughs, smoothing out his shirt and dropping his hand back to his side. "Tell me more."

"Ryan offered all the Paradise 11 employees jobs at Current and Coast. He gave us first choice of where we want to work before he fills all the positions. Matt took a job as a bartender, and I'm really happy for him. His bartending skills are far beyond a dive bar. He'll excel at Current and Coast."

"That's nice. Ryan must be impressed with his staff. Are you switching?"

"I love working at Paradise 11, but Current and Coast is more upscale, and I would earn more money. I was torn until Ryan offered to give me the brunch shifts on Saturdays and Sundays while still working at the bar. I jumped at the opportunity. It means giving up a few hours on Saturdays at Paradise 11, but the tips at the restaurant will more than make up for it," I explain Ryan's offer.

"Ellis, that's great! Congratulations."

"Thanks! I'm excited for the opportunity at Current and Coast without having to give up a job I love."

"I know you love working in the food service industry and the call center is just a way to make ends meet. Have you thought about asking Ryan if you can pick up some lunch shifts at the restaurant?"

"Can't. They're only open for happy hour and dinner, except on the weekend when they add brunch."

Jagger squeezes my hand as we stop at the corner and wait for the light to change. He doesn't say more about my job. I know he worries about the hours I work, but I don't have a choice right now. One day I might, but I'm not there yet.

Chapter 23

Jagger

Ellis' hand is warm in mine and it's sending shock waves through me. When he walked into the studio dressed like a wet fucking dream, I considered skipping out on tonight and dragging him back to my apartment all caveman style. I want to rip his clothes off and fuck him until we both forget our names. Instead, I chose to behave like an adult and go to this damn art opening. I *have* to go, but I also want to bury my dick in Ellis.

The gallery is only two blocks away and the walk is quick, but the cool breeze helps me calm down a little, so not everyone in the room will know how turned on I am. There's a short line, which is a good sign. The doors will open in about ten minutes.

"Gallery Expresso," Ellis stops, reading the sign out loud. "What's this?"

The name is kind of silly, but it works. "It's an art gallery with an espresso bar. Express yourself and drink espresso," I explain.

Ellis snorts a laugh. That's stu… actually, it's kind of genius."

"You think so?"

"Yeah, I do. They're having a special event tonight?" he questions.

"An art opening. There will be some food and drinks and most of the art pieces are for sale."

"I love it! I've never been to an art opening." I wasn't sure if Ellis would like coming here, but his eyes light up when he talks, and I can see the excitement on his face and hear it in his voice. Score one point for me in the cool date column. "Come on, let's get in line."

"This way." I lead him past the line to the alley where the back door is located and knock. Mindy, the gallery owner, opens the door.

"Jagger!" I kiss her cheek. "Come on in." She motions for us to pass her.

"Mindy, this is Ellis. Ellis, Mindy. She owns the place."

"It's so nice to meet you," Mindy says, shaking Ellis' hand.

"Nice to meet you, too."

"Go on in. I'll be out in a minute," Mindy offers.

Not letting go of Ellis' hand, I pull him through the office area and into the gallery.

"Mr. Ward, welcome. Can I get you a drink?" Mindy's assistant offers as we enter the room. I can never remember her name. I have got to do better.

"Water for me and," I look at Ellis, "champagne?"

"Sure. Thank you." Confusion is etched all over his face and his voice is unsure.

"Champagne for my boyfriend, please."

When I venture another glance in Ellis' direction, his mouth is hanging open and he's staring at me wide-eyed like I'm some sort of celebrity.

"What?" I ask.

"Is there something you aren't telling me, *Mr. Ward?*"

A server returns with our drinks. I accept them both and hand the champagne to Ellis, buying myself all of five seconds. He takes a sip of the bubbly with raised eyebrows, waiting for me to respond.

Putting my hands on Ellis' shoulders, I turn him around so he can see the wall behind us with my name sprawled across it. He gasps and turns around so fast he almost spills the champagne.

"This is *your* art opening? Why didn't you tell me?" Ellis rushes out in shock.

"Surprise?" It comes out as a guilty question if that's even a thing. "There is something else." I rub the back of my neck, worried this next part is going to freak him out and have him running out the door.

"What?" Ellis narrows his eyes at me.

"My family will be here tonight."

His jaw drops again then he starts to shake his head vigorously. "No. I *cannot* meet your family."

"Why not?" I do my best to keep the humor out of my question, but flustered Ellis is fucking adorable. And apparently adorable gets me hot.

He lifts his hand up and down, indicating his body. "Look at me. I'm wearing a blouse and… *eyeliner.*"

"So?" I question.

"So, if you had told me I was meeting your family, I would have dressed appropriately! I wouldn't have worn makeup or dyed my hair." Ellis' voice rises a few octaves as he speaks and his eyes glisten with unshed tears.

Cupping his cheek, I look him directly in the eyes, so he knows my words are sincere. "I like you just the way you are. I don't want to introduce my family to some fake version of you. You are my boyfriend, and there is *nothing* I would change. My family is going to care about two things— the way we treat each other and how I feel about you. Clothes, shoes, hair, and makeup aren't going to factor into their opinion of you. Your kindness and how damn sweet you are will. Be yourself, Ellis." I step back and let my gaze rake over his body. "This is the Ellis I fell for, and the one I want my family to meet."

"Are you sure? I know I can be a lot... too much." His voice quivers as he speaks. Fuck everyone who ever made him feel shitty about his choices.

"Whoever made you believe that is a moron. One day, I'm going to convince you that you are so much more than what you see and what other people have told you." Every time Ellis says these things it pisses me off. How dare anyone make him believe he is less in any way. My parents pick that precise moment to walk in the door. Of course, they were at the front of the line. I smile when I catch their eyes. "Deep breath, baby. My parents are here. You're going to be great."

As Ellis turns around, I take squeeze his hand gently, hoping it calms his nerves. I probably should have warned him, but I suspected the real Ellis wouldn't have shown up. Apparently, I was right.

"Mom, Dad." I let go of Ellis long enough to hug my parents then immediately take it again. "This is Ellis. Ellis, these are my parents."

"Hi, Mr. and Mrs. Ward. It's nice to meet you." Ellis offers his hand and my dad shakes it.

"I'm a hugger. Is it alright if I hug you, Ellis?" Mom asks, kindly.

"Um, yes." Mom gives Ellis a quick hug and I see him relax a little. "And please call us Tom and Joy.

"Oh, okay. Tom and Joy."

"Jag tells us you live in Anchor Point. What a beautiful town. I just love going to the beach." My mom is brilliant as starting a conversation and putting people at ease.

"It's nice. I grew up there."

"Do you enjoy the beach.?"

"Oh, yes. I enjoy walking on the beach. It's a good place to think."

"Jag told us you work at a bar. How do you like that?"

"I love it so much. Meeting new people from all over the world is fun."

"Mom," I interrupt their conversation. "I'm going to show Ellis around a little. Your other children just arrived. Can you entertain them for a few minutes?" I ask, hoping she understands. Meeting everyone at once will be overwhelming. My family is big and loud. Ellis needs to meet them in small doses.

"Of course, sweetheart. Go enjoy yourselves. And congratulations. We are so proud of you." She beams.

"Thank you." I lead Ellis away.

For the next two hours, I introduce Ellis to my family, mingle, and give a short speech thanking everyone for coming. It's a whirlwind, and by the time the opening ends and the guests have left, I'm exhausted. Ellis did great and my family was tame. They didn't all rush him at once, but he did meet them all. My mom pulled me aside before she left to tell me how much she likes him. My family's opinion doesn't dictate who I choose to date, but it makes me happy to know they like him.

"You did amazing," I say, wrapping my arms around him. "My family loves you."

Ellis smiles brightly. "They do?"

"Absolutely. Mom wants us to come to the house for dinner next Sunday."

"I'd like that."

"Good." I kiss him quickly. "I need to handle a few things then we can go."

"Do you need help?"

"Sure. Come on." I lead Ellis back to the office where I find Mindy.

"Hey, Mindy. Sorry I haven't had a chance to speak to you tonight."

"No worries. This was your night to shine." She faces Ellis. "Did you enjoy yourself?"

"Oh, yes. Thank you for having me. The gallery is beautiful," Ellis responds excitedly. When he met my family, he was so shy, which I didn't expect. I never pegged Ellis for shy, but I guess meeting a bunch of people is hard for him.

"Congratulations are in order," Mindy says, returning her gaze to me. "You had a successful show."

"Yeah, I think it went well." I smile. "I made several contacts, and a few people picked up brochures for classes. I met the owner of a gallery in Tallahassee. Mr. Klein, I think. Anyway, I have his card, and he took mine. Said he's interested in featuring some of my pieces."

"That's all wonderful, but I meant the sales," Mindy explains.

"Sales? I sold a couple of pieces?"

"Not a couple. Almost all of them."

"Jag, that's great! Congratulations!" Ellis beams at me.

I'm still frozen in shock. "Are you serious?"

"Very. You had thirty-five pieces on display and twenty-seven of them sold. A few are being shipped, but most will be picked up this week. All paid in full. I'd like to keep the other pieces here for a few days. Often when people come back to pick up their art, they end up buying something else. Do you mind waiting a few days for me to cut you a check in case the others sell?"

"Yeah, that's fine. I can't believe so many sold."

"I can! Your glasswork is phenomenal," Ellis pipes up. "I'm proud of you."

"He's right. Let's meet soon. I want to schedule another opening in a few months."

"That sounds good. Thank you, Mindy."

We say our goodbyes and I lead Ellis out of the gallery and back toward his car. When we reach the car, he looks a little lost or concerned. I'm not sure.

"Um, I… uh, never mind." He waves his hands and turns for the car but stumbles a little.

I catch him before he falls. "Are you alright?"

Ellis' face heats and turns an adorable shade of red. "I think the champagne is hitting me. I felt fine at the gallery, but now I feel a little tipsy. Can you drive me home? I'll pay for an Uber to get you back."

"I'm happy to drive you home." I consider offering for him to stay with me, but surely, he would ask to crash there if that's what he wanted to do. "Let's go." I'm not worried about the Uber home, I can pay for it. But I hope he'll let me spend the night.

It takes about thirty minutes to get back to Ellis' place and I'm glad I put his address in my GPS because he fell asleep five minutes into the drive. I was with him the entire night. He didn't drink that much. Maybe he's not a big drinker.

When I turn onto his dirt road, it's dark. Like extremely dark with no streetlights. Faint lights come from the few houses we pass. After a mile or so the GPS tells me to turn left. There's a narrow dirt road, so I ease onto it. A few hundred feet later a small silver trailer with an outside light casting a dim glow appears. Behind the trailer there are some more low lights and a handful of other trailers. Several trees surround Ellis' place, making it feel secluded.

The voice on the GPS tells me I have arrived, so I stop in front of the Airstream and gently shake Ellis.

"Baby, I think we're here." He jolts up so fast he hits his head on the car window. "Are you okay?"

"Uh, yeah. It didn't hurt." His eyes dart around for several seconds. "Okay, yeah. This is my place. We can wait here for the Uber. I feel better. I can drive you down the road to the gas station if you'd rather wait there," he rambles.

Taking off my seat belt, I pull Ellis to me, crashing my lips on his. It's gentle at first, but as I push my tongue inside, the kiss becomes heated and frantic. I need Ellis. I want to be inside him. I've been half hard since he walked in my studio almost five hours ago.

Forcing myself to stop before I come in my pants, I pull away but stay in his space, gripping his shirt in my hands.

"I'd rather go inside and fuck my boyfriend then curl up with him in my arms, letting the thump of his heartbeat lull me to sleep."

Ellis' eyes focus on his home instead of me. "You want to see where I live?" Even in the low light of the car, I can see the shame in his features.

"I would love to see where you live. I want to know everything about you."

"But it's just a crappy trailer," he whispers.

"It's your home. That makes it perfect."

A smile tries to tug at the corners of his mouth, but he keeps the frown firmly in place. "It's far from perfect. It's not even nice."

"You don't have to be embarrassed. This is your home. *Yours*. Be proud of it. How many people your age still live at home?"

"I don't know." He shrugs then slumps his shoulders.

"A lot. Several of the people I know still lived at home when they were twenty-one. Hell, most of my siblings are in their thirties and still live on the same property as my parents."

"Okay," he reluctantly agrees. "You can come inside but don't laugh."

"I'll never laugh at you," I promise then hop out of the car before he changes his mind.

Slowly, Ellis emerges from the passenger side and leads me to the front door. It creaks open when he pushes it and a flash of protectiveness rushes through me. Is he safe out here alone? The door was locked, but I bet if I yanked on it hard enough, I could have torn it open without much effort. Pushing my concerns aside for now, I follow Ellis up the three small steps and into the home. He flips on a light, and I get a view of the entire place. It's small, but tidy and clean. To the left is a small counter with a sink and stove. Next to the counter is a refrigerator, not a full sized one, but not one of those mini dorm-style ones either. Across the back wall is a small table with two chairs and a loveseat. To the right is an open door leading into a bedroom, I can tell from here that the bed takes up most of the space. Next to the bedroom, there is another door I assume is a bathroom. Straight across from the entrance is an empty wall with a window near the top and a few canvases leaning against it. The first one is a beach sunset painting.

"Did you paint that?" I ask, pointing to the art.

Ellis smiles shyly then glances down, focusing on his feet. "Yeah," he practically whispers.

"It's gorgeous," I gush in amazement.

His head snaps to the painting as if he's trying to figure out if we're looking at the same thing. "It is?"

The painting is phenomenal. Walking over, I pick up the canvas carefully and inspect it closer. The shades of pinks, yellows, and oranges are beautiful. From the other side of the room, it could have been mistaken for a photograph if I didn't see the canvas. Up close, I can barely make out the brush strokes. It's flawless. "Yeah. Ellis, you have some serious talent." He beams at my praise while still looking a little unsure. Has no one ever told him he's talented? Behind the sunset is a painting of a lighthouse. "Do you mind?" I ask, pointing to the others.

Ellis shakes his head, so I squat down and sift through the dozen or so paintings— lighthouses, a boat, some beach scenes, a few green spaces, some abstract pieces and his trailer set against the woods. I wonder if that's what it looks like in the daylight. How can I even describe it? Old and rustic but loved. That painting exudes the pride he has in his home even though he doesn't want anyone to see it.

"Do you want something to drink or a snack?" Ellis offers as I stand up and walk back to where he still stands by the door.

"I'd like to snack on you."

I pull him into my arms, pressing my lips to his, searching for entrance. He smiles against my mouth then slowly opens for me. I push my tongue in, tasting a hint of champagne lingering from the gallery. Ellis melts against me with his hands in my hair, letting my strong arms hold him up. I guide him toward the bedroom, but he stops, freezing just short of the door-way. He breaks the kiss and darts his eyes from the bed to me and back to the bed. Suddenly, my confident man is anything but. He's unsure and… something. Scared. Embarrassed.

CHAPTER 24

ELLIS

"What's wrong?" Jag asks, cupping my cheek. Guess I didn't cover my mood well or at all.

"Uh, yeah." I fidget, not sure how to say this. "It's just... well... sorry." I wave my hands around, gesturing to my home.

"Your place is fabulous. I like it. It's you from the colorful dishes and floral curtains to the bright-green couch." The kindness in Jag's eyes when he speaks means everything to me. With one look, he makes me feel special. Wanted.

"The couch is a built-in, but I bought the cover to give some sparkle. This whole place was beige and drab." I shudder, remembering what it looked like when I first moved in a few years ago. "You like it?" I hate the skepticism in my words. It's hard for me to believe Jag. I've been told too many times I'm not good enough and even though his words make me feel better about myself the negative voices still nag in the back of my mind.

"Yes. Now, can I get back to kissing you? My lips are lonely," Jag pouts, drawing a laugh from me.

"Mine, too," I agree right before Jag's mouth lands on mine. The kiss is frantic and needy all teeth and moans. Our hands are everywhere, and there are too many clothes between us. I can't wait to be naked for him. I want us to explore every inch of each other's bodies with our fingers and tongues.

Jagger breaks the kiss, leading me by the hand to my couch. It's been a while since I brought someone back here. Usually, I don't care enough about my hookups to be bothered with what they think. Since I've been doing a better job of keeping the place clean I was more comfortable letting Jag inside tonight. It's bad enough that I live in an old, tiny trailer. There's no way I would have let him in if it was also filthy.

He sits down as he pulls me onto his lap. I straddle his hips, grinding his erection through our clothes. I'm half hard, and the feel of him under me is causing me to plump up, fast. Jagger's lips find mine again. This time the kiss is gentle, like he's memorizing the way I taste. His tongue sneaks in slowly as one hand runs through my short locks, softly massaging my scalp. There's nothing rushed or rough about and it feels amazing, sensual.

Sex has never been sensual for me. It's always been quick and dirty even with Jagger. This is already better than any sex I've had and we're both still fully clothed.

I tenderly scrape my fingers up Jagger's arms,

squeezing his muscles then grabbing onto his shoulders with more pressure when he licks my neck from ear to chin and back, sucking and biting the lobe. A small whine escapes me as I drop my head back, giving him more access. Accepting the invitation, Jag tracks circles over my Adam's apple with his tongue before moving to me neck.

"Oh, yes," I whimper as he sucks bruises into the skin, pushing the blouse off my shoulders to suck there, too. I grind against him, my hips moving on their own. Every sense is heightened. Nothing has ever felt this good.

"Delicious. I want to taste every inch of you," Jagger groans against my neck.

All I can do is whimper and moan as he continues to explore my body. He leisurely unbuttons my blouse. He's barely touching me and I'm losing my mind. The heat of his fingers and the bruises on my neck pulse deliciously on my skin.

Jagger pushes the blouse down my arms, letting it fall to the floor behind us. He relaxes back against the couch, letting his gaze rake over my chest and I've never felt more exposed, not even when I've been completely naked and spread open for him.

His thumbs graze lightly over my nipples, sending waves of pleasure through me. "Fuck," I hiss when he suddenly pinches then both twisting slightly. He laps at one then slowly moves to the other. The pain lessens for an instant then he bites down hard and a mix of pain and pleasure rock through me. "Oh, fuck, yes!" I cry out. "I'm so fucking close, Jag. I want you inside me. Please."

"Patience. I haven't finished tasting you." His tongue flicks against my nipples as his voice vibrates my chest.

"If I come in my pants, it will be over."

"Who says?" he challenges me with bright eyes.

"What? I can't come in my pants."

Jagger traces lines over my ribs with his tongue, still playing with my nipples. "Go ahead. If you come in your pants, I'll lick it clean when I get to that spot."

"Damn, I love your dirty mouth."

"Good. I plan to use this mouth to get *multiple* orgasms out of you tonight. I'm taking my time and having my way with you."

"Yes. Okay. Please." Words are almost impossible at this point. I'm not sure what I'm saying, all I know is I want more of this.

Jagger ruts against me as he grazes his fingers along my ribs, looking smug when I whimper. Seriously, I'm about to come in my damn pants. He must sense my desperation because he moves fast, eliciting moans and curses from me.

"Shit. Fuck. Yes. Baby. More."

He bites down on my neck, and I freeze in a failed attempt to hold back my orgasm. Cum spurt into my underwear and embarrassment floods me.

Jagger runs a hand through my hair. "Dirty boy," he whispers against my ear. "Good job."

My heart soars as all embarrassment disappears. Jagger likes what I did. He wants me to be dirty for him. Fuck. I like it, too. Having sex in public is adventurous, but it's all been basic and vanilla. No dirty talk. Blowjobs and quick fucks are the entirety of my experience. Sex with Jag is different. It's intimate, sensual, animalistic, and familiar. I want to do all the things I've fantasized about but never experienced with him and only him.

My cock is sticky and my underwear is uncomfortable, but I don't care. I'm already getting hard again as Jagger stands up holding onto me, He turns around, dropping me on the couch and falling to his knees. He pulls off my shoes then unbuttons my pants, dragging them down my legs and flinging them over his shoulder. Once again, I'm fully naked and Jagger is completely clothed.

This is starting to become a thing with us and I kind of like it. I like being naked and exposed for him. I like the way his eyes rake over me hungrily. I like the way I feel under his intense glare.

"Gorgeous. Fuck, you're perfect." His hands travel from my ankles up my legs to my thighs, leaving a trail of goosebumps in their wake. Then he follows the same trail with his tongue, tasting me from feet to hips just like he promised. "Pull your legs up," Jag instructs giving them a gentle push. I do as he says, opening them and giving him access to every inch of my body.

Jag runs his tongue from the tip of my cock to the root then over my balls and down to my ass, devouring the mess I made for him. He kisses one cheek then the other, biting down hard enough to leave a mark, and I hiss. But the pain turns to pleasure when he licks over the mark.

"Fuck!" Do that again." He moves to the other side and leaves what I'm sure is a matching mark. God, the pain feels good. Maybe I'm a pain slut and didn't know it.

"You like that?" Jagger asks with a grin.

"Yes!" I breathe out. "More, Jag. I need you."

He leans down, peppering kisses over my hole then licks across it, and I almost blow another load. What the hell is he doing to me? How can I be this hard again so quickly? Jag places his hands on my ass and spreads me open before he swirls his tongue around my entrance then trails long strokes up and down. Holy fuck! My vision blurs and my eyes roll back. I drop my head on the back of the couch as Jag pushes his tongue past my rim and does something with it that drives me insane.

"Shit. Yes. Jag. Do it again. More. Please," I ramble on and on, spewing words that turn to gibberish as he eats me out like I'm the last meal he'll ever get.

Jag grabs my aching cock, stroking it roughly, twisting his wrist with each pull. My hips jerk into his hand on their own. I can't even form a coherent thought at this point, my body is making decisions without my brain. His hands and tongue are fucking magic. My hips thrust up and down, riding his tongue and using his hand as my personal sex toy. I'm so fucking close for the second time in minutes. My breathing is heavy. Jagger's moans vibrate against my ass, sending more shock waves through me. Then my balls draw up and I let out a primal wail as I empty onto his hand and spurts of cum hit my stomach.

"No. Stop," I beg as Jag continues to work his tongue inside my hole. My whole body is a ball of nerves, and I can take the sensation. He sits on his heels with a smug grin. Bastard. "Proud of yourself?" I ask as my breathing slows.

"Very." He stands up and reaches a hand toward me. "Come on. I want to fuck you in your bed."

"No." I cross my arms, refusing to go with him.

He freezes. "No?" he asks in shock.

"First, I want to undress you and enjoy your body then you can fuck me in my bed."

"Deal!" he agrees, excitedly. "Where do you want me?"

"Right where you're standing." I roll off the couch and step into Jag's space. I've never taken my time with a man before, and I want to savor every inch of his body the way he did mine. This is a dream come true, one I didn't know I was missing until Jagger spent the past hour worshiping my body. It was the hottest sex I've ever had, and the man didn't even stick his cock in me. Not yet anyway.

CHAPTER 25

JAGGER

Spending this time exploring Ellis on an intimate level means everything to me. His body is beautiful. I like every muscle, curve, and dip on him. He's so brave and confident, being completely naked for me, letting me touch and lick every inch. I'll never get enough of this.

My body trembles slightly. I've never allowed a man to take time with my body the way I did with Ellis'. With him standing in front of me, eyes blown wide, naked and sated, my nerves ratchet up. I want this with him, but it's all new to me. Sex has always been about getting release, not this intimate exploration. Even when I had boyfriends, we didn't spend this kind of time exploring each other. We'd get caught up in the moment, fuck, and be done. I prefer this intimacy over the quick and dirty.

Ellis pulls on the hem of my shirt, and I raise my arms as he lifts it over my head. He buries his face in my armpit before I have a chance to let them fall back to my side. He inhales deeply, gliding his tongue over my pit and swirling it around. *Holy fuck.* I've never let a man do that, but shit, I like it. I drop my hands to my head, giving Ellis the access he wants. He runs his tongue from one pit across my chest, lapping and nipping at my skin to the other side, giving that pit the same attention. I moan loudly. It's not a sexy moan, but I can't control it. My cock is painfully hard, and the longer Ellis spends with tongue in my pits like it's the best thing he's ever tasted, the needier I get.

"Oh, fuck! Yes!" I groan, wondering if I can come just from his face buried in my armpit. That's an idea to test another day. Ellis trails kisses along my neck, biting lightly as he goes. How can his mouth feel this damn good?

"You taste amazing," he purrs, biting hard into the sensitive skin on my neck then sucking long enough to leave a mark. That's going to earn me an earful from Mel, but who cares. *Shut up brain.* Why am I thinking about my damn sister? I shudder at the thought, but thankfully, Ellis thinks it's him.

He pulls off my neck with a pop. "You like that?"

"Mmm." His fingers rake over my stomach and ribs leaving goosebumps in their wake. Fuck, I love his touch. His fingers work open my pants as his mouth finds mine. I part my lips, letting him in. His tongue moves against mine and my mind goes blank. All I can do is feel— his touch, his tongue, his erection. My pants pool around my ankles as Ellis breaks the kiss. The loss pulls me out of the fog as I watch him fall to his knees, never taking his eyes off me.

I thread my fingers through his hair as he grazes his fingernails along my thighs and kisses across my stomach, jutting his tongue out to lap at the precum leaking from my slit.

"Mmm, yummy."

My legs shake with anticipation. I need his mouth on me. "Suck me." My voice is rough and gravelly.

Ellis doesn't hesitate. He envelops my head with his warm, wet mouth, sinking down agonizingly slowly. Every inch of his mouth feels like heaven. He hollows his cheeks sucking hard and swallowing at the same time, working my cock almost to release.

I throw my head back, letting go of his hair and grabbing onto the table behind me for support. He does something with his tongue and my knees buckle. Ellis grabs my ass, steadying me enough to keep me from falling, never hesitating his momentum. He bobs up and down, driving me to the brink.

"Slow down. I want to fuck you." He smiles around my cock then pulls off with an audible pop.

Ellis stands up and grabs my wrist. "Yeah, let's do that." He pulls me to his small bedroom and climbs on the bed, reaching onto a small shelf then tossing a bottle of lube behind him. I catch it right before a condom lands in front of me. "How do you want me?" he calls over his shoulder, wiggling his ass.

"Brat," I mumble under my breath. "On your back. I want to see your face when I make you come again." Ellis flops onto his back, pulling his legs up to his chest and spreading open for me. "Gorgeous. I love the way you look spread and ready. That perfect pink hole begging for my cock."

"Fuck me, already. I'm not going to be happy if I come from your words," Ellis teases with a sassy smirk.

I flick my eyes to his, holding his gaze. "But *I* will be very happy if that happens. Proud," I add with a wink, shoving two lubed fingers into his hole without warning. Ellis gasps, clenching the sheet as his back arches off the bed.

"Ready." His breath becomes ragged when I find that little bundle of nerves. "Don't need prepping," Ellis growls. He's so responsive and coming completely undone just from my fingers. One day, I'm going to see how many orgasms I can get out of him untouched and without my cock in his ass.

"I don't want to hurt you." He narrows his gaze at me, silently begging me to quit screwing around. It's fucking adorable.

"Please, Jag," Ellis begs. Reluctantly, I pull my fingers out and push my tip in. Ellis winces when I push past his rim and I stop.

"Are you alright?"

"Yeah," he pants. "Keep. Going." I look into his eyes and when all I see is lust and need, I slam the rest of the way in. No hesitation. No mercy. Ellis cries out, grasping my shoulders. He pulls me down until our lips meet. "Move," Ellis demands, against my mouth. I was so lost in his lips, I forgot to move inside him.

Climbing onto my knees, I pull almost all the way out and drive back in, drawing another scream from Ellis. His eyes heat with desire and a sated smile forms on his lips. I do it again and again, faster with each jerk of my hips, the sound of our bodies slamming together growing louder and more frantic with each thrust.

"Ung, yes, there," Ellis pants when I find that sensitive spot.

"There?" I ask, rubbing the head of my cock over his prostate.

"Uh, ye—" His words become an incoherent stream of moans as I piston in and out, hitting that spot with each thrust.

Ellis is a mess of whimpers, sweat, and pants. His cock is leaking onto his stomach, red, and begging to be touched. I grab it in one hand, stroking to the rhythm of my hips. His noises get louder, the small trailer rocking as I frantically pound into him. Ellis grips the sheets again, knuckles turning white as he stiffens under me and comes, streams of his release landing on his chest and chin.

Several seconds later, I follow, filling the condom with a grunt. I collapse onto the bed next to him, falling from his body in the process. I wrap my arms around my boyfriend and pull his back to my chest. Ignoring the sweaty, sticky mess, I kiss his cheek.

"That was amazing!"

"Mmm," he returns as his breath evens out. I lift my head enough to see that his eyes are closed. I love the happy, satisfied look on his face, but we need to clean up before we fall asleep.

"Come on, baby. We need to shower."

"You go ahead. I need a nap."

"You can't sleep covered in cum." I crawl to the end

of the bed and grab his ankles, dragging him to me. He squeals at the unexpected movement and groans in protest when I ignore him and pull him to his feet. He trudges behind me, disgruntled and stomping lightly. The little tantrum is fucking cute as hell.

Ellis leans against the wall, watching with hooded eyes while I start the shower. The space is too small for both of us, so once the water is warm, I guide Ellis inside. He showers while I discard the condom and take the soiled sheets off the bed.

"I'm done," Ellis calls a few minutes later.

"I stripped the bed," I tell him as I climb under the warm spray. It feels great against my sore body. Damn, that was a workout, but worth it. Spending so much time exploring each other before I fucked him means everything to me. It might sound sappy, but I like being intimate with Ellis. I enjoy getting to know every inch of his body. What we have is so much more than sex. The sex is fucking mind-blowing, but I want something deeper with Ellis. I want forever.

CHAPTER 26

ELLIS

As much as I was afraid to let Jagger see my home, he didn't make fun of me or my lack of... stuff. I guess I should have expected it. Jag has been nothing but nice to me, and he isn't the type of guy who will make fun of others, but my dad's voice is always playing in the back of my mind filling me with negative thoughts.

It's been a weird day. Having Jag in my space while I work is throwing me off, but in a good way. I like having him close. I made breakfast for us before I had to sign onto the call center site. He played on his phone and washed the breakfast dishes while I worked. Around one, he slid a plate in front of me. I'd been so focused on the call that was taking forever, I hadn't noticed him making lunch. I ate my sandwich and chips as soon as the call ended then hopped onto the next one. I don't usually break for lunch. My shifts are only six hours, so I power through and get them done.

I offered to drive Jag after work, but he asked if he

could take me to dinner first. Apparently, he had spent the day coming up with a plan for a date and that's how we ended up at Ocean Shack.

The outdoor restaurant sits on the boardwalk and has some of the best seafood in Anchor Point, not that it's hard to get amazing seafood living on the Gulf Coast. There's something special about sitting on the boardwalk, smelling the salty air, and listening to the waves while you eat that hits me just right. It's been one of my favorite things for as long as I can remember. Maybe I love it because it's one of the few things I have in common with my parents and we have a lot of amazing family memories that mostly involve food at the beach.

"What are you thinking about?" Jagger asks, popping a shrimp into his mouth.

"The beach is one of my favorite places. I have great memories spending days on the beach with my parents."

"Yeah?"

"My parents are firm believers in hard work. During the week my dad always put in long hours at the office, but almost every Saturday, we packed up the car with coolers of food, a small grill, beach games, a big tent, chairs, table, the works. We'd come down early, like eight in the morning. Dad has a huge variety of cast iron, so he'd make breakfast on the grill. We'd swim and play games all morning then Dad grilled burgers or hot dogs, sometimes steak or chicken for lunch. Then we'd spend the afternoon playing more. It was so much fun. Some weekends, we even grilled out dinner."

"That sounds fun and relaxing." Jag smiles widely while I share my favorite childhood memory.

"It was. They would invite other couples to join us with their kids, but most of my parents' friends had kids older than me, so they would let me invite my own friends. It really was special."

"Do you still come out to the beach often?" Jag's eyes flick to the sand and waves.

"Not really. It's strange because I still live right here and could easily walk or drive down, but I work a lot of hours. When I'm not working, I'm tired and tend to spend the time lounging around."

"We should spend a day down here soon. One Sunday after your brunch shift."

My heart does this weird stutter thing in my chest, and I can't stop myself from smiling. He's so thoughtful. "Yeah, that sounds fun."

"Do you want to walk on the beach?" Jagger asks as he wipes his mouth and crumbles up the napkin, tossing it on his empty plate.

"Yeah, that sounds great." We carry our trash to the cans then walk down the wooden steps to the beach. I kick my shoes off, carrying them in my hand and letting my feet sink into the cool sand.

Jagger holds my hand as we walk toward the waves. When we get close, we both drop our shoes on the sand and roll up our pant legs before taking a few steps into the water, letting it lap against our ankles. A small squeal escapes before I can cover it. The late March water is colder than I expected. It shouldn't surprise me. I've lived here my entire life and spent countless days on the beach even in the winter. Winter in Florida isn't really winter. I've been swimming on Christmas Day more than once. The water is cold, but not unbearable.

Jagger chuckles beside me, seemingly unaffected by the cold water. "What? It's cold." My feet have acclimated to the temperature, but I play up the whole 'woe is me, I'm so cold' act for him.

Instead of feeling sorry for me, Jag kicks water up, wetting my legs. I gasp and shriek simultaneously, extricating my hand from his grasp and splashing water on him then running away. I don't get far before two giant arms wrap around me, lifting me off the ground and spinning me around. Jag slowly puts my feet back on the sand, but he doesn't let go of me. He nuzzles against my neck, kissing and licking the sensitive skin. I moan loudly, tilting my head to the side, giving him more access. He nips at the skin then bites lightly, sucking hard before releasing my neck and licking up to my ear. My body becomes jelly in his arms, and he has to hold tighter to keep me from falling. He stops licking and sucking long enough to turn me around. Then his mouth is on mine, hot and sloppy, tongue pushing inside. He tastes like shrimp, cilantro and lime.

My cock is painfully hard, and so is his. I can feel him against my thigh as I get lost in thoughts of having a hell of a lot more than his tongue in my mouth. Reaching down, I play with the button on his jeans, trying to pop it open so I can get my hand in there.

"Whoa." He pulls back, stopping me. "What are you doing?"

"I want to suck you."

He glances around frantically. "Not here."

"Why not? It's dark-ish."

"There are people walking on the beach, houses with big windows, and some of the shops are still open." Jag's voice becomes more frantic as he points out his fears at being discovered.

"Oh, come on, where is your sense of adventure?" I bite my bottom lip in what I hope is sexy as fuck and will get me my way.

"Not in a jail cell."

"We won't get arrested." The more I think about having sex on the beach with Jag, the harder I get.

"Yes, we will," Jagger argues.

"I've never been arrested." The sentence flies out before I realize what I've said. Jagger stumbles back a few steps and gawks at me.

"What does that mean?" he asks, cocking head to the side.

"What?" I play the innocent card, but I can tell by his expression he's not buying it. "I haven't ever been arrested." I repeat. "Have you?" I ask, hoping like hell he takes it a simple statement of fact, not the underlying truth.

"No, but that isn't what you meant. We were talking about having sex on the beach and you said, 'I've never been arrested,' implying that you *have* had sex on the beach."

Fuck. "Well, yeah. But everyone's had sex on the beach."

"That's not a thing," Jag deadpans.

"Are you sure?" I ask with a playful smile. "I'm pretty sure it's a thing. And I *know* it's a thing I want to do again. Tonight. With you." I grab Jagger's wrist and lead him down the beach toward the boardwalk. "Come on. I know a place."

Jagger lets me pull him past the boardwalk, and past where the houses are, to a small area surrounded by rocks. It's semi-private and this part of the beach is much darker because there are no lights from homes or businesses.

We climb over the rocks, and I sit down on one, waiting for Jagger to sit beside me. He eyes me warily. "What are we doing here?"

"Sitting," I reply innocently.

"Bullshit," he coughs into his hand, cracking up. He's figured me out, not that I'm discreet.

"Ryan brought Grayson here on a date. Grayson was so excited like it's some huge, secret hideout just for the two of them, but everyone knows about it. People always come here to fuck."

"Deflecting much?" he asks with an unreadable expression. I don't answer because I'm pretty sure it wasn't a real question. "Are you going to tell me what you meant by the 'not getting arrested' statement?"

Damn, the man *cannot* let something go. "Are you sure you want to know the answer?" I stare at him, eyebrow cocked in challenge.

He lifts my hand and kisses it. "I want to know

everything about you." And I swoon! It's becoming a problem— the swooning. How can I possibly not when Jag is so perfect and says all the best things?

"Sometimes, I like my sex a little public."

"Public," he repeats. "How public?"

"Bathrooms, clubs, the beach, alleys."

"Well, shit. Um, wow." Jagger lets go of my hand and I feel the loss completely. Is this the thing that's going to run him off? The deal breaker? He scrubs his hands up and down his face a few times then through his long locks. "I thought the back of my studio was pretty public."

"With the door locked? Oh, my sweet, innocent child, *that* was private sex."

"Do you think I'm a prude?" Jagger suddenly looks scared, fear mars his words, like he's in the wrong somehow.

"Absolutely not! Trust me, there is nothing prudish about the sex we've had." Fear settles in my gut. The question I have to ask him is one I'm not sure I want the answer to, but I need to know what he really thinks of me. "Do you think I'm a whore?"

"What? No! Why would you ask me that?"

My entire body heats with embarrassment and I can't look at him. It hasn't registered yet. He doesn't understand what I am. *Stupid.* Why the fuck did I bring this up? He'll never be able to look at me the same again. Jagger runs a gentle hand down my back, and it takes everything inside me not to sob. It's so sweet. Calming.

I take a deep breath and let it out through my nose

as slowly as possible. "I've been with a *lot* of guys. Nameless guys. In public places."

"You are not a whore. Frankly, I kind of like your slutty side. It's hot as fuck. Just because I've never had sex in public doesn't mean it isn't appealing."

"Yeah?" I ask skeptically, still not looking at him.

He takes my chin in his hand and turns my face, holding me tightly so I can't look away. "You are hot. Gorgeous. Sexy. I want you all the time. When you aren't with me, I can't get you out of my head. I want to experience new things with you. Things that you like."

"Like a beach blowie?" Excitement tinges my words. Now we're back on track and my dick takes notice.

He looks around the small alcove. It's not private, but it's also far enough away from the main part of the beach, so we likely won't be seen in the dark.

"I take it I'm not the first guy you brought here." he deadpans but doesn't sound angry or upset. In fact, there's a hint of humor in his voice. Might as well stick with the truth.

"It's a good place for high school blow jobs, a few handies, and one time a decent fuck."

"High school blow jobs? Please tell me you aren't—"

"I'm not a pervert," I cry out in horror. "*I* was in high school and so were the other guys. Trust me, I quit screwing around with high school guys before I graduated." Well, except for that baseball player. Story for another time... or never.

"Good to know." He drops his hand from my face and rests it on my thigh. "Thank you for being honest. What you did before we started dating is none of my business. But I was curious when you started talking about public sex and not going to jail. I hope I didn't cross any lines or make you feel like you had to tell me something you weren't comfortable sharing." Jag pauses briefly with a hint of desire in his eyes. "The thought of having sex out here is appealing, but to be honest, it makes me nervous." He throws his hands up in the air. "Damn, now I *do* sound like the biggest prude."

"My sex life is basically an open book. Megan knows every sordid detail. If I didn't want to share, I wouldn't. And you don't sound like a prude. We've just had different experiences." I absently rub circles on his thigh. "We don't have to do anything you aren't ready for. You don't have to like something just because I do."

"But I want to try it. Once. Just to see."

"We can start with a hand job, or I can blow you. We don't have to go full on naked fuck our first time. Start slowly. If you like it, we can try something else another day."

"Are you sure?" Jag looks relieved.

"Of course. Like I said— no pressure." Jagger looks all around us to make sure the beach near us is clear. "No one is coming, Jagger. We'll be fine." Leaning in, I softly press my lips to his. "Relax," I whisper as I pepper kisses over his neck from one side to the other.

He moans when I bite his ear. Moving to my knees, I push his legs open and settle myself on the sand. He reaches for his pants, but I grab his hands and set them on the rocks on either side of him.

"Let me." I unbutton and unzip his pants. He pushes

up enough for me to pull them down below his ass, leaving him in his underwear. Without a blanket, it's going to feel gross sitting on those rocks, so I pull his erection free without exposing his bare ass. He's probably more comfortable this way, too.

I stroke him lazily, watching to make sure he's okay with what I'm doing. His pupils blow, and he moans when I run my thumb over his slit. Fuck, he's sexy when he's blissed out. I run my tongue over every vein, tasting him— sweat, soap, salt. It's a heady combination. I lick over his head, drawing out another groan. Abandoning the hand job idea, I swallow him down to the root in one motion, reveling in the feel of his cock in my throat and the noises he's making. I bob up and down a few times then pull off with a pop.

"Don't stop, Ellis."

Just making sure he's still into this and apparently, he is. I swallow him all the way back down, holding him there and working his cock with my throat. Then I pull almost all the way off, but before I can release him, Jag grabs my hair and pushes me back down. I smile around his length. It's fucking glorious when he gets a little aggressive streak. I freeze, waiting for him to take control.

"Fuck," he growls as he pulls me all the way up, shoving my head back up, repeating the motion over and over, setting a rough, fast rhythm. He lifts his hips off the rocks, thrusting into me, using me in the most delectable way. All I can do is take it. Spit runs down my chin and down his cock, wetting his underwear. Tears form at the edge of my eyes, falling as he uses me harder and abuses my throat. I relish the moment, not wanting it to end.

With one hand, I brace myself on his leg and pull out my own cock with the other. I frantically jerk myself off, trying my best to match his rhythm, but he's fucking my throat so damn fast I can't keep up.

"Oh, yes, *fuck*. Take it, baby. That feels so fucking good."

I work my cock furiously, as my orgasm builds. I want to wait for him, but my balls are tight and there's no way I'm going to last. Jagger's words become incoherent mumblings mixed with a few 'fucks.'

"Ellis," he cries my name as he shoots down my throat. I follow with my own release covering my hand. When he's empty, he lets his cock fall from my mouth.

We both sit there, breathing heavily. When he looks down and sees my cum-covered hand, he lifts it to his mouth and licks it clean. I whimper when he sucks my fingers into his mouth. If I wasn't completely spent, I'd be hard again. Jag pulls me onto his lap and shoves his tongue in my mouth mixing our tastes together.

"That was the hottest thing I've ever done," he admits, breaking the kiss.

"Did I create a public sex fiend?" I feign innocence, batting my lashes for show.

"Maybe." Jagger winks. "It was exhilarating." He puts my cock away then sets me on the rock next to him while he pulls his own pants up. "*Definitely* want to do it again."

"Me, too." I stand up and reach for Jagger's hand. "Come on, let me get you home. It's getting late."

"Look at you being all responsible," Jagger teases. We walk hand in hand to my car. Another date with Jagger. I might never get used to this. I've never had a real boyfriend, and I didn't believe I was worthy of one. Then I met Jagger, and everything changed. Well, not overnight. It took me a long time to agree to being his boyfriend. I'm still not completely convinced this is for real, but I'm enjoying the ride. Jagger is an awesome man— strong, sexy, loyal, caring, and brave.

CHAPTER 27

JAGGER

It's been almost a week since our date on the beach and I haven't seen Ellis. I miss the hell out of him. This week our schedules have been busier than usual. He's working more hours now that Current and Coast is open, and the spring crowds are starting to converge on Anchor Point.

I've been putting in more hours, too. I decided to give summer camp a try since the studio is having so much success with classes, but that means planning the camp. This summer I'm only going to offer four sessions. Each session will be from eight in the morning until noon with a snack break and last for one week. Each week, I will offer the camp to a different age group, starting with high school in the middle of June. I'm hoping to recruit some kids from week one to help the following weeks for the community service hours they need to graduate. Week two will be for middle school. Then weeks three and four will be younger kids in July. I opted for two weeks with the younger kids because I'm not opening as many spaces for that age group each session. They will *definitely* need more attention.

I've met with a few other camp organizers in the area this week to learn more and get a better understanding of what I need to do and how best to plan for camp. It's basically like having kids come for field trips but with longer hours and for multiple days. Melanie is helping by creating flyers to bring to area schools and graphics for social media. She also made a registration form and updated the waiver and paperwork for camp instead of a field trip. I've been planning the curriculum. If this summer goes well, I might add more weeks next year.

Friday night, one of the art galleries in Tallahassee had a huge opening for a local artist. It's the same gallery that is displaying a few of my pieces, and I'm hoping to eventually get my own show there. I wanted to go to the opening, but it's something I want to experience with Ellis, and he had to work, so today, I'm taking him to see the show. The artwork will be on display for two weeks, but today is the only day we both have time.

My apartment door opens, and Ellis calls my name. "In the bedroom," I call back.

I texted him before I hopped in the shower to let him know the door would be unlocked and to come right in. It's time to give him a key.

"Hey, sexy," Ellis purrs from the bedroom doorway.

I'm barefoot in nothing by a pair of off-white linen pants. I freeze when my eyes land on Ellis. Fuck I love everything about his look, from the purple hair and modest makeup to his painted nails and outfit. He has black eyeliner, purple eyeshadow, and light pink lip gloss. His nails are the same shade of purple as his hair, but the eyeshadow is a lighter shade. He's wearing black capri pants that hang low on his hips and an open blouse with several shades of purple in an abstract pattern. Underneath is a black mesh crop top showing off his flat stomach. As usual the look in complete with his combat boots and silver hoop earrings.

I open and close my mouth several times, but no words come out. Lust fills every pore and my brain fogs as my cock hardens. He's a wet fucking dream come true.

I finally manage a strangled, "Fuuuck."

"You like?" Ellis twirls around, giving me a mouth-watering view from the back where the pants deliciously hug his pert ass.

Staying here and ripping his clothes off sounds like a much better plan than driving almost two hours to an art show.

"You look fucking gorgeous… sexy, edible." Ellis beams at my words. Seeing him confident in himself makes me happy. He struggles to be himself when we go out, and I hate that he worries I'm going to be embarrassed to be seen with him. Damn his parents for making him feel like he's too flashy or in any way not good enough because the man standing before me is absolute perfection.

It takes every bit of willpower I have not to walk

over to Ellis and kiss him. But if I do that, we will end up naked in my bed and miss the exhibit. Instead, I pull on a navy polo and slip into a pair of brown boat shoes. Then I shove my wallet and phone in my pockets.

"Ready?" I ask.

"Yeah. Where are we going?"

I take Ellis' hand I walk past him. "To an art show in Tallahassee. I thought we'd have a dinner there before we head back."

"Sounds fun."

I grab my keys off the hook by the door, lock up and lead Ellis to my truck. Being in this enclosed space isn't helping the situation growing in my pants. Ellis smells like the beach. He always smells like coconut, sunshine, and salt. Yeah, I don't know if sunshine is a smell, but that's what I think of when I'm close to him. When I was at his place a couple of weeks ago, I snooped in his bathroom, smelling everything. His scent comes from the shampoo and body wash he uses. Next time I'm there, I'm taking a picture so I can buy some for my bathroom.

Ellis keeps one hand in mine while I drive. He connects his phone to my truck then scrolls through his music app until he finds a playlist he likes. Music fills the cab. It's upbeat and sounds like something you'd dance to in a club. It isn't a song I know, but Ellis sings along, loud and out of tune. I fidget in my seat, trying my damndest to calm the fuck down because apparently, my dick gets all hot and bothered by off-key singing.

I smile as he belts out songs and dances in his seat

never letting go of my hand. It's hard to focus on the road when all I want to do is watch Ellis. I have no choice but to settle for listening to him. For over an hour, I enjoy a private concert as Ellis sings song after song.

"Oh, shit," he yells suddenly. "Sorry."

"What's wrong?" I ask, concern lacing my words.

"Nothing. I'm sorry. Sometimes I get lost in the music. I didn't realize I've been singing for so long."

"I love listening to you sing. You're fucking adorable, and you were having fun. I feel special. How many people can say they've had their own private Ellis concert?"

"Counting you?" he asks.

When I nod, he starts counting on his fingers. Then he hums softly and says, "Including you, that makes," he pauses as if figuring out a difficult math problem. "One." I bust out laughing.

"One?" I question. "With all that counting, I thought you were going to tell me you're some secret pop star."

"Nope. No secret identity. I just like to sing." He smiles widely. "Thank you for being nice about it. I know I kind of suck at it."

"Off-key and sexy happens to be my favorite type of singer. You can give me a private show any time."

"Oh, really? Will that show involve anything *other* than singing?"

"Depends." I shrug nonchalantly.

"What do you have in mind?" he asks in that flirty voice that gets me revved up.

"Oh, I can think of a lot of things."

"Name three," he challenges.

I let go of Ellis' hand and hold up one finger. "A strip tease." I raise a second finger. "An entire two-hour concert with you singing *and* dancing completely naked." I put up a third finger. "You sing to me while I fuck you. Shall I go on? Because I can think of more."

Ellis adjusts himself. "No," he squeaks then clears his throat. "Uh, no. I-I get the idea."

As we walk from the parking lot to the art gallery, I pull out the paper tickets I pre-ordered and printed. A girl in her early twenties with long, blonde hair greets us at the door.

"Hi! Welcome to Creative Collective. Do you already have tickets?"

"Yeah." I hand her the papers. She scans them then hands us each a brochure.

"This has information about the artist and each of his pieces. Enjoy and let us know if you have any questions."

"Thank you," Ellis and I say in unison. We step around the wall in the center of the entryway and enter the gallery. Paintings line the walls, several pedestals around the room hold ceramic and glass pieces, and a long table in the center is lined with framed sketches.

"Wow," Ellis gasps, glancing around the space. "I can't believe he works with so many different mediums." He flips through the brochure, lips moving as he reads quietly. Even that's sexy.

"Let's start on this side," I say, pointing to the wall on the left. Ellis nods in agreement. We walk to the first painting.

"Tranquility," Ellis reads from the brochure. "Michael was inspired by his childhood in the mountains of West Virginia. He found peace and solitude at the top of a mountain amidst a tumultuous upbringing."

The painting is beautiful, and I understand why it's called tranquility. The view is from a mountain top with a bright, blue sky overhead and a valley below with a serene lake surrounded by mountains.

I flip my own brochure over and find the paragraph about the artist. "Michael Masters was born and raised in the West Virginia mountains in a town where coal mining was king. While large corporations got rich, the poor families in Bentonville struggled to make ends meet. Long, stressful days with little money made life difficult. Michael found peace from his rough upbringing in the mountains surrounding his small town. He discovered his passion and talent for art early on and used it as a way out of the coal mining industry. He earned a full scholarship to Raigus Art and Design in Tarlow, Georgia, where he pursued bachelor's degrees in sculpting and painting. Since college, Michael has traveled the world, showing his work in galleries in over forty countries."

"Oh, look," Ellis gasps as soon as I finish reading. I glance to where he's pointing at the table with framed drawings of men, women, and children in the town where he grew up. Some look like they just walked out of a mine, others look tired and dirty, and the children are all sad. In the center, is a small sign that says, 'Life in Bentonville.' The drawings are hauntingly beautiful and give me a sense of people doing their best to survive from one day to the next.

We walk over to get a close look. Several of the drawings are of a mine in various stages of what appears to be an explosion. Others depict women and children crying, some holding one another and some facing anguish alone. It's a heartbreaking scene.

Ellis flips through the brochure, quickly finding what he needs. "In 1982, when Michael was seven years old, disaster struck Bentonville. The largest mine in the area suffered an explosion, trapping and ultimately killing thirty-one miners. The town never truly recovered from the heartbreak or financial collapse. To this day, more than forty years later, poverty is rampant in the area, and its residents struggle to survive and keep the town alive."

"Wow, that's awful." I blink back a few tears and notice Ellis doing the same. The drawings and story behind them are tragic, but Michael did a beautiful job depicting the events.

We spend the next hour looking at the art and discussing some of our favorite pieces. Then I excuse myself under the pretense of having to find the bathroom, but I'm on a different mission. Ellis is talking to the girl from the front, so I seek off to the offices in the back. I find an open door with a man sitting at a desk. I knock lightly and he looks up.

"Mr. Klein?" I ask.

"Yes," the older gentleman acknowledges me as he stands. "You must be Jagger."

"I am. Thank you for taking time to see me." He motions for me sit. I gather my thoughts as I walk the few steps to the proffered chair. I hope the gallery owner in front of me sees what I see when I show him the pictures on my phone, and I'm able to give this gift to Ellis.

CHAPTER 28

ELLIS

Jagger looks like an overexcited little kid. He's bouncing from one foot to the other, and I swear he lets out a squeal when I open the studio door, but it was hard to hear over him clapping like a fool.

"What has you so... whatever this is?" I wave my hand at him.

"Come!"

"I really can't do that on command or with a soft cock," I quip with a bratty smirk.

He shakes his head. "Later. Right now, come with me."

He grabs my wrist and drags me across the lobby, through the glass blowing studio, and to a door at the far end. He swings the door open and drags me inside. My mouth drops. Like to the *floor*. I may never be able to pick it up again. The room is about five hundred square feet with several easels and canvases in every size imaginable. Boxes of acrylic and oil paint, brushes upon brushes, and cleanup supplies stored on shelves and in cabinets. Two walls have large windows with plenty of natural light. Under one window is a desk with sketch pads and packs of pencils in every style and color.

"What is this?" I ask in utter shock.

"An art studio," he deadpans. "For you."

I turn on him so fast, I almost lose my balance. Somehow, I manage to keep myself up right. "Wh-What?"

"Well, if you're going to have an art show, you need a place to work. Prepare."

"An art show? What are you talking about?" None of this makes sense. "I'm not an artist."

"You are very much an artist," he disagrees.

"Jagger," I growl. "Start from the beginning and explain everything."

He pulls me against his chest and rubs his hands up and down my arms. "Don't get mad."

"Oh, *fuck*," I groan. "Never start a sentence that way, Jag."

"Sorry." He takes a deep breath like he's trying to get up the nerve to tell me. This feels big. Important. Nerves gnaw at me. If he doesn't start talking soon, I might vomit or scream or pass out. "When I was at your place a few weeks ago, and you were working, I took some photos of your paintings. I know I should have asked, but I wanted to surprise you. I showed them to Mindy at Gallery Expresso and Mr. Klein, the owner of Creative Collection. They were both very impressed. Mr. Klein wants to display two in his gallery to see if there is any interest, and Mindy wants to offer you your own show, similar to the one I had."

"I can't do an art show. I'm. Not. An. Artist." I punctuate each word, hoping he understands this time.

"*You* are very talented. You deserve this. But you need a place to create, so... Tada!" He gestures to the space surrounding us, spreading his fingers and shaking his hands.

'Tada' and jazz hands are not something I ever thought would come from Jagger and it takes every ounce of willpower not to laugh out loud. This is *not* a laughing situation. This is serious. He gave me a studio, a freaking studio.

"Jagger," I breathe out, and it sounds all whispery and whiney. It might be too much, but the gesture is turning me on. No one has ever supported my art dream. I've basically given up. The more time that passes, the further away my art aspirations get and the less time I spend doing anything artistic. It's been weeks since I've sketched and months since I've painted. "This is all too much. All this stuff costs a fortune."

He wraps his arms around me from behind and rests his chin on my shoulder. "You deserve this and so much more."

"No, I don't. I'm not even good," I protest.

"You're right." I swallow the gasp that almost escapes me. I know I'm right, but I didn't expect him to agree so easily. "You are amazing, phenomenal, great, special. You are *so* much better than good."

"Jag—"

"Stop," he cuts me off. "Don't put yourself down." I huff at his very correct observation. That's exactly what I was about to do. "I believe in you, and I see how talented you are. How about this? The offer from Mindy is there. Take some time to see what you can create in this space. If you find inspiration, paint. If not, then step away for a while. I understand you can't force art if the muse isn't speaking to you, but you also haven't had a space to work. Who knows what you'll be able to create in this room?"

"Maybe…"

"In the meantime, let Mr. Klein display two paintings from your house in his gallery. You'll never know until you try."

"I guess you're right. Mr. Klein did see the photos, so if he wants to display my work, it can't hurt." Jagger has really thought this through on my behalf.

"Yes!" Jagger cheers, punching the air with his fist.

"Just to be clear, I'm *not* making any promises about the art show."

"I understand, but will you at least spend some time in here and see how it goes?"

"Okay," I relent. I wiggle loose from Jagger's arms enough to turn around so I can look at his face. "Thank you. This is a wonderful studio. I really do love it." I kiss Jagger quickly then pull away from him, so I can get a good look at the space.

He went all out. He chose the same things I would have chosen if I was stocking the space myself. The brands, paint colors, canvas sizes, and various brushes are all the best on the market. Damn, he's good. I walk around the room, picking items up, feeling the brushes in my hand, running my fingers along the edge of the canvases and taking it all in. It's a little overwhelming. Understatement. It's a *lot* overwhelming, but my stomach does this weird fluttery thing, and my heart picks up speed. I miss painting. Not having space to be creative has been weighing heavy on me without me even realizing it. As I walk around the room, I feel my entire body start to relax. *This* is home. This is where I feel strong and confident. How did Jagger know how much I need this when I couldn't see it myself?

A large, white canvas rests on one of the easels with an empty palette leaning against it. I pick up the palette and walk over to the rows of paint, choosing several and squeezing them on the white surface. I fill a cup with water and place it in the holder on the edge of the easel then gather several different size brushes, returning to the canvas with my supplies.

Instinct takes over and I start painting without a clear picture in mind. My entire focus is on the canvas as I block out everything else around me.

When I finally stop sometime later, probably hours, the scene on the canvas steals my breath. It's the little alcove where Jagger and I ended up on our date last week. The sun is setting, casting the alcove in gorgeous shades of pink, yellow, and orange. A man sits on one of the rocks with his head thrown back and back stiff. There's a hint of someone in front of him, but the other person is almost entirely blocked by the man sitting.

"Jesus, fuck!" Jagger gasps behind me, scaring the

shit out of me. I thought I was alone. "That's hot. Ellis, that painting is… fuck. Is that me?"

"I… yeah. Sorry. I didn't mean to paint this." Embarrassment fills me.

"It's beautiful." Jag's face is full of awe. He stands next to me, getting a closer look.

"It is?"

"Yes. Is this how you see me? Who knew I was this fucking hot getting a blow job?" he muses with a chuckle.

That cracks me up and I cackle, big and boisterous. "Well," I say through the laugh. "I've never actually seen you from the back when you're in the midst of ecstasy, but I bet this is a pretty close representation." I turn to look at him. "Are you mad?"

"Mad? Why would I be mad?" Confusion etches his words and face.

"Because I painted us having sex."

"No! I'm not mad at all. This is beautiful. You should display it at Mr. Klein's gallery." Jagger glances at me then looks away quickly like he has something else to say. Gently, I place a hand on his arm. He still doesn't look at me, but he continues. "Please don't sell it."

"Okay." I shrug. "It probably wouldn't sell anyway." I don't even try to hide my disappointment. I knew this was a bad idea. I'm not an artist. I'd be lying if I said it doesn't hurt, but it does. It's breaking my heart to know Jagger doesn't think I'm good enough to sell my work.

"Ellis," he says, placing a hand on my shoulder and

gently turning me to face him. "You misunderstand. I don't want you to sell this because I want to hang it in my apartment. It's selfish, and I'll pay you for it because I know it would sell for a lot of money in a gallery, but it's intimate, and it's the first painting of us. I want it."

"Wait. You think it's good enough to sell?" Now I'm the one confused.

"One hundred percent."

"You don't mind that I painted us?"

"No."

"And if I paint something else with us, you won't care if I sell it?" I ask skeptically.

"I would love that." I shake my head at his words. I just can't wrap my head around Jag's excitement and encouragement. Am I really good?

"How long have we been working?" I ask through a yawn.

"You've been in here for about four hours. I made a couple of glass pieces and did some paperwork in the office."

"Sorry. I know we were supposed to spend the day together."

Jag cups my face. "As much as I want to spend time with you, I'm glad you found your creative side again. I hope this proves to you that you can do this. I know one painting doesn't make an art show, but it's a start."

I feel better than I have in a while. More centered. Creative. I haven't felt that in far too long. My hands are already itching to pick up the paintbrush again. Scenes play in my head, some star Jagger, others are of the two of us, and more are of nature. Maybe I can do this.

"If… and this is only an if, but *if* I do the art show when would it take place? Like how long do I have and how many pieces will I need?"

If," Jagger starts, playing along with me, "you do the show, you can pick the date. Obviously, it would have to be a time when she doesn't have another show on the books, but it doesn't have to be soon. As for how many, what are you comfortable with and what kind of free time do you have? This only took you four hours, and you had nothing in your head. No plan. I guess my question is— how long do you need to finish, say, ten paintings?"

"I can only paint on Sunday afternoons, and maybe Monday night, with my work schedule. If we don't spend any time together, which I am *not* okay with, it would take me about a month to finish ten."

Jagger smiles. "Yeah, I'm not okay with not spending time with you, either. But on Sundays, we can split our time. You can come over when your brunch shift ends and paint for a few hours then we can have dinner and spend time together. If you want, you can spend the night on Sundays and work from my apartment on Monday then you're right down the street from the studio," he suggests.

"I like that idea. Okay, so maybe six weeks or two months if I only do ten and we spend time together. Is that enough?" My voice shakes as I try to understand all of this. I'm so out of my league with this entire art show idea.

"The quantity isn't important. You have this one, you can display it and just mark it 'Not for Sale.' Then you have all those paintings at your house. You can sell or display them. I would suggest having at least ten to sell, though. You're *going* to sell them."

"How can you be so sure?"

"Because you are an artist." He pulls me into his arms. "And I will keep telling you that no matter how many times I have to until you believe it."

"Can we do it together?"

CHAPTER 29

JAGGER

"Together?" I'm not sure I understand what's he asking.

"Can we have a joint art show? My paintings, maybe a few sketches, and some of your glass pieces. I can even frame the sketches like Masters did at Creative Collective." The excitement in Ellis' voice is contagious and makes my heart soar. I'm happy he is seriously considering this.

"We can, but I want this for *you*. I want you to be the main focus."

"Please." His voice is suddenly unsure. Afraid, almost.

"Will it make you more comfortable if we do it together?"

"Yes. This is the first time anyone has supported my art. I'm having a lot of trouble believing I'm good enough," he admits. The sheer sadness in his voice breaks my heart. All I want is for him to see how talented he is and have confidence in his art and himself.

"I believe in you, and I know you're good enough to carry a show on your own, but I will be happy to plan it together if it makes you feel better."

"Thank you. Oh, we should do a theme!" Ellis' excitement returns as soon as I agree to the show. "Like maybe something nautical— boats, lighthouses, sea turtles, seahorses, beaches." His eyes go wide in the middle of listing ideas. "Wait, can you make those things with glass?"

"Absolutely, and I love that idea."

"How much time do you need?" Excitement grows in his voice and it contagious.

"A couple of months will work. I have the advantage of being here every day."

"Alright, so June?"

I pull Ellis into my arms and kiss his forehead. "June it is, baby. I'll talk to Mindy this week and nail down an exact date."

"Can we do something else? This has all been a little much. I need… I'm… I don't know."

"You're crashing. You've been overstimulated, and you've had to think about a lot today. You're probably hungry, too."

"All of that. How did you know?"

"It happens to my sister, Max, sometimes. Having a calm, quiet place to decompress always helps her. Come on, let's go to my apartment." I take Ellis by the hand and lead him out of the studio, turning off the lights as we walk through his space then mine. Once on the sidewalk out front, I lock the door and lead him down the street. Today has been a big day and I'm super proud of Ellis for agreeing to the art show. It's so far out of his comfort zone, but damn he deserves it. Fuck everyone who has ever squashed his dreams and his creativity.

When we get to my apartment, I walk him to the couch and push his shoulders down until he sits. "Wait here." He doesn't argue, just sinks into the soft cushions with heavy eyes. I cover him with my softest blanket.

In the kitchen, I fill a plate with strawberries, grapes, salami, cheese cubes, and some crackers like some poor man's charcuterie. It's the best I can do with what I currently have in the kitchen, but it will hold him over until dinner.

I set the plate and a glass of water in front of him. "Eat and drink then take a nap until dinner." I turn to walk back to the kitchen then remember a text I got from my mom earlier. "Hey, I totally forgot, but my family wants us to meet them for dinner tomorrow. No pressure if it's too soon."

"I've already met your family. Dinner sounds nice." Ellis yawns through his words.

"Cool. I'll let Mom know we'll be there."

"I can help cook tonight, or we can go out. I'm awake now. I can rally."

"Ellis, you're exhausted. Let me take care of you. Please."

He nods, giving in because honestly, he probably

doesn't have the energy to argue. I leave Ellis with his snack and return to the kitchen to figure out dinner.

———

WHY AM I SO NERVOUS? Ellis is right, he's met my family. I feel like every nerve in my body is on fire. It's one thing for them to meet him briefly in a large group when I can pull him away from them. It's entirely different for us to be in a restaurant with my whole family and no way to escape.

I'm not worried about them liking Ellis, they already do. But I know my family, and given the chance, my brothers will give him the third degree just to see if he can take the heat. Truthfully, I don't care what they think. I love Ellis. I never thought I'd fully love anyone other than my family, but the truth is, Ellis is my family, too. I care about him deeply and want to spend my life with him. My feelings for him have grown into something I wasn't expecting. When he showed up at my studio just before Christmas and we had sex, I was sure that was it. One and done as was Ellis' motto, but I knew when he walked out that day, one time would never be enough. Maybe I do love him, but we aren't ready to go there.

It took me a while to convince him that my feelings are real, but now we spend every minute of free time together and I'm falling for Ellis more and more each day.

When I finally emerge from the bathroom, dressed and ready to go, Ellis is still sitting on my couch where

I left him. He looks perfectly content and not nervous at all. That's good. I want him to be comfortable around my family.

"You look nice," Ellis says with a smile.

"Thanks." I picked out a pair of black jeans and a green polo. The restaurant is casual, but I like to look nice. Ellis is dressed conservatively today, which is his way of hiding. I understand because I know he worries people I care about will judge him, but I like when he's himself and dresses in those sexy crop tops, blouses, and mesh shirts. Who knew I was a sucker for shirts? Today he's in a pair of royal blue dress pants and a white button up with the sleeves rolled up to his elbows and several buttons undone, showing off the tattoos on his forearm and chest. It's hot, but it's not Ellis. In fact, it looks like something his mother picked out. I almost ask him, but I don't want him to think I'm being mean to his mother or to be self-conscious about his outfit. "You look great, too."

We walk hand in hand to the restaurant, located two blocks from my apartment. When we arrive, the hostess leads us to a small room where most of my family is already waiting. With a group of nineteen, we need an entire room for ourselves.

"Jag! Ellis!" Mom gushes, pulling each of us in for a hug. "I'm so glad you made it. "How about a glass of wine?" she offers, picking up a glass from a small tray and handing it to Ellis.

"Thank you." Ellis takes a sip as he smiles at my mom. Leave it to my family to have an entire tray of drinks waiting.

"Ellis, Jagger tells me you're quite the artist."

"Mom," I groan, dragging the word out like an annoyed child.

"You hush," she scolds. "Go bother your brothers and let me talk to Ellis about his art." She shoos me away, and I swear I hear Ellis giggle under his breath. I think those two are conspiring against me or something.

I wander to Lex, glancing over my shoulder a few times to check on Ellis. He is smiling widely, hanging on every word Mom utters.

"Looks like Mom has your boyfriend trapped," Lex comments, patting me on the shoulder.

"Yeah."

"Don't worry. She's probably just telling him about all the guys you dated in high school and college."

My eyes snap to my brother. "She better not." Those are secrets, not secrets exactly. But there are some embarrassing dating stories in my past that I want to forget. My mom will not do me any favors by giving Ellis her version of them. She doesn't always remember the facts correctly.

Lex laughs and pats me on the back. "All of our spouses have been the victim of Mom's stories. He'll survive and so will you. Trust me, if her stories about me didn't run Amanda off, you seriously have nothing to worry about."

Lex has a point. He was an asshole to the girls he dated in high school. In fact, Amanda is the only girl he's ever treated right. I guess when you find your soulmate, it's different. Scratch that. I *know* it's different.

Yep, that happened. I just thought of Ellis as my soulmate, and it's absolutely true. The other day after our multiple-hour sexcapades, I thought of him as my forever. I've got it bad, and I'm not afraid to admit it. Well, I might be a little slightly terrified to admit it to Ellis. I've only said 'I love you' a couple of times. He's doing great and is fully on board with the whole monogamy thing, but I'm scared to harp to much of my true feelings. Like the deep down forever ones. I don't want to run him off.

A few minutes later, I find Ellis holding court with my sisters and sisters-in-law. He is animated, waving his hands around as he talks, and they are all full of smiles, laughing at whatever story he's telling, eating up every word. My heart clenches at the sight. They genuinely like him and he looks right at home.

I walk up behind him and wrap my arms around his waist, planting a kiss on his cheek.

Stephanie squeals, "Eeek! You two are so freaking cute."

"Ellis is hilarious. You need to bring him around more often," Max tells me.

"We really like him," Amanda adds.

"Maybe more than you," Mel teases.

I gasp at her words. "More than me? No one is better than me. That thought is absurd."

"Don't worry, babe, I still like you even though you will clearly never earn the top spot again," Ellis teases, eliciting giggles from the girls.

I turn Ellis in my arms and pin him with a glare. "My sisters love *me*. I will always be number one," I growl. I mean for it to come out angry, but it falls flat, and Ellis shakes his head, smiling.

"You're so cute when you pretend to be all angry and offended." He pats my cheek and turns back to the girls as I lean in for a kiss. Instead of lips, I'm met with a mouth full of hair. When I glance up, slightly embarrassed, all I see are heart eyes from the four women. They adore Ellis and it makes me ecstatic to see him getting along with them even if it means getting teased in the process.

CHAPTER 30

ELLIS

I need a break from the painting, and dare I admit, sex. My entire body shudders at that admission. Who knew needing a sex break was even a thing? Jagger is a fucking beast in bed. The best I've ever had. But I'm exhausted. For weeks, every free minute has been spent painting and preparing for the art show. When we finally stop working to get some rest, we end up fucking instead of sleeping, cutting into the hours of rest my body craves.

A few days ago, Jag convinced me to go to Cosmos one night. Exhaustion was shoved to the side. I tried to say no, but he countered with 'I'll fuck you in the bathroom.' He reeled me in like a goddamn fish on a line with the promise of public sex. Being used by him, knowing everyone in line could hear me scream was the hottest sex I've ever experienced. It's all finally catching up with me.

I spent the morning trying to sleep, but after lying in bed for hours with sleep eluding me, I forced myself to shower and go outside. I've barely seen the sun for days. I'm walking down the boardwalk when I hear someone call me.

"Ellis. Hey, Ellis!" Turning, I find Ryan walking toward me with a guy close to my age. They look a lot alike, and I can only assume it's his brother. I heard his younger brother recently moved to Anchor Point.

"What's up, Ryan?"

"Enjoying the nice weather and a little time off."

"Yeah. Me, too." I smile at them both, taking the other guy in. He's an inch or two shorter than me with shaggy, brown hair and dark-brown eyes. He's objectively hot but not my type. Ha! I'd totally let him fuck me if I was single. But he's a little too clean cut and All-American for me.

"This is my brother, Nicky." Ryan gestures in the kid's direction. "This is Ellis. He works at the bar."

"Hey, it's nice to meet you." I hold my hand out for him to shake. Nicky flinches slightly but tries to cover it with a fake smile. Reluctantly, he lifts his hand and shakes mine. Either this kid is painfully shy, or he has some *serious* trauma. I hope it's the former. I hate to think of anyone being hurt.

"It's good to meet you." His voice is quiet, and I can barely hear him over the waves crashing against the shore. There's a storm offshore and the waves are bigger than normal today.

"We were going to grab some lunch at Ocean Shack. Wanna join us?" I'm about to decline when I see the hopeful look in Nicky's eyes.

"Um, I don't want to intrude."

"You're not intruding." Nicky shocks me with his words, more confident now, but still guarded.

"Okay," I concede, not sure what's going on. If the kid needs a friend, I can have lunch with my boss.

I follow Ryan and Nicky to the Ocean Shack window and wait for them to order. As I step up, Ryan says, "Get whatever you want. It's on me."

"No, I can—" I start to protest, but Ryan cuts me off.

"My treat. I insist."

"Thank you." After placing our orders, Nicky follows me to a nearby table with our drinks while Ryan pays for our meals.

Surprising me, Nicky takes the seat next to me and puts Ryan's drink on the other side of him. I expected him to sit across from me. He seems a little more relaxed now, but nerves still dance across his face when he looks at me.

"How do you like Anchor Point?" I ask in a feeble attempt to break the ice.

"It's okay, I guess. I like the beach." He shrugs. "I've never seen the beach before."

"Never?" I question as Ryan sits, placing a large number 26 on the edge of the table.

"Never what?" he asks.

"I told Ellis this is the first time I've seen the beach."

"Oh, yeah, we didn't grow up near the water. I had never seen the beach either when I moved here," Ryan admits, adding to my shock.

"Wow. Growing up here, it didn't occur to me that some people have never seen a beach. I guess it makes sense— I've never been to the mountains."

Nicky's eyes widen. "What?" As soon as he says it, he starts laughing. "The mountains are great. Lots of places to hike and be alone."

"Do you like the mountains more than the beach?" I ask as the server brings our food, interrupting the conversation.

"Buffalo shrimp," he says, and Ryan reaches over taking his food. "Shrimp Po Boy," he continues, and I raise my hand. He sets my food in front of me then places a basket of fish fingers in front of Nicky. As the server walks away, I take a huge bite of my sandwich.

Nicky smiles at the basket of fried goodness in front of him. "The beach. I *definitely* like the beach better."

"Is that just because of the food?" Ryan asks with a teasing tone.

"The food and you. Is that what you're fishing for?" Nicky shoots back with a small smile.

"Yes. Thank you. I'm glad I make your list of reasons why you like the beach."

"Well, it certainly isn't the damn heat," Nicky grumbles with a pout. "I hate the heat."

"Oh, sweetie, this is nothing. Wait 'til July and August. It's hotter than the devil's ass." Nicky and Ryan both crack up. "What? It's true."

"It is," Ryan agrees.

"Fuck, me, maybe I don't like the beach." Nicky mumbles, biting into one of his fish fingers. He lets out a groan. "Never mind. I love it here. This is *delicious*."

For a few minutes, we enjoy our greasy, fried seafood. The boardwalk is busy with families and tourists. The season is in full swing. With most of the spring break crowd gone, families and couples are starting to filter through. Even though it's hot, I love this time of year. Work is busy, but the tips are great.

"Ellis," Ryan grabs my attention. He wipes his face and hands with his napkin, dropping it into his empty basket. "I've been wanting to introduce you to Nicky. I thought maybe you could show him around."

"Oh, God, shut up. Just stop, Ryan." Nicky's face turns red as he shakes his head.

"What?" The innocence on Ryan's face is comical. He has no idea what he did.

"I don't need you to make friends for me."

"Why is that bad? I thought introducing you to someone your age would be a good thing."

"Basically, you just told Ellis that I'm desperate and can't make friends without my big brother's help."

"No," Ryan objects.

"You kinda did," I agree with Nicky. "I think it's sweet, but if my parents did that to me, I'd be *mortified*."

"Thank you." Nicky relaxes against the back of his chair.

"You're welcome, but I am happy to show you around. How old are you?"

"Nineteen."

"Okay, so not Cosmos," I think out loud.

"Definitely, *not* Cosmos," Ryan growls.

"What's Cosmos?" Nicky sits up, intrigued.

"A club," I say.

At the same time Ryan barks out, "Not a place for kids."

Nicky jerks back, glaring at Ryan. "I'm *not* a kid."

"Well, you aren't going to Cosmos even when you're twenty-one."

"I'm totally going." Nicky's grin is mischievous and challenging. Oh, I like this guy. We are going to have fun together. "If you're this worked up, it has to be fun."

"It's just a club," I say with confusion.

Ryan stares at me a few beats too long, and it makes me nervous. "What do you do when you go to Cosmos?" he asks.

"I dance, have a few drinks, flirt, hoo... oh, uh... dance and drink," I amend quickly.

"And..." Ryan motions for me to continue. "Finish that thought, Ellis."

Suddenly, I am very uncomfortable with this conversation. Cosmos is known for being queer friendly, like Paradise 11, but it is also known as *the* place to hook up. I should know. I've been fucked by plenty of guys in those bathrooms. Most recently, Jagger. Discreetly, I move around in my chair. Thinking about the things he did to me in that bathroom are getting me worked up.

"No." I shake my head, vehemently.

"Fine. I'll finish." Ryan looks pointedly at his brother. "People go there to fuck random strangers. It isn't the place for you." Nicky sinks into his seat at Ryan's harsh tone. Ryan gathers the trash and carries it to the can.

As soon as he is out of earshot, Nicky looks at me. "I need to find a good hook up. Can you help me?"

I choke on my water. "Um, help you how?"

"Like meet people or," he rakes his eyes over me, "fuck me." His eyes and tone are hopeful.

"No. *We* cannot fuck. One, I have a boyfriend. Two, Ryan is my boss. And three, I like to be fucked."

Nicky deflates. "Oh, alright."

"We can hang out and I will introduce you to people."

"You don't have to do that."

"I might not have to, sweetie, but I want to. Going out and hooking up are my specialties."

Nicky perks up. "Yeah! Okay. Thank you."

"Ready?" Ryan returns, still tense to the point it's comical. He's acting like an overprotective father.

"I guess," Nicky responds, sadly as he pushes himself up. My heart aches for him. Poor kid needs a friend.

"Wait. Here, put your number in my phone. I hand him the phone and he quickly types his number in and sends himself a text. His phone vibrates on the table. "Now I have yours, too."

"Fabulous! Thank you for lunch, Ryan." I wave them away. "You two go have fun." Once they are out of sight, I push myself up from the chair and head in the other direction toward my car.

Fifteen minutes later when I pull up to my trailer, I find Jagger pacing in front of it. I silence my phone and toss it in the glove box when I'm driving. I'm the worst about texting and driving, looking for songs, or scrolling social media. I get distracted too easily when it comes to my phone, especially when I'm driving. I hit a tree when I seventeen, a mailbox when I was eighteen, and a fence when I was twenty all because I was distracted by the phone. I'm lucky none of them involved other cars and no one got hurt.

Megan was with me when I hit the fence. She always yelled at me when I was on my phone, but I never took her seriously. The only reason I hit the fence is because I swerved in front of oncoming traffic, and she screamed. I yanked the wheel in time to avoid the other car, but I didn't hit the brakes quick enough. Luckily, I wasn't going fast when I hit the fence. I paid to get the fence fixed, but my car still has the damage. It will cost more than the car is worth to repair it, so I drive around with a huge dent in the bumper, and the paint scraped down the passenger side. After almost hurting my best friend, I changed my attitude about the phone. Now I stay off it when I'm driving.

When I grab my phone, I see two missed calls from Jagger. I shove the phone in my pocket and run to him, jumping into his arms and wrapping my legs around his waist.

"Hey, sexy! What are you doing here?"

Leaning in, I kiss him, pushing past his lips and running my tongue along his. One hand squeezes my ass while he caresses the other one up my back and into my hair. Slowly, without breaking the kiss, Jagger walks us to my car and sits me on the hood.

He pulls back. "I needed to see you."

I preen at his words. "Like what you see?" I ask, faking shy as I look down at the crop top, capris, and ankle boots I'm wearing. It's super feminine and one of my favorite outfits.

"So. Fucking. Much. Everything you wear is sexy, but I love your crop tops and skirts the most."

The first time I wore a skirt to his apartment, he fucked me against the front door before we left for dinner then again as soon as we got home. He couldn't stop touching me the entire time we were out. Part of me was terrified when I chose that outfit, he would hate it.

Jagger runs his hands up my legs then lightly across my stomach. "Can I fuck you right here?"

"On top of my car?"

"Yeah. Or on the steps. I have a blanket in the truck if you want to do it on the ground. I want to fuck you outside." His breath against my ear as his sultry voice says those words, send all my blood rushing straight to my dick.

"None of my neighbors are close enough to catch us," I whine with a pout. That's not entirely true, but they are all on the other side of the trailer and behind a few trees.

"Isn't that a good thing?"

"Theoretically." I lean close and whisper. "I like the thrill of knowing I can get caught or the possibility that someone might be watching." Jagger's entire body shivers and goosebumps cover his arms. His cock hardens against my leg. "You like that, don't you."

"Honestly, I literally just learned something about myself."

"Ooh, what's that?"

"The thought of someone watching us, someone seeing you naked and whimpering, unable to do anything except take my fucking cock as I slam into you."

My breathing is heavy, and my cock is painfully hard. Fuck. "Are you serious?" I ask with a hint of excitement. "You want people to watch?"

He thinks about it for long seconds never breaking eye contact with me. "Yeah. Shit, Ellis. I think I really do want that. Is that wrong? Does that make me a horrible boyfriend? I'm sorry." He tries to step away, but I grab onto his shirt.

"Whoa." I turn him back toward me. "I've never fucked when I knew for sure people were watching, but I have had sex in alleys, bathrooms, and on the beach, where it is likely someone saw me, and I didn't know. It's hot as fuck. And knowing you want people to see us, fuck... that's a whole new level of sexy."

"Is this something we can make happen?" Jagger looks like an embarrassed kid learning about sex for the first time.

"Sweetie, it is definitely something we can make happen."

"How?"

"Lots of ways. Clubs, like Cosmos. We can turn any private place public, your studio for example. If we know the right people to invite, we can do it there."

"You know the right people?" he asks with a little hesitance.

"Yes. But the Cosmos bathroom is also good."

Jagger leans in and kisses me roughly. He pulls my shirt over my head, licking and kissing my collar bone then down my chest and stomach. Squatting down, he unbuckles my shoes and slides them off. Then he lifts me off the car, pulling off my pants and underwear in one go. Standing in front of my trailer completely naked while Jagger is fully clothed, does something to my insides. My hearts races and my dick leaks. I might be broken, but I don't give a fuck. This is sexy as hell.

Jagger rakes his eyes over every inch of my body at an agonizingly slow pace. For a brief moment, I imagine we have an audience watching. Chairs full of people, seeing my naked body, waiting for Jagger to make his move. My cock hardens more. If that is even possible. Fuck, I want to do that soon.

"Turn around." Jagger surprises me, and I jolt slightly. As I drop my feet to the ground and turn to face the car, Jagger steps closer. He gently pushes my back. "Arms and chest on the car, baby." I lean over, arms above my head, chest against the warm car hood.

Jagger traces his fingers down my spine, following the trail with his tongue, lighting me on fire. He nips along the curve of my ass then smacks each cheek softly. His lips kiss along the small of my back, tongue dancing over the intricate tattoo of a snake wrapped around several flowers.

He stops abruptly, his fingers digging painfully into my hips, and he makes a noise somewhere between a sigh and a growl. "Does your tattoo say, 'Cum Slut?'"

"Uh, yeah." I do my best not to sound embarrassed. I'm *not* embarrassed. Not exactly. Most of the guys who figure out what it says are filling me with their cum, making the name fit. With Jagger, it hits a little differently. I want to be more than a cum slut to him. I've never felt this way about anyone. I was perfectly happy being everyone's cum slut and never settling down with a boyfriend. Now that I have Jagger, things like this fucking tattoo make me feel self-conscious, like he's going to eventually realize that's all I am and leave me.

Suddenly, he isn't touching me at all, and it feels scary and vulnerable. "Why?" His tone is a mix of anger and agony.

I glance back to find him staring at the offending tattoo, his breathing ragged, his features seething and his eyes glistening with unshed tears. My heart skips a beat or four. What the actual fuck is happening?

"Jagger?" Standing up I turn to face him, reaching out my hand. He spins me around and pushes me back onto the hood of the car, holding me in place with one hand between my shoulders and the other tracing a finger over the tattoo.

"Is—?" he chokes then clears his throat and tries again. "Is this what you think of yourself?"

I let out a laugh. "It's what everyone thinks of me."

His hold tightens. "It isn't what *I* think of you," he bites out.

"Can you just fuck me?" As much as I love public sex, being outside naked and having this conversation is getting a little weird even for me.

"No, I can't just *fuck* you." I push off the car, shoving Jagger back with my body, so I can have some room to breathe. How the hell can all the air feel like it's been sucked up when we are literally outside is beyond me, but that's exactly how it feels.

I grab my clothes off the ground and dig my keys out of my pocket, storming to the front door like a petulant child. Once inside, I leave the door open. He can follow or not. At this point, I don't fucking care. My body is shaking, but my brain can't decipher if it's anger, fear, or something else.

After I drop my dirty clothes on the floor outside of the bathroom, I step inside and turn the shower on, locking the door behind me.

Chapter 31

Jagger

By the time I get inside, Ellis is in the bathroom with the shower running. I try the door, but it's locked. I park myself on his couch and wait impatiently for him to emerge. He's mad at me, at my reaction to his tattoo. Hurt is probably a better description.

It isn't the first time I've seen it, but I've never been that up close and personal with it. I thought it was just a snake with flowers, and I thought him having a tramp stamp was sexy as fuck. When I read those words, it ripped my heart in two. How can he think that about himself? I know his past. He's been with a lot of guys. I don't know his exact body count and truthfully, I don't want to know. It's none of my business. Having a high body count doesn't make him a slut. There is nothing wrong with a healthy sex life.

The opening door scares me, and I jump embarrassingly high for someone sitting on a couch. Ellis doesn't seem to notice. Hell, he doesn't even glance my way as he walks into the bedroom and closes the door. I consider going after him, but instead I stay put, waiting for him to come to me. Is it the right choice? Who the hell knows? But it's what I do.

A few minutes later, Ellis walks back out barefoot, wearing a pink crop top and a pair of gray capri sweatpants, hanging low on his hips. Damn, he's alluring. He stops in the small kitchen and takes two water bottles from the fridge, offering one to me. He folds his legs under himself and drops onto the couch, facing me. He twists the cap off and swallows several gulps of water then recaps it and lets out a long sigh, relaxing his entire body as he does.

"Why does the tattoo bother you so much?" he finally asks.

"Because it's degrading."

"No, it isn't," he argues. "I am a cum slut."

How can he be so matter of fact about this? "No, you aren't. Quit degrading yourself," I growl.

"It isn't an insult or degrading. I love cum. I love the way it tastes. I love the way it feels to be used. I love how it feels to be covered in cum. It isn't degrading if I enjoy it."

"But you said it's all anyone thinks about you, and that sounds derogatory."

"Okay, you're right, I did say that. Look, I've never been good enough for anyone until you. A lot of guys have called me shitty names, and it didn't feel good at the time. Eventually, I became somewhat immune to it. One day, I decided to embrace it, so I turned the name calling into something positive. That tattoo gave me all the power. No one could make me feel bad about being a cum slut because it's what I am and what I want to be." He takes my hand and holds it over his heart. "Now I'm *your* cum slut and no one else gets to have me."

"It really doesn't bother you?"

"Not now. It did for a long time, but not since I got the tattoo. It was… empowering."

"I'm sorry I got so upset. I never want to see you hurt."

"Thank you." Ellis lets go of my hand and swings his legs out from under himself, climbing over to me, straddling my hips. "Now, I think my boyfriend owes me a good railing." He grinds his growing erection against my cock, pulling a needy, unattractive whine from me. The feel of his cock rutting against mine is almost more than I can take. By the way Ellis' eyes flutter, it must feel just as good to him.

"You know, I was kind of excited about fucking you outside." The disappointment is evident in my voice.

"Jagger Ward, have I unlocked a new kink in you?"

"Definitely." I pull Ellis flush against my chest and lick my tongue over his ear. He melts against me. "But now that I have you here, I want to fuck you like this."

"Pull your cock out," Ellis commands.

He climbs off me long enough to step out of his sweatpants. He isn't wearing anything under them. I push my own pants off, stroking my cock as I watch Ellis. He straddles my lap again in nothing but that tantalizing pink crop top.

"I prepped in the bathroom," he says, voice low and

sensual. Ellis takes my cock, lining it up with his hole and slowly sinks down.

"Fuck." That's all I can manage.

He feels so good in this position, not that I've found a position that doesn't feel good with him. There's something hot about knowing he prepped for me even when he was angry. He knew we would figure our shit out. Huh, maybe I learned something new about him today. If he's upset, give him time to process it. I shove that thought to the back of my mind to store for next time.

Grabbing Ellis' hips, I guide him up and down my length, digging my fingers into him. I watch him intently as he bounces on my dick. His eyes are closed, and he's biting his bottom lip. He moves up and down my length, rolling his hips. Shit, the scene is sultry.

"That feels good, baby. Ride me harder." Ellis picks up the pace, Fucking down on me over and over. His own cock bouncing with every movement. The sounds coming from him are obscene, only making it more erotic to watch. He clenches around me every time he slams against my thighs. "Fuck, Ellis, I'm gonna come."

"Let go baby," he coaxes.

"It's too soon."

He leans forward, never breaking his momentum. "You can fuck me again later." His warm breath skates across my ear then his tongue laps at the lobe right before he bites down, sending shock waves straight to my dick. "I want to feel your cum fill me. Make me your cum slut." My dick jumps inside of him, unloading as his ass tightens around me. Ellis throws his head back, grunting and moaning as he comes on my cock, his tight hole convulsing around my spent dick.

"Sorry. That. Was. Amazing." I breathe out, panting heavily. I start to stand up, but he shakes his head and leans against me.

"Later. I want to curl up in your arms and enjoy the feeling of your cum leaking out of me."

My cock twitches at his words. How the hell am I already getting hard again? "Shit." A thought hits me at that moment.

Ellis chuckles. "There it is."

"What?" I ask. My brain is still not firing on all cylinders.

"You were about to freak out because we didn't use a condom."

"Yeah, I got caught up in the moment." I don't want to say it out loud and upset Ellis, but he's been with other guys since we started fucking and I'm a little concerned. A lot concerned if I'm being honest

He climbs off me and picks up a piece of paper from the counter, handing it to me. He stands in front of me, bouncing from one foot to the other, biting his cuticle nervously. I glance over the information in front of me. It's negative test results. He got tested. We talked about it once but never agreed to get it done. This is the only time we've gotten caught up in the moment and forgotten to use protection.

"I wanted to surprise you. I got them a few days ago." He smiles adorably as he curls up in my lap.

"Aren't you worried about me?" I question with a smirk.

Ellis scoffs. "No. You don't fuck around like me. Well, I don't fuck around anymore."

I lean down and grab my pants off the floor, searching the pockets until I find my phone. I open the photo I took yesterday then flip it around to show Ellis. He reads the results, eyes going wide.

"You got tested, too? But you were negative before..." his words trail off.

"Best to know for sure. No reason to risk your health."

"Because I was with other people when we first started fucking." He half questions, half states with a resigned sigh. "I'm sorry I did that to you."

I pull him back into my lap and cup his cheek. "No need to apologize. At the time we were just fucking. We were both free to do what we wanted."

"But you didn't."

"Ellis," I sigh. It's time to tell him the truth. I don't talk about my past relationships much, but I need him to know this. "The last person I fucked was my former boyfriend. We were together for two years. My family and friends all hated him, but I refused to see the truth. He was an asshole, not abusive, and he didn't cheat, but he didn't care about me, not truly. He was nice a lot of the time, but had massive mood swings and would go days without talking to me when something set him off. When he dumped me, I was heartbroken because I was convinced if I didn't marry him, I would never find someone. We broke up almost a year ago, and until I met you, I had no desire to date, let alone, have sex."

"I'm sorry you went through that. You deserve better."

"Yeah, well, my track record isn't great. It's basically a string of jerks since I was sixteen. Then you. I'm glad I waited for you and didn't jump into marriage with any of those asshats."

Ellis stiffens. "You want to marry me?"

I smile even though my heart might beat out of my chest. "I know it's fast and I don't want to scare you, but yes, one day I want to marry you. I love you, Ellis." He looks a little green and very unsure. "Hey," I say, squeezing his thigh. "You don't have to say it back. It's the truth of how I feel, but I don't expect you to say it to me until you are truly ready."

He nods his agreement but doesn't look any better than he did a few minutes ago. "I've never said that to anyone," he admits, refusing to look at me. "And it isn't something people say to me, not even my parents. I don't know if I'll ever be able to say it, Jag. What if I'm never ready?"

"One day you will be, and I'll *never* pressure you or make you feel bad for not saying it."

"I really care about you. I like being with you and want to spend all our time together. I hate being away from you. You're the first person I can see spending my life with." He finally looks at me and all I see in his eyes is love, whether he's ready to say it out loud or not. "Thank you for telling me how you feel and respecting that I can't say those words yet."

He leans in and kisses me passionately. Without breaking the kiss, I stand up, and Ellis wraps his legs around me. I carry him to the bed and drop him on it, crawling on top of him. I'm going to spend the rest of the night showing Ellis how much I love him.

CHAPTER 32

ELLIS

The art show is in less than two months, six weeks to be exact. It's not close enough for me to be nervous, but I am stressed out about it anyway. I hope I'll have enough paintings completed by then to warrant a real art show. I have seven in my trailer that I need to bring to the studio, so I have everything in one place.

Over the past few weeks, I've finished four others, and I have eight more planned. I'm not sure I have enough time to complete all of them, but I'll do my best. Jagger and I have been spending as much time as possible preparing for the show, but that hasn't given us any time together until late at night when we're both exhausted.

"Princess," Jagger calls from the other room, and I swoon!

"Yeah," I holler back.

He pokes his head in the door. "Mel wants to know if we're hungry."

"OMG, yes! I'm starving."

"Alright, drama queen," he teases. "What do you want?"

"From where?"

"Wherever."

"I could totally go for some tacos. Tacos are life and I need some like yesterday."

"Oooh, yeah, that sounds good. Any preferences?"

"Nah, get a variety and some guac. Oh, and cheese dip. Lots of chips."

Jagger chuckles quietly. "Anything else, Princess?"

"Nope, that should do it."

Jagger types away on his phone as he disappears back into the other room. I watch him go, my heart full. I love when he calls me Princess. He started doing it about a week or so ago and I can't get enough. I feel special every time he says it. Mel is officially my favorite of all his siblings. She brings me food.

The blank canvas stares mockingly at me. I was doing so well a few hours ago, but now I'm stuck. By the time my shift ended last night, and I drove all the way to Jagger's apartment, it was almost four in the morning. Then we had sex. I was too tired to get up early, so I didn't drag my ass to the studio until almost ten. The first painting was one I started a few days ago, so it didn't take long to put on the finishing touches.

Now, I need a new idea. Okay, I have an idea, but I can't figure out how to get started. Grabbing a pencil, I make a few light sketches on the canvas, an outline of an old, wooden ship. It's not speaking to me like the others, but I have to start somewhere and none of my other ideas excite me, either. Mixing up a few different colors, I return to the canvas, but all I do is stare at it.

By the time I hear Mel in the other room, my canvas is still blank with the exception of a few pencil marks. A quick glance at the clock on the wall, tells me I've been staring aimlessly for almost an hour.

This fucking *sucks*. I was doing so well, and now, nothing. Nada. Zilch. Grabbing my paint brush, I spread brown paint across the canvas in one long stroke. Then another. Then another. Switching colors and brushes, I do the same with the orange, red, blue and purple.

"What are you doing?"

I squeal and jump, dropping the cup of yellow paint on the floor. It splashes all over me, Jagger and the easel. A few small spots even make it onto the bottom of the canvas. I don't bother responding. All I can do is stare at the mess as tears prickle my eyes. Why am I so upset? What the hell is wrong with me?

"Hey, Ellis, what's wrong?" Jagger pulls me into a hug and I lose it. Sobs wrack my body, and he has to use all his strength to hold me up. He walks us over the desk chair, sits down, and sits me onto his lap like a small child as if we aren't the same height. He rubs my back in gentle comforting circles, making shushing sounds while I cry large, crocodile tears all over his shoulder.

When I finally calm down, my face is covered in tears and snot, and so is Jagger's shirt. He waits patiently for me to wipe my face and sit up. He doesn't force me to talk. He simply holds me on his lap and runs his fingers along my back over and over, soothing me.

"I'm sorry." I try to stand up, but he holds me tighter against his body.

"Tell me what's wrong."

"I don't even know. I was doing great, getting ideas, painting them then boom. Nothing. My brain is empty. Creativity turned *completely* off. Closed for business. Then you came in and scared me, I dropped the paint and that sent me over the edge.

"You need a break before *you* break."

"Pretty sure it's too late for that." I point to myself, letting out a humorless chuckle.

"No, this is a small meltdown. You're going to really break if you don't get some rest." Jagger picks up my phone from the desk and hands it to me. "Call Ryan. Tell him you won't be in tonight."

"What?" I can't do that. It's Friday night. The bar will be packed."

"And he can pick up the slack. You need a night off from the bar and painting. You're running yourself ragged working three jobs and trying to get ready for the show. You can't do this for six more weeks."

"I'm not calling out. I'll clean up this mess, fill my belly with tacos and head back to Anchor Point. After my shift, I'll come back to your apartment, get a few hours of sleep, and be good as new tomorrow. Then the creativity will come flowing through me. All good." I try to stand again, but Jagger refuses to let go.

"Are you even listening to yourself? That is an

insane schedule. You can't keep doing this to yourself. Call Ryan or I will."

"You can't call my boss for me."

"Here's the phone. Go ahead," Jag challenges.

"Ugh! Fine. But if I get fired, you're gonna be my sugar daddy."

"It might be more like your Splenda daddy."

"W-wh-what?" I stutter laughing my ass off. "What does that even mean."

"Well, I don't make enough money to be anyone's sugar daddy. Splenda is a sugar substitute, but sugar substitute daddy is a mouthful, so— Splenda daddy."

"You're ridiculous."

"But I got you to laugh. Feel better, Princess?"

"A little," I admit. Jagger nods toward the phone. With a heavy sigh, I pick it up and hit Ryan's name then press speakerphone.

"Hey, Ellis, what's up?"

"Um, hi. Sooo… I need the night off." The words rush out and part of me hopes he will just make me come to work. I need the money more than my sanity.

"Is everything okay? Are you sick?" Concern laces his questions

"Everything is fine. I'm not sick."

"The why do you need the night off?"

"Because Jagger said I do," I say reluctantly.

"Jesus," Jagger groans through gritted teeth. "Hey, Ryan."

"Jagger, what's going on with Ellis?"

"He needs to rest. He's going to run himself into the ground if he doesn't take a break soon. Between his jobs and preparing for the art show, he's going nonstop for eighteen plus hours most days. He's exhausted and burnt out. So, yeah, I told him to call because he won't listen to his body."

"I'm sorry, Ryan. I know it's last minute and if it's an issue, I can be there. I'm fine. Really. Like I don't feel tired at all. Jag is being dramatic." The words rush out again. I can't afford to lose this job.

"No, Jagger is right. You need a break. You can take the whole weekend off from the bar and the restaurant. I can get someone to cover your shifts. Two jobs is a lot to handle, so don't worry about either of them until Tuesday."

Jagger looks at me in complete disbelief. Without taking his eyes off me, he throws me under the bus. "Ellis works another day job during the week."

"What? Another job? Ellis, how many hours a week do you work?" Ryan practically roars.

"I don't know. Like eighty-ish."

"And you're preparing for an art show? Ellis, you can't keep this up." Ryan's tone is full of concern.

"*You* work a lot," I argue.

"I own two businesses and don't work that many hours. This has to stop. I can get someone else to cover brunch for a while."

"No!" I cry, panicking. "Please don't fire me. I need the money."

"I'm not firing you. I'm asking you to take the brunch shifts off your plate until after the art show."

"I can't do that." All I envision are my bills piling up without the brunch tips.

"Let him rest this weekend," Jagger suggests. "Can you hold off on offering his brunch shifts to someone else for a few days. We'll talk about it over the weekend and get back to you on Monday."

"Okay, I can do that. Under one condition," Ryan states.

"What's that?" I ask, with glassy eyes and a quivering bottom lip. I am barely hanging on.

"This weekend, you rest. Take the break you deserve."

"Yeah, I can do that," I promise. We say our good-byes and Jagger ends the call.

"I'm proud of you. I know that was hard, but it will be good for you to have the next few days off. Tonight and tomorrow, we rest. Then Sunday, we'll see how you feel. If you're up for some painting, we'll come back to the studio."

"What are we going to do? I can't just do nothing," I protest.

"Sure you can. Tacos are waiting in the other room. We stuff our faces, clean up the studio, and get it all closed up. Then we walk to my apartment, take a shower together and dress in comfy pajamas. For the next day and a half, we lounge around in our pjs, binge crappy movies, order take out and junk food to be delivered, and have sex."

"That sounds amazing."

"It will be. You deserve it. I'm going to take care of you, so you can get some much-needed rest. No deadlines. No timeline. No alarms. No schedule. Sleep. Eat. Sex. That's it."

This time, Jagger lets me stand. As I rise, I grab his hand and pull him up. "Let's taco!"

TWO HOURS LATER, my belly is full, the studio is clean, and we're freshly showered, lounging on Jagger's couch. He has his feet propped up on the coffee table and his arms wrapped around me. My head rests on his chest as he gently strokes his fingers through my now purple hair. An old B-rated horror flick plays on his television, but I'm too tired to pay attention. I keep dozing off, but then Jag will shift or laugh at something on the screen, and I force my eyes open, temporarily unsure about where I am or what's happening. If Jagger notices, he doesn't say anything. He simply continues to focus on the TV while absently running his fingers through my hair, coaxing me back to sleep.

"Ellis." Something gently rocks me.

"No. Sleepy." I moan without opening my eyes.

"Come on, Princess, wake up." Slowly Jag's words register, and I blink my eyes open. The lamp next to the couch is on, but the rest of the apartment is dark except for the light above the stove, casting the kitchen in a dim glow.

"What time is it?" I ask, rubbing my eyes and pushing myself up to a sitting position. "And I thought you were playing pillow for me," I pout.

"It's after nine. And I was for about a couple of hours then I wiggled out from under you, did some laundry and cleaned the kitchen. I ordered us dinner."

He reaches for me. "Come on. We'll eat then crawl into bed. It's a lot more comfortable than the couch."

Letting Jag pull me to the barstools, I ask, "Did I really sleep for five hours?"

"Yes. I hated to wake you, but you need to eat, and I want you in my bed where you belong, not out here all night like some couch-surfing acquaintance."

"And what are we going to do in that bed of yours?" I tease.

As much as I wanted shower sex earlier, by the time we got to the apartment, I could barely keep my eyes open. Jag had to wash me and help me get dressed. I probably should be embarrassed, but it felt nice to have someone take care of me.

"That depends," he growls, low and sexy.

"On what?" I ask, adjusting my growing erection.

"Whether or not you fall asleep," he teases.

"I'm well rested now. Good to go."

CHAPTER 33

JAGGER

Ellis finally agreed to introduce me to his parents. We've been to Sunday dinner at my parents' house a few times, but Ellis has never invited to his meet his parents. He doesn't talk about them much and I don't think he goes to see them often even though they also live in Anchor Point.

Ellis fidgets nervously as I drive us the short distance from his trailer to the small neighborhood where his parents live. It makes me wonder what I'm getting myself into. I don't give a fuck if his parents like me. Ellis is the only one who matters.

Now I'm getting nervous. What if they hate me and then Ellis decides he doesn't want to be with me because their opinion matters to him? *No. Calm down, Jag. Ellis has already told you his parents aren't supportive of his dreams, but they don't care that he's gay.* He needs me to be strong today. I push my nerves down and focus on Ellis, reaching over and taking one of his hands in mine.

"Take the next left," Ellis states absently from the passenger seat. I follow his instructions as we wind through the neighborhood. I've never been through here. It's closer to the center of town than the beach and dons several tree-lined streets with small cottage and ranch-style homes. Most are painted in pastel colors fitting perfectly in the beach community. "Turn right." Ellis points to the upcoming street. I take the turn, and he gestures to a ranch-style home painted pale blue with yellow shutters. "That one. You can pull up behind the minivan."

When I put the truck in park and get a good look at Ellis, he's a little green. If this starts to go bad in any way, I'm taking him home. I'm not going to let them make him feel bad about anything.

"Ready?"

"Yeah," he breathes out, shaking his head. I don't question him because he pushes open the door and climbs out, waiting for me in front of the small porch. I take his hand again, pressing the lock button on my key fob then pocketing my keys.

When we get to the door, Ellis turns the knob, finding it unlocked. "I keep telling them to lock the door," he mumbles. Anchor Point is safe, but I have to agree with Ellis. His parents are elderly and shouldn't have their door unlocked. Anyone could walk right in. "Hey, Dad."

The door opens into a small foyer with a large living room to the right. His dad is sitting on the couch with the TV blaring at max volume. He looks up when

Ellis speaks, but I bet it was because he saw movement not because he actually heard Ellis speak.

Ellis picks up the remote and turns the volume down as his dad scooches to the front of the couch and slowly pushes himself up. The act seems difficult for the man, but once he's on his feet, he looks strong and sturdy. I half expected him to be feeble with no balance.

"Samantha, the boy's here." Ellis' dad motions to me. "Who's this?"

"This is my boyfriend, Jagger. Jag, this is my dad, Bob Young."

"Hi, Ellis, sweetheart," his mom says, coming around the corner, drying her hands on a kitchen towel.

"Hey, Mom. This is Jagger. This is my mom, Samantha."

"It very nice to meet you both," I say to Ellis' parents.

"Good to meet you, too," his mom says sweetly. His dad doesn't say anything. He simply returns to the couch and turns the volume back up on the TV.

Ellis rolls his eyes as we follow his mom into the kitchen. "Can I get you something to drink?" Ellis offers, pulling a pitcher of water from the fridge.

"Water is fine. Thank you."

"Mom, are you ready for me to set the table and get everyone a drink?" Ellis offers, falling back into a role he seems to know well.

"Oh, that would be lovely, dear. Dinner is ready," she replies.

Ellis busies himself, pouring four glasses of water then taking plates from the cabinet and silverware from a drawer. He picks up a stack of dishes and walks to the small table on the other side of the kitchen. I follow him with two glasses of water, setting them on the table then grabbing the other two. By the time the table is set, Mrs. Young has platters and bowls of food on the counter.

"Go get your father," she says to Ellis, carrying a platter of fried chicken to the table. I pick up a bowl of green beans and a bowl of mashed potatoes, handing them to Mrs. Young when I reach the table. She seems like the kind of woman who has a special spot for each dish. While she places them on the table, I get the platter of rolls and the bowl of corn. "Thank you, Jagger. Such a nice young man. I hope you can teach Ellis some manners. He needs a lesson in helping his parents."

Is she fucking kidding me? The first thing Ellis did was jump in to help. She didn't even ask him to set the table. He *offered*. I stay quiet and wait until Mr. and Mrs. Young are seated. Ellis points to one of the remaining empty chairs, and I drop onto it while he takes the other one. The table is a small, round four-seater, but somehow, his mom managed to get all the food on it.

Mrs. Young uses the tongs to choose one piece of chicken then picks up the platter and hands it to her husband. I wait for Ellis to put food on his plate and pass the dishes to me. I'm not sure what the etiquette is here. At the Ward house, it's usually buffet style and a free for all. Between my brothers and brothers-in-law, there's usually a shoving match to get to the food and sometimes elbows and fists enter the mix. We don't hurt each other, but we all know the food will be gone if we mess around and take too long to fill our plates.

Once our plates are full, everyone starts eating. The silence is like nails on a chalkboard. It's absolutely horrible and sending my nerves into overdrive. I don't think there has been a second of silence since Law was born. I'm assuming it was quiet for the three years when Lex was an only child. All I know for sure is it's been a mad house as long as I've been alive.

"How is work?" Mr. Young asks gruffly when his plate is almost empty. "Still working at that damn bar?"

"Work is good. Yes, I'm still working at Paradise 11. Have you seen the new Current and Coast restaurant downtown?" His parents both nod.

"It looks expensive, especially for a beach town," his dad grunts out.

"It is upscale, but the prices are reasonable. Ryan owns it, and I work the brunch shift there on the weekends." His mother perks up at those words, sitting taller in her chair.

"Oh, how wonderful. I'm surprised Ryan offered it to you with your limited skill set, but that's good news nonetheless." Condescending bitch. I keep my mouth shut, but I'd like to say a few choice words to his mother. Ellis flinches slightly but recovers quickly and takes another bite of potatoes. How many times have words like that been thrown at him for him to have such a small reaction? If either of my parents ever said something like that to me, it would break my heart.

"Jagger, tell us about yourself. What do you do for work?" his mom turns the conversation to me.

"I'm an artist," I answer smugly. "I own a glass-blowing studio in Orange Grove."

"Oh, an artist. How exciting! You must be very talented *and* smart to own your own business." Ellis practically chokes on his food. She can't be serious. Ellis has told me how unsupportive his parents were when he wanted to go to art school, and now they're acting like me being an artist is the greatest job out there.

"It's a lot of work, but I love my job." I set my fork on my now empty plate and place my elbows on the table, resting my chin in my hands. I smile at Ellis, knowing this move is probably frowned upon in this house. I can practically hear his mom scolding him for putting his elbows on the table, but she doesn't correct me. "You know, Ellis is very talented. His paintings are incredible."

"He's always been a dreamer. Dilly dallying with paint and making a mess." His mom's annoyed tone grates on my nerves.

"Yeah, I had to repaint and re-carpet his room after he moved out," his dad adds. "Everything had paint on it. Even the furniture. Cost us a fortune, purchasing new furniture for that room."

Ellis deflates next to me. For a brief moment when I spoke, he looked hopeful. Then his parents squashed his dreams all over again.

"He has a studio now where he can paint and be creative." I skip the part about me gifting him the studio. They will turn that into something negative for sure. "He has been asked to do an art show in a couple of weeks. His paintings will be the prominent feature of the exhibit. And a gallery in Tallahassee recently sold two of his paintings for a great price," I smile as I speak.

"An art show? What exactly does that mean? No one is going to pay to see a room full of his paintings," Mrs. Young sneers.

"Mom—" Ellis starts, but she cuts him off.

"Don't get upset. It's my job to keep you grounded. I don't want you to be disappointed if no one comes to see you. Art shows are for famous, talented people."

"The show is almost sold out. They had a hundred and fifty tickets to sell and well over a hundred have already been sold." I reach into my pocket and pull out two tickets. "In fact, I would love for the two of you to be my guest." I offer the tickets to his mom. Hesitantly, she accepts them.

"Well, we will try to be there," Mrs. Young states in her snooty voice.

"His paintings will be for sale. He will have a beautiful one of a sunset over the beach that would look lovely on that wall." I point to the empty wall behind Mrs. Ward, using the word lovely because she's said it several times since we arrived.

No one responds to my comment about the painting and the urge to smack some sense into both his parents is strong. His father leaves his dirty plate on the table and shuffles back to the living room. His mother starts clearing the table. Ellis and I stand at the same time and start picking up dishes and carrying them to the sink. While Mrs. Young puts away the leftover food, Ellis starts loading the dishwasher and I sit back at the table with nothing to do.

Once the kitchen is clean, Ellis and I say our goodbyes. It's time to get him out of here. I can't stand to be here any longer. I can't imagine how he must feel.

"Thank you for dinner. It was delicious."

"You are welcome, Jagger. Come back any time. I am so impressed with you and your entrepreneurial spirit." She squeezes my arm. "And thank you for all the help today."

"Mr. Young, it was nice to meet you. Have a good afternoon." He grunts a goodbye from the couch without taking his eyes off the television.

"Bye, Dad. Bye, Mom. Dinner was yummy as always." How can Ellis sound so cheerful after that debacle?

"Goodbye, dear." She leans close to Ellis but speaks loud enough for me to hear. "I hope you don't run him off with your depressing trailer and bad job. I think Jagger will be a good influence on you."

"Truthfully," I jump in, not allowing Ellis to respond. "Ellis has been the good influence on me. He's helping me with new ideas for glass pieces. As I said, he's very talented." Fuck, I'm tired of these two people saying whatever they want to Ellis.

I grab him by the hand and pull him to my truck, not giving his mom a chance to say anything else. He has heard enough and so have I.

Ellis climbs into the truck without a word and his entire demeanor changes. He slumps into the seat and sighs heavily. He lets me hold his hand as I drive out of the neighborhood, but he's staring out the window, refusing to look at me. That was the worst 'meet the parents' situation I have ever been in. They are horrible to Ellis, constantly belittling him and making him feel like he's worthless. No wonder he has such a hard time believing in himself and his talent.

We were there almost two hours and neither of his parents touched him. No hugs. No back pats. No arm squeeze. Nothing. Now I understand why he is always touching me, not that I'm complaining. I love when Ellis holds my hand, places a hand on my back, touches my leg when we sit next to each other, and cuddles up to me on the couch or in bed. I can't get enough of his hands, and I always want to have mine on him. Like right now, I can't even drive without his hand in mine. It feels empty and lonely when we aren't touching. I will spend the rest of my days making sure he is never touch-starved again.

Them not even hugging their son was bad, but they never once said 'I love you,' 'good job,' or 'I'm proud of you.' His mom gave me plenty of compliments and even thanked me for helping when Ellis did a shit ton more work than me. But did she thank him? Hell no. How can they be so blind to their son's talent, kindness, and love. And so unsupportive?

"It's okay, Jagger. They're old." Ellis' voice is hollow, and my heart breaks for him.

"It isn't okay." I say calmly even though I'm seething

on the inside. "You deserve to be treated so much better. Don't let their words or lack of support get in your head. You are one of the most talented people I've ever met. Your paintings are better than most of the ones currently hanging in Gallery Expresso."

He scoffs at my words. I want to argue and beat my words into him until he believes me, but that isn't going to help. Ellis has to accept his talent in his own time. One day, he will see what other people see. If I tell him what I see and others show him by buying his artwork then one day he will see the truth and his parents' words will be buried deep inside him.

Ellis' phone vibrates in the cup holder. He let's go of my hand and picks it up, reading something then gasping.

"Eleanor had the baby! OMG, she is the cutest! Nicky said she is allowing visitors at the hospital for the next two hours if we want to meet the baby."

"What do you want to do?" I was planning on taking Ellis home and wrapping him in my arms for the rest of the afternoon, but I'm happy to make a pit stop at the hospital. I don't know Eleanor, but she's part of the Paradise 11 group, so I will leave it up to Ellis.

"I want to meet her. I love babies. But I'm wrung out from dinner and want to go home, each some junk food, and go to bed."

That sounds like the perfect way to spend the rest of the night.

CHAPTER 34

ELLIS

J agger has been extra attentive these past few weeks. Between my mental breakdown then dinner with my parents, he has been hovering, constantly checking on me, and making sure I'm eating and taking care of myself. I appreciate it, but honestly, I'm fine.

After I lost my shit and freaked out over the art show, I felt better. More grounded. Creative took over and the paintings started pouring out of me. It was amazing. Every time I finished a painting, my confidence increased, and I was able to create another one. Selling two paintings at Creative Connection helped also. Mr. Klein requested four more, so I brought those to him last Sunday. One has already sold.

As for my parents, dinner really showed me that they will likely never support my art dream. On some level I knew this, but I held out hope. I haven't talked to them since dinner, and I doubt they will come to my show even though Jagger gave them tickets, but I am still going to enjoy my day. My friends will be there, Jagger's family is coming, and, of course, Jagger will be by my side.

The show is set up and ready. Jagger and I went by the studio earlier today and made sure everything was all set and to see if Mindy needed anything else from us. The displays looked beautiful and having a nautical theme was a great idea. My paintings combined with Jagger's glass pieces make a gorgeous scene. When we came back to Jag's apartment to get dressed, the caterers were arriving to set up the food and bar. The show starts at six and we need to be there about fifteen minutes early.

Ryan gave Megan and Matt the night off so they can come to support me on opening night, and he is bringing Nicky. I'm excited to have my friends with me. Chelsea and Grayson promised to come see the show while it's on display over the next week.

Strong arms wrap around me as I stare at myself in the mirror trying to decide if my outfit is too much. "You look amazing," Jag whispers against my ear.

I meet his eyes in the mirror. "I don't know. What if my parents are there?"

"How do you feel in these clothes?"

"Sexy. Confident. My figure looks fabulous!" I tell him honestly.

"That's all that matters. You feel good." Jag kisses my cheek then trails his nose along my jawline before turning my head so our lips can meet. I part my lips, opening for him. He dips his tongue in, searching mine out. His hands thread into my hair as he turns me in his arms. I grip his shoulders with both hands, digging my fingers in and moaning into his mouth. "And you look damn sexy," he says into my mouth.

Slowly, I turn back to the mirror and Jag rests his chin on my shoulder. "Wear skirts more often. I am one hundred percent into it. I want to see more of this." He rakes his eyes down my body and lets out a low growl. "On second thought, I want to see less of it on you and more of it on the fucking floor." He pushes his erection against my thigh, letting me know just how much he loves what he sees.

"Thank you. I like the way I look and feel in this, but other people might not like it." My insecurities are getting the best of me.

"Fuck them. I dare one person to make a negative comment." The edge of anger in Jagger's tone is a clear challenge and one I know he'll follow through on if given the chance.

I chuckle softly. "Okay, caveman, let's go before I decide to change clothes."

"If anyone is mean to you, I'll show them just how 'caveman' I can be." Jag hugs me against him and kisses my cheek before letting me go.

We both grab our wallets, keys, and phones before walking the short distance to the gallery. Mindy has been a dream. She's knowledgeable, kind, and easy to collaborate with. She took care of everything. All we had to do was create and deliver our art. She also involved us in every step, allowing us to approve food and drink options and placement of the art.

Jag squeezes my hand as we step through the back

door of the studio. "I'm so proud of you," he whispers right before Mindy greets us. I beam as I face her.

"Perfect timing. We'll be opening the doors soon. We sold the last fifteen tickets at the door and are expecting a full house," Mindy gleefully claps her hands. "We did have to turn away about ten people unfortunately but offered them free admission to the exhibit any day this week. Congratulations on selling out your first art opening, Ellis. That's quite an accomplishment. You are going to do great things."

"Thank you." I manage to get the words out, but they are choked. My eyes sting with unshed tears. I never imagined this day would come and I certainly didn't believe the tickets would sell out. A supportive boyfriend and sold out art exhibit... these are things I never believed would happen to me.

"Go ahead into the gallery and grab a drink." She motions to the doorway leading to the next room. I don't move. Suddenly, I'm frozen in place and can't breathe.

Jag turns me to him. "Breathe, baby." When I don't respond, he cups my cheek, and I snap my eyes to his. "You're going to be amazing. The work is done. Tonight is about you enjoying yourself and what you've created. That's all."

I take a stuttered breath then another. Finally, I get in a few deep breaths and start to feel my body relax. "I'm ready."

Jagger takes my hand and leads me into the gallery, stopping at the bar to get a glass of wine for me and water for himself. I sip the wine as the doors open and the crowd starts to filter inside. Some people head for the bar or table of hors d'oeuvres, others start looking at the artwork, and a few walk toward me. I take another deep breath as a gentleman in a dark jeans and orange polo steps up, holding out his hand.

"Fredrick Carson," he states, shaking my hand. "Do you mind if I ask you a few questions and take some photos?"

I stall for a second and my brain goes completely offline. Jag nudges my back gently and I notice the man has a press badge.

"Um, yes, of course," I respond in a voice a few octaves too high

We step away from the crowd and Fredrick pulls out a notepad. Jag stands between us and the crowd, giving us a little privacy.

"First, I want to confirm the information I have is correct. Your name is Ellis Young. You are twenty-one and from Anchor Point."

"Yes, that's all correct."

"Great. I write for an online artist blog called Art Connect. I'd like to run a story Monday. Will that be okay?" he asks.

"What will the story entail?" I ask, surprising myself. I hope it's alright to question him.

"I will include personal information like name, age, where you're from, and your background. I will also include my experience at the opening and personal thoughts on your work."

My stomach plummets. He's going to write his opinion of my art. That might go horribly wrong, but then again, anyone in here can post something negative online.

"Okay," I agree.

"Excellent. I know you live in Anchor Point? Were you born there?"

"Yes. I've lived there my entire life."

"Is it somewhere you plan to stay or do you have big city dreams?"

"I love Anchor Point, but I also feel at home here in Orange Grove. I can't see myself living somewhere like New York City." I glance at the back of Jagger's head. I'll never move away from him. "I plan to continue living in Anchor Point or moving to Orange Grove."

"What would keep an artist here?" he asks.

"Anchor Point is my home. I love the beach, and my friends and family are there. Orange Grove has a thriving art community. There are larger cities like Tallahassee, Orlando, and Jacksonville that are a short drive away. I'm young and just starting out. I want to explore my art and learn who I am as an artist and how I fit within the art community before I consider a life-changing move."

"Wow, that's very smart and insightful. How did you get started with art? What inspires you?" he continues.

"I've loved art for as long as I can remember. As a kid, I was constantly drawing and painting. Even as other kids outgrew finger painting and elementary art classes, finding different hobbies in middle and high school, art stuck with me. It's always been a part of me and something that grounds me. When I create, I feel at peace." My words are true, but I'm not sure where they are coming from. These aren't things I've actively thought about, but as I say them, I know it's my truth.

Fredrick asks me questions for another ten or fifteen minutes then he takes a few photos of me in front of some of my paintings and one with Jagger and me. Once he disappears into the crowd, I lean into Jagger. That was exhausting. I've never been interviewed. Before I fully recover, several other people come over and tell me how much they love my work. Jagger stays by my side the entire time but talks about his art if someone asks or if I mention it. This is his show, too, but he truly is making the night about me.

He only agreed to be part of the show because I was too scared to do it alone. He even scaled back the number of glass pieces he's showing, so the focal point can be my art. I appreciate his love and support so much more than I can possibly put into words.

Over the next hour, Jag's family comes to tell me how much they love my art, Megan and Matt are here and rave about my paintings. I've seen Ryan, but we haven't had a chance to speak. It's been a whirlwind, but I'm happy with the turnout and positive words from everyone. For the first time, I feel supported and seen by someone other than Jag.

Taking a moment for myself, I walk over to Matt and Megan. Talking to all the guests and reporters is overstimulating, and I need a moment to decompress.

"Ellis," Megan gushes. "I always knew you could do this! I'm so proud of you!" She hugs me tightly and I kiss the top of her head.

"Thank you, Megan." Standing between her and Matt, I glance around the crowd still perusing my paintings. "I'm so shocked that the show sold out! Have either one of you overheard what people are saying?" I'm not sure I want to know the answer, but the question is out there now.

"Ellis, trust me, I've heard nothing but great things," Matt reassures me.

"He's not lying," Megan agrees. "Be right back. I want to grab a refill," she says, holding up her champagne flute and waving it. "Ryan's my DD, so I can partay on my night off!"

As she beelines for the bar, I turn back to Matt. Lately he's been acting out of sorts. I brushed off the weird interaction right before Christmas and the marks I saw the following month because he still seemed like himself— upbeat and happy. But I'm getting worried. I only see him during my brunch shifts now that he's working at the restaurant, but since April, things seem to have gotten worse. He avoids any real conversations, his smile feels forced, and he's evasive when you ask him simple questions like, 'What are you doing this weekend?' or 'How was your night?' Something is definitely off.

Matt reaches up to scratch his neck and moves the fabric of his shirt to the left. That's when I see it. Several bruises along his collarbone that look like they dip below his shirt. Glancing down, I also see a thumb-shaped bruise on his forearm.

"Hey, Matt. What's up with your neck?" I ask him,

hoping something weird happened at work like he bumped into something.

"Wh-what are you talking about?" he stutters out, adjusting his shirt to cover the bruises. When my eyes fall to his arms, he crosses them.

"Are you sure everything is alright?" I probe a little further. I am past the point of concern and in full worry-mode.

Jag chooses that moment to walk up behind me and wrap his arm around my waist. I relax into him, turning and kissing him quickly. When I look back to Matt, I find him halfway across the room, rushing out the door. I move to chase after him, but Jag holds me in place with his arm.

"Another time, baby. Tonight is about you," he whispers into my ear. I want to argue, to tell him what I saw, but I honestly don't know the truth, so I let it drop.

"Ellis," Mom's voice shocks me. My eyes widen as I stare at them. Jag moves to my side, smiling as he faces my parents.

"Mom, Dad. Thank you for coming."

"Yes, well, it was nice of Jagger to give us tickets. You didn't tell us he was showing these exquisite glass pieces." She looks at Jag. "You are truly talented."

"Thank you, Mrs. Young, but today is about Ellis. This is *his* art opening. I was just fortunate enough to be invited to include a few pieces. If you notice the name on the wall, it's Ellis Young." Jagger's words are nice, but I can hear a little bite in them, and my heart swoons. He's all sexy when he sticks up for me. Mmm, I love when his caveman side comes out.

My mom ignores Jag's comments and keeps her focus on me. "We just don't want you to throw your life away because you think coloring is going to make you money. You aren't a real artist, Ellis." Wow, stabbing me in the chest would hurt less.

"Your mother is right," Dad jumps in before I can respond to Mom. "Your art is good, but this is still not a future. It's time to get serious. Take some notes from your boyfriend. Jag is a good influence. He has direction and a future. I just hope it lasts with you two. We have told you for years that no man is sticking around if you are poor, unfocused, and work dead-end jobs. It's time to grow up, Ellis."

"Now wait just a damn minute," Jagger starts, but is cut off.

"No, son," Jag's mother's voice comes from my left. I glance over and see Joy with a hand on his bicep shaking her head. "These are Ellis' parents, and you are not to be disrespectful."

Great. Is everyone against me? Jag was going to stick up for me, but his mother won't let him. Does she think he can do better than me, too?

"At least, she sees the truth," my mother mumbles.

Joy pins my mom with a glare. "I in no way said I agree with you. We have spent time with Ellis on several occasions. He is focused, smart, and talented. Our family adores him, and we are thrilled Ellis and Jag are together. Your son works harder than any twenty-one-year-old I've ever met. Certainly, harder than any of my children did at his age. Ellis is a talented artist and is in the middle of his first art opening. That is a huge accomplishment and something he, and you as his parents, should be extremely proud of." Joy turns to me and says, "I am proud of you, Ellis. Your art is gorgeous. Thank you so much for including our family in your special day. We'll see you on Sunday for dinner." She kisses my cheek then tells Jagger goodbye and leaves.

My parents are shocked silent for a minute. Before they can say anything, Mindy approaches. "Ellis, congratulations on a wonderful opening. Please stop by my office before you leave. I would like to speak to you about another show and a position at the gallery's summer camp, starting in two weeks."

"Wow, yes! I'll stop by. Thank you." She nods with a smile and turns to go, but Jagger stops her.

"Mindy, do you happen to know off-hand how many paintings Ellis sold tonight?"

Mindy looks a little confused and my stomach drops. Zero. I bet the answer is zero and my parents are going to know they were right all along. I'm not an artist. I'm a failure."

"They all sold, and several people inquired about commissioning work from him." She smiles at me. "Congratulations, again. You are going to be a *huge* success in the art world."

My mom looks like she's been slapped. It might be wrong but seeing that look on her face brings me great joy.

CHAPTER 35

JAGGER

After my mom and Mindy praised Ellis, his parents didn't have much to say. They half-heartedly congratulated him then left. I know he's disappointed by the way they treated him, but I hope the success of the show overrides their negativity. He was hard to read before he went into Mindy's office. As much as I wanted to go with him, I stayed behind. This is the start of his art career, and he is more than capable of handling it himself. I don't want me following him to offer moral support to be misinterpreted as him thinking I don't believe in him or his ability.

By the time he comes out, I'm surprised I haven't worn a hole in the floor where I've been pacing. I can't wait to find out what Mindy offered him.

He looks happy, no, more than happy. He looks ecstatic. "Ready?" I ask, grabbing his hand and pulling him against my chest and kissing him quickly. "I'm so proud of you and can't wait to hear all about your talk with Mindy, but only if you want to share."

"Yes, I want to share!" He pulls me toward the door. "I'm starving. I need you to feed me."

"Oh, I have something to feed you," I tease.

"As much as I want to eat your dick, I need actual food first." I adjust myself as we step onto the sidewalk. Damn, his dirty mouth turns me on. That and the thought of shoving my cock down his throat. "Problems?"

"Nope," I lie with a pout.

"Don't worry. I promise to take of that for you as soon I get some food."

"Well, maybe not as soon as you get food. Getting arrested for fucking in a restaurant is not on my bucket list."

"You know how I love public sex. How about in the bathroom or the alley behind the restaurant? I'm easy."

I stop in the middle of the sidewalk and flip him around until we are nose to nose. "You are only easy for me," I growl possessively. "And quit talking about fucking before I drag you to the first semi-private place I can find and shove my cock inside you without any prep."

Ellis cocks his head to the side. "One, that isn't the threat you think it is. Two, why do you think I brought a small purse. It does look fabulous with this outfit, but I also tossed some lube in it, just in case." Without giving me a chance to respond, he saunters toward the row of restaurants in the next block, swaying his hips as he goes.

It takes a second for me to catch up with him after he leaves me stunned on the sidewalk. When I get to him, I hesitate to take his hand. I'm already worked up and touching him always gets me going. I walk in silence beside him, willing myself to calm the fuck down. I can't go into the restaurant like this.

"Are you mad at me?" Ellis questions, but then he looks at my face before glancing down at my crotch. "Oh! Never mind." He winks and smirks, clearly proud of himself.

I'm sure the expression on my face is pained, and I'm trying my best to get my erection to go away. If his response is any indication there is no way to hide how turned on I am. And now Ellis knows how much the idea of public sex excites me. It isn't something I ever thought about, but since he blew me on the beach months ago, all I can think about is when and where we can fuck.

We end up at an all-night diner. It's one of our favorite places for a late-night meal or middle of the night cravings after sex. After we order, I look at Ellis expectantly. "Tell me! I can't wait any longer."

"You heard Mindy say all twenty-four paintings sold. She didn't tell me how she priced them. She just asked me to trust her, so I did. The smaller ones sold for two hundred each, the larger ones sold for five hundred, and those two massive canvases sold for a thousand a piece. One. Thousand. Dollars. Jagger, I made over ten thousand dollars tonight. Can you believe it?" he squeals.

"I absolutely can believe it. You are extremely talented."

"She wants me to do another big show in six months, but in the meantime, she said she wants a few pieces to keep on display. She also said Mr. Klein stopped in tonight and was *very* impressed. He is going to contact me about doing a show at his gallery with a small group of up-and-coming artists."

"That's amazing!" I'm happy for Ellis. He deserves this.

"It's scary. That's a lot of paintings."

"Does she want twenty-four again?"

"She actually wants at least forty but thinks I should do some smaller ones that can sell for a hundred each."

"It only took you about nine weeks to get ready for this show."

"Yes, but I already had eight paintings done."

"And six months is a lot more time than nine weeks," I remind him.

"True. I already told her yes, so there's that." He smiles with a shrug.

Our food arrives and the conversation wanes as we both shovel it into our mouths. I went for the burger and fries, it's my go-to comfort food. Ellis order waffles covered in strawberries and whipped cream.

"She also mentioned summer camp. What's that about?" I ask

"Oh, she wants me to work at the summer art camp. She thinks I'll do a great job teaching the kids how to paint. I can't start until the second week because I have to quit my call center job and fill out some paperwork for a background check. I also have to take a class online this week about working with kids and what's appropriate and what isn't."

"Ellis, that's great! I'm glad you'll be able to quit the call center job. Working at an art camp will be a lot of fun for you. We'll have to compare art camp stories."

"Deal. I'm excited! The hourly pay is the same as the call center. There will be fewer hours since camp is only from eight to one. But since it's summer, tips should be better at the bar. And I'll have the money from the art show, so I should be fine. I guess I'll see how the summer goes. If I need another job, I'll worry about it then." It's been less than an hour and Ellis has already thoroughly thought this through.

"I'm sure you'll be fine. Do you have a budget?"

"Hell, no. Do I look like I have a budget? I pay my bills first, but then I spend the rest on clothes or eating out or other frivolous things. Plus, I have some debt I'm trying to pay off. I never save money."

"Can I help you make a budget?"

He thinks about my offer. "Sure. If you think you can stretch that ten k so I can stay away from call centers, I'm willing to listen. It would be nice not to have to take another job after summer camp ends."

"We'll figure it out, so you don't have to work anymore shitty jobs." I reach over and take Ellis' hand. "I love you. You were amazing today."

Ellis squeezes my hand in return. "I love you, too. Thank you for everything— the art show, my parents, all of it. What?" That innocent 'what' sends me over the edge and a few tears fall down my cheeks.

"You said you love me."

"I *do* love you. I love you so much, Jagger. I was going to say it at a more private, intimate moment, but I couldn't wait any longer." A huge grin spreads across his face.

I slide out of the booth and scoot into the other side next to Ellis, kissing him slowly, lingering longer than I should in a restaurant, but I don't give a shit.

"Let's get out of here." I pull Ellis from his seat, stopping at the front to pay the cashier then we're heading to my apartment. "Ryan wants to meet us at Current and Coast Sunday at eight. He said he has something he wants to run by us both before your shift."

"Yeah, okay," Ellis agrees.

As we pass the alley that runs behind the restaurant we just left, I pull Ellis into the shadows and push him against the wall. "Where's the lube?"

"Uh, in my bag." He fumbles for it while I use the time to undo my pants and pull my cock out. As soon as he produces the small packet, I take it from him, coating myself with a few strokes then pushing his skirt up.

My eyes snap to his, and I find a smug smile and heated eyes staring back at me. "No underwear. Nice touch." I lift Ellis and he wraps his legs around me. It's awkward, but I'm able to get a finger inside him, working him open.

"It's enough. Come on." I know he can take me without much prep, but I don't like to see the pain on his face when he isn't properly prepped. "Jag, I need you." I remove my finger and line my cock up with his hole. Slowly, he works himself down on me, pausing to breathe through the pain.

"We can stop if it hurts."

"All good." He sinks down more then moves up before gliding down further. With my hands holding him up, he works himself up and down my cock. "Fuck, that feels good." I try to move my hips with his rhythm, but it's difficult in this position. It doesn't matter. He clenches his ass around me as he moves, drawing me closer and closer to orgasm with every movement.

"Yeah, baby, ride me." Ellis adjusts his hips slightly, letting out a strangled moan when I hit the spot. "Is that it?" I ask, voice husky.

"Yes. Again." I hit the same spot with each thrust of my hips. "Harder," he begs, moving down my cock as I slam my hips up.

"I'm close, baby."

"Me, too, Princess." When I bite down on Ellis' neck, he cries out as he clenches his ass and comes undone, I can feel his release hit my wrist. As soon as he tightens around me, I lose control and fill him. I lean us against the wall as I pull out of him. We both pant, trying to catch our breath. Ellis drops his legs, but I keep my arms around him, making sure he doesn't fall.

"Let's go home," I say, straightening his skirt and fastening my pants. All I want to do is fall asleep with Ellis in my arms, right where he belongs.

CHAPTER 36

ELLIS

J agger met me at my trailer last night. He was waiting for me when I got off my shift. I was so thankful not to have to drive all the way to Orange Grove. We don't always spend the night together but, as the weeks pass, it's becoming more and more common. The late-night drives to Orange Grove are grueling.

He came to me last night since we have to be at Current and Coast so early this morning to meet with Ryan. I'm dragging. Between the hours I've been working and the art show, my tank is on empty. I need a day off, but that isn't happening any time soon. After my brunch shift, I have to meet Mindy at the gallery to sign some paperwork then we're having dinner with Jagger's family.

"Princess." Jagger shakes me gently.

"I'm awake. I just closed my eyes to rest."

"Come on. We're here."

Huh, maybe I did doze off on the short drive to the

restaurant. I don't remember Jag parking. I blink a few times and stretch then follow him out of the truck. Ryan is walking up to the door in front of us. He unlocks it and waits for us to catch up. When I step inside, I stop in my tracks. A large painting of the beach with waves lapping the shore and the sun setting in the distance hangs on the wall behind the hostess stand. My painting. One that sold for a thousand dollars Friday night.

"It looks beautiful there, doesn't it?" Ryan says.

"Ry... I... Wha?" I can't form words. What do I even say?

"I've been looking for something to hang there since we opened, but nothing was quite right. When I saw this, I knew. It's perfect. The colors match the aesthetic of the restaurant, and since it has land and water, it works with our name," he explains.

"Thank you, Ryan." I finally look at him with damp eyes. "This means so much to me."

"You're very talented, Ellis. I'm proud to have your painting on display. Let's sit. There are several things I want to talk to you two about."

"Good morning," Grayson greets us as Ryan leads us to a booth near the back, where three mugs, a carafe of coffee, a three glasses of water wait.

"Mornin'," Jag returns.

"Hey, Grayson," I add with a small wave.

"I'll be right out with some food." Grayson leaves us for a few minutes while we all take our seats.

Nerves chomp at me. This feels all business-y and formal. What is happening? I venture a glance in Jag's direction, but he's relaxed like this is all perfectly normal. Grayson returns with several dishes of food and three empty plates.

"Looks delicious, honey. Thank you," Ryan tells Grayson. He pulls his boyfriend down for a kiss then Grayson disappears into the kitchen to prepare for the brunch crowd.

"Please, dig in. I'm going to go ahead and get started while we eat so Ellis can get to work when we open," Ryan starts. "Ellis, do you have a brochure or rack card about you and your art with contact information?"

"What? No. Is that even a thing?" I feel stupid. Are those things I need?

"It's fine if you don't have anything. I know you're just starting out, but I also know people are going to ask about the artist when they see that painting. When you have time to put together something, bring me a stack and I'll leave them at the hostess stand. A business card is fine, too."

"Oh, yeah, okay, I can do that. Thank you," I mutter my reply.

"The other thing I want to discuss with both of you is an idea I have for an art district here in Anchor Point. I want to create something similar to what Orange Grove has, but on a smaller scale. I am considering two locations, either the line of stores across the street that are still empty from Hurricane Nichole or the south end of the boardwalk. I personally think either could work. The stores across the street would require a complete gut, but the buildings are there. They are stable and already have utilities. The south end of the boardwalk is completely empty, so the building would have to be built from the ground up. Thoughts?" Ryan asks while eyeing both of us curiously.

"I think Anchor Point would benefit greatly from something like this," Jagger states. "I like the idea of revitalizing this area around the square. People tend to flock to the boardwalk already. Downtown could use something to help draw people in."

"That's a good point." Ryan mulls over Jag's idea.

"What types of stores or galleries are you thinking about?" Jagger asks. I'm completely lost and not sure why he needs me here. Jagger knows what to do. He owns his own studio and works in a thriving art district already.

"I'm hoping to bring in a few art galleries, maybe an educational studio, a café, and some smaller spaces artists can rent. Those spaces would be open so the public could see the artist at work."

"Do you have potential artists to fill these spaces?" Jagger questions.

"I spoke to Mindy on Friday, and again yesterday, when I picked up my painting. She's interested in expanding and opening a Gallery Expresso here. I want to offer both of you a store or studio space. Both, if you prefer." Ryan's offer is generous, but I have no idea what to do.

"Me? A store? I don't think my art will sell enough to warrant a store."

"It will sell. I think you more than proved yourself on Friday," Jagger tells me.

"I agree with Jag. You're an incredible artist, Ellis. I also want you to design the logo and paint a sign for the art district. Eleanor is going to do all the marketing."

"This is a lot to think about," I say, averting my eyes.

"Ellis is right. Can we take some time to discuss everything? I'm concerned about the number of hours Ellis is already working. Adding any of this to his plate might not be feasible." Part of me is happy Jag is sticking up for me, but the other part is a little hurt and offended. I *can* do this. I *want* to do this. My art dream is coming true and he's going to squash it.

"Absolutely! Take some time. Ellis, if this is something you want to do, we can discuss cutting hours here or at the bar. Or you can quit one or both. Look at all your options and decide what you want most," Ryan offers me a lot to consider.

"Thank you," is all I say. I want all of it, but I'm going to have to choose. There really is no way I can do it all. I have bills to pay, and art isn't a steady income. I can't physically do it all, so I'm stuck keeping the serving jobs and giving up on my art. "I need to get to work." I offer a fake smile, kissing Jagger on the cheek then heading to the back to clock in.

I'M EXHAUSTED by the time we head toward Jag's parents' house for dinner. The brunch shift was busy with an hour wait forty minutes before closing. The hostess was turning people away at one-thirty and the last group on the waitlist didn't get seated until almost three and we usually close at two. Needless to say, it was after four before I could leave work and had to push the meeting with Mindy back, which made us late leaving for dinner.

I don't know what Ryan is going to do, but something's got to change. It's great that Current and Coast is seeing so much success after only being open for three months, but having brunch run long cuts into happy hour. I heard him and Grayson talking about revamping some things, but I don't know what they are planning.

"You look worn out," Jag says, starting the truck and taking my hand. "We can skip dinner. My family will understand."

"No, absolutely not. I am not canceling on your family at the last minute. They will hate me for keeping you away from them."

"They would never hate you. I stayed away from family dinner for years and they still love me."

"They're your family. They're stuck with you. No one has to like me."

"Ellis, you're exhausted. You can't keep up this schedule," Jag nags.

"I know," I snap, voice full of venom. Jag cuts the ignition. Staring out the window, I refuse to look at him. If I do, I'm going to break down completely.

"Talk to me, baby," he encourages softly.

"Nothing to talk about. I can't add anything else to my already busy schedule."

"You have to make some choices because you can't

do it all," he agrees. "But you can change your current jobs for something different."

Closing my eyes, I let the first tear fall. "No, I can't." My voice cracks on the words, and my shoulders slowly begin to shake. I try to keep the crying at bay, but there's no use. I can't stop myself.

Jagger unbuckles my seatbelt and pulls me across the bench seat until I'm practically in his lap. He wraps his arms around me and breathes me in, causing me to relax against him. I always feel safe and protected in his arms.

"What do *you* want to do?" he asks softly.

"Go to dinner, sleep, get up and go to work. Repeat forever. Die."

"Alright, drama queen," he teases, but I don't laugh. "Ellis, what do you *want* to do? Forget about bills and money for a minute and think about what you truly want. Don't even think about repeating some bullshit your parents fed you."

"I don't know," I whisper.

"Yes, you do. Stop being infuriating and answer my question."

I hate being called out when I'm acting like a child. Instead of answering Jagger, I want to leave him sitting here alone while I run back to my car and drive home to wallow in self-pity. But I choose to behave like an adult. "Artist. If I didn't have to worry about money, I'd choose all the art things— gallery shows, art district, my own storefront. But it doesn't matter what I want. Money is the problem, and I have bills to pay."

"Would you quit working at Paradise 11 and

Current and Coast if it meant you could do all the art things?"

"Maybe. I mean, I'd have to. It's just that I love those jobs so much. Part of me hates to even think about giving them up."

Jag opens the driver's side door and pulls me the rest of the way across the seat, setting me on the ground. "Come on." He nods his head toward the front of his apartment building.

"Jag, we have dinner. We're already like super late."

"We aren't going. I texted my mom and told her I was tired and had something I needed to take care of. We'll go next week."

"You lied to your mother for me?" I question, completely taken aback.

"I am tired, but not nearly as exhausted as you are, and I need to take of you. No lies. I just chose not to put the blame on you. I know my family will under-stand, but I also know it will bother you if you feel like you let them down."

Jagger knows exactly how to make me swoon and fall harder for him without even trying. I follow him into his apartment, ready to fall into bed.

CHAPTER 37

JAGGER

Ellis looks completely distraught. He trudges slowly behind me as we make our way to my apartment. His hands are stuffed in his pockets and his shoulders are drawn inward. He's closing himself off from me and I fucking hate it. All I want to do is fix everything for him. I want him to be taken care of and happy. I will do anything to make that happen.

When we get inside, I walk toward the bedroom, pausing briefly at the door. "Have a seat on the couch. I'll be right back." Without a word, or even a glance in my direction, Ellis collapses onto the couch. I walk through the bedroom to the ensuite bathroom and turn the water in the tub on, waiting for it to get hot before plugging it and pouring in some lavender-scented bubble bath. My mom always did this for us when we were kids and had a shitty day. It would help me relax and feel better no matter what happened.

Now I keep it under the sink and use it when life

gets me down. I hope it helps Ellis as much as it helps me. Once the tub is full, I go to the kitchen and make Ellis that sweet, fruity drink he likes that has vodka, grenadine, pineapple juice, and Sprite. I make one for myself without the vodka and carry both to the bathroom.

Walking back to the living room, I strip off my clothes as I go. Ellis looks at me but doesn't question why I'm naked. I pull him to his feet and strip his clothes off then lead him to the bathroom. I test the water to make sure it's not too hot before I step in, reaching for Ellis' hand. He puts his hand in mine and climbs in. After I sit down, I situate him between my legs then hand him his drink and pick up mine.

We sit in the tub, sipping our drinks until Ellis finally lets go and sags against my chest. Took him long enough. I was starting to think he was immune to my mom's magic lavender bubble bath.

With my free hand, I rub circles on his stomach. "Let's talk this through, Princess. I have an idea that I think can work. In order to pursue your art with the gallery shows and the art district, you have to quit your other two jobs. I know you're worried about money, and I'm not discounting that for one second. It isn't easy to start an art career, but you have someone to help who has been there." I pause while I sip my drink. Sometimes I wonder if it would be easier to say things if I drank alcohol because right now my nerves are waging a full-blown war in my stomach. "There is something I've been wanting to ask you for several weeks, but I was waiting for the right moment. Please listen to this next part, Ellis. What I'm going to ask will help your situation, but money is *not* the reason I'm asking. It was a decision I made before any of this art stuff was a possibility."

"Um, okay, I'm listening."

"I want you to move in with me." Ellis sucks in a breath, but I continue before he has a chance to speak. "We spend most nights together already. Living together will save us both on rent and utilities."

"No. I'm not taking a handout." Ellis tries to move away from me, but there is nowhere for him to go. The tub is small, and we barely fit, so it's easy to hold him in place.

"You didn't listen. This is not a handout. This is me asking my boyfriend, the man I love, to move in with me. You will pay your way. I'm not offering to be your sugar daddy."

Ellis laughs suddenly, and it's the best sound I've heard all day. "Ew, never say 'sugar daddy' again."

"How about 'daddy?'" I goad, hoping to hear him laugh again. It works, he laughs then makes a gagging sound.

"Nope. No way. Never."

Setting my glass down, I wrap both arms around him and kiss along his jaw. "I love you, Ellis, and I want to live with you. My apartment is bigger, but if me moving into the trailer is the only way you'll say yes, then I'm there."

"What's the rest of the plan?" Ellis is getting interested in my idea. This is a good sign.

"Well, I think you should keep the camp job. For

now, ask Ryan to cut back your bar hours, but keep working brunch at the restaurant. The money you make from painting sales will help make up the difference. It will take time for the art district to get up and running, possibly six months to a year. That gives you time to have at least one art show. We can cut costs by eating at home. Save as much as you can and when the art district opens, quit working at the bar and restaurant so you can focus on your own storefront and studio. Maybe we can share a storefront to cut down on rent."

"That all sounds nice, but I still feel like it's a dream. What if I can't make enough money with my art?"

"Ellis, you'll never know unless you try. Ask Ryan if he can keep you on as a filler like when people go on vacation or are out sick. If you pick up a few shifts a month, it will help supplement your income."

"It's scary. But it's also exciting. It would be great to make money with my art."

"You already make money with your art. You can do this, Ellis. I believe in you."

"Thank you."

Ellis stays still for a long time, sipping his drink and relaxing against my chest. He still hasn't answered my question, but I don't push him. He needs time to process everything. He's had a lot thrown at him these past few days. I can't imagine the rollercoaster of emotions he's feeling from the highs of selling out his show and Ryan offering him a space at the new art district and wanting him to be a part of the planning to the lows of listening to his parents' negativity and him feeling like his dream in unachievable. After long minutes of silence, he finally speaks.

"I'm getting cold." Okay, not what I expected, but the water is chilly.

"Can you pull the plug?" He reaches down and yanks out the white disc, setting it on the side of the tub.

I stand up, pulling him to his feet and turning us so I can block him from the spray. After pulling the shower curtain closed, I turn on the water, flinching when the cold downpour hits my back. I hold Ellis in my arms until the water turns warm then I move so he is under it. Taking my time, I wash his body and hair, not lingering in one spot for too long. This is about taking care of him, showing him my love, not getting us off. That can come later. Once he's clean, I quickly wash my own body and hair. I try to hurry, so Ellis doesn't get cold, but it takes a few minutes to rinse the shampoo from my long hair. Once I'm clean, I turn off the water and dry Ellis then myself.

In the bedroom, I pull on a pair of gym shorts and a t-shirt then hold out a pair of gray sweats. Ellis steps into them, letting me dress him. I pull one of my favorite t-shirts over his head. I like the way he looks in my clothes. Note to self, make him wear my clothes more often.

After we're both dressed, I lead Ellis back to the couch where I leave him while I grab our glasses from the bathroom. In the kitchen, I make him another drink and pop a frozen pizza into the oven. While the pizza cooks, I join Ellis on the couch. I don't like silent

Ellis. I usually know exactly how he feels because when he doesn't say it with words, he says it with his face. I love that Ellis hides nothing. But right now, he's hiding everything. I can't read him at all and it's killing me.

"Dinner will be ready soon." It's the only thing I can think of to break the unbearable silence without pressuring him to give me an answer.

"Okay. Thanks," he replies absently.

"Do you want a snack while we wait?" This is more awkward than our first date.

"No." he rests his head on my shoulder. "Thank you for taking care of me. The bath was nice. Smelled super great."

"Lavendar. It reminds me of my childhood."

"Hmm, that's nice."

"Ellis, I will always take care of you," I assure him, doing my best to keep the worry out of my voice.

"I know. I love you, Jagger." He sits up and turns pulling one leg onto the couch and taking my face in his hands. "Like I really love you so damn much it hurts. I've been kidding myself, thinking this was some fleeting thing, but it isn't. I'm completely and totally in love with you."

"Good because I'm in love with you, too. You're it for me. I wasn't lying when I said I want to marry you one day."

"I want to say yes to the living with you, but I need a little more time to think about it. Is that alright?" His shaky voice breaks my heart. I hate seeing this unsure side of him. The one that still believes he isn't good enough.

"Of course. I will never pressure you to do something you aren't ready to do."

"Thank you." Ellis crashes his lips to mine. The beeping oven timer interrupts our make-out session. I could spend the rest of the night on the couch kissing Ellis. He looks better, more relaxed. He still needs to rest, but at least he's thinking rationally now and looking at what he truly wants rather than all the crap his parents have filled his head with. Reluctantly, I sit back and smile at Ellis.

"I'll bring the food over. Do you want another drink?"

"No, thanks. Just some water."

While I get our plates, I keep watching Ellis. How did I get so lucky? I love that man so damn much. And I'm going to spend the rest of my life showing him.

CHAPTER 38

ELLIS

I t's been three days since Jagger asked me to move in with him, and I've made three excuses not to see him. After spending Sunday night at his apartment because I was too tired to drive home, I've been a chicken shit and basically ignored him. I've responded to his texts, but I haven't seen him. Monday night, I told him I was still tired and needed to do some cleaning up at my trailer. On Tuesday, I told him I wanted to stay at my place, but not to drive over because I had to be in early on Wednesday. Like that's ever stopped us from seeing each other. Tonight, I'm hanging out with Nicky after work. I texted Jagger and told him I had plans with work friends, which technically isn't a lie. I *do* work with Nicky. He started working at Current and Coast not long after we met. Jag told me he was going to his parents' house for dinner and spending the night at the house he owns on their property.

I know I'm being dramatic and probably mean, but

I don't know what to say to Jagger. It's easier to ignore the situation completely than to confront it.

"Ready?" I ask as I walk into the back office.

"Yep. Where are we going?" Nicky asks.

"Most everything is closed, so how about we hang out at my trailer? You can crash on my couch, or I can drive you home later."

"Cool." When we pass Ryan on the way out, Nicky slaps his back. "Gonna hang out with Ellis. Probably crashing on his couch. Don't really know yet. You and Grayson can be as loud as you want. Just don't fuck in the kitchen." Nicky makes a gagging sound and Ryan looks mortified.

"Okay," he finally chokes out.

When we get to the end of the pier, Nicky pulls out a vape and takes a long drag. He blows out the smoke before he gets in my car. "Want some?" he offers.

"No thanks."

"Probably smart since you're driving."

"Wait. Is that a weed pen?"

"Is that a problem?" He looks at me warily as if second-guessing this entire friendship idea.

"Not at all."

"So... weed good, nicotine bad?"

"Something like that. I'll take a hit when we get to my place if you're crashing."

"Got any beer?"

"Yeah."

"If we can party, I'm all for crashing on the couch. Ryan will go all 'dad' on me if I come home drunk and high. I can't even smoke on my break because Grayson will tell Ryan." Nicky takes another hit and blows the smoke out the window. "Where's your boyfriend? Y'all still together?"

"We're together."

"Nice. Where is he tonight?"

"Home. Well, not home exactly, but sort of."

"That makes no sense, man. Am I high as fuck already? Damn this shit's good." He holds the pen out, lazily examining the cartridge. If it's that good, I'm definitely taking a hit or two.

"No," I say through a laugh. "It's not you. I mean he has a house on his parents' property. He's there tonight. He has an apartment in Orange Grove where he lives."

Nicky turns so fast, he almost chokes himself with the seat belt. "Let's go there."

"Where?"

"To Jag's apartment. We can raid his fridge, and you can be there all romantic-like waiting for him in the morning."

"How will you get home?"

"Figure it out tomorrow." He waves his hand, blowing off my question.

"We can't break into his apartment." As I argue with Nicky, I pass the turn for my road and head in the direction of Orange Grove.

"We *can* break in," he retorts.

"We *shouldn't* break in," I amend.

"You know you passed your road and this bridge we're on takes us off the island and in the direction of Orange Grove?"

"I'm aware."

"It's pretty easy to convince you to commit a crime. I wonder what else I can get you to do?"

"I have a key." I choose to ignore his comment and all the innuendos with it.

"Score. Do we need to stop and buy alcohol or does he have some?"

"He has plenty." Jagger might not drink, but he keeps alcohol on hand for his friends, siblings, and me.

The closer we get to Orange Grove, the more I question this decision. If I was already high, there would be no doubt in my actions. I make shitty decisions when I'm high, which is why I rarely smoke. But tonight, I've already passed the bad choice threshold, so I might as well go all in. It will be fun for Jag to find me in his bed... right?

The drive passes quickly with Nicky rambling on about crazy people who come into the restaurant and me questioning my life choices, but by the time I park in front of Jagger's building, my nerves have disappeared, and adrenaline runs through me. I take a hit off Nicky's pen then lead him to the elevators and up to the eighth floor.

Nicky finds his way to the kitchen and starts opening cabinets, the pantry, and the refrigerator, pulling out liquor, mixers, glasses, and a shaker as he goes. For someone underage and from a strict, religious family, he knows his way around alcohol. He places two shots in front of me and pours two for himself. I don't bother asking what it is before tossing one back then the other.

Taking another hit from his pen, I park myself on

one of the barstools and watch Nicky mix a bunch of ingredients together. He even muddles fresh strawberries, blueberries, and mint in the bottom of the glass before adding ice, coconut rum, and club soda. He hands one to me, holding up his glass to cheer me. I clink mine against his then take a sip.

"Yummy. That's fucking amazing," I gush.

"It's one my faves. Fruity and delicious."

"Like meee!" I squeal, spinning on the barstool. Okay, maybe I took too many hits. Every time I mix alcohol and weed, I get all hyper then crash hard. Nicky laughs at my antics then plops himself on the stool next to me.

"What do you want to do?" His voice is low and conspiratorial.

"Besides drink?" Laughter bubbles out of me. This is fun.

"Yeah. Is there anything fun to do here?" Nicky glances around the space. "It kinda looks old and boring. All 'adulty' like Ryan's place. Oh, fuck! Are we going to be old and boring before we're thirty?" Nicky dramatically throws his hand over his forehead.

"No! That will never happen to us. And I can assure you, Jag is not old and boring." I wink at Nicky.

"Do tell. Is the sex fire?"

"Yes! The best sex I've *ever* had. And I've had a lot of sex. He's so hot with his muscles and long, curly hair." As I think of Jagger's defined chest and lickable abs, my jeans tighten a little.

Nicky suddenly hops off the stool, taking our empty glasses to the counter, tossing some concoction into the shaker before pouring the liquid into our glasses. This one is an orange color.

"What's this?"

"Coconut rum, vodka, orange juice, and Sprite.." I take a sip. Dang, he makes a yummy drink. "Your boyfriend has so much stuff. He must like to try new concoctions."

"He drinks the juices for breakfast. He doesn't drink alcohol but keeps stuff here for me."

"He doesn't drink alcohol at all? Like never? Is he an alcoholic or something?"

"Nope. Never. He just doesn't like it." I leave it at that, choosing not to share Jaxon's story. It isn't a secret, but I don't feel like talking about anything sad.

Nicky sucks down his drink and makes himself another one before I finish my second. Then he starts opening drawers and searching through stuff.

"What are you doing?" I ask.

"Let's snoop. Find out what kind of man Jag really is. See if he has any secrets."

Nicky leaves the kitchen and walks to the living room before I have a chance to respond. He searches the entertainment center but only finds video games and a photo album. He brings the pictures to the couch. Carrying my drink with me, I flop down beside him. The album is old and worn like it's been looked through a hundred times.

He opens to the first page where there is a picture of his family. I recognize his mom immediately, and when I look closer, I see a baby version of Jagger, two actually.

"Who are these people?" Nicky asks, pointing to the picture.

"Jag's family." He keeps flipping without questioning me further. It's a glimpse into Jag's entire life. More pictures of him and his siblings at different ages fill each page. Some are group photos, and some are individual. Apparently, Jag and Jax both wrestled in high school, and damn, he looks good in that tight uniform.

"Your boyfriend is a twin. *Hot,*" Nicky says, voice filled with lust. I snap the album closed and take it from him.

"Enough of that." My words come out strained and clipped.

"Come on. Twins are hot. Do you ever get them mixed up? Have you fucked them both?"

"No," I bark, shoving the album back on the shelf where Nicky found it. There is no reason for me to be this upset. Nicky doesn't know. "Sorry," I say on an exhale. "Jax, Jag's twin, died when they were seventeen."

"Oh, shit. I didn't know." For some reason, serious Nicky cracks me up, and I start laughing. Not a simple, quiet laugh. Nope. Full on fold myself in half, falling to the floor, belly hurting laugh.

"What's so funny?" Nicky asks as he starts to laugh, too. Next thing I know, he's on the floor beside me and we're both laughing like a couple of idiots. Minutes later, when we finally gain some composure, Nicky stands up and heads for the kitchen. "I need another drink."

"Me, too. Make me something pretty and fruity."

"Like you."

"Yes, queen!"

This time Nicky hands me another shot before giving me something in a tall glass. It's pink and sweet and I might need two of these.

"This one has coconut rum, orange juice, cranberry juice, genadine, and lime," Nicky explains.

"You should be a bartender. Delaci… delico…," I slur, trying to form the word. "Yummy," I finally say.

"Let's see what else we can find." Nicky grabs my free hand and pulls me into the half bathroom across from the kitchen, but it's empty except for basic items. He drags me to the master bathroom, where he finds some more interesting items, like lube, a large box of condoms we never used, and a plug. "So… which one of you takes this?" he asks, waving it in my face.

I grab it from him. "None of your business."

"You. I know it's you!" When I pin him with a glare, he holds up his hands. "I'm not judging. I like things in my ass, too. Anyway, you already told me you like to get fucked."

Nicky leaves me in the bathroom a little stunned, but the thud of an opening door pulls my attention to the bedroom. I find him sitting on the floor in the large closet. His drink is on a shelf, and he's taking a hit off the pen while using his free hand to open a box. I drop onto the floor next to him, accepting the pen when he offers it.

"Can I ask you something?"

"Sure." He flips through the box then puts the top

on and shoves it back under a shelf, pulling out another one.

"Jag wants me to move in with him." I glance over to see what's in the box, but it's just a few trophies and some award ribbons.

"That's cool." Nicky's focus is on the box, so I'm not sure he's listening.

"Do you think it's too soon?"

"How long have you been together?"

"That depends- fucking, dating, or actual boyfriends?"

"All of them?" Nicky responds but it sounds more like a question. Like he's confused by my answer.

"Fucking for six months, dating just over four months, and boyfriends for like three and half months."

"Okay, but even before you were boyfriends, you were hanging out and getting to know each other. We'll say six months then. That's not super-fast if you love him," he fires back with a shrug.

"I do love him, but shit is changing so fast. It's too much. My job is changing, I'm trying to do this art thing, Jag wants me here with him..." I trail off. "I guess, I don't want to lose myself or my independence. I've been taking care of everything alone for almost four years."

"You're afraid to let someone else have some of the power."

"Maybe."

"Do you trust him?"

"I do," I reply without hesitation.

"You are killing yourself, working constantly. I

barely know you and I can see the exhaustion on your face. You're getting burnt out, and it isn't healthy. If he wants you to move in and take some of the stress off you, let him." Nicky acts like it's such a simple solution.

I think about his words for several seconds as I take a few sips of my drink. He's right. "I thought you were supposed to be a dumb kid always looking for a good time, not a wise man passing out decent advice."

He ignores me and powers through his thoughts. "Even better if he wants to pay for shit." Nicky sighs with a grin. "Sugar daddies are God's gift to young, gay men. Damn, I need me a sugar daddy. I'd let him pay for everything."

"There it is."

"What?" I deserve to have a hot older man take care of me. I would make such a great house husband. My man can work, while I spend my days being pampered," he muses.

"I think the idea of house husband means *you* take care of the house while your man makes the money."

"Ew, no. I don't want to cook and clean all day." Nicky shoves another box under the shelf then pulls out a shoe box.

"What's that?" The box is full of cards with different colored envelopes. Nicky opens one then another one. He shifts through them quickly.

"Birthday cards."

"Birthday cards?" I grab one out of the box and open it. It's dated February 16th. "He had a birthday and didn't tell me."

"You don't even know how old your boyfriend is." Nicky rolls on the floor, laughing his ass off.

"It's not that funny."

"It's hilarious." Nicky eventually gets control of himself and finds another shoebox to search. "Jag really does have a bunch of nothing in here. All these boxes are like taxes and business stuff. Boring" he singsongs the last word. "Well, except for the secret birthday stash. Ellis, your boyfriend is a stand-up guy. Like he's one of the good-" Nicky stops talking mid-sentence and gasps.

"What? What is it?" Panic rises in my chest. What kind of bad shit did he find?

"Nothing." Nicky slams the shoebox closed before I can see what's inside. "It... it's not bad. You don't want to see it."

My heart plummets. Whatever is in that box *has* to be bad. Why would he be acting so weird if it was good? I grab the box from him, pulling the top off and tossing it onto the floor, forcing myself to look inside even though I'm terrified.

What is this? I pick up each item, reading the information, and digging through the entire box. "Nicky," I breath out. Heat floods my body as I begin to shake. I blink back tears. "He, this is a ring. Is he going to propose?'

Nicky picks up a piece of paper and holds it up so we can both read. "Seems so. In like ten days. Dolphin cruise, ring, one night stay at a fancy hotel. Looks like he has a fun night planned," Nicky chuckles holding up a blindfold, some zip ties, and a plug. "Also, why did he print everything? He knows phones are a thing. There are apps for this stuff. Are you sure he's twenty-five... oops, twenty-six?"

"Jag wants to marry me," I whisper, ignoring Nicky. "Fuck, I'm being such an idiot. For days, I've been freaking out about living with him because I can't fathom someone wanting to be with me all the time, and he's planning a freaking proposal."

Nicky carefully takes the box from me and puts everything back inside then slides it onto the shelf. "What are you going to do?

"I don't know."

"Do you want to marry him?"

I consider his question for a minute. I'm completely in love with Jagger. I want to spend my life him. "Without a doubt."

"There's your answer. Move in with your man and when he pops the question say yes. Nicky finishes his drink and hops up. "Now, come on, I need another one."

We stumble out of the closet a little more wasted than I felt while sitting on the floor. When I walk out of the bedroom, I smack right into Jagger's broad chest.

An audible gulp escapes me. "Fuck. Jag! What are you doing here?"

"I think the better question is what are you doing here?" Jag's eyes narrow on me. His tone is strained, and I can feel the anger rolling off him.

"We were just hanging out. Remember, I told you I was hanging out with work friends. This is Nicky, he's my work friend," I rush the words out then hiccup a bunch of times as my stomach churns.

"I know who Nicky is, but I don't know why you two are in my apartment."

"Are you mad? Sorry. I didn't think you would mind. I was going to be all sexy and in your bed in the morning when you came home. You know naked and waiting!" I run my fingers down his chest, hoping my words sound sexy and tempting, but then I hiccup again and dry heave.

"And where was Nicky going to be?" Jag bites out through gritted teeth.

"Oh, um, on the couch." Nicky is cracking up behind me, making it hard to focus on Jag and my freak out and whatever apology... oh, yeah! Apology, that's what I'm doing. Damn, my brain hurts. "I'm sorry, Jag. We shouldn't be here. We can leave." I start to step around him, but he stops me.

"You two are wasted. Completely fucked up. You aren't going anywhere." He points to a chair and says, "Sit there and wait for me." I do as I'm told while Jag tells Nicky to go the couch. A few minutes later, Jag is handing a glass of water to Nicky. He waits until Nicky drinks it all then he covers my friend and tells him to go to sleep.

Once Nicky is situated on the couch, Jag takes my hand and leads me to the bedroom, closing the door behind us. He strips me down to my underwear and helps me crawl into bed. He makes me drink a glass of water, too, then climbs in next to me and covers us both.

"I'm sorry, Jag."

"Shh, get some sleep. We can talk tomorrow."

CHAPTER 39

ELLIS

When I blink open my eyes, it takes me several minutes to adjust to the light and remember where I am. My head is killing me, my mouth is dry, and it tastes disgusting. Suddenly, last night comes flooding back. I feel like there are some missing pieces, but I remember the gist of it. Nicky and I got blitzed. Fucked out of our minds. And not in the fun, sexy way.

"Oh, shit." We snuck into Jag's apartment, snooped around, found a ring, and got caught. A few hours ago, I was happier than I've ever been, but today, I'm likely getting my heart crushed. Jag isn't going to want me anymore. I broke into his home. That's unforgivable. "What the fuck were we thinking?" I mumble. My stomach lurches as I groan and roll over.

The bed next to me is empty and cold. Jag's been up for a while. Hell, he probably got up as soon as I fell asleep. I doubt he wants to be near me. When I sit up, I find a glass of water and two Tylenol on the bedside table. I take the pills and slowly get dressed. After I go to the bathroom and make sure I have my keys, wallet, and phone, I slowly walk to the closed door, taking a deep breath before I face whatever is on the other side. Hopefully, Jag is gone, and I can slink back to Anchor Point and forget last night ever happened. Jag won't be forced to break up with me in person and I won't have to face his disappointment.

When I creak open the door, I hear voices. Fuck my life. Jag and Nicky are in the kitchen. My stomach rolls at the smell of frying bacon. I turn around and run back to the bathroom. By the time I finish emptying the contents of my stomach, Jag in sitting behind me, rubbing my back.

"Get it all out, baby." I dry heave a few times then collapse against his chest. He hands me a cup of water and wraps his arms around me as I take a tentative sip. "Are you okay?"

"I think so. Sorry. The smell of bacon got me."

"If it makes you feel better, Nicky spent most of the morning in the other bathroom."

"We both deserve it." My stomach churns again, but this time nothing comes up.

"Stupid choices get you stupid prizes," Jag mumbles behind me. "My dad always said that when we did dumb shit growing up and had to face the consequences."

"It's not wrong. What were we thinking?" I cover my face with both hands. Jag is the last person I want to see this morning, but I feel warm and safe in his arms. I hope this isn't the last time he ever holds me.

"You weren't," Jag teases. "I'm glad you did that here and not somewhere, else. Please don't ever get hammered like that unless you are with me or safe at home." Jag's voice hitches and my heart constricts. He's probably thinking about Jax. *Good job, Ellis. You're an idiot.*

"I won't. It was dumb and I'm paying the price today." I groan. "I hate feeling like this."

"Let's get some food in you. It will help."

"No bacon," I pout as Jag helps me to my feet.

"No bacon," he agrees.

Leaning heavily on Jag, I let him walk me to the couch where I drop down, pulling a blanket over myself. Nicky comes over and joins me while Jag goes back to the kitchen.

"You look like I feel," Nicky grumbles.

"I feel like ass."

"Me, too." Nicky covers himself with half of my blanket.

"Do you think he hates me?" My voice breaks on the quiet words.

"Not at all." Nicky glances over to where Jag is busy in the kitchen. "I don't even think he's mad. Definitely worried, but not angry."

"I hope this doesn't change anything. I thought he was going to kick me out this morning."

"Nah, he won't do that. He loves you."

I clamp my mouth shut when Jag heads our way, he hands us both a plate with toast and grits. "Thanks," I mumble.

"Eat every bite." He sets two glasses of water on the

coffee table. "And drink all the water. Nicky, when you're finished, I'll call you an Uber."

My heart constricts a little at that. With Nicky here, Jag and I don't have to talk about last night. I can live in my bubble of bliss where everything is perfect, and I didn't do something stupid that might make my boyfriend break up with me. If Nicky leaves, I will be forced to face reality and whatever Jag has to say.

We eat our food in silence while Jag cleans the kitchen, which looks better than it did last night. Nicky looks at me with pity in his eyes, but he keeps his thoughts to himself. He has to see the fear in my eyes. I don't know what's going to happen when he leaves, but I guess it's a good sign that Jag isn't sending me away, too.

"It's gonna be okay. He loves you," Nicky whispers, taking my empty plate and carrying it to the kitchen with his own.

I burrow further down into the couch cushions and pull the blanket all the way up to my chin while Nicky and Jag talk quietly.

"Princess." My body is gently shaken awake. My head feels foggy as I blink open my eyes. Jag stands over me, smiling down. I must have fallen asleep. "Hey, how are you feeling?"

"Um, better. Where's Nicky?"

"He left almost two hours ago."

"Two hours?"

"You fell asleep. I hated to wake you, but you need to eat and hydrate. You also should call your boss. I know tomorrow is your last day, but you didn't show up at the call center."

"Oh, shit. What time is it?" I forgot I still have a day job.

Jag picks his phone up from the coffee table. "Uh, ten after two." Well, it's too late to worry about my call center shift, but I have time to get to the bar.

"I'm up." I stretch and yawn. My head feels better and my stomach growls. That's a good sign. "I'll take something to go. My shift starts at three, so I have less than an hour to drive home, shower, get to work."

"You need to call in."

"What? No! I have to work." Staying here and getting my heart ripped to shreds is also not at the top of the to-do list for this afternoon.

"We have to talk, and you need some more rest."

"I've been hungover before, Jag. I can work." My words come out a little harsher than I mean for them to, but this is the whole reason I'm hesitant to live with him. I can make my own decisions and pay my own way.

"I know you can work, but I think we need to talk about last night. At least shower here and let me drive you to work. Then I'll pick you up later. Or call and ask Ryan if you can come in an hour or two late."

Dropping my shoulders, I concede. "Let me text Ryan and see what he says then I'll go take a quick shower."

"Thank you. I'll make us some lunch." Jag turns for the kitchen as I force myself off the couch. He turns back and steps into my space, cupping my cheeks with his strong hands. "I love you, Ellis. We need to talk about what happened last night, but it doesn't change how I feel about you or me wanting you to move in with me." Then he kisses me quickly, pressing his lips to mine, but not pushing his tongue inside. Yeah, I don't blame him. I haven't brushed my teeth today. I feel kind of gross all over. A shower is a smart choice.

I fire off a text to Ryan as I walk to the bathroom.

> Me: Hey, so, I need a huge favor.

> Me: Had a rough night and feeling sluggish.

> Me: Can I come in a little later? Like 6-ish?

WHILE I WAIT FOR A RESPONSE, I start the shower and open Jag's dresser, searching for something to wear. A sense of dread and guilt wash over me. I can't believe Nicky and I snooped through his apartment. What the fuck was I thinking?

I find a t-shirt and pair of gym shorts. They will be loose, but at least these have a drawstring I can tie to hold them up. I'll need to swing by my place to change into jeans and a Paradise 11 shirt.

Then I remember I have to contact my asshole boss at the call center. I hate him so much, so I text instead of making a call. He's going to be an ass either way and I really don't care if I burn a bridge. I'll never go back to work there.

> Me: Personal emergency. Sorry I didn't text sooner.

> Me: I won't be in tomorrow.

I decide the last part on a whim. Tomorrow is my last day and I have no desire to log in and deal with six hours' worth of calls.

> Asshole: Fine. Don't expect a recommendation for any future job.

I don't bother responding. His recommendation is meaningless to me, so why engage? Ryan still hasn't responded, so I take a quick shower, letting the warm water relieve some of the tension. After I brush my teeth and dress, I check my phone again, finding a response from Ryan.

> Ryan: Yeah 6 /6:30 is fine.

> Ryan: You doing ok?

> Ryan: Nicky feels like shit.

> Me: Tired.

> Me: Just need to handle something with Jag.

I don't bother responding to the Nicky comment. It's not my place to talk to Ryan about Nicky, and if he starts asking questions, I might accidentally say something that Nicky won't appreciate. Ryan might be my boss, but Nicky is my friend, and he trusts me.

When I get back to the other room, Jag has two

plates of food and two glasses of water on the coffee table and he's waiting for me on the couch.

"Feel better?" Jag asks, reaching out his hand to me. Taking it, I let him pull me onto the couch. He positions me right next to him and passes me a plate.

"Yeah. I needed that." My stomach growls loudly at that exact moment. "I need this, too." Holding up the sandwich, I take a big bite. How does Jag make something as simple as a ham sandwich taste delicious? "I'm really sorry about last night," I say around the bite of sandwich.

"No more apologizing. You made a mistake. You apologized. I forgive you. But I do want to know why you and Nicky were here."

"It was stupid. He was high and we were going to go to my house. Then I said something about you not being home, and Nicky had the bright idea to come here, so I could surprise you and be in your bed when you got home. It would have worked better if you hadn't come in the middle of the night." I pout, hoping it comes across cute and innocent.

"Were you high in the car?" His words are clipped and terrified. He hates it if anyone drives under the influence.

"No," I assure him. "I was high and drunk when you got home, but I didn't do anything until we got here." I take another bite of the sandwich mostly to have something to do. This conversation is making me nervous and I'm slowly losing my appetite.

"Good. Please never drive when you're smoking or drinking."

"I won't. I promise."

"Let me see if I understand. You two came here to get wasted, so you could surprise me in bed? What was Nicky going to do?"

"Crash on the couch." I shrug.

"How romantic," he teases. "My hot, naked boyfriend completely fucked up, waiting in my bed with his friend passed out in the next room," he deadpans.

"We might not have thought through all the details."

I shove the last bite of sandwich in my mouth and lean over to put the plate on the table, but almost drop it when Jag says, "Did you find anything interesting?"

"What?" I choke on the food in my mouth.

"Drunk Ellis doesn't clean up after himself. Or maybe it was Nicky snooping." Jag pursues his lips and taps his chin thoughtfully.

"Shit. I'm so sor-" Jag puts a finger over my mouth.

"Do *not* apologize."

My shoulders drop as my body deflates. "It was Nicky's idea, but I didn't try to stop him. I was on board. I don't know why. I trust you, but it seemed like a good idea. I never meant to break your trust or break into your apartment."

"I will tell you anything you want to know. Hell, if you ask, I will let you go through every drawer, cabinet and box in this apartment. I have nothing to hide from you, Ellis."

"I know," I whine. "It was dumb and I hate myself—"

"Nope. You're not doing that. Do not get down on

yourself. You made a mistake. *One* bad choice. That's it."

"How can you not be angry?"

"Oh, I was. When I walked in, I was pissed. But taking care of you was more important than anything else. Enough people have put you down and made you feel less than or worthless. I am not going to do that to you. Ever. No matter what. After I made sure you and Nicky were both safely sleeping, I got some rest, too. I waited until I was calm and you were sober, so we could have a rational conversation." He tips my chin up and kisses me. "I love you, Ellis."

"It won't happen again. If I want to know something, I will ask."

"Did you find anything interesting?" he asks again.

I think about telling him I found the ring, but instead I say, "You had a birthday."

Jag lets out a long sigh. "I did."

"Nicky found it quite hilarious that I didn't know how old you were."

"We weren't together then. Celebrating my birthday is hard for me. I prefer letting the day pass like any other."

"It was the day you came to the bar, and I was so mean to you."

"The two have nothing to do with each other."

"But I ruined your birthday." Jag wraps his arms around me and pulls me onto his lap, so I'm straddling him.

"You did not ruin anything. Those cards are in a box for a reason. My family insists on acknowledging my birthday, so I indulge them. We're together now. That's what matters."

"Nicky says you're boring," I blurt out.

"Boring," he gasps, grabbing his chest in mock offense. "I am *not* boring."

"Mmm, I know. Nicky probably doesn't think you're boring since he found the plug in the bathroom."

"Serves him right." Jag lightly scrapes his nails up and down my arms. "Can we talk about you moving in?"

"You still want me to live here?" Shock doesn't begin to describe how I feel. How can he still want me after what I did?

"More than anything. It was torture not seeing you for three days. I hate being away from you." The neediness in his tone is turning me the fuck on. I've given him so much push back on... well, everythin— dating, being boyfriends, and now living together. The truth is, I love him and want to spend my life with Jag.

"I'm ready. When Nicky and I were sitting in your closet, looking through boxes of taxes and boring crap, I realized how much I truly want to live here and be with you all the time. I love you so much."

"You're sure? We're going to live together?" he asks, sounding unsure. *Super. Way to make your confident boyfriend insecure.*

I wiggle on Jag's lap, letting him feel how sure I am. Cupping his neck in my hands, I look him directly in the eyes. "I want to live with you, Jagger. You are the only person I want. You're the first person I have ever seen a future with. You see me. You support me and that never wavers, no matter what dumb shit I do. The whole saving money thing is an added bonus. For the first time, I truly believe my art dream can come true."

Jag crashes him mouth to mine, kissing me deeply, never breaking contact as he stands and carries me into our bedroom.

CHAPTER 40

JAGGER

Sunday morning, I wake up with Ellis wrapped around me. His left arm and leg are slung over my body and he's practically lying on top of me, snoring softly. He so fucking adorable when he sleeps with his vibrant, pink hair sticking up at all angles, and a trail of drool puddling on my chest.

Once Ellis was on board with moving in together, everything else fell into place. At first, he wanted to wait to move because his landlord won't let him break the lease, so he has to pay rent for one more month. It took some convincing, but he eventually agreed not to wait. I want him with me in our bed every night, but it isn't right for him to have to pay double everything for an entire month because his landlord is a douche, so he isn't going to pay rent and utilities here until August.

I helped him pack up his trailer and we moved everything here in an afternoon. Living in a trailer, the furniture stayed behind, which is fine since I have a fully furnished apartment.

We moved the art supplies still left in the trailer to his studio. I cleaned out my dresser and closet to make room for his clothes. It's a tight fit but will work for now. His dishes were all mismatched items he bought at discount stores and garage sales, so he opted to donated all the kitchen stuff.

As much as I want to stay like this for the entire day, nature calls. Carefully, I wiggle out from under my boyfriend and go to the bathroom to take care of business. When I come out, he's still sleeping, so I go to the kitchen to start a pot of coffee. Ellis sleeps like the dead until the smell of food hits him. Then he'll be up and ready to go. That boy can put away some food.

It's been over a week under the same roof, and I can't wait to spend my life with Ellis. The plans I made for today will secure our future together. Hopefully. Part of me is terrified that this step is too big and too soon for Ellis. I don't want to scare him off, but he is it for me and I want to make it officially official. It's a silly saying between us, but when we first became boyfriends, it's what we said. Now it's time for the next step in our relationship. I just hope I'm not rushing Ellis or putting too much pressure on him.

Breakfast is almost ready when a naked, disheveled Ellis appears at the counter. He's half asleep, looking completely wrecked with dried cum on his chest from last night. We fell asleep before we were able to clean up. Last night, we were too cum drunk and exhausted to care, but this morning, it feels gross.

"Good morning," I greet him, passing a mug of hot water and the basket of tea bags across the bar to him.

"Officially official day one eighteen." I love counting the days we've been together. And today is going to be one of the best so far... hopefully.

"Morning," he mumbles back with a grin, choosing his tea and dipping it in the hot liquid.

Walking over to him with a damp cloth, I wipe the cum from his smooth chest and kiss him on the cheek. "You look hot as fuck still dirty from last night." Ellis blushes and playfully pushes me away as his cheeks and ears turn pink. That look when he gets all embarrassed and shy as if he's some young virgin, does something for me. How can someone with the words 'cum slut' tattooed on him be so shy sometimes? It baffles me, but I secretly love this about him.

After tossing the cloth in the hamper, I wash my hands and finish preparing breakfast. "This is nice," he muses with a content sigh. "It's all domestic and shit, but I love it. Being here with you. Living here. This is going be perfect." I'm not sure if he's talking to me or trying to convince himself he made the right decision.

"It already is perfect. I love having you in my space. Our space. You belong here." I place two plates with crustless veggie quiche and fresh fruit on the counter.

"Do you want to put on some pants before we eat?"

Ellis' eyes flick to his soft cock and he giggles. "BRB!" He bolts to the bedroom and comes back a few second later, pulling on a pair of fuzzy purple pajama bottoms. These have sex toys all over them. He returns to his seat at the counter with a blissful look on his face.

"I do belong here." His eyes brighten and he starts to

perk up as he eats and sips on his tea. It always takes Ellis a little while in the morning to get going. He needs a cup of tea and about a half hour.

"I have a surprise for you."

"You do?" Ellis drops his fork and claps his hands. "Tell me. I love surprises!"

"After breakfast and a shower, pack a bag for one night."

His face falls. "But I start working at camp tomorrow."

"I promise you will be at Gallery Expresso on time."

"Okay. I can't be late on my first day."

I kiss his cheek as I stand and pick up our plates. "Why don't you go pack while I clean the kitchen then we can shower together," I suggest.

"Oooh, shower sex?" he asks with a quirked eyebrow.

I lean in close to his ear and purr, "If you're a good boy, I'll let you choke on my cock." Ellis practically knocks me over with his enthusiasm for getting to the bedroom.

"I'll be good. Everything will be packed by the time you get you get in here," he calls over his shoulder running to the bedroom.

I clean the kitchen in record time. Visions of Ellis on his knees in the shower are running rampant in my mind and I'm painfully hard by the time I turn on the shower. While the water warms, I lean against the door jamb and watch Ellis zip his suitcase then strip out of his pants.

"Ready!" he squeals, pushing past me.

I quickly undress and join him. As soon as I step foot in the shower, Ellis drops to his knees. He braces himself with his hands on my thighs and sucks my cock to the back of his throat. My hands go to his head, holding him against me. Fuck, I love the feel of his mouth wrapped around me, the sounds of him gagging on my cock, and the sight of his nose buried in in my trimmed pubic hair. It's a heady combination. Hot as fuck.

I loosen my grip and he pulls back a little, inhaling deeply through his nose. He bobs up and down, hollowing his cheeks and sending me spiraling toward the edge. Grabbing the back of his head, I thrust into his throat, setting my own pace. He drops his hands to his side, letting me use him. Fuck, I love when he lets his body go limp, giving me complete control. I slam into him hard and fast, barely able to hear his whimpers over the water as my cock hits the back of his throat over and over.

"Look at me." His eyes snap to mine. Tears mix with the shower spray as I use him. "You take me so good." His eyes brighten with pride, "Such a good princess for me."

The look in his eyes— love, pride, lust— has me ready to explode. The way he responds to my words revs me up. Ellis is a slut for praise and dirty talk. No matter what I say, his body reacts to it and it's fucking hot. I rock into him a few more times then unload down his throat. He swallows my release before leaning back on his heels, working his own cock furiously. A few seconds later his release is running down the drain.

I help Ellis to his feet and wrap my arms around him. "Cum slut," I whisper against his.

"Only for you," he pants out.

———

LESS THAN AN HOUR LATER, we're checking into Nautilus, a boutique hotel in Ashton Bay— a small beach town just north of Anchor Point. Our room overlooks the gulf with a gorgeous view of the marina and water.

"Jagger, this is beautiful," Ellis muses, taking in the view.

The room is large with a king bed as the focal point. A large painting of sailboats hangs above it. There is a small couch and table. The bottle of champagne I ordered is chilling. I pop open the champagne and fill a glass for Ellis. Then pour water in the other flute for me. Taking Ellis' hand, I lead him to the balcony.

"I love you."

"I love you, too. Thank you for bringing me here. This is nice."

"Princess, this is only the beginning." We watch the boats in the bay while sipping our drinks for a few minutes. Ellis declines a second glass, so I cork the bottle and put it in the small fridge for later. "I will always take care of you," I promise with a kiss. "We need to get going. I have more surprises in store tonight."

"I can't wait," Ellis says excitedly.

We stroll hand in hand toward the marina. "Wait here," I tell Ellis outside of a small café. He looks at me with curiosity but doesn't ask questions, parking himself on a bench while I walk inside.

"Hi, welcome. Table for one?" the hostess asks.

"No. I'm here to pick up an order."

"I can help you with that. What's the name on the order?"

"Jagger Ward."

She types something on her screen then looks back up at me. "It's ready. I'll be right back." She disappears into the kitchen, returning quickly with a picnic basket. She sets it on a nearby table and opens it. Inside I find everything I ordered arranged neatly.

"This looks wonderful. Thank you."

"You're welcome, Mr. Ward. Enjoy your evening."

"What's all this?" Ellis asks, standing as I walk outside.

"This is dinner." We walk down the dock to the waiting boat.

"Mr. Ward, it's great to see you again."

"Hey, Captain Mac. This is Ellis." I introduce the two. I met Captain Mac a few weeks ago when I planned this excursion. He's been doing sunset cruises for over twenty years. He came highly recommended and is one of the few in the area that offers private cruises. I don't want an audience tonight.

"Welcome. Please come aboard." Captain Mac takes the basket from me as I offer a hand to Ellis and help him on the boat.

The captain already has a blanket laid out for us with a battery-operated lantern for later and the flowers I ordered. I set up the food and pour some white wine for Ellis. We sit down and enjoy our food while Captain Mac maneuvers us out into the Gulf.

"It will take us about fifteen minutes to get to the best spot for dolphin watching. Relax and enjoy the ride. I'll let you know when we arrive."

"Dolphins, food, wine, flowers," Ellis squeals. "What a great date!"

You have no idea, Ellis. Instead of saying that out loud, I smile and kiss him, slowly sliding my tongue inside. He tastes like wine and hummus, but I don't care. I deepen the kiss, threading my fingers through his hair and pulling him closer.

"I love you," he says, breaking the kiss.

"I love you, too."

We spend the next few minutes eating and enjoying the ride until Captain Mac stops the boat. It idles while he comes back to speak to us.

"We'll anchor here for a couple of hours. You'll be able to watch the dolphins and the sunset." I'll be on the bridge if you need anything. It's a little after seven. You have about an hour and a half before sunset. Then we'll head back to the marina around nine if that works, Mr. Ward."

"Yes, thank you."

Ellis and I move to the edge of the boat where there are seats turned to look out over the water. Within minutes, three dolphins surface then dive back under the water.

Ellis gasps. "Did you see that?" He sits up a little and leans closer to the edge as the three surface again. "OMG! This is so exciting."

"Have you ever seen the dolphins out here?" I ask

"Yeah, once when I was a kid. I've seen them from the beach tons of times, but only once from a boat and that was like thirteen years ago. My parents love the beach but aren't really boat people. 'We prefer the safety of dry land,' was my mom's favorite response any time I asked to go on a dolphin cruise."

"Then I'm glad I brought—"

"Jag, did you see that?" Ellis interrupts, grabbing my arm and squeezing. His face lights up like he's watching the most amazing sight. Another small group of dolphins surface right next to our boat.

"Yeah, baby. I saw."

"They're close enough to touch," he says in awe as the same group breaches the water. "Beautiful and majestic."

"Be right back," I tell Ellis. I fill a plate with some snacks— raw vegetables, hummus, salami, olives, and crackers, then grab the bottle of wine. After I refill his wine glass, I set the bottle down and return to my seat, holding the plate out to Ellis. He takes a carrot, dips it in the hummus, and pops it in his mouth then sips his wine.

We watch the water as the sun slowly starts to dip down. A few more dolphins put on a show while we enjoy the food. As the sun gets lower in the sky, I take the plate back to the blanket and nod to Captain Mac. As I return to Ellis, Captain Mac steps out with his camera, making sure to stay just out of Ellis' line of sight.

I pull Ellis to his feet and hold both his hands in mine. "Ellis, I love you so much. Our relationship has been a whirlwind, but I knew from the moment I met you, I wanted you. As I got to know you it became clear that I can't live without you. You are it for me and I want to spend the rest of my life making you happy." I sink to one knee as I pull out a silver band with a diamond in the middle and several smaller diamonds on either side. It's bright and a little sparkly. When I saw the ring, I thought of Ellis' personality and knew it was the perfect one. "Ellis, will you marry me?" Captain Mac takes pictures of the entire proposal. Tears fill Ellis' eyes then flow down his face. I'd be concerned if he didn't have a huge smile.

"Yes! Yes, I will marry you, Jagger." After I slide the ring on Ellis' finger, he holds his hand up and gets a good look at it. "Jag, it's gorgeous! I can't wait to show everyone! All my girlfriends are going to be *so* jealous."

Standing up, I pull my fiancé into a slow, lingering kiss. I'm going to marry Ellis Young. I might be the luckiest person on the planet. Nothing I said to him was an exaggeration. I knew from the first time we fucked in my studio, he was the man I would marry one day.

I break the kiss and cup his face in my hands. "I want a short engagement. Like I would marry you tomorrow, but I know you probably want to plan some things. I'm not waiting long to make you my husband."

"I can live with that. We should pick a venue and then take the first date they have available."

"Nautilus."

"What?"

"The hotel where we're staying has an event space. Why don't we get married on the beach in front of Nautilus at sunset and have a reception in their event space? It has floor to ceiling glass doors that all open to the beach."

"I feel like you've already planned the wedding," Ellis teases.

"I have some ideas, but I want *you* to have your dream wedding."

"A sunset beach wedding sounds a-may-zing!"

"Let's go back to the hotel and start making plans," I suggest.

"Only if we can discuss this naked in bed after my fiancé fucks me." Ellis waggles his eyebrows at me.

"That's the best idea I've heard in a long time," I agree.

Ellis rests between my legs with his back against my chest and my arms wrapped around him as we return to shore. After he was resistant to the idea of moving in together, I wasn't sure if asking him to marry me was too soon. He seemed genuinely surprised even though I know he and Nicky found the shoebox where I had everything hidden. I came home a little earlier than he thinks, but there's no need to spoil this magnificent moment. One day we'll talk and laugh about it. Tonight, I'm going to enjoy making love to my fiancé and planning our future.

For a long time, I didn't think I would ever find someone to love me the way I crave. And I never imagined finding a man like Ellis who deserves my love and encouragement as he makes his dreams come true. My mother always told me that finding support in a partner was the key to a happy relationship. My support, my happiness, my everything is in my arms and I'm never letting him go.

Epilogue

Jagger

Ellis and I are neck deep in wedding plans. It's all happening so fast. We'll marry at sunset next Sunday on the beach in front of Nautilus then spend a week in Maine for our honeymoon. But before our late August wedding, I want to give Ellis a pre-wedding gift he'll never forget.

There is a private room behind Cosmos with its own bar and entrance. I've spent weeks making sure everything we need is in place. Tonight will be everything Ellis desires. It has been almost impossible to keep this secret from my fiancé. I can't wait for the big reveal.

"Hey, sexy," Ellis purrs, walking into the living room, dressed in the outfit I left out for him— a black, leather, knee length skirt with a pink, mesh crop-top and his combat boots. His hair is dyed lime green and he's wearing green eye shadow and black eye liner.

"Fuuuck," I let out on a long exhale. Pushing up

from the couch, I stalk toward him, pushing him against the wall, wrapping my hand around his neck, and grazing a finger over his pulse point. "You look absolutely gorgeous."

Ellis blushes and it goes straight to my cock. Damn, I love this shy side of him. "Are you sure?"

"Perfection."

Whatever he was going to respond is cut off when I press our mouths together and lick along his lips until he opens for me. He tastes minty from his mouthwash, but I imagine the way he'll taste later when my release is on his tongue.

Breaking the kiss, I step back and force myself away from him. If I don't calm down, we aren't going to make it to our destination. Skipping tonight isn't an option. I did this for him. And to be honest the more I think about tonight, the more excited I get. I want this as much as he does.

"Are you wearing the jock strap?" I pass Ellis a bottle of water as I question him. He nods as he takes a sip. "Did you prep?" Another nod and another sip. "Good job, Princess. Are you wearing the plug?"

"Yes," he responds in an almost exasperated tone. "Are you going to tell me where we're going?"

"No. Drink the entire bottle," I instruct, loading a few more bottles into the bag holding the other supplies. Leaving it on the counter, I pull my soon-to-be-husband into my arms, remembering there's something important I need to tell him before we leave.

"Happy officially official day one hundred and eighty-four."

He rolls his eyes but can't hide the huge smile that spreads across his face. "I can't believe you still count our days."

"For one more week. Day one ninety-one will also be day one of the rest of our lives. Then I'll have to come up with something new. Maybe... 'husband day one' or 'mine forever day one.'"

"Or... maybe you should go back to the drawing board," he teases. Smacking him on the ass, I step away from him and grab the discarded bag.

"Ready?"

"Very."

He takes the hand I hold out to him, and I lead him downstairs to my truck. Once we're on the road, heading toward Anchor Point, he finishes his water and shoves the empty bottle into the cup holder.

I put his favorite playlist on, but he isn't singing. Ellis fidgets nervously in his seat. Keeping my left hand on the wheel, I reach over and place my right one on his bouncing leg, squeezing lightly.

"Do you need me to tell you where we're going? I want tonight to be everything you crave, and if that means telling you before we get there, I'm okay with that."

Ellis releases a heavy sigh, drumming his fingers on the dash. "I don't know. I trust you and I know anything you plan will be amazing. You'll never put me in danger, but I'm wearing a plug, and you made me prep. This is not a typical date and that scares me."

"You like surprises. You trust me. And you're right, I will never hurt you or put you in danger. So, what about tonight is scary?" Ellis doesn't respond. When I pull up to a red light, I glance over and see his bottom lip quivering. Well, shit. "Hey, it's okay. You don't have to do anything you don't want to do. We can turn around right now and go home."

"I'm sorry. I don't understand why I'm scared." The light turns green, so I continue to the next block and turn onto the street where Cosmos is located. Ellis' breath hitches. "Are you taking me to Cosmos?" The relief in his voice is palpable.

I park in a space near the small building behind the club and put the truck in park. "Sort of." I grin mischievously as Ellis' eyes dart between me and the building.

"What is happening?"

I turn in my seat, and Ellis does the same so we're facing each other. With both hands, I cup his neck just under his ears and run my thumbs gently over his cheeks. "You can say no to some or all of what I'm about to tell you. No pressure, but through those doors is a pre-wedding present. I've invited seven men to watch us."

"Watch us?" Ellis chokes out, shock piercing his words.

"Yes. Remember back in the spring when we talked about letting an audience watch us?" Ellis nods in response, so I continue. "Well, I thought about that scenario a lot over the summer. Jerked off to it a few times, honestly. The more I thought about it, the more I realized it isn't just a fantasy. It's something we both desire, and I want to give that to you. But if you're not ready to have an audience, we won't go in there."

"You *want* people to watch us?" He cocks an eyebrow, still surprised by my plan.

"Truthfully, yes, I do," I admit. "Only if you want it, too. I will *not* be upset in any way if this isn't something you still desire."

"I want it." His voice is breathy, and his pupils are blown. A quick glance down, shows me how much my naughty boy is turned the fuck on. The tight skirt was a brilliant idea. There's no way to hide his growing erection.

"A couple of things before we go inside. First, there are people you know and others you don't know. Is that okay?" There is no way I'm doing this if he isn't comfortable with every aspect.

"Who do I know? Like, if it's my boss, fuck no!"

"Ryan was not invited. But Nicky is in there and so is Flynn. I know we'll be working with him on the development of the art district."

"Both of them are fine. Anyone else?" Ellis buzzes with excitement.

"My friend, Gentry." That one surprised me. When I approached Gentry for his opinion of my plan, he asked if he could come watch. I've known him my entire life and he's inly ever dated girls. But I trust Gentry and have no problem with him being here. Ellis only met Gentry once in passing, so I have no idea what he'll think. I pause for a reaction and when one doesn't come, I continue. "Carter, the owner of Cosmos."

"They're fine, too. Can we go now?"

"Patience. The others you don't know. Gentry knows them and they are all part of the BDSM community. They will be respectful, and we can trust them."

"I approve," he rushes out. "C'mon?"

"Not yet." He's fucking adorable, vibrating in his seat unable to control his excitement. Is there anything you aren't comfortable doing in front of those men?"

"Are you kidding? You're offering to make my fantasy come true and you think there's something I don't want to do. No. I want it *all*. Fuck me. Suck me. Use me. Make me you're fucking toy and show those men what a fucking cum slut I am."

"Jesus fucking Christ, I'm going to come in my pants like a goddamn teenager if you keep talking like that."

"Then. Let's. Go. Inside." He claps his hands on each word, imploring me to get the show started."

"Keep it in your skirt," I tease. "At least until I tell you to take it out."

We climb out of the car and Ellis practically runs to the door. I grab his bicep before he can open it, pulling him to the side of the building and through a door that leads to a small private area just outside of the larger room where the men wait.

In the center of the room is a fucking bench, an armless chair and a small table with several items I brought over earlier today. It was imperative for me to set up everything myself. Ellis' safety and comfort is the most important thing.

Several chairs are in a circle for viewing. The bar is open, but Carter assures me he will limit everyone to two drinks. I move the curtain enough for Ellis to see. He has to be comfortable with everything or I will put a stop to this and take him home.

He sucks in a breath. "Jag, this is… everything. Thank you." He looks at me, concern suddenly on his face. "Are you okay with all this?"

"Absolutely! I can't wait for them to see you naked and spread for me, knowing they will never have you."

"Aww, sweetie. You say the nicest things to me." Ellis is serious. "Best wedding gift ever!"

Leaving the bag behind the curtain for later, I slide open the curtains and lead Ellis into the room. All eyes turn to us immediately. Most of them land on Ellis and take him in. I don't blame them, he is fucking stunning. Without stopping to have any conversations, I guide Ellis across the open space. This is about us and my sole focus is him. If he wants, we can stay and hang out after, but right now, I need him naked and at my mercy.

When I turn Ellis, so his back is against my chest, every man in the room is staring at him with hunger in their eyes. I run one hand over the bulge tenting his skirt while I unzip the back with the other hand, letting the fabric fall to the floor. Squatting behind him, I pull off his boots and shove everything to the side. As I stand, I graze my hands up his legs and over his thighs, resting them on his stomach, tracing gentle circles there. Ellis purrs softly.

My hands move up to his chest lifting his shirt as I

go. I pinch his nipples, rolling them between my index fingers and thumbs, eliciting a pained cry from him. His cock leaks leaving a growing wet spot on his pink jock strap. Shit, I love him in pink. The color does so many things to me. Pulling the shirt up more, Ellis raises his hands over his head, and I pull it all the way off, tossing it behind me.

"How are you doing?" I whisper in his ear.

"Good. Ready."

I turn him to face me and kiss him gently. "What's your safe word?" He rolls his eyes. Ellis hates having a safe word. He claims it isn't necessary, but I insist. I always want him to have a way to stop anything we're doing at any time, especially if we're going to start exploring other sexual interests. I have one, too. At my insistence, we chose them a couple of months ago. "Ellis," I scold.

"Banana." Ellis hates bananas, so he chose it, not wanting anything he enjoys associated with something potentially scary. Sticking with that idea, I chose raspberry. Those little red fruits are gross. They always taste hairy for some reason.

"Good boy. I love you. Relax and have fun, baby. This is all for you."

"I love you. Thank you." Doing what I asked, he relaxes against me, waiting for me to take control.

"Anything for you. No more talking unless it's to use your safe word."

I press my lips to his and kiss him until he melts into me. Breaking the kiss, I move us, so everyone has a side view then I push down on Ellis' shoulders. He goes to his knees without question, and I step back just out of his reach while I remove my clothes. With a quick glance at the group, I notice several of them are sitting and some have their own cocks out, stroking themselves lazily.

Focusing back on Ellis, I step up to him and gently push his arms behind him. He complies, clasping his hands behind his back. I stroke my hard, throbbing cock a few times then rub the precum across his lips, making them glisten.

"Open. Tongue out." Ellis obeys and I slap my cock against his tongue several times, pulling a groan from him.

Slowly, I sink into his warm, wet mouth until I reach the back of his throat, holding myself there. When Ellis squirms I wait several more seconds before pulling out enough to let him get a little air. I slam into his throat again, repeating the motion a few times, causing him to choke. Fuck! I love that sound. Tears stream down his face and drool coats his chin as I abuse his throat.

"Fuck, yes, take it, Princess. You look so hot with my cock down your throat," I grunt out, holding his head and fucking his mouth.

Ellis groans and gags, vibrating around my cock. Damn, he feels amazing. I'm getting close and there's a lot more I have planned for him, so I slow my thrusting before pulling completely out, trails of drool linking my cock to his mouth.

Ellis breathes heavily, struggling for a second to catch his breath. "You look fucking wrecked," I tell him, running a thumb across his lips. "Stand up." I help Ellis to his feet then push him face down onto the bench, standing behind him to block everyone's view. Bending down, I whisper. "You're doing great. Still good?"

"Yes," he pants. "More, please."

I hook my thumbs into the band of the jock strap and rip it off him, dropping it to the floor. As much as I love him in a jock, I want his cock out. I step to the side so everyone can see his plugged ass on full display. I roughly tap the toy several times and Ellis moans.

"Ung, shit."

"Shhh," I warn with another thump against the plug. "I didn't give you permission to speak." There's no way Ellis is going to stay quiet. He is a very vocal lover, but I enjoy telling him to be quiet just to see how long he can obey. "Take it out," I command with one final tap to the black plug.

Ellis reaches behind himself. It's awkward and he struggles to reach the plug, but he does what he's told and slowly works it out of his ass, leaving his hole gaping. Falling to my knees, I pepper kisses over one thigh then the other, pulling his cock down and stroking it a few times as I lick and suck his balls. Ellis' breathing increases and he writhes as I trace my tongue up his crease and lick over his hole. When I swirl my tongue as I push inside, I hear the plug clatter to the floor. Ellis screams and moans, making incoherent noises.

Fuck, he tastes so good. Eating him out is becoming one of my favorite things to do. He bucks under me, forcing me further inside.

"Jag, fuck, more. Need. You."

Standing, I pop one ass cheek then the other. "Turn over." Again, I step away, giving our audience a perfect view of Ellis' ass. Walking to stand near his head, I help him get comfortable on the bench. "Pull your legs up." Ellis pulls his knees to his chest, and I push them apart, spreading him wide for everyone to see. He clasps his hands on the back of legs to hold them in place.

The men are in various stages of undress, cocks out. Two of the ones I don't know are jerking each other get off. Nicky's hungry eyes are locked on Ellis and full of desire. He bites his bottom lip, working his cock furiously. A streak of jealousy courses through me. I trust Ellis will never cheat, but I have often wondered if Nicky has a thing for him. Every eye is on Ellis, and I fucking relish it.

Ellis whimpers, pulling my attention back to him. He looks fucking gorgeous laid out in front of everyone. My heart soars and I swell with pride. Mine. Ellis is mine. Forever. Witnessing those men watching Ellis with lust in their eyes makes me fucking feral. I need to be inside him *now*. I need to take him, fuck him.

I give Ellis a chaste kiss. "They can't take their eyes off you. Now, I'm going to fuck you. Take what's mine."

Ellis smiles with more love in his eyes than I deserve. "Yes, please," he begs.

Picking up the bottle of lube as I move into position, I coat my aching cock then drop the bottle on the floor. I line myself up and push in, balls deep in one quick motion, sliding in with ease. Thank you, plug.

Not giving Ellis time to think or adjust, I start

moving immediately, setting a hard, fast pace. I'm too worked up to make it last. My hips slap against his ass, filling the room with the sounds of skin slapping together mixed with grunts, moans, and groans.

"Fuck, yes. Take it."

I grab Ellis' hands and hold them above his head, forcing his legs further back with my body, pushing me into a different position. Ellis whimpers when I hit the right spot over and over. I'm not going to last, but that's fine. The night's young.

Ellis cries out without warning and explodes all over his stomach and chest, clenching around my cock, dragging me over the edge. If the sounds coming from behind me are any indication, most of them have found their own release.

"That was hot, Princess." I let my weight rest on Ellis as I kiss him passionately. He threads his fingers through my hair, holding me to him as if I'm going to get away. Our tongues rub against each other and my cock twitches inside Ellis. He smiles, breaking the kiss. "I love you. I'm so proud of you," I praise Ellis, and he preens under me. "Thank you for giving me that."

"Can we do it again?" he asks with excitement.

"Let's take a break. Then we can do it again tonight or plan another night."

"Yes. to both. I love you, Jagger."

The other men give us some privacy while they clean themselves up and retreat to the other side of the room to talk quietly at the bar. Helping Ellis to his feet, I wrap a blanket around him passing him a bottle of water. Then I guide us to the waiting chair and pull him into my lap, holding him close. He needs to rest before we go again. I have plans for that bag full of goodies. Arranging this night for us was a brilliant decision. One more week and I get to call Ellis Young my husband. I can't wait to promise him forever in front of our friends and family.

Acknowledgments

I would like to thank the following people for their support as I worked to complete Finding Support.

First and foremost, to my amazing readers. Without your support, I wouldn't be able to do what I love. You have made my lifelong dream a reality.

Rick, my husband, for his constant support and love. I am grateful for everything you have done for me over the years. You are a true partner when it comes to cooking, cleaning, errands, kids, laundry, and so much more. I appreciate you sharing my excitement, helping me work through scenes, and answering questions.

Anders and Grady for your love and understanding. It has been an amazing adventure, and I am blessed to have sons as awesome as you. Thank you for standing by my side and helping me with new ideas.

My cover artist, Erin, who brought my vision to fruition even when I struggled to know exactly what I wanted.

My proofreader, Michelle. Thank you for correcting my grammar!

The amazing team at Brittany Montano Management for helping to make this book a success even though you had to work with a crazy fast timeline. I appreciate your unwavering support.

EMERSON GAIL

Emerson Gail was born and raised in southeast Georgia. She has been married to her husband, Rick, for over 24 years, and they have two sons. She has always found peace and solitude in books - reading or writing. Emerson expresses herself through stories that relay her deep appreciation of relationships and finding one's people, whether biological or chosen. Her hobbies include writing, reading, listening to music, wine tasting, and watching football.

Books by Emerson Gail

Finding Forever Series

Finding Home

Finding Support

Books by Pamela Gail

SERIES
WHERE THE PATH LEADS
Path of the Heartbeats

Fixing My Path

Changing My Path

The Empty Path

An Unexpected Path

The Wrong Path

STANDALONE
Young Adult
Soul of Eli

MM ROMANCE
Miami Vices